M000287579

# SEQUENCE OF PROTOCOL

## John Griffin

AHMED PUBLISHING
Point Breeze Station
P.O. Box 11977
Philadelphia, PA 19145-0277

Copyright @2012 by John Griffin

ISBN#: 978-0-615-84435-0
Printed in the United States of America

Published July, 2013
Cover designed by j. griffin and friends
AHMED PUBLISHING
Point Breeze Station
P.O. Box 11977
Philadelphia, PA 19145-0277

# Acknowledgements

I owe special thanks to my extraordinary editors, Joan Behr and Staci Gorden, who spent many hours correcting my errors.

For their financial support, I would like to thank The Prison Literacy Project, who has assisted me with defraying the costs of publishing this book.

## Dedication

---

THIS NOVEL IS DEDICATED TO MY BROTHERS

"WE LOVE EACH OTHER MORE AS WE GROW"

# PREFACE

This novel is fictional and in no way means to denigrate the Nation of Islam under the leadership of the Honorable Elijah Muhammad or those dedicated brothers and sisters who demonstrated courage and dignity by strictly adhering to his teachings. The writer recognizes that the Nation of Islam, under the leadership of the Honorable Elijah Muhammad, was a unique religious organization, established for the redemption and development of black people who had experienced over 400 years of self-destructive tutelage and savagery, under white America.

The Author

# PROLOGUE

Are there no mirrors in America,
so your flaws your may detect?
Or is it because of your vampirism,
that your image will not reflect?
Haven't you noticed that your armor is tarnished,
and your crown is slightly bent?
That your slave has risen from his grave,
to become your embarrassment?
He marches in your streets,
at your Capitol steps he sings,
proclaiming and loudly lamenting the burdens
from which his injustice springs...

--- It is from this retrospect that this writer shares measured steps toward lacerated dreams and encrusted nightmares...

From the time the first black man set foot on its soil, America produced the distinct understanding of difference. Despite it being the choice of God to make the African black, for his color alone, he was loathed, brutalized, humiliated and enslaved. His history in this country, from the cradle to the grave, has been one of suffering and ill-treatment that are unequaled in the annals of history.

Although in the early to mid – 20th century, white Americans spent a great deal of time telling themselves and the world that these intense feelings of racial loathing for the black race were largely a matter of the past. Yet, the fact remained that feelings of white revulsion and rage caused many black men, women and children to be lynched, both physically and psychologically, for no other reason than being who they were. In the 1950s and 1960s, the disgusting images of blacks being brutalized leaped from television sets and into the living rooms and minds of people around the world. Blacks all over the country witnessed the odious acts of humiliation being perpetrated upon their people by vicious whites.

These blatant racial attacks helped generate a climate of change in the black community and as a result, various groups began speaking out and conscious awareness began sprinkling down to the grassroots. Although the precipitation didn't completely saturate every black person with racial pride and cultural understanding, most who had become dissatisfied now sought collective action to bring about change.

Dissatisfaction was mostly demonstrated by the youthful segments of various black communities. They had lost faith in and respect for some of the leaders who had previously represented their mothers and fathers. Those leaders and their persistence in nonviolence in the face of so much violence against black people had become unacceptable to many of them. They were tired of watching black leaders in the name of Christ, march black people down streets where white police joined with white civilians to beat, kick and sic dogs on them. Many saw that as being a bit too Christian, especially when the whites administering these beatings claimed to be acting under the sign of the same cross. Most inner-city black youth didn't want lessons in how to be non-violent in the face of white rage. What they yearned for was black leadership creating acceptable ways in fighting back.

These youth began to hear and see young black men and women speaking loudly in front of crowds, some were teenagers; some were in their early twenties and thirties, shouting words like "Black Power," "Black Solidarity," and "Black Liberation." These strong phrases permeated the black neighborhoods and pricked the youthful black minds, and the most important factor to them was that the word "Black" preceded these phrases. Someone was finally reaching out to them. Names like Huey P. Newton of the Black Panther Party, Stokely Carmichael and H. Rap Brown of the Student Non-violent Coordinating Committee and Elijah Muhammad and Malcolm X of the Nation of Islam, became synonymous with strength and defiance.

Although these men and women, and the organizations they headed, became synonymous with courage and strength in some black communities, they were viewed as a threat to the American way of life in the white communities. Under the dictatorship and direction of J. Edgar Hoover, a devout racist, the FBI embarked on a plan to disrupt, discredit and destroy the Black groups that white America, hypocritically labeled, "Hate Groups."

Hoover, who rarely bothered to conceal the vengeance of his racial prejudices, had once stated, "As long as I am the director, there will never be a negro special agent of the FBI. For more than forty years, he only allowed blacks in the Bureau to be dubbed "honorary agents." In reality, they acted as little more than personal servants, retainers, chauffeurs and office boys to Hoover.

J. Edgar Hoover's notorious racial attitude played a large role in determining the FBI's investigatory agenda. He insisted that the Bureau practice selective enforcement of the nation's civil rights laws. He was protective of whites committing massive disobedience in the South and he created special units, such as the infamous Counter Intelligence Program, that became known as COINTELPRO. The program was created for the sole purpose of infiltrating, disrupting, misdirecting and neutralizing the black organizations he personally viewed as Hate Groups.

# CHAPTER I

## NATIONAL SECURITY AGENCY
## COUNTER INTELLIGENCE

| INTERNAL MEMO: | TO ALL DEPARTMENTS: |
| --- | --- |
| DATE: | JULY 26, 1967 |
| SUBJECT: | HATE GROUPS |
| FILE: | NUMBER HG-0064-67 |

[THE CURRENT VIOLENCE ON THE STREETS OF DETROIT, MICHIGAN, THAT IS BEING COMMITTED BY MEMBERS OF THE NEGRO COMMUNITY, INCITED AND INFLUENCED BY OTUSIDE AGITATORS CONNECTED TO THE COMMUNIST/ SOCIALIST PARTY, FURTHER DEMONSTRATES THE URGENCY FOR THIS AGENCY TO TAKE EFFECTIVE MEASURES TO NEUTRALIZE THOSE PARTICULAR COMMUNIST EFFORTS TO INFILTRATRE AND INFECT OUR AMERICAN WAY OF LIFE. SINCE MOST NEGROES OUTSIDE THE DEEP SOUTH LIVE IN OUR LARGEST METROPOLITAN AREAS, i.e., NEW YORK CITY, LOS ANGELES, CHICAGO, PHILADELPHIA, DETROIT, BOSTON, SAN FRANCISCO-OAKLAND, PITTSBURGH, ST. LOUIS, WASHINGTON, CLEVELAND, AND BALTIMORE – THE AGITATORS, UNDER THE GUISE OF CIVIL RIGHTS, SEEK MAINLY TO CONCENTRATE THEIR EFFORTS THERE.

TO EFFECTIVELY MAINTAIN ORDER, BY CONTAINMENT AND CONTROL, AS OF THIS DAY, JULY 26, 1967, ALL SUPERVISORS WILL INSTRUCT ALL OPERATIVES CURRENTLY SITUATED INSIDE THE FOLLOWING HATE GROUPS, FOR THE PURPOSE OF COMPLETE NEUTRALIZATION OF SAID GROUPS, TO BECOME MORE INVOLVED IN THE PLANNED COURSE OF ACTION OF SAID GROUPS, BY FACILITATING SCENARIOS THAT WILL DISRUPT AND BRING AN END TO THOSE ORGANIZATIONS:]

TO:  THE SUBJECT GROUPS INCLUDE, BUT ARE NOT EXCLUSIVE

THE BLACK PANTHER PARTY (BPP)
THE NATION OF ISLAM (NOI)
STUDENT FOR THE NON-VIOLENT COORDINATING
COMMITTEE (SNCC).

\*\*\*

Wade Coleman didn't work as an operative for the U.S. National Security Agency, so he didn't get to read that memo. But Wade, who lived in Philadelphia, could tell from the article appearing in the July 26, 1967 morning edition of The Philadelphia Bulletin, that more black people were about to die at the hands of white folks.

As much as he loved his job, working as a clothing salesman, at Frankenfields Clothier, he dreaded going to work on this particular morning. He knew that his co-workers, all of whom were white, would be there gloating, and waiting, with a smug look on their faces, to engage him in conversation about the ineptness of blacks in America. Of course, they referred to it as the state of urban affairs, but he knew what they meant. He always felt put off by their superior attitudes and dismissive tones.

The Bulletin reported that: "...On Monday, July 24, amidst the wide spread looting that has continued in riot-torn areas of Detroit, Michigan, for four days, the police came under sniper attack, and one police officer was killed. The sniper was never found. On Tuesday, July 25, National Guardsmen, Highway Patrolmen and the Detroit Police were called to the Algiers Motel in response to reported sniper fire. Though no sniper was found, eight black youths and two white girls were lined up in the hallway and interrogated by law enforcement officials. It is unclear what happened next, but it is reported that some officers conducting the questioning, began playing a game of intimidation with the suspects. One by one, the youths were isolated in a room and a shot was fired. The police would then return and tell the other suspects that the isolated suspect was killed because he refused to tell who the sniper was. Though it was said to be only a game; a war of nerves, according to the officials, three black youths were left dead in the bedrooms of the Algiers Motel and there is now an investigation into those deaths..."

They killed them guys, Wade thought, as he exited the Broad Street subway, tossing the newspaper in the waste basket. I know it, and those so-called investigators know it, too.

Recalling his own experience with the Philadelphia Police, there was absolutely no doubt in his mind that those black youths were murdered. His encounter had been three years earlier, in the summer of 1964. He'd just graduated from Edison High School that June. And exactly one month later, there had been a riot on Columbia Avenue, one of the black neighborhood shopping areas in North Philadelphia.

A week after the riot, while on his way to a job interview, Wade visited the riot-torn area. Most of the businesses had been burned out, and those that weren't were boarded up. And even after a week, one could still smell the scent of burned wood and cloth, and singed metal.

It was about 6:00 p.m. when Wade finished the job interview at the Great Wall Restaurant on Roosevelt Boulevard and Adams Avenue. A mostly white community, in the northeast section of Philly, the police patrolled that area constantly. And now that there had just been a violent riot in the city, the cops were out for blood, going everywhere, looking for black men to arrest.

While leaving the job interview, Wade was accosted by two white police officers who wanted to know why he was in that neighborhood.

"Wha'cha doing out 'ere, boy," one of them asked.

"I'm just leaving a job interview," Wade responded, not liking being called a boy.

"Where at?"

"The Great Wall Restaurant."

"They ain't hiring no niggers out 'ere."

"Then I should get the job, cause I ain't no nigger."

Wade heard the driver's side door open, and saw the cop begin to step out. "We gon' get all you niggers off the street before the weekend," the cop said, walking around the front of the car. Just then, the cop sitting on the passenger's side opened his door and stepped out. He had his nightstick in one hand, and his other hand on the top of his holstered 38 revolver.

Wade stiffened, staring at the cop closest to him, while also keeping the other cop in eyesight. Though his heart was thumping, he was actually surprised that he felt no fear. He pivoted sideways, ready to defend himself. When he swings that nightstick, Wade thought, I'll crouch down and block it with my arm, then leap forward between them. Beyond that, Wade had no strategy other than to fight as hard as he could. As far back as he could remember, white police had been coming into black folk's neighborhoods, beating up men, women and even children. And though he knew it wasn't wise for him to resist them, this evening, he would.

"Hey! Hey!" a yell came from someone standing on the steps of the Great Wall Restaurant. "You, Mister," the owner of the restaurant called out. "You forgot to sign papers. You forgot to sign papers."

Seeing the alarmed looking Chinese man standing on the steps watching their every move, both cops backed off.

"You better get out of this neighborhood, boy," one said, as they both got in the car and drove off.

Not only had Mr. Tsung-Dao Lee saved Wade's life that evening, he hired him, as well. Wade worked there for a year before leaving to take his present job at Frankenfield's Clothier.

As Wade reached 15th and Ridge Avenue, he knew he had to get his frustrations under control before he reached the store, lest he might go off on his co-workers time they started in on that, why black people do this and that talk. Concentrating on the sights around him, he smiled at the two wide hipped sisters, wearing their hair in teeny-weeny afros, and walking in his direction. They smiled back, and why wouldn't they, he looked good in his beige silk suit, off-white shirt and pleated chocolate tie. If he didn't know anything else, Wade knew about clothes, and he knew how to put 'em on. That was probably why Saul Frankenfield had hired him in the first place. Not that Wade wasn't a good salesman, he was. But the Jewish owners wanted more than just a good salesman in that neighborhood, they wanted someone who would appeal to their customers, all of whom were black.

The sun was bright, and there was a slight breeze that helped cool the heat.

"It's a beautiful day, today, Mrs. Bee," Wade said to the old black woman who owned Soul Spoon Restaurant, where he ate lunch every day.

"You got that right, honey," she replied. "Will we see you at noon, sweetie?"

"Yes, ma'am."

Across the street, Larry Davis had already opened up his record store. The music playing up and down the street that morning was, "Boogaloo Down Broadway," and the little kids were out on the sidewalk, doing just that.

"You early this morning, Larry," Wade hollered.

"Yeah, bro," Larry yelled back across the street. "I got to hire a new girl today." Larry said that everyday. That was his joke about him going to get rid of his wife. They had been together about 20 years, and still acted like two love-sick teenagers.

Wade took a deep breath as he crossed 16th street, walked passed the firehouse, turned in between the display windows, and entered the store.

# CHAPTER II

Tall and light-skinned, and carrying a brown paper bag, the muscular young man wore an old faded gray wool suit, a washed-out bluish broadcloth shirt, and a pair of rugged brown boots.

It was almost noon, and Wade, who was busy stacking shirts and trying to ignore the provoking comments coming from his two white co-workers, hadn't noticed the man enter the store and walk over to the clothing racks lined up near the side wall.

"What about it, Wade?" Randy, one of the white workers asked, while standing at the cash register, but with his back to the door.

"Why do colored people, who are supposedly protesting the so-called injustices of the world, always riot and loot from stores, then burn down their own neighborhoods?"

As Wade turned to reply, he saw the tall man in the faded grey suit standing in the corner examining the suits on the rack.

"Can I help you, sir?" He asked, ignoring Randy's question, and quickly noticing that the customer was about 6 feet 5 inches tall. "We have a very fine collection of suits, but the ones on that rack wouldn't fit you. If you'd like, I can show you our collection of Tall Men suits."

"I know you're not saying that it's justice to burn down your own neighborhood," Randy continued, still unaware of the customer. "That's just plain stupid, if you ask me."

Joel, the other white salesman in the store, nudged Randy, then nodded toward the customer.

"Can we help you, sir?" Randy said, stepping from behind the counter and approaching as if Wade hadn't already acknowledged the customer's presence, by moving over to him.

"No, I'd prefer him," the man said bluntly, pointing to Wade.

"Uh, perhaps Wade can help you," Joel said, pulling on Randy's arm. "He's more familiar with our Tall Men selections."

Glancing back over his shoulder, Wade took note of Joel's maneuver. It was a common one. Whenever a black male, who looked somewhat suspicious or intimidating entered the store, both white clerks would ask Wade to wait on him.

"My name is Wade, sir. May I show you to our Tall Men section?" Wade asked, extending his hand toward the back of the store, while also taking note of the set of clothes the man had on. Wade had seen clothes like that before, and he was sure that Randy and Joel had been quick to notice them as well. The clothes were obviously state issued. The Eastern State Penitentiary was over on 21$^{st}$ and Fairmount Avenues, which was about nine blocks away from the store. So they often got a few men in the store, who had just been released from prison, and would come in to buy a new set of clothes before going home.

"Yeah," the man said, jokingly, as he looked Wade up and down. "Where do y'all keep the suits cut like the one you're wearing? Is that a Bill Blass or a Pierre Cardin?"

Wade smiled. He could see that the man would wear about a size 50 long, and the pants would need altering because the man had a narrow waist.

"It's a Cardin. But we don't sell them here. However, we do have an excellent factory selection I can show you."

"Never mind," the man remarked as he placed the brown paper bag on the floor. "Show me a few mohair sweaters and a couple of gabardine pants. That's if y'all carry them in my size. And I'll also need underwear; boxer shorts, v-neck t-shirts, and six pair of black stretch socks."

"Where were you at, Eastern?" He asked the man, while pulling out stacks of v-necks, crew necks and cardigans from the sweater case.

"Yep, for seven years. Do you have any v-necks with pockets at the bottom?"

"I think we do. We just got in some silk knit v-necks that you might like. I'll be right back. I have to go down in the storeroom to get them."

Lucius noticed that Wade was going out of his way to accommodate him and he liked that. He also noticed the two white salesmen eyeing him from across the room. He stared back at them, which made them both nervous. When Wade came back upstairs with the knits, he saw a slight smile on the man's face.

"When I walked in the store, I couldn't help but overhear your conversation," the man told Wade. "Oh, by the way, my name is Lucius. And you should never feel as if you have to define the actions of the oppressed."

"Glad to meet you," Wade said, shaking the man's huge hand, but failing to respond to his comment. "I think you'll like these knits. I brought up all the ones we have in your size."

"These three will do fine," Lucius said, picking out three different colors and smiling to himself, as he realized that Wade felt uncomfortable speaking in front of his white co-workers.

"How about the pants I picked out, do y'all do alterations here?"

"No, but there's a cleaners down the street that will do them," Wade enthusiastically replied. "I'm getting ready to go to lunch. If you don't mind, you can have lunch with me, and pick your pants up afterward. That way, you won't have to wait in the cleaners."

"You buying?" Lucius joked.

Lunch for Lucius was a salad and juice. When Aunt Bee tried to get him to try her steak and fries, he respectfully declined. When Wade asked if he was a vegetarian, Lucius replied, "Oh, I eat meat. I just don't eat pork." And when Wade pointed out that steak wasn't pork, Lucius responded by pointing out that Aunt Bee was using lard on her grill and that she also cooked all her meats, both pork and beef, on that same grill. "That means people are eating pork, without even knowing it."

"Well, I admit, Wade said, grinning, most of my family has always ate pork, and they seem fine to me."

"Perhaps if we run into one another again," Lucius related, not wanting to get into that conversation just yet, "I'll explain why I don't eat pork. But right now, I'd like to know why you are intimidated by your co-workers. Is it because they're white or is it because you work for them that you feel you must steer the conversation away from racial matters?"

"No, they're not my bosses. And I'm not intimidated by them. It's just, well, we were talking about the riot in Detroit and the three black youths they found dead. I just get frustrated when they try to excuse the actions of the police, that's all. Be they black or white, they should be held accountable for their actions, too."

"There's an old saying," Lucius said, putting some salad in his mouth. "To excuse one's self is to accuse one's self. Look, Wade, white folks have always viewed blacks, and especially black men, as criminals. They have long viewed criminal behavior as a thing that comes natural to blacks. To many whites, we're just a biological flaw."

Wade stopped eating his steak and fries and sat staring at Lucius. He sounded more like a college professor than someone who was just out of the state penitentiary.

"How old are you?" Lucius asked.

"I'm 20," Wade answered.

"Well, you were probably too young to remember 1954, but I was 14 then. White men in Mississippi mutilated and killed a 14 year old black boy named Emmit Till. He was from Chicago and was down there to visit his family. The white men who killed him said that he had flirted with some white woman. Those men were found not guilty, just like the ones in Detroit will be found not guilty. Whites like to believe that their lynch mobs are punishing real crimes by dangerous Negroes. If they happened to lynch the wrong person, well, that too serves a purpose by reminding other Negroes of their place. Frustrations are born out of a lack of action, Wade. Don't defend the actions of the oppressed to the oppressors. Make the oppressors aware of their crimes and let them try to defend that."

Wade was almost speechless. He admired this man, and the way he talked about black people. He could see the emotion in Lucius' eyes as he spoke.

"Lucius, can I, uh, ask you a question?"

"Sure."

"Why were you in prison? I mean, the way you speak and carry yourself, one wouldn't think... well was it something criminal?"

"I don't believe so. But the white man said I assaulted three people, and incited a riot."

"When, the 1964 riot on Columbus Avenue?" Wade asked.

"No. In 1960. I beat up three white Mummers at the New Year's Day Parade. They were strutting around wearing black stuff on their faces, like they did every year. They wouldn't allow blacks in the parade, but would strut around playing their banjos and insult the dignity of our people by making a mockery. I got tired of it. I hit one of them devils so hard that I almost knocked all the smut off his face."

Wade had heard the term, devils, before. It was one the Muslims used to refer to the white man. He must be a Muslim, Wade thought.

"And they said that was inciting a riot?"

"Yeah, 'cause when some brothers from South Philly saw the police grab me, they started beating all those black face wearing mummers. They don't wear that shit on their faces no more."

"You did seven years for that?"

"They gave me three-and-a half to seven years. But when I came up for parole, after four years, I was denied because they considered me an organizer of some of the prison groups, and they gave me a year hit. So I just decided to max out."

"What does max out mean?"

"It means I did the whole thing so I wouldn't have any parole people following me around."

After Lucius picked up his pants from the cleaners, he thanked Wade for lunch and an enlightening conversation. Wade, so impressed by Lucius' graciousness, couldn't help but think he should be thanking him.

"You know, Lucius, if you're interested, I know of a place to get some really good suits, sport jackets and even overcoats, at a cut-rate price.

"What, are they seconds?" Lucius asked.

"No. They're not seconds," Wade responded. "I don't tell many people about this, but I have a hookup with one of the buyers from Frankenfields Clothier. Of course my boss don't know about this. And, especially not those two white boys that work with me. If they knew, I'd be in jail."

"Tell you what," Lucius said, reaching inside the paper bag he had with him, and pulling out three books. "I have to leave town for a few weeks, but when I get back, I'll holla at'cha, okay. In the mean time, read these books and tell me what you think. These are my prize possessions, so take care of them."

"Okay," Wade said, glancing at the titles: <u>How to East to Live</u>, <u>Message To The Black Man</u> and <u>The Miseducation of the Negro</u>. All three books were in perfect condition, though it was obvious they had been thoroughly read.

"I like you, Wade," Lucius said, looking Wade directly in his eyes and presenting his hand to shake. "I think we will become good friends."

Later that day, while flipping through the pages of The Message To The Black Man, Wade thought about the question Lucius had asked him. He was right. I have been trying to manage the conversations with my co-workers. It seemed I'd rather talk about little innocuous things, so that I would feel accepted by them. Because when we would talk about racial matters, I would often tense up, seeing that questioning look in their eyes that said, "Quiet, the negro is trying to speak."

# CHAPTER III

Seated around a table at the Salaam Restaurant, on 117th and Lennox Avenues, in New York City, were six well-dressed black men from Philadelphia's Muhammad's Temple Number 12. All of them were in their mid to late twenties, and all but one dined there before.

As they sat there talking and laughing, no one would have suspected that at one time in their younger lives, they had all been members of different Philly street gangs and enemies of one another. However, geographic rivalries soon disappeared when they joined together under the banner of the Nation of Islam for the common cause of spiritual brotherhood and nation building. And, at the moment, they were there to celebrate Brother Lucius X's release from prison.

Dressed in one of his new sweaters and gabardine slacks, Lucius felt honored, not only to be at the Salaam Restaurant for the first time, but also that these particular brothers had been the ones to ask him to dine with them. They were men who had experienced pretty much what he had experienced while growing up on the streets of Philly. Men who had been, and still were, regarded as courageous, respected and even feared by many throughout the city. But between them, the respect was mutual. And where they came from, that was important.

The other five men at the table were Brother Milton X Hines, who was an Assistant Minister and originally from South Philly; Brother Lester 2X Edwards, from West Philly; Brother Ethan X. Siswell, Brother Josh 8X Clarkson, and Brother Christopher 4X Williams, all from North Philadelphia.

According to their spiritual leader, the Honorable Elijah Muhammad, who they believed to be the Messenger of Allah, their surnames represented slave names that had been given to Negro slaves by their slave masters. And, since only Allah knew the true nature of each man and woman, only He or His messenger could provide them with original names and enter their names into the official Muslim registry, called the Book of Life. Until then, the "X" which as in algebra represented an unknown factor, would represent their surnames.

All new members joining the religion were advised to write a Letter of Submission to headquarters in Chicago to register with the Nation of Islam and receive their "X." If a brother or sister wrote a letter of submission and received a letter granting them their "X," the brother or sister was to take the acceptance letter to the Temple in the city in which he or she lived, to be registered as a member. If there were other registered Muslims in that city with the same first name, the "X" of the newest Muslim would follow in numeric order, the one preceding it. Thus, Sister Pearline 2X would follow Sister Pearline X.

With the exception of Lucius and Assistant Minister Milton, all other brothers at the table were lieutenants in the Nation of Islam.

"I see that we have some brothers from Philly seated out front," shouted one Muslim waiter, as he peeked through the window of one of the kitchen doors.

"Yeah," proclaimed another waiter. "Brother Minister Milton is with them."

"Then let's show them how the Muslims from Temple 7 treat their beloved brothers from Temple 12," shouted the head chef. "Let's prepare and served them one of our best meals."

The Salaam Restaurant was huge and immaculate. It wasn't one of those greasy spoons so often seen in the black neighborhoods. There were orange and white drapes at each of the huge windows, and white table cloths covered each circular table. And, all the waiters wore black pants, orange waist length jackets and white cloth gloves. Neatly folded across their left arm were white cloth napkins. They greeted each customer with politeness and proficiency. Dashing from table to table, they moved quickly, with polish and precision.

Approaching their table, the waiter greeted the brothers from Philly. "As-Salaam-Alaikum, My Brothers! I heard Temple 12 was in the house. The top of the clock."

"Wa-Laikum-As-Salaam," came the joint reply. Then, after a brief conversation, as the waiter filled their water glasses, Brother Minister Milton asked the waiter if Brother Carlton, the head chef was there.

"Yes, sir, Brother Minister, he's in the kitchen."

"Would you please ask him to prepare something special for our prodigal brother, here," he asked, pointing at Lucius.

"Actually, Brother Minister," Lucius commented, smiling. "I never left. I was more like Jonah, snatched away and then swallowed up by a whale of a prison system run by some odious devils."

They all laughed, including the waiter. And, as he made his way back to the kitchen, he called out, "That special meal is already being prepared, Brother Minister, Brother Carlton took care of that time he saw you arrive."

Placing his hand on the minister's arm, Lucius remarked, "Brother Minister, I was sorry to hear about Malcolm. I know that you and he had become close."

"Yeah, it was a tragic situation," Minister Milton replied. "He was a good brother at heart."

There was a pause, then Lucius recalling an earlier time, stated, "I remember the day I received my acceptance letter from Chicago, stating that I had received my X, I brought it to the Temple, and you were there. You were about to take some Junior F.O.I. to New York, and told me that I could go with y'all, if I liked. "You remember that, Brother Minister?"

"Yeah," Brother Minister said, grinning. "I'd almost forgotten about that. Seems you were a bit confused about what the F.O.I. really stood for."

"Yeah, you told me that it meant the Fruit of Islam."

"Mmm Hmm," Brother Milton said. "I remember telling you that white folks wanted people to believe that it meant just a paramilitary training unit that only certain brothers were a part of. I told you that every Muslim male was the Fruit of Islam. That you were the Fruit of Islam, and that it was your responsibility to defend your family and community and to protect and respect all women and children."

"Yeah, I remember you telling me that in the car. And when we got to New York, I got the chance to see Malcolm. He even spoke briefly to us before you and he had your meeting. Man that was out of sight!"

"What you actually met Malcolm?" Brother Lester asked.

"Well, no. I didn't meet him personally. He spoke to the entire New York City Fruit of Islam class that day, and I just happened to be there with the Junior F.O.I from Philly."

"How old were you then? You weren't a junior, were you?

"No, I was 19 then. But Brother Minister allowed me to go because I'd been so enthusiastic about receiving my X and had hurried to the Temple with my acceptance letter."

Brother Minister Milton smiled as he remembered that day. It had been 1959, and over the next four years, he had gotten the opportunity to travel with Malcolm a few times.

"Malcolm was greatly loved," remarked Brother Lester. "A lot of brothers left the Temple when he was suspended."

"Yeah, but most of them came back." Lucius stated. "They realized how much they loved the Dear Holy Apostle. Although I was in prison, I could see that."

"Actually," Brother Minister quietly remarked, "I think had Malcolm not commented about Kennedy's assassination on the Today Show, things might have turned out differently. He was truly remarkable and had the potential to become a great leader. Though some might misunderstand or disagree with me, our date with destiny may well be altered by too much hatred among our own. We can't become like our brothers in Africa, killing off our own talented leaders at the behest of our white oppressors."

Silence could be heard around the table. For a moment at least, it seemed that Malcolm was there. And Minister Milton was remembering the last time he had spoken with him. It had been the spring of 1963, and they had just left a news conference in Harlem, where Malcolm had discussed the need for black leaders to overcome their differences and sit down together.

"Do you think they'll respond to your message?" Milton had asked Brother Malcolm.

"Well, Malcolm said, pausing for a moment, "What's important is that it was said. All of our brothers must realize that the black man's blighted existence in this country requires more than one approach toward a solution."

Milton had found that statement memorable because to him it indicated a first in Malcolm's softened stance toward his ideological adversaries.

"Hey, Lucius," Minister Milton remarked, finally breaking the silence around the table, "You see Brother Andrew yet? You know he and Sister Earline are planning a dinner for you."

"No, I haven't seen anyone yet.  But I planned to see them when I get back from Chicago.  I think the good brother really wants me to meet his wife's youngest sister, Livia."

"Yeah, I've seen her at the Temple," Lester said.  "She's a very pretty sister.  A *very pretty sister.*"

When Brother Minister excused himself from the table to go to the bathroom, Ethan took the opportunity to ask about Lucius' trip.

"I'm leaving tonight.  Brother David is driving me out there.  He has to go to Pittsburgh to deliver some Muhammad Speaks newspapers, so I asked that he allow me to tag along and then he and I can go on to Chicago."

"Well, when you get back," Josh whispered, "we have to sit down and talk.  Ethan and I had a meeting the other day with some old acquaintances of yours."

"Who you talkin' bout?"

"Mo and Big Cil."

"I heard that they're slingin' powder, now."

"Yeah, and branching out.  But we can wait 'til you get back to fill you in."

"How long you gonna be in Chicago, anyway?"  Chris asked.

"Don't know.  Brother Captain Khalil sent a letter to Philly six months before I was even released.  He said that he heard that I could be an added benefit to the recruiting of Temple 12, so he would like to see me when I got out."

"He's on the Supreme Captain's staff, isn't he?"  Lester asked.

"Yeah," Brother Josh said.  "And he's been shaking things up in all the mosques around the country since he was appointed to that staff."

"Wha' cha mean?"  Lucius asked.

"He wants the numbers up, head count and papers sold."

"Well, we're doing pretty good in the sale of <u>Muhammad Speaks</u>, aren't we?"  Lester asked.

"We could always do better," Brother Minister said as he sat down, "Our food is arriving."

They watched in amazement as a string of waiters arrived with trays and platters of baked and fried fish, short ribs, and fried chicken legs simmering in hot sauce.  Separate bowls filled with brown rice covered in lamb stew, hot peppers and onions followed.  They were served hot buttered dinner rolls, glazed carrots, sweet corn and Fatima salad.  For dessert, they enjoyed banana pie, bread pudding and fruit cocktail and they sipped on Akbar juice, spring water and coffee.

Later, while leaving the restaurant, Brother Ethan slipped Lucius a piece of paper.  "It's from Redtop, she knows you're home and asked me to give you the address to her new place."

"New place?"  Lucius asked.  "She closed the one on Fairmount Avenue?"

"Yeah. She got a much bigger spot now. It's much nicer than the other. It's on Germantown Avenue."

Lucius had always admired Brother Ethan's ability to be discrete. Of all those at the dinner, he and Brother Ethan were most alike. They grew up together and had started attending the Muslim Temple around the same time. Both being teenagers back then, and highly motivated by their sex drives, spent a lot of time chasing the girls. They caught most of them and learned to practice the art of discretion.

Brother Ethan knew that Lucius wouldn't have wanted the other brothers to hear anything about Redtop. Ten years his senior, she had played a big part in Lucius' sexual growth and development as a young man. Though the others may have known of her business acumen, her personal interest in Lucius was a well-kept secret, shared only by the three of them.

"How is she doin?" Lucius asked.

"Hey, that's Redtop," Ethan said with a shrug of his shoulders. "She's a survivor who always lands on her feet."

"Yeah, I heard about her husband getting' killed. They ever find out who shot him?"

"No," Ethan answered faintly, "But at least she was able to get the insurance money."

Lucius stared at his much shorter but broadly built friend as they moved toward the car. But Ethan, sensing the stare, kept his light eyes diverted.

# CHAPTER IV

By the time the second bullet entered Stretch's neck, he was already dead and slumped over the steering wheel of his car. The first shot fired entered right behind the left ear, killing him instantly. But Rushard wasn't one to take chances. His military training had taught him that. So when Stretch fell forward from the first shot, Rushard quickly placed the gun to Stretch's neck and pumped in another bullet.

Just a few moments earlier, as the sun was fading from the hot July sky, Walter "Stretch" Cole and his partner, Sheldon Bland, had wheeled into a small cul-de-sac behind the Carlyle Hotel on 7th and Chestnut Streets in Camden, New Jersey. As he had done a few times before, Stretch eased his 1967 coco brown Buick Electra 225 up to the garage door and waited for it to open. The garage belonged to Pete, "Fat Pete" DeFazio, a small-time hustler who often acted as a courier, delivering money from the prostitution and gambling houses run by the South Jersey mob. Because of his loose affiliation with the mob, Fat Pete often times had privileged information about the gambling spots and drug deals that were going down. On a few occasions, when he thought it worth the risk, he'd set up drug buyers to be robbed after they had made the buy. Pete would always use Stretch and Sheldon for the robberies, and they would then distribute the drugs to their workers in Philly.

Knowing the dangers of stealing from the mob, Fat Pete was always careful to only set up certain buyers. However, he had an Achilles heel. His girlfriend, Lisa, couldn't keep her legs or her mouth closed. And to make matters worse, she was also sleeping with one of the young mobsters from the same crime family Pete was stealing from.

Two days before driving to the Camden garage, Fat Pete had Sheldon wait in a motel room just off the highway outside Easton, PA. A drug buy between a female courier, sent there by Anthony Pacetti, a capo in the Farnese crime family, and a pusher from Maryland, was to go down there. However, earlier that morning, Stretch had kidnapped the buyer outside the motel and driven him across the state line into New York's farming area. There, in the surrounding woods, the buyer was robbed of the $200,000 he was carrying for the purchase of a kilo of heroin, then shot to death and buried behind an old farmhouse.

When the female courier arrived at the motel, she was robbed of the heroin and killed. Her body was left there to be found, so the mob would be looking for the buyer from Maryland. It might have worked, if not that very same night, Lisa hadn't inadvertently opened her mouth, while opening her legs and revealed Pete's sudden fortuitous windfall and his secret association with two black drug dealers from Philly.

The next morning, Fat Pete and Lisa were awakened by the man Lisa had been pillow talking to. With him were two burly associates who tortured Pete until he gave up Sheldon and Stretch's name and location. The men then made Pete contact Sheldon and set up a meeting at the garage so that they could split up the money and heroin. After calling Anthony Pacetti and reporting what they had learned from Fat Pete, the men were given a Philadelphia phone number and the name, Maurice "Mo" Barton.

"Call'im, and tell'im you're callin' for me," Pacetti whispered into the phone. "Giv'im the address to the garage and tell'im what that fat bastard said about the drugs and money being hidden in that car."

"You want us to go there, too?" the man asked. "You kno' justa check on them Mooliyans?"

"No. Mo will kno' to contact me."

Before leaving, the men put a bullet a piece in Pete and Lisa's heads.

When the garage door opened, Stretch drove the Buick inside. Seeing Fat Pete's silver Lincoln, he and Sheldon expected nothing out of the ordinary. It wasn't until Sheldon saw Rushard leap from behind the Lincoln and placed the blue steel .38 revolver against Stretch's head that he knew they were in trouble.

Having been yanked from the car by Rushard's partner Dalton Lance, Sheldon now stood frozen in fear as he watched Rushard search the interior of the car.

"Where the fuck is it?" Dalton yelled, as he reached inside Sheldon's suit coat and removed the .45 automatic from his waist band. "We ain't got all day. Either you die with yo'r stupid-ass friend, or you give it up, now!"

Sheldon tried not to, but he couldn't help but look at the blood seeping from his friend's head and neck. It had all happened so quickly that he didn't even have time to reach for his own gun.

Sheldon knew Rushard well. They were about the same age, and had even played basketball against each other on opposing high school teams. Rushard had attended Southern, and he went to West Philadelphia High. After graduating, Rushard went in the army and Sheldon didn't see him for awhile. Once Rushard was discharged, however, he would sometimes visit Sheldon's sister.

"We ain't gonna ask you again." Dalton snarled.

"Hold up," Rushard said, climbing from the car. He still looked the same to Sheldon. Though they were both 23 now, Rushard still looked like that light-skinned, curly haired teenager he played ball against.

"Don't do this, man," Rushard told Sheldon. "It's obvious that the drugs and money is 'ere somewhere. Don't make us kill you when you kno' that we gonna find it anyway."

"I'ma dead man anyway, Rus," Sheldon managed to say, " you kno' tha'." Sweat was running down his face. He felt like he had to pee but was too afraid to even move.

"You got tha' right," Dalton mumbled, his eyes darting nervously back and forth, as his nostrils flared. "You punk-ass motherfuckah."

"Check under that hood," Dalton yelled to Rushard, "I'll check the trunk and tires."

Rushard lifted the hood and began to look around. Although it wasn't easy to see, he located a converted compartment that someone had soldered on the inner-side of the wheel-well.

"Hey, man," Sheldon heard Big Cil's raspy voice whispering from behind him. "You and Stretch finally fucked up big time, huh?"

Before Sheldon had time to respond, Cil pushed him toward the back of the garage. And if Sheldon had any hope of getting out of there alive, it faded as soon as he heard Big Cil's voice. Cil had those cold deadly eyes that frightened even those who were considered to be stone cold killers. And at that very moment, he was casting that deadly stare at Sheldon.

"I found it?" Rushard yelled out, as he pulled a well-wrapped package from the compartment.

"Can we work something out, Rus?" Sheldon managed to say. "We go back too far for this, man."

"We just snuffed yo'r life-long partner, man. Ain't no way we leavin you alive." Dalton yelled. "I told you last year 'bout dealin' wit' them white boys. Now they gave us the contract on you."

"It's all 'ere," Rus yelled. "Let's get the fuck out of 'ere."

Without blinking, Cil turned and hit Sheldon in the neck with an ice pick. He worked it in and out until he was sure Sheldon was dead and then he let him drop to the cement floor.

"I don't know why you don't just cap a motherfuckah, instead of using that damn ice pick." Dalton said, as he stepped over Sheldon's body and peeked outside.

"Cause there's no noise and little blood," Cil mumbled in his raspy voice. "He bleeds to death from the inside."

Outside the garage, waiting in a 1967 green Fleetwood was the fourth man of the group, Maurice "Mo" Barton. He and Cecil "Big Cil" Sampson, Rushard "Rus" Braxton and Dalton Landers had known each other for years. All but Maurice had grown up in South Philly. Mo, who was like a brother to Rus, was from West Philly.

Less than a minute later, the dark green '67 Cadillac was backing out of the cul-de-sac. Only then did they remove the rubber gloves they all wore. They put everything: the drugs, money, guns and the ice pick in a plastic bag and handed it to the man standing on the corner. Harvey Rollins, who was also part of their crew and from South Philly, then got into an old beat-up 1961 black Ford Falcon and drove off in the opposite direction.

# CHAPTER V

"I'm coming," she yelled, upon hearing the knock at her door. She had just stepped from the shower.

"I hope that's Lucius," she gleefully whispered. "I heard he was released this morning. I hope he spends his first night out with me." As Babysis ran the towel over her dark curly hair and wiped the beads of water from her round copper colored baby-face, she thought about the one and only time she had spent the night with Lucius. That had been seven years ago, and they were teenagers then. She had literally tricked him into bed that night and was hoping to get that chance again.

Again, she heard the knock. It was louder this time and sounded more impatient. Thinking it was Lucius behind that door, she remembered his big hands. "Damn, even as a boy he had big hands."

Wrapping her bathrobe around her fully developed body, she stared in the full length mirror at how it hugged her big hips. "Shit, I'ma woman, now. He gonna love this night." The fleshy cheeks of her ass jiggled as she hurried to the door and opened it, only to find Joe Napoli standing there.

"Hey, honey!" she cooed, hesitantly, trying not to sound disappointed. "I been waitin' on you. Wha' took you so long?"

Actually, she hadn't expected him. He wasn't supposed to be there on Wednesdays. He always came on Thursday nights.

"Yeah, I know," Napoli said, glancing around before stepping inside. "You just couldn't fuckin' wait, right?"

Before she could say another word, Napoli grabbed her arms and pressed her short full body against his huge belly.

"Wha'cha been up to, girl?" he asked, suspiciously. "You been in touch with any of your old friends, today?"

"Nah, Joe, I ain't been in touch with nobody. I jus' been trying to get my things together. You kno' how we do."

"You sure ain't nobody contacted you from the past?"

"What you talking 'bout sugar. Ain't nobody been 'ere."

Kicking the door closed, he pushed her across the room and back against the bed. He forced his thick tongue deep inside her mouth. The sour taste of tobacco sickened her so that she had to swallow to keep from vomiting.

Feeling her legs pressed against the side of the bed, she sat down seeking momentary relief from her revulsion. But the relief was short-lived. In less than a minute, Napoli had his suit coat off, his gun, badge and handcuffs on her night table and his pants down. He snatched open her robe to reveal her nakedness. The sight of her damp naked body caused his sour expression to change. But, though his lips smiled, his eyes remained as hard and mean as they always were.

Joe jabbed two clumsy fingers between her thighs to feel for her wetness. She wasn't wet. So he began to roughly twist and turn his fingers. "You're not ready, huh? I thought you said you were waiting for me." The sight of her discomfort excited him.

- 19 -

"I'm always ready for you, sugar," she answered and ran her hand mechanically over his groin. She shuddered at the feel of his dick, a reaction he misinterpreted for her excitement.

This was a game she had played for him over the years that was now getting so much harder to play, and tiresome for her. Babysis found herself almost in a panic, running her mind through various scenarios that might help her cope. But it was hard to detach her spirit from her body with no time for preparation.

"You ready, whore?" He snapped.

"Yeah, baby, I'm ready for you," she murmured, feeling overwhelmed by the stench of the tobacco on his breath and the cheap cologne he always splashed on his fat body.

Joe pushed her back on the bed, the weight of his body squashing the air right out of her. She felt his erection press against her belly and felt sick. She wished she was drunk. She held her breath as she felt him sliding down her body, his head going between her thighs, and she felt the vague sensation of his tongue licking her, then wiggling up inside her. She tried over and over to disavow her body. She didn't want it to be her lying there under this white slob of a man. Not tonight, especially, not tonight. She wanted it to be Lucius. She needed his big black hands pulling her thighs apart.

But it seemed useless. As quickly as Joe had moved down her body, he was again on top of her, his dick wildly poking the edges around her crotch like some dog in heat. Babysis squeezed her eyes closed and bit on her tongue to stop herself from crying out. When she tried to speed the ordeal by guiding him in with her hand, Joe hissed, "Don't!" and pinned her wrists to the mattress.

I jus' hope he's as quick as he usually is, she thought, as her mind finally assisted in giving her relief from the moment.

In her mind's eye, she was laying back on a soft bed with clean floral printed sheets and big, fluffy pillows that smelled of rose petals. At the foot of the bed stood a huge vanity mirror in which she glimpsed herself dressed in a white silk nightgown with lace and ribbons at the neck. From somewhere distant, she heard a familiar sound that reminded her of the old hymns she used to hear her grandmother sing. Again, she caught sight of herself in the pretty looking glass. The soft black curls of her hair, clinging to her copper-colored face, and the sensual curves of her breasts and lips being gently touched and caressed by huge strong black hands.

When Joe was finished, Babysis heard herself whispering, "Take it out! Take it out!" And as he always did, Joe dressed quickly, as if in an attempt to hide his fat, pig-like body. If she hadn't been so disgusted by the feel of his semen seeping from inside her, she would have laughed out loud. But instead, she coldly watched him as she wiped his putrid filth from between her thighs.

For some reason, he didn't run out the door as he usually did. And she believed she knew why.

"We need to talk, Gloria," he said, in an official manner. He sat down across from her bed, as if he didn't want to be too close to her.

Gloria Smith didn't like the sound of her real name coming from his mouth. It reminded her of when she first met him, and what he and his partner had done to her then. They both were rookies on the police force, and in uniform. Babysis was 15 years old, and they had picked her up for being out too late. When their sergeant at the station told them to drive her home, they drove her to the back of an old abandoned building instead, and Joe Napoli watched as his partner, Officer O'Brien, brutally raped her.

That's the night she met Lucius Please. He had saw her stumbling out in the street and came to her aid. When he took her to the hospital, he, not the police, was blamed for the rape. And though she insisted that Officer O'Brien had raped her, while Officer Napoli watched, nothing was ever done about it. Lucius, who was 17 at the time, was not charged, but he was extremely affected by the incident. The only good thing to come from that night was that Lucius became her friend.

"Talk 'bout wha' Joe?" she asked, sarcasm dipping from her lips. "Wha', you didn't like the taste of my pussy this time?"

"Get serious," he shot back. "I need to know if your friend Lucius Please has contacted you. I know he's out."

"I haven't heard from Lucius in years. We're not friends anymore. I'ma prostitute, a whore. Why would he contact me?"

Though Babysis hoped Lucius would contact her, she had no intentions of telling Joe Napoli anything. She knew why he was so concerned about Lucius. About two years after Officer O'Brien had raped her, the police found him in the back of that same abandoned building. His pants were pulled down below his knees, and his throat had been cut from ear to ear. Though the police suspected Lucius of killing him, they had no proof. Shortly after that, Lucius went to prison for beating up the Mummers for wearing black face at the New Year's Day Parade.

She looked right into Joe's narrow eyes and said, "The only people who call me are those seekin' a cheap, but damn good fuck, that they can't get from their wives and girlfriends."

"Don't make me get official with you," he spat. "I can make things real bad for you and you know that."

"Things have been bad for me ever since I met yo'r ass Joe, you kno' tha'. You stood there and watched that Irish bastard rape me, and you enjoyed it so much, tha' when I was forced to start workin' the streets, you couldn't wait to lick my shit."

Joe Napoli picked up his badge and gun, then backhanded Babysis with the handcuffs, knocking blood from her mouth. She flinched, but didn't cry out. Instead she stared at him and smiled. "You're scared of him, ain't cha? He might be the only black man you ever been scared of."

"Scared of him?" Joe yelled. "You tell that black bastard that if he crosses my path, he's a dead nigger."

Babysis pressed her lips tightly together and swallowed hard. "Mmm hmm. I'll tell 'im. If I see 'im."

With that, Joe Napoli was out the door.

# CHAPTER VI

### "The Vilest Deeds Like Poison-Weeds
### Bloom Well in Prison Air."

Lucius recalled the words, by Oscar Wilde, he'd read so many times while he was in prison. They had become a part of his psyche, his motivation, his purpose. They came to mind each time he thought of the dying man to whom he had given his word, while in the hole at Eastern State Penitentiary. It was that vow of vengeance that he'd made to Brother Fred that he was now about to fulfill.

Concealed by the darkness of night and the dense scraggly shrubs that grew beneath Interstate 95's exit ramp, Lucius watched, unseen from the brushes, as Nick Pulaski moved around behind the counter inside his gas station. Located on Trenton Road, on the outskirts of Levittown, in Bucks County, the gas station had just recently been purchased by Pulaski.

The lone female customer inside with Pulaski had already purchased gas, and she was now buying a few packs of cigarettes and other small items.

Herc had been right. Pulaski's station was located in the perfect spot to attract daytime customers. The exit ramp led off the Interstate and merged into Trenton Road, giving motorists an opportunity to purchase gas right after a long drive. However, in the late night and early morning hours, the area was isolated. With few houses and pedestrians, this made it the perfect spot for Lucius to wait for Nick Pulaski.

Wearing a pair of dark colored coveralls over his clothing and galoshes over his shoes, Lucius had parked Herc's black Chevy about a block from where he stood hidden beneath the exit ramp. In the 30 minutes he had been standing in the shadows, waiting and watching, he had seen only two customers drive up to the pumps.

Herc did a good job gathering information for me, Lucius thought, as he watched two white boys in a pickup truck stop to get gas, just as the female customer was getting in her car to leave.

"Look at 'im, fuckin' devil," Lucius mumbled. "He probably never even gave a second thought to what he did. To him, the brother was jus' another niggah. But I haven't forgotten."

Nick Pulaski had been a prison guard, working the hole, at Eastern State Penitentiary. Four years earlier, he'd been one of two guards who had beaten and stomped a Muslim inmate to death. Lucius, who had been instrumental in converting that inmate to Islam, had been locked in his cell and couldn't get out to help the brother. Later that night, while the beaten man lie dying on the cold floor of his cell, Lucius called out to him through the vent over the sink. He promised the brother that he would find a way to make them pay for what they had done to him. The next morning the inmate died. And the prison officials, fearing problems, moved both guards to the towers so they wouldn't be inside the prison.

Lucius never saw them again. But, over the years, in his darkened cell, he was trying to figure out a way to revenge that brother. He asked his longtime friend, Hercules "Herc" Williams, who came to visit him about twice a month, to help by learning everything he possibly could about the two guards.

Lucius trusted Herc. They came from the same North Philly neighborhood, and had been friends since they were six years old. They used to fight each other's battles, share toys, food, and even girls. And, because they were always about the same size, they often wore each other's clothes to school.

When Herc would visit Lucius at the prison, they would talk about what needed to be done about the guards. About a month before Lucius was to be released, Herc reported that Pulaski had retired and bought a gas station in Bucks County.

"That other cracker died of cancer last week," Herc told Lucius. "You should let me handle Pulaski before he dies, too."

"No," Lucius responded, his eyes staring into space. "On the day I come home, if that devil isn't already dead, you can rest assure, he'll die that day."

"Yeah, but Lucius, I kno' his routine. Like you said, I followed him for a month. That gave me a good idea of what he does and how he does it. Just like the Jews, these Pollacks follow a set pattern. What he did on Monday one week, he did on Monday the next. Always took the same route, never deviated."

"I appreciate your diligence, Herc, but I have to do this myself. I gave my word."

"Don't you think the cops will suspect you?" Herc asked.

"Yeah, they might. But I gotta plan. And I'll need you to help me with it."

"No problem," Herc responded, "I'm here for you Bro, you kno' tha'."

"On the day I get out, Brother David is s'posed to drive me up to Chicago. But on the way, we have to pick up some <u>Muhammad Speaks</u> newspapers so that we can take them to the brothers in Western Penitentiary in Pittsburgh. Since we'll be picking the newspapers up from a brother in Dauphin County, we won't be driving all the way through to Pittsburgh. I'll need you to meet us there and stay at the motel in my place."

"Yeah, I can do tha'. But why?"

"Cause, you and I look so much alike, people will think you're me. If anyone comes around later, asking questions and showing a picture, they'll say, yeah, he was 'ere. But while you're at the motel with David, I'll take yo'r car and drive to Pulaski's gas station. Once I've handled my business there, I'll meet you and switch places before it's time to leave the next morning."

"So you want me to be seen by people," Herc asked. "Like buying some food or som'um?"

"Yeah, something like that."

"You still kno' how to get to Bucks County?" Herc joked.

"I ain't been away tha' long, man. I bought my first car in Langhorne. I kno' it's a few hours drive from Harrisburg, but I'll be back in time."

"Do David kno' bout this?"

"No. We'll get different rooms. He won't kno' tha' I've left. I'll tell 'im that I need som' sleep and will meet him at the car in the mornin'. You jus' make sure he doesn't see you movin' 'round tha' motel."

Emerging from the shadows of the exit ramp and into the glow of the street light, Lucius kept his eyes firmly fixed on the man as he stepped back inside the station. The two kids in the pick-up truck were driving off. Lucius could see the clock on the wall inside the station. It was 2 a.m. Herc had said that Pulaski usually closed up around that time.

"I have to move now," he mumbled. "I gotta get back on the road."

With eyes narrowed, he moved swiftly. The shinny blade of the straight razor in his right hand flickered in the glow of the street light. Pulaski had just bend over to pick up some crates and moved them inside the door. He didn't see the tall muscular black man creeping up from behind.

"Hey, Pulaski," Lucius whispered, as he took a position behind the former prison guard. "Stomp any brothers lately?"

Nick Pulaski shivered from a cold spot between his shoulder blades, as he remembered, with frightening vividness where he had heard that voice before. As he turned, his eyes were met by a pair of stone cold eyes staring back at him.

They stood toe to toe, face to face. Both about the same height, though Lucius was 202 pounds of solid chiseled muscle, Pulaski was more like 280 pounds of flab. Gripped in fear, and unable to move, Pulaski first tried to protest, then beg. His lips moved, but the sound was quickly turned into a grunt and then a gurgle. He didn't see the swift movement of the blade, but recoiled as it slashed open his throat. Falling backward, Pulaski's body went into a violent spasm, then folded over. But Lucius wasn't finished. He immediately grabbed hold of Pulaski's shirt and pulled him upright again.

"Oh no, devil," Lucius growled. "You're not going out without a fight! Are you? Well, take this wit'cha."

And with that, he sliced Pulaski's neck from the opposite direction. Creating an "X" across his neck and opening the wound even wider. As spurts of blood gushed from Pulaski's neck, Lucius held him up and stared into the dying man's eyes.

"Think of Brother Fred." He snarled through clenched teeth. "Remember how you stomped him to death. He may not be where you're going, but I'm sendin' you his way jus' the same."

Though Lucius was now speaking to a dead man, gone limp in his hands, he let him drop to the floor then used his size 14 foot to press on his neck and force out more blood.

As Lucius drove back toward Dauphin County to meet Herc, all thoughts of Pulaski had gone the way of the discarded coveralls, galoshes and straight razor. They were in a sewer somewhere in Montgomery County. It was over, and he could now move on.

After arriving at the motel, Lucius spoke briefly to Herc, then met David so that they could first have breakfast, then leave. Things had gone according to plan. Brother David never suspected that Lucius had left the motel.

As David drove, Lucius, unable to sleep, took in the sights and wondered what this Chicago trip was really about. How did Brother Captain know that I existed? He asked himself. What have I ever done within the Nation of Islam that would cause him to write a letter to the Temple, asking to see me? Well, I guess I'll find out soon enough."

As he marveled at the Pennsylvania countryside, one range blended into another. For Lucius, who had never seen the rural areas, the twist and turns of the roads through the Allegheny Mountains went past the greenest trees he'd ever seen; it was like something out of a picture book. Finally, after about 30hours since his release from prison, he felt rested enough to close his eyes. He felt sleep approaching.

When Lucius awoke, they were in Pittsburgh. After checking in with the Chaplain and Muslim Minister at the Penitentiary, David was able to get a special pass for Lucius to visit, as well. They were allowed to eat lunch with some of the Muslim brothers, then left three bundles of the <u>Muhammad Speaks</u> newspapers.

# CHAPTER VII

Lucius enjoyed the sights along the route to Chicago, as well. It seemed the drive from Philly to Pittsburgh was about as long as the drive from Pittsburgh to Chicago. It was around 8 p.m. when they arrived. Lucius was amazed at how different the city looked from Philadelphia.

He asked David about the Brother Captain he was going to meet, but David knew very little about him.

"I only met him twice before," he answered. "And both times it was at monthly joint security meetings for captains and lieutenants."

"What's he like?" Lucius asked.

"Seems real serious. Very soft spoken and gives the impression of someone who might have come from a professional background."

Lucius smiled to himself. It sounded as if David was describing himself. He was around 35 years of old and had graduated from Lincoln University. He became a guidance counselor at a local junior high school before leaving to teach at the Muslim elementary school.

Brother Captain Khalil, a short, well-dressed, soft spoken man with deep set eyes, met them at the Salaam Restaurant. After giving a lukewarm greeting of, "As-Salaam-Alaikum," to Brother David, Brother Captain turned and extended both his hands to Lucius.

"As-Salaam-Alaikum, Brother Lucius," he said warmly looking the tall man up and down. "I've heard a lot of good things about you, brother."

"Wa-Laikum-As-Salaam," Lucius courteously replied, while gripping both hands in a brotherly handshake. "If there's some good to be said about any of us, sir, it's due to the blessed wisdom Allah has bestowed upon our dear Holy Apostle.

"You're right about that my brother." Brother Captain replied. "We must thank Allah daily for the Honorable Elijah Muhammad."

Captain Khalil didn't look much older than Lucius, and for some reason, this surprised Lucius. He had expected to meet a much older brother. Probably because when contacted about coming to Chicago, he had been told that the newly appointed captain to the security staff was a seasoned brother who wanted to meet with certain brothers from temples around the country.

"We can't talk here." Khalil told them. "They're quite busy today. Follow me in your car down to the store, we'll talk there."

The store was a very fashionable haberdashery on East 51st Street on the South Side. Lucius would later learn that it was owned by the Chief of Security for the Nation of Islam, Raymond Sharrieff. Once inside, Brother Khalil asked David to remain in the front of the store with the salesmen, while he and Lucius went in the back to talk.

"Have a seat, Brother Lucius," he said, barely over a whisper. "This won't take long. Actually, I hated bringing you all the way here for such a brief conversation, but I was needed here and was unable to come to Philly at the moment."

As he nervously sat, Lucius felt the soft leather of the chair creases beneath him. "Really, I didn't mind coming here, sir. As you know, I was just released from prison, yesterday. It was an honor to be asked to come to Chicago."

"Well, I hope that you are still impressed after hearing what I have to say."

***

It was 1 a.m. Friday morning, when Lucius pulled up in front of the Spinning Top Night Club on Germantown Avenue and Cumberland Street in Philadelphia. He was amazed to see how the building, originally a three-story house, had been converted. The facade of dark and light grey shaded masonry went from the first floor to the roof. Beneath the second floor windows, an illuminated spinning red top flashed on and off.

"Damn," Lucius mumbled. "Girl is talkin' loud."

Still, he hesitated before ringing the doorbell on the side of the black and white door. Torn between his memories of her soft loveliness and the vow he'd made to himself, that he would follow the dictates of his religion, Lucius stood at the door as if it was the crossroads of life. While in his prison cell, he had prayed and told Allah and himself that he would never fornicate or commit adultery again. Though he had never been with another man's wife, he had been with Redtop and Babysis after he had accepted Islam. That caused him to partly view those years in prison as punishment for his sins.

Still, he had to admit, he needed to see her even if they didn't have sex. The sound of the doorbell was low and almost musical. At that moment, he stood, a man considered by many to be fearless, waiting for the person he feared most.

The tall bow-legged, red-haired woman with a sprinkle of freckles on her pretty face, looked like a million dollars as she strode through the crowd. Men and women alike, stared. Their eyes traveling up and down her shapely body. Most men desiring her, most women envying her. She just had that look, that easy self-possessed assurance of someone who was used to having the eyes of strangers on her.

The emerald-green knit dress, slightly flared, showed off the rhythmic bounce of her hips as she moved toward the door. However, as exciting as she was to look at, all glances from the customers weren't for her. Each time the doorbell rang, all eyes in the dimly lit, fashionable nightclub looked up to see who the new arrivals would be.

"It's been a long time," she whispered, holding open the door. Her voice still had that soft husky sound. And in that instance, he recalled her last words to him when he had asked her not to visit him while he was in prison.

"Why are you punishing me?" she had asked. "You're gonna be punishing me for a long time?"

"Hello, Red," he finally said, gathering himself enough to step inside the club and into the view of all those eyes. "You're right, it has been a long time."

He wasn't surprised at how beautiful she looked. She had always been a pretty woman. Cinnamon colored skin, with a few brown freckles and penny sized dimples. She was a natural red head, and very rare in the black community.

"You look wonderful," he said, bending so that only she could hear. All eyes were on them. Those who knew him had heard he was home and had expected he would soon be there.

"Thank you," she answered. "So do you."

He looked so good to her that she wanted to just take him in her arms right there in front of everyone. But she didn't.

"I had hoped that you'd come to see me yesterday," was what she wanted to say. But Redtop understood Lucius better than most, even after not seeing him for so long. So she just showed her genuine happiness to have him there now.

Tearing his eyes from hers, he noticed the crowd, some standing on a dance floor, others sitting at the bar that ran the length of what used to be a living room and dining area.

"You have a very nice place here," he whispered, while nodding to and acknowledging some of the people he recognized in the room.

Redtop didn't answer. She took hold of his hand and led him passed the crowd and up the stairs. On the second floor, there were other people sitting at tables and listening to live entertainment. He glanced at the jazz trio as she guided him toward another set of stairs. As soon as they reached he third floor, she turned and faced him, taking both of his hands in hers. She studied him, smiling, her eyes loving and filling with tears.

"I can't tell you how glad I am to see you, Lucius. I always wondered how it would be. How you would look. You were so young when they took you away. But now, look at you. So handsome, so big and strong. You have always been a pretty man."

Though he tried not to, Lucius found himself blushing. He wanted to say something loving to her, but was too afraid he would weaken.

Redtop turned and went into the living room and Lucius followed. The dimly lit room was sparsely furnished with a couch and a coffee table and two chairs catty-cornered at the window. The walls were painted pastel, the floor hardwood. Off to the side, he could see her bedroom. Lit only by candlelight, the bed was huge. It was nothing like the paper thin mattress he had been sleeping on for the past seven years.

"I was saddened to hear about your mother," she said, for the moment, bailing him out of his thoughts, and motioning for him to take a seat beside her on the couch. "I know how much you loved her."

"Thank you," he answered. "Seems we both lost a loved one in the past few years."

"Yeah," she shrugged. "But my husband don't deserve to be mentioned in the same breath as your mom. She was a fine upstanding woman."

"Yes, she was."

"And my husband. Well, that's a horse of a different color."

"Why did you marry him?" Lucius asked. "I never really understood that."

"After your trial, when you wouldn't let me visit, I felt abandoned, so to speak. Not that you and I were ever a couple, in that sense. But, you were important to me. When I met Rother, I was at my lowest point, emotionally. He became my ladder, someone to lift myself back up on, I guess."

"How long were y'all together?"

"About a year," she said, in a murmur. "About six months after we separated, he was killed. As a matter of fact, right here in this club. Some thugs were trying to rob him, and instead of just giving them the money, the idiot tried to fight."

"Was this his club?"

"One of them," she said, reaching for his hand and rubbing it between both of hers. "The other two went to his daughters from a previous marriage. This one was left to me."

Lucius didn't mention his suspicions about her husband's death. He would leave that alone, for now. As he began to feel a bit more comfortable with her, his body relaxed and her closeness began to affect him. Emotions made him tremble and she detected it.

"It's been a long time for me, too," she said, staring into his eyes. "I still remember how we were together. I miss that."

His voice was thick. "I miss it, too." Again he felt torn between his desire for her and the principles of his faith. It was made even more difficult when she leaned closer and kissed him on the mouth. He felt her breath on his skin. He wanted so desperately to kiss her in return, to hold her, to experience the comfort of her body he remembered from so long ago. But still, he hesitated.

"I know you don't love me," she whispered with her lips on his ear. "We were so good for each other because we had no expectations. But still, we had something connecting us. And that something is pulling at us right now."

Trying to sound strong and regain control of the situation, Lucius said, "You're right, Red. But that something springs from desperation and loneliness. If we weren't desperate or lonely would we …?"

"Hush," she whispered. "If loneliness and desperation are the only reason you miss someone, you never really needed them in your life in the first place. You don't desire me out of loneliness and desperation, alone. How can something so good between us be a sin?"

Lucius needed her more than anything right then. At that moment, he had been stripped of that noble steerage he had previously relied on. He pulled her closed and squeezed her tightly. He needed her to make him feel whole again, like a man again. His head dropped to her breasts and she started moving against him.

"Are you sure?" she asked.

"Yes. I just hope I don't disappoint you."

"Don't worry about me," she whispered huskily. "I just wouldn't want you to wake up in the morning disappointed in yourself."

Lucius now welcomed those memories he had tried so hard to suppress over the years. As he felt her hand move to his crotch, he raised his head from her breasts and mashed his lips solidly against hers.

"You're so good for me, Lucius," she breathed over and over in his mouth. "Carry me to our bed, baby, carry me."

***

When he awoke, Lucius realized that he had lost a battle of virtues. But like an onion, which one peels layer by layer, he knew there would be more battles before the war was won.

He looked down at Redtop breathing slow and easy in a restful sleep. Her head lay on his chest. She was beautiful, exciting, intelligent and prosperous. A man would be a fool not to consider her for marriage, he thought. Then, as quickly as he had thought it, he put it out of his mind and recalled the conversation he'd had with Brother Captain Khalil.

The Brother Captain had said someone from Philadelphia had called him about Lucius' ability to organize the men who were at the prison with him.

"They really respected you," Brother Khalil had said to him. "I'm told that many of the letters we received from the men at that prison, inquiring about the Nation of Islam, came as a result of you talking with them."

When Lucius insisted that he had done nothing more than other Muslim brothers recruiting inside the prison had done, Brother Captain leaned forward over his desk and looked directly into Lucius' eyes. "None of us is the same, my brother. Different results often come from men using similar tactics. Some are leaders, others are followers. You are a leader with a very different ability. You must recognize it and take advantage of it."

"What is it you want me to do, sir?" Lucius asked.

"Some on the Supreme Captain's staff, people whom I will not name, have asked me to speak with you about recruiting and organizing certain brothers in Philly."

"I'm not sure of what you mean by certain brothers."

"At this time around this country, there are black men who are beginning to stand up against the oppression by the white devils. Though many might be sympathizers, not all will join the Nation of Islam. But, they can still be of service to us. Like in prison, because of the oppressive conditions, there were men who banned together regardless of their personal beliefs. And, I hear that you were very good at using that to our advantage there."

Brother Captain Khalil went on to tell Lucius that a few other brothers in Philly would be available to assist him in this.

"But you're the only person who reports to me. No one else. Understand?"

"Yes, sir, I think so."

"I don't want you to think so, Brother Lucius. I want you to know. The men you will be expected to recruit are, like yourself, courageous. Right now they are doing things that would not be accepted within the Nation of Islam. This means you'll have to deal with them on their level. Can you do that?"

"Yes, sir."

"Any regrets?" Redtop asked, raising her head from his broad chest.

"No," he murmured. "Not a one."

"Good, cause you haven't lost a thing, you know that."

"I had a good teacher," he grinned.

But as Lucius left her that morning, he was filled with remorse. Recalling his studies while in prison, he remembered reading about the struggles of Prophet Job, in the Bible, and the conversation between God and Satan. The devil had told God that Job was only an obedient servant to God because God had a protective hedge around him. "Remove that hedge," he told God, "and Job will be as the unfaithful. He will curse you and love me."

Had prison been his hedge? Lucius thought. But unlike Job, once his hedge was removed, had he failed the test of faith?

# CHAPTER VIII

A slight drizzle, through which the morning sun shined, created a rainbow off in the distance. As Lucius parked Redtop's maroon Mustang on the corner of Cumberland and Jessup Streets, he noticed the brilliant colors arching in the sky and smiled. Once again, he was enjoying the gifts that lay beyond prison walls.

Instinctively, he glanced at the doorways and windows as he made his way up Jessup toward Huntington Street. His strides, long and steady, his shoulder dipped, as he strolled that walk innate to those brothers who had grown up in Philly.

He saw no one on the street and was thankful for that. The 2500 block of Jessup held lots of memories for him, but he didn't need to be distracted by them now. His only concern at the moment was seeing Fat Hank and speaking with Babysis, if she was there.

The thought of seeing Babysis invoked memories of last night with Redtop. Though he had showered since being with her, he could still smell the scent of her perfume and feel the gentle essence of her womanhood upon his body. For the sake of his own reality, he knew he had to rid himself of her effects.

Fat Hank was standing at the window of his restaurant and saw Lucius approaching. A smile stretched across his aging face. He had known Lucius since he was a little boy and had always loved him like a son. When Lucius went to prison, it was Fat Hank who put up the money for a lawyer and made sure Lucius had funds for commissary and books while there.

The door opened and the floor board creaked as Lucius stepped inside.

"Damn, old man, you ain't fixed that floor board yet?"

"Shit, that's my alarm system." Fat Hank grinned, his arms outstretched. "C'mere boy and give me a hug."

Lucius pulled the older man into his arms and hugged him tightly. He could tell that Hank was still sturdy and he seemed in good shape. For that he was thankful. While he was away, he had worried a lot about Hank. He'd also heard a rumor about someone trying to shake Hank down for money. But Lucius wouldn't mention it unless Hank did. He knew that Hank was a proud man and might not want to ask for anyone's help.

"I see you still eatin' up yo'r product," Lucius joked.

"Shit, if I don't eat my cooking' who else will?"

Now that Lucius was standing in front of him, Hank could see just how much he had grown while being in prison. Lucius had always been tall, but now his frame was thick and muscular.

"How you get 'ere?" Hank asked. "You catch the bus or som'um?"

"Yeah." Lucius said, not wanting Hank to know he was driving one of Redtop's cars.

"You ain't gotta ride no bus. I got four cars that ain't doin' nut'in but gatherin' dust. Shit, two of 'em practically brand spankin' new."

"I'm alright," Lucius assured him. "The brothers at the mosque got a car for me to use. I jus' ain't pick it up yet."

"Yeah," Hank mumbled, glancing down at the floor for a moment before again flashing his broad grin. "Boy, you sho look good," he continued. "I really missed you. C'mon back 'ere and let me feed'ja."

"Hey, fat man," Lucius said, grabbing Hank by his arm and stopping him before he got behind the counter. "I hope you kno' how much I appreciated what you did for me while…"

"Lucius," Hank whispered, "Please, don't thank me for doin' wha' comes nat'chu'ly. You like a son to me, boy. I'll always be 'ere for you."

It was while Lucius was filling his mouth with a mess of grits and scrambled eggs, covered in butter and hot sauce that Hank finally mentioned Babysis.

"You kno' that girl's upstairs," Hank whispered.

"Who?" Lucius asked as if he didn't already know who Hank was referring to.

"Babysis?" Hank said. "She been 'ere for the last few days. I guess she figured since you wouldn't com' to her, she'd com' to you. Sooner or later, she knew you'd come 'ere."

"I'ma go up and see her, alright?"

"Yeah," Hank answered. "I gotta go down in the basement, anyway. I gotta get som'um out the safe for ya."

"Som'um like what?"

"I saved som' money for ya while you was off in that place. It ain't much, but it'll keep the hawk from your do'r."

"I can't take any more money from you."

"Take the money, boy. I'ma give it to you, anyway."

"Old man, you ain't changed a bit," Lucius said, laughing, as he headed for the steps leading to the apartment upstairs.

"Yeah," Fat Hank yelled after him. "And I can still turn this 'ere left hook over on yo'r young chin, too."

It was easy for Lucius to smile at her as he reached the top of the stairs and turned into the large living room. She was sitting on a couch, her dark curly hair cut the way she had worn it when he last saw her. Babysis had matured into a woman over the years, and he thought she was even prettier than he remembered.

She didn't smile as she rose to meet him. Dressed in a floral print silky robe that wrapped her shapely body like a glove, she moved voluptuously toward him. Her eyes stared directly into his. It was a look that was hard but not cold. She was angry and wanted him to know it.

"Give me a hug, Sis," he mouthed as she closed the distance between them. "You're surely a sight for sore eyes."

She managed a smile before getting on her tip-toes so she could stretch to wrap her arms around his neck.

"I should strangle you," she whispered, as her body stretched out against him.

The feel of her warm softness pressing against him caused him to recall the many lonely nights he had spent in prison desiring such a woman. His body reacted to her just as it had reacted the night before with Redtop, only quicker.

"It's really good to see you," he said, removing her arms from around his neck and stepping back out of her reach.

"I can't tell," she shrugged. "If it's so good seeing me, then why did it take you so long getting here?"

"C'mon, Gloria, I only been out a few days. I had to go to the Temple and they sent me out of town, to Chicago."

There was nothing pretentious about Babysis. She had long ago accepted her lifestyle and knew that Lucius was aware of what she had been doing while he was away. So, though hurt that he hadn't come to her first, she would now enjoy him as much as he would allow. Where Lucius Please was concerned, she had no pride to swallow. Since the night she was raped by the cops and he had come to her aid, she had loved him. And though she felt he could never understand that love, she would always be there to accommodate, if he asked.

"Don't call me Gloria," she said, rolling her eyes and still playing the game. "You only call me that when you wanna sound like my big brother. I don't need no big brother this morning. I need you!"

"That's incest," he joked, walking her over to the couch and sitting down. "How are you, really? You know, I thought about you every day while I was in that place."

"Were you worried about me?" she asked, her eyes again staring into his. "I'm fine. I'ma always be fine."

Those feelings began to stir in him again. Regardless of how much he tried not looking at her in that way, he wanted her. That little teenager who had tricked him in her bed years ago was gone. In her place sat a full figured beautiful woman who wanted him to take her in his arms and make love to her.

"I'm sorry I didn't come to see you earlier. I…"

"It's alright," she interrupted, sounding calmer. "I know you have other people in your life. I was just being childish like I always did when it came to you. I'm just glad you're here, now."

A tinge of guilt swept over him. H wanted this woman, yet he was willing to allow her to think that because of her choices in life, he didn't desire her.

Jumping up from the couch, Babysis exclaimed, "C'mere, Lucius, I got something to show you."

He watched as she hurried across the floor, her full round hips bouncing under the silk robe. Her excitement, like that of a little child, caused him to smile. He rose slowly and crossed the room to where she stood at the window.

"I bought it," she proclaimed, pointing out the window at a mint-green 64 Impala. "I paid for it with my own money! Hank wanted to let me have one of his cars, but I wanted to buy my own."

"It's nice," he remarked. "You should be very proud of yourself … speaking of Hank, have you heard of any problems he's been having?"

"Yeah, you mean with Dabney, don't you?"

"Who is Dabney?"

"He's this guy that shakes down older drug dealers by making them think he's got backup."

"So I take it that Hank is still dealing, huh?"

"C'mon, Lucius, you know what's going down. Even while you were away, people kept you informed about me and just about everybody else you know."

"I guess I was just hoping, that's all."

"The only reason Hank pays Dabney is because he works for the police."

"Dabney works for the police? What, he's a snitch?"

"Mmm Hmm, he was here last week. Probably won't be back until September, now."

"September?" Lucius mumbled, as if talking to himself.

"Please be careful, Lucius," she said, squeezing his hand in hers. "You already got that cop trying to put you away, talking about you killed his partner."

"Yeah, I've heard rumors," he said. "Is it that same cop from before?"

"Yeah, to be truthful, he's been coming around asking questions."

"He's been protecting you from arrest?"

"Yes," she sheepishly murmured, glancing down at the floor. "I've…"

"No need," he said, lifting her chin with his finger.

"Please take this key," she said, pressing her apartment key into his hand. "I don't live here. I stay at …"

"I have your address," he smiled.

They looked at one another in silence. The longer they stood there, the deeper the silence became. She now knew he wanted her, but she wouldn't push it. It had to be at his asking and not at her request.

"I have to go," he whispered, kissing her on the cheek.

"I know."

As he descended the steps, Hank tossed him a brown paper package and a set of keys. "It's the 66 black Riviera parked in my garage. Pick it up whenever, it'll be there for ya."

After walking back down the block and climbing in the front seat of Redtop's Mustang, Lucius counted the contents of the bag. It was $10,000.

# CHAPTER IX

## September 3, 1967

In the six weeks since Lucius had left the books with him, Wade did nothing but go to work and return home to read. He sometimes even carried one of the books to work with him to read during his lunch hour. He had no distractions. Frankie, his girlfriend, was away visiting her family in another state and wasn't due back in Philly for another week.

The book, How To Eat To Live, conveyed the message of how one should eat healthy to preserve one's life. Until then, Wade had never fully understood why the Muslims didn't eat pork. But now he was learning more about different kinds of food that was unhealthy, as well.

But it was the book, Message to the Blackman in America that really got Wade's attention. Though he had heard the voices of people like H. Rap Brown, Huey Newton, and Stokely Carmichael, their messages were very different from that of Mr. Muhammad's. Wade learned that Elijah Muhammad had been teaching for years. He had been the teacher of Malcolm X and the inspiration for others.

What most impressed Wade was Mr. Muhammad's direct approach to the race problem in America. Unlike other black leaders, he didn't mince words while pointing out the injustice meted out by whites toward blacks in God's name. In one passage he had written, "If God was your father, you would love me." The book caused Wade to recall the many incidents in his short life, where he'd seen or heard of whites victimizing blacks. How many times had he seen blacks, regardless of their station in life, trying to appease and love white folks, only to be rewarded with rejection and humiliation?

The depth of their cruelty were conjured when those seemingly innocuous things he hadn't thought of in years now crept into his mind as embarrassments. They had corrupted things as innocent as cartoons he had watched as a child, by portraying caricatures of Africans shuffling shiftlessly through the jungle with rings around their necks, big lips painted white, while singing, "Salami, Salami, Baloney." He'd laughed at those cartoons without even knowing that their purpose had been to degrade the culture and religion of his own people. The white man had him and countless other black children laughing at themselves.

Then there were the all-white divine images from church, the little pink faced angels in the clouds. Even in his school books, he'd seen blacks serving whites. Standing in the heat of the sun while holding umbrellas over the heads of their masters. And he cringed as he thought of past and present lynching's and what blacks were now experiencing in both the South and North; marching and singing about freedom, while being beaten and kicked. It was on the news everyday, white police joined with white citizens to sic dogs on blacks, beat them with batons, and flush them with water hoses.

<u>The Miseducation of the Negro</u> by Carter G. Woodson, was equally impressive. In it, Wade saw a passage which seemed to exemplify exactly what Mr. Muhammad had said about the controlled inferior thinking of the Negro in America:

> *"When you control a man's thinking, you do not have to worry about his actions. You do not have to tell him to stand here or go yonder. He will find his proper place and will stay in it. You do not have to send him to the back door. He will go without being told. In fact, if there is no back door, he will cut one for his special benefit."*

The enthusiasm Wade was experiencing that Sunday morning while on his way to the Blue Horizon Ballroom was like nothing he'd ever imagined. After spending night after night reading those books and doing research on his own, he felt as if someone had come to make sense of the inklings he'd had all his life, but never knew what they were. Like a key turning a rusty lock, his mind began to open up. How could I not have known, he thought. The white man must be the devil.

Wade smiled while recalling an incident that had occurred a few years earlier when a Muslim brother once tried to sell him a <u>Muhammad Speaks</u> newspaper.

"I don't know nothing' about no Muhammad." Wade had said, with a look of agitation.

"What's your name, brother?" the Muslim asked calmly.

"My name's Wade."

"You know, Brother Wade, the ignorance plaguing our people is comparable to triple darkness. When a people don't know that they don't know something, that's a darkness void of any light, whatsoever."

Wade didn't know what the brother meant. He thought it was just the man's way of insulting him, personally. But after seeing the brother a couple of times on the subway, he came to view the brother as just being philosophical. However, Wade still never bought a paper from him. That is, not until after he had read Elijah Muhammad's <u>Message to the Blackman in America</u>, and realized what the brother had meant by triple darkness.

That past Saturday night, Wade had just gotten off work and walked down into the subway. Standing on the platform was the brother who had always tried to sell him the paper. Seeing him, Wade walked right up to him and asked for a <u>Muhammad Speaks</u>. The brother didn't hesitate, nor did he charge him for the paper. He just smiled, handed Wade the paper, and said, "This one is on me. The next one you can pay for."

When Wade told him about the books he had been reading, the brother informed him of the Temple meeting that would be at the Blue Horizon Ballroom the next day. "Sunday at 1 pm," he said. "You should go. It's a joint meeting. Brothers and sisters from all the Temples in the area will be there. You might even see the brother who lent you the books."

When Dabney's 1966 Grey Continental came to a stop on the corner of Huntington and Germantown Avenues, he pulled the brown paper bag from under the seat and handed it to Ralph.

"When you see me wave to you, bring this bag down to the restaurant," he said. "Leave the car here."

"I kno', man," Ralph replied in a slur. "We go through this shit ev'rytime."

"And get the fuck outta the mirror pickin' yo'r face, man," Dabney yelled. "If the rollers pull up and see you doin' that, you'll get my shit busted."

He got out of the car and glanced at his watch. "12:45," he mumbled. "And that fuckin' Ralph already shot-up over half of my monster. I gotta get'im off that fuckin' meth befor' he fuck up all my shit."

Crossing Germantown Avenue, Dabney relished the sound the heals of his shoes made on the cobblestones lining the street. Somehow it made him feel dressed up. He glanced at his reflection in the store window as he passed. I like this suit, he thought, as he turned and climbed the steps of Fat Hank's restaurant. Less than two minutes later, he reappeared outside, waving his arms at Ralph, who was still picking at the bumps on his face.

"Yo, Ralph," Dabney yelled. "Bring me my overcoat."

Ralph grabbed the bag of heroine, placed it under a coat and leaped from the car. But none of this went unnoticed. As she had done every Sunday afternoon, for years, Babysis had come to Fat Hank's restaurant for a meal. She sat in her nearly new Impala and watched from down the street as Ralph handed the coat to Dabney.

"Tha' cheap-suit-wearin-faggot," she mumbled. "He's back again. Tryin' to get hank to sell tha' fucking garbage for 'im. Okay, I'ma call Lucius. He should be at the Temple by now."

Creeping out of her car so Dabney wouldn't see her, she headed for the phone booth on the corner. No, wait, she thought to herself. They got tha' joint meetin' thing down at the Blue Horizon today. I'll catch'im later. Maybe this time I'll get 'im to spend the night wit' me, too."

She waited until Dabney and Ralph had driven off before she emerged from the phone booth. Walking swiftly to the restaurant, she yelled out her familiar cry, as she opened the door.

"Hey, hey, hey. Little Momma 'ere for som' ribs and fried chicken, Big Daddy."

As usual, Fat Hank grinned, then replied. "Ain't nuttin' little 'bout tha' wide ass of yours, girl."

"Yeah, well, I wish Lucius would notice it," she sighed.

# CHAPTER X

The Blue Horizon was a ballroom where banquets, cabarets, and other events, like boxing matches or fashion shows were often held. Every first Sunday of the month, the Muslims from all the temples in Philadelphia and surrounding areas held a joint meeting there and filled it to capacity.

It was a hot Sunday afternoon. There were so many cars parked in front of the Blue Horizon, and up and down Broad Street, that many of them took up the middle divide which separated the north and south-bound lanes of that wide street.

Wade arrived at the Ballroom around 12:30. He had been told that services wouldn't start until 1 pm, but he wanted to be early. He hoped to see Brother Lucius, so he could thank him for the loan of the books and give them back.

Just inside the door were two rooms with curtains hanging over their entrance. Everyone entering the services had to be searched. Males in one room, and females in the other. As the Muslim brother began searching Wade, he greeted him. "As-Salaam-Alaikum." When Wade returned the greeting, the brother said, "Welcome to Muhammad's Temple. We ask that you understand we have rules we conduct ourselves by."

He was standing directly in front of Wade and spoke in a voice just above a whisper. "Here at Muhammad's Temple, we ask that you remove all items from your pockets and allow us to view them. If any of those items have to be checked, we will place them in a bag, give you a receipt and return them to you when you leave. If you are carrying a weapon, we will return it and ask that you leave immediately. We do this for your protection as well as ours."

Though he'd earlier been told about this procedure, the brother's mannerism impressed Wade. If there was anything he had noticed about the Muslims, he had met on the street, it was that they always acted polite and respectful. Wade handed the brother the books he had bought with him, and was given a claims ticket. As he left the small search area, he noticed two men standing by a wide entrance-way that was also covered by a curtain. They brushed the curtain aside and Wade walked into an auditorium that was filled with about a thousand folding chairs. They were arranged in rows and separated by an aisle with men sitting on one side and women sitting on the other. Wade would later learn that Islam teaches that men and women should be separated in times of instruction and prayer. There was also a second level balcony there, which extended around the sides of the hall and overlooked the wide floor and stage below.

On the stage were three chairs that sat behind and to the right of a podium. To the left of the podium was a blackboard, where on one side, someone had written the words: "Slavery, Suffering, and Death = Christianity." Under those words were drawn symbols of an American flag, a cross, and a black man hanging from a tree. On the other side it read, "Freedom, Justice and Equality = Islam." And in the middle of the board were the words, "Which One Will Survive Armageddon?"

Wade was ushered to his seat by an elderly brother in a black suit and a skinny black bow-tie. As more people began arriving, Wade sat there soaking in the surroundings. It was awe-inspiring; jittery, but not frightening. Soul-stirring and subdued at the same time. He watched wide-eyed as the procession of beautiful multi-shaded brown-faced women, dressed in long ankle-length white dresses, walk up and down the center aisle. Most wore matching head-pieces, while others had their hair covered with different colored scarves. Wade noticed that some of the sisters standing post wore white box-hats with flaps tied under their chin. On their hats were the letters, M.G.T. and G.C.C., which stood for Muslim Girl's Training and General Civilization Class.

To Wade, all the women there looked like beautiful, soft angels. He smiled as he realized that he had never before thought of angels as being black. He had been conditioned, like so many other blacks in this country, and elsewhere, to think in terms of only white divinity.

With the exception of those brothers immaculately dressed in their blue, high collared F.O.I. uniforms, and caps with the star and crescent on them, most of the men wore suits. But they weren't all the same color, either, and didn't all look like the one the usher had on. This was important to Wade. He hadn't made up his mind to join the Nation of Islam, yet, but he had concerns about the dress code. Some of the brothers he had seen wore dark bland looking suits, and he didn't like that. Though his style wasn't necessarily conservative, he preferred subtle and subdued colors. Most of his suits were pin-striped, tweeds, checks, glen plaids, and shadow-stripe silks. There was nothing plain about the way he dressed, and because of his job in the clothing industry, his suits were expensive.

There were brothers standing post on the men's side of the room and sisters on the women's side. At the bottom of the stage, just below where the speaker would stand, two brothers sat and stared directly into the crowd. Their eyes constantly moving from one person to the next, watching the movements and gestures of everyone there.

Wade spotted a cocoa-butter brown sister, who for some reason, reminded him of his girlfriend, Frankie. Damn, he thought, as he watched the sister walk toward the stage. What about Frankie? It definitely won't be easy getting her to cover up that fine body she got. But the thought of her big hips bouncing under a long skirt or dress somehow excited him.

"As-Salaam-Alaikum," said a brother, startling Wade, as he slid in the seat next to him. The man wore an Afro and had on a multi-colored dashiki.

"Wa-Alaikum-As-Salaam," Wade replied, surprised that he hadn't seen this colorful brother approaching.

"I hear the Minister from Boston is the guest-speaker this week, "the brother whispered. "At the last joint meeting, I heard Minister Uriah speak. He's the head Minister in the Delaware Valley."

Just then Wade noticed two brothers crossing the stage and taking their seats behind the podium. A hush went through the crowd, as an older brother approached the podium from behind the red and white curtain.

"As-Salaam-Alaikum," he shouted into the microphone to the crowd, who immediately responded, "Wa-Alaikum-As-Salaam, Brother Minister."

"I'm Brother Minister Milton. I'm not your principle speaker this afternoon, but I would like to talk to you about the teachings of our beloved leader and teacher, The Honorable Elijah Muhammad." The entire place was completely quiet. You could hear a pin drop.

"The Honorable Elijah Muhammad is the Messenger of God. He teaches us that those formerly known as American Negroes, are actually the Original Man who were stolen from their homeland and deprived of the knowledge of self. Messenger Muhammad says that the white man robbed God of a whole nation of people, and used them for his vile and evil purpose. The Messenger says we must regain our knowledge of self so we can again do for self. Our beloved Holy Apostle says that we have to shed our habit of depending on the white man ..."

Wade could feel the energy in the room. And every so often he would hear a collective, "Teach Brother Minister, Teach," coming from the congregation. By the time the main speaker took the podium, the sisters were fanning and the brothers were hollering. "That's right, Brother Minister. Wake'em up!"

The main speaker was Brother Minister Joseph, who stood about 5 feet 4 inches, but had a voice that boomed throughout the hall.

"There's a lotta talk about black-power these days," he said, already wiping his forehead as if in preparation of the sweat to come. "But most people don't know where it came from. Well, I'm here to tell you. It came from our beloved leader and teacher, the Honorable Elijah Muhammad, who has restored pride and dignity to the black man and woman. He tells us that without power, we are nothing in this world. Though Allah will deliver us from our enemies, we must still put forth an effort to deliver ourselves up from the musk and mire. Without power, nothing is accomplished. History shows us this. When Lincoln freed the Negro from his physical slavery, it was done without placing the necessary power in the hands of those who were supposed to benefit. When the United States Supreme Court ruled that segregation in the school system was illegal, it was done without the necessary enforcement that would've assured that the individual states would obey the law. And when the Voting Rights Act was recently passed, it was done without the necessary enforcement to allow for equal political power in the hands of the so-called Negro."

In a quiet and orderly manner, two brothers from the first row stood and walked swiftly toward the two brothers sitting at the foot of the stage. Those two brothers rose and stepped aside, allowing the other two to do an about-face and take their seats. This procedure happened so quickly and smoothly that very few people were even aware of the change. The audience was on the edge of their seats, and Wade's attention hung on every word coming from the Minister's mouth.

"The liberated slaves were utterly lacking in the economic and political powers necessary to exploit their newly found freedom. Just as black families with school age children and black voters desiring for change in the electoral process lacked power to enforce the laws."

Walking out from behind the podium, the minister pointed at the audience, and said, "No man holding power will freely hand it over to those without it. If you want it, you must seize it by gaining self-knowledge. By establishing support for your own self-improvement and self-empowerment. The Honorable Elijah Muhammad has the plan for us. A plan which comes directly from the lips of God, Himself ..."

# CHAPTER XI

After the service, Wade caught a quick glimpse of Lucius as he and a few other brothers escorted Minister Joseph from the hall. Wade had hoped Lucius would've seen him, but with all the excitement and people rushing to leave, he just put it out of his mind. As he waited for the men in front of him to file out of the row, he was surprised to see Lucius coming his way.

"As-Salaam-Alaikum, Brother Wade," Lucius said with a grin. "It is Wade, right?"

"Yeah?" Wade said gleefully. "Uh, Wa-Alaikum-Salaam. I'd hoped to run into you. I, uh, wanted to give you your books back. I read them. I read all of them. I…"

"Let's walk over here," Lucius said, guiding Wade out of the center aisle. "Let's let the sisters pass."

Once they got to the other side of the hall, Lucius turned and called over three brothers.

"This is Brother Ethan, Brother Lester and Brother Christopher. Brothers, this is the first man I met when I got outta the joint. This is Brother Wade."

They greeted Wade with warm handshakes and asked how he liked the service. He admitted that he liked it and was thinking of becoming a Muslim. "But one of the reasons I came today, he chimed, "is to return these books to Brother Lucius and thank him for allowing me the opportunity to read them. I read them all and I really learned a lot."

"Keep them," Lucius replied. "They're a gift. If you wanna pass them on to someone else, feel free to do so."

"Thanks, man. I mean…"

"No thanks needed, brother. Where you goin', now? Are you hungry? Wanna go get some good tasting food?"

"I dunno, I, uh."

"C'mon, let's go," Lucius said, turning to Brother Ethan, "It's alright, isn't it? Think Sister Geraldine will mind one more mouth?"

"It's fine." Ethan said, smiling. "Gerri loves feeding hungry Muslims."

"Didn't you go to Edison High?" Christopher asked Wade as they walked toward the door. "I think I remember you from the football games."

"Yeah, I thought you looked familiar," Wade answered. "I used to go to all the Thanksgiving Day games between Edison and Dobbins. I was goin' with a girl who went to Dobbins then."

"Yeah, if we lost the game, we'd win the fight," Chris laughed.

"Hey," Wade smiled. "I haven't heard our old school motto in a long time."

"I like that suit," Brother Ethan said.

"Thanks," Wade replied, feeling a lot less nervous than before. "I got it at a spot down on 4th & Callowhill."

With envious eyes, Wade sat watching Brother Ethan's eight year old twin daughters play Jacks on the surface of a small folding table. Ethan and his wife, Geraldine, had a beautiful home in the Germantown section of the city. The atmosphere in their home seemed one of family warmth and genuineness. The little girls, sitting there dressed like grownup Muslim women shyly looked up at Wade and giggled as they tossed the rubber ball in the air and picked up each jack with precision.

Brother Ethan and his wife both looked to be in their late twenties. He was medium height, muscularly built, with rugged but handsome features. She was a very pretty light brown-skinned woman. Her long brown hair, which was uncovered, because she was in her own home, was pulled back and twisted into a bun. And though she wore the traditional Muslim dress, one could tell that she was a firm and finely built woman. Her down-home southern mannerisms added to an attractiveness that reminded Wade of Frankie.

Again, he found himself wondering how he would be able to get Frankie to enter into a religion that called for women to fully cover their bodies.

He recalled their first meeting. It was a year ago. He was working at one of the Center-City clothing stores, and would take his lunch breaks at Horn & Hardarts restaurant on 8th and Chestnut. On occasion, he'd see her coming out of one of the office buildings across the street from the diner. Though she sometimes ate lunch at the same place, he could never get up the nerve to speak to her. Always fashionably dressed, she was a thick and shapely sepia beauty, with small breasts, a narrow waist and a big bouncy behind. Her wide hips rolled with each stride, and Wade wasn't the only man stealing quick glances from afar. She got plenty of attention.

But it wasn't until one Friday evening, when she happened to come into the store, that he got the chance to talk to her. She was looking for a cardigan sweater, size XL, and Wade rushed over to her. After all, she was now on this turf and this was where he was most comfortable. Finally, getting the chance to see her up-close, she had light-brown eyes and big dimples; her reddish-brown hair hung loosely around her face.

After quite a bit of probing, he learned that her name was Francine Finney. She was from Danville, Virginia, but staying in Philly while attending Cheney State College, majoring in business law. She worked part-time at Nasuti & Miller Law offices for the experience and extra credit. When Wade found out that the gift she was purchasing was for her father, and not a boyfriend, he smiled, and she smiled back.

After convincing her that an Italian knit would be the better gift, he asked if they might have lunch together that upcoming Monday. "We might," she flirted. "That is, if you don't forget me."

As he watched this well-dressed, well-built young woman walk away from him, he wondered aloud, "How could any sane man forget a face and body like that."

***

Brother Lucius was in the kitchen using the phone, and the others, Brother Lester and Brother Christopher sat across from Ethan and Wade. Wade listened as they talked about a bazaar planned for sometime after their Ramadan in December.

"You think we'll be able to raise the money?" Chris was asking.

"Hey, we don't have a choice." Lester replied. "We have to put the down payment on the building by March. The only way we can raise that kind of money is to have the bazaar."

"Think we can get the champ to come?" Lucius asked, walking into the room. "I never got the chance to meet'im."

"He hasn't been back to Philly since them devils took his title," Chris frowned. "Them devils want the brother to go off to another country and kill for them while they givin' us hell in this country."

"Well, wha' else would you expect from the devil," Ethan said.

"Y'all kno' Ali?" Wade asked, realizing he was who they were talking about.

"Yeah," Lester responded. "He's our Muslim brother."

"That was Stanley Coulter on the phone," Lucius said, changing the conversation. "He had left a message for me to call'im. He wanna kno' when we gon' meet with him about this Community Activity Center thing. Says he needs help with ..."

"Yeah, he called me last night," Ethan interrupted, his eyes darting in Wade's direction. "I told him that we have things to do first."

"Right," Lucius nodded, taking the hint. "We'll talk wit'im later."

"Dinner's ready," Sister Geraldine yelled. "You men c'mon in 'ere."

The food looked delicious and tasted even better. Between bites of chicken-fried-rice, macaroni and cheese, yams and navy bean soup, the conversation went from light and humorist to serious and thought provoking. Wade listened admiringly as these young men spoke historically and politically of the plight of blacks in this country. They didn't sound like the average black from the corner. He felt as if he was in a room of young Malcolms. And then once the sister and the children had left the dining room, the topic became current. Lester, stuffing his mouth with banana pudding, asked Ethan how his meeting with the Assistant Minister had went. "What did he say about the suspension? Can you avoid it?"

"He said I could avoid it if I went to Temple Number One, in Detroit for about a year. But I told him I couldn't do that. My family would suffer if I left, and I can't afford to take them with me."

"All this shit over some punk-ass negro trying to prove himself to a woman?" Chris asked.

"Well, he was hurt pretty bad," Lester added. "Brother Lazarus didn't want Ethan talking to his woman about the respect women get in our religion. He stepped up cussin', callin' Ethan a nigger, and blowin' whiskey breath in the brother's face. Well, you kno' Ethan. He stretched' im."

"Yeah, but I hit him too hard," Ethan added. "His head bounced off the concrete like a rubber ball. Now Brother Lazarus is filing a police report, claimin' I hit'im with a weapon or som'um. But it was my fist."

"So, you gotta go to court for that shit?" Chris asked.

"Yep. Just like when you shot that dude's Doberman Pinscher," Ethan laughed, "And you had to go to court."

"So what's the Minister saying?" Chris asked, ignoring the dog comment.

"He's gonna suspend me until the issue is resolved."

Lucius reached over and tapped Wade on the shoulder. "Wade, stay away from Chris and Ethan," he laughed. "They stay in trouble."

"Hey, I ain't jus' got outta the joint," Chris joked, and everyone laughed, including Lucius.

"You gotta gig?" Ethan asked Wade. "If you need work, we can get you hired down at the union hall."

"Yeah, I work at a clothing store, on Ridge avenue," he answered. "But I appreciate the offer."

Though the thought crossed his mind, Wade didn't mention how much he hated working with the white boys on his job. But, he did ask what kinda work they did.

"Right now, we're renovating office buildings," Ethan replied. "All the old radiators and pipes have to be removed so that a central-air system can be installed. We junk all the metal, but make most of the money off the copper."

Wade really liked being with these brothers. They had helped him make up his mind. He would joint the Nation of Islam, and he told them so before leaving that evening. "Now, all I have to do is figure out how to get my girl-friend to become a Muslim," he joked. Lucius then suggested that he spend some time with Ethan, Chris and Brother Josh, who Wade was yet to meet, because they were sincere about the religion, and all three were married. "Perhaps they can give you some advice on how to convince the sister," he said.

# CHAPTER XII

It was 9:45 on Friday night, her eyes were closed, but she wasn't asleep. The dull rumble of the train rolling along the steel rails was almost hypnotic. Leaning back in her seat, Frankie thought about all she would have to do once she arrived back in Philadelphia. Since July, she had been in Virginia, helping her mother care for her father who had earlier been diagnosed with throat cancer. Fortunately, the chemo-therapy had worked, and he was doing much better. It was now September and time for her to leave.

She had only seen Wade twice since she had been gone. And on neither occasion had they shared any alone time. And now, with the new semester at Cheney already starting, there was still so much for her to do.

But the first thing Frankie planned to do was spend time alone with her man. Afterward, she would try to convince the registrar to let her take some classes. And, of course, she'd have to find another job. She had hated giving up her job at the law firm, but since they couldn't hold the position open, she had no choice. However, at least she hadn't lost her apartment. While she was away, Wade had moved in and kept the rent up for her. Now, they could just share the apartment.

As the train pulled into the North Philadelphia station, Frankie readied herself for departure. Glancing out the window at the crowd gathered on the platform under the lights, her eyes searched anxiously for Wade. I wonder if he rented a car like he promised, she thought. The last thing I wanna do now is catch a cab or take public transportation.

As soon as she saw him, her face lit up. She smiled and forgot about the concerns she had experienced a few moments earlier. He was standing there, his eyes searching for her, in the wrong direction, as usual.

"I'm over here, stupid," she yelled, laughing, but admiring how good he looked. He wore a pair of sky blue silk pants and dark green silk v-neck knit with no shirt. Flashing his even white teeth, his smile was as big and bright as ever. She loved everything about Wade Coleman, his dark skin, thick black hair and mustache. But it had been his style of dress that first caught her eye.

"Damn, girl, you look good!" He proclaimed, stretching out his arms to embrace her.

"Expecting anything different?" she joked, before kissing him full on the mouth. It was a long wet kiss. A kiss between lovers who really enjoyed being together again.

"How's your father?" Wade asked, picking up her bags and walking her toward the steps. "Is he up and about?"

"Yeah. He's doing much better. And mom is happy and healthy. How's your mother?"

"Fussy as usual," he said, placing the suitcases down and again reaching for her hands. "You know she wants you to come by for dinner next Sunday."

For a moment, they stood there looking at each other. Not speaking, just breathing. Wade grabbed her around her waist and pulled her to him. She melted against his body and felt him come alive.

"We better get a room, huh?" She smiled. Then they both laughed out loud and headed down the steps and out into the parking lot. Her eyes widened with surprise when he lead her to the 1967 smoke-grey Mustang sitting at the curb.

"This a rental?" She asked.

"Nope. This is ours."

"Wade, what did you do? Did you buy a brand new car?"

"Yeah. And if you ride me right," he grinned, "I'll let you drive it."

She didn't wanna press him about how he could afford a new car, at least not yet. She had just gotten off a train after being away for two months.

He glanced over at her and broke into laughter. "Baby, you kno' I wouldn't buy a car without talking it over with you. I want you to be a part of all my decisions." And no sooner had he said it, did he think about his choice to become a Muslim.

She smiled and kissed him on the cheek. Another thing she liked about him was his sense of humor. He could always make her laugh.

Leaving the parking lot on Glenwood Avenue, Wade drove north on Broad Street then west on Germantown Avenue. Frankie, leaning back, with her eyes closed, relaxed against the headrest. Her thoughts were of Wade and how much she enjoyed being with him.

From the moment she walked into that clothing store, she liked him. After getting her to have lunch with him, the next day he was waiting outside the office building for her when she got off work. He convinced her to take in a show with him at the Postal Card on South Street. A terrific jazz vocalist named Little Jimmy Scott performed that night. One of the songs he sang: "Someone to Watch Over Me," really touched her. She loved it. Later that evening, they strolled hand in hand through center city, talking and laughing about what seemed like everything and nothing at all. The next day, he took her to Pat's Steaks for cheese steaks and sodas, and they ate them sitting on a bench in Fairmount Park. That Sunday, he took her to Bookbinders' Seafood House and bought her lobster. And a month later, when she finally let him into her apartment, she experienced the same seething between her legs that she felt at that exact moment. It had been a year since they met, and he still excited her.

Wade turned off Germantown Avenue and onto Washington Lane, where he now lived with Frankie. "We're here," he said, pulling the Mustang over to the curb.

***

It was 2:30 am, the bars had closed, and folks from that neighborhood and beyond were now filling the many speakeasies around the city. Mamie Johnson, a/k/a Miss Mamie, had one of the best known after hour joints in North Philly. She had lowered her backyard to the level of her basement floor, walled it in, and extended her basement all the way out to the alley. There was a horse shoe shaped bar in the center of the floor, booths lining both walls, and a dance area. Soul food was prepared upstairs. Mamie, who was Jamaican and had a way of making people feel at ease, did more business than most bars.

Ethan and Lester could hear Arthur Conley's "Sweet Soul Music," blasting from the Jukebox as soon as they entered Miss Mamie's front door. As they strolled through her living room, the enticing aroma of that special Jamaican sauce she smeared on her fried chicken, ribs and roast pork, filled their nostrils.

"Do you like good music, sweet soul music," vibrated in their ears, as Ethan and Lester shuffled, bounced and danced their way down the narrow staircase, leading to a basement full of underground partiers like the pretty red-bone who Ethan knew from earlier times. Engaging her in conversation, was some guy Ethan didn't know. As he squeezed by her, Ethan nodded, and she responded with a wink and a quick smile.

"Think he'll get anything in return?" Lester asked, scanning the room.

"If he does, it'll be worth ev'ry penny."

The place was packed with people they both knew. Some were crowded around the bar, dancing and popping their fingers to the music. Others, mostly couples, were crammed into booths, awaiting delivery of their food and liquor. Ethan was very familiar with this spot. Before becoming a Muslim, he had pulled quite a few women out of it. Some of them were there now. And on one occasion, he and Josh had to actually shoot a joker down there. Fortunately, he didn't die. They drove him out to Fairmount Park and told him to never come back down that end, again.

"Wha'sup Easy-E?" Mamie asked, referring to Ethan.

"Nuthin' much," he replied, watching her strut her wide frame across the floor. She was carrying two plates of fried chicken and two bottles of Ballentine beer on a tray. As she headed toward the booth where a young couple sat waiting, she looked back over her shoulder and yelled, "I ain't got time fo' no trouble tonite, y'all. You 'ere?"

Mamie sensed that Ethan and Lester were there looking for someone. She didn't know who but pitied them just the same. Before he became one of those moose-lums, as she called them, Mamie felt as though she knew what to expect from Ethan. But now, it wasn't about just getting his dick wet, anymore. It was about money. And, as far as Mamie was concerned, and she figured she knew men better than most women, that fact alone made Ethan much more dangerous than he'd previously been.

Now, Lester, she thought, tha's a horse of a different color. I'd handle his fine yellow-ass. He's been tryin to get som' of my stuff since Ethan first bought'im 'round 'ere. But if I put it on'im, I won't be able to get rid of 'im.

His head still bobbing to the music, Ethan grinned as he scoped the room. "Mississippi ain't here, yet," he said, glancing at the two afro-wearing women dancing together near the bar. One had a mini-skirt so short, he could see her pink panties as she rocked her hips from side to side.

"Wha'cha wanna do, wait or come back later?" Lester asked, focusing on Miss Mamie's fat ass. He liked big women. She had exotic features, and the fact that she was older than he, made her even more attractive.

"Let's wait," Ethan said. "You go keep Mamie busy for a minute. I'm gonna sit over there in the corner.

No sooner had Lester walked over to where Mamie was standing, did Mississippi, whose name was Steward Franklin, walk through the door. He wore a brightly colored plaid suit and a wide brim hat. Originally from Natchez, Mississippi, he had told everyone who'd listen that he was one helleva gambler.

When he got a job at the Philadelphia Shipyard, he met some Italian mobsters who he convinced to let him operate their card games in the black neighborhoods. "How do we kno' you can keep our money safe?" they asked. "Because I got backup," he said, "I got som' good people who'll protect your money."

However, Mississippi had no backup, what he had was a plan that included Ethan and Josh, whom he'd previously met at Mamie's speakeasy. His scheme was to make the Italians believe he had real protection. And as payment, Ethan and Josh would receive part of Mississippi's cut, plus whatever he skimmed off the top. "Jus' so you kno'," Josh had told Mississippi, "We won't go to war with no brothers 'bout white boys' money. And as an incentive, you gotta promise to arrange for them Italians to provide vending machines and three months supply of stock for our grocery stores tha' they'll think you own."

"How many stores we talkin' bout?" He joked. "Tha's kinda small potatoes for you guys, ain't it?"

"Right now, just three," Ethan answered. He didn't like that small potatoes remark, but he let it go for now because they needed him. "We'll be opening more later on."

Actually, the stores were to be opened and operated in neighborhoods where they wanted to reach out to the local corner-boys and stop the gang wars.

The scheme had worked. Mississippi had been hosting the games for six months, now. But he had yet to get the machines and produce that he had promised.

Too busy running his mouth with the two high-yellow girls he had with him, Mississippi didn't see Ethan approaching him from the darkened corner.

"Wha'sup?" Ethan asked, placing a hand on Mississippi's shoulder and smiling at the high-yellow girls.

"Hey, bro," Mississippi said, flashing a gold tooth as he turned to face Ethan. "I hoped to see you tonight. I got y'all money, ratch'ere."

Mamie was asking Lester why he always looked at her like she was food, when Lester finally noticed Mississippi.

"Uh, 'cause I wanna taste some of tha'," he said, his eyes now focusing on Mississippi and what he was pulling from his pocket.

"When?" She asked, jokingly.

"But Lester didn't hear her. His hand went immediately to his waistband, his fingers gripping the handle of his .357. When he saw that

Mississippi had nothing but money in his hand, he released the handle and returned his focus on Mamie.

"Is all of it 'ere?" Ethan asked.

"Yeah. I had to make a few moves, but I got all of y'alls."

"Wha' about the vending machines?" Ethan asked narrowing his eyes. "We had a deal. Now you got us on hold. Tha's not good business."

"I talked to Vinnie. He assured me tha' he'd have the machines ready by February. As far as the produce, he can do tha' now."

"We'll wait til February for ev'rything," Ethan said, counting the money. "But if you can't deliver on tha' we'll have to arrange som'um else."

Mississippi knew that meant the brothers would start focusing on his games. There was a lot of money passing hands there, and he didn't have the power to stop them if they decided to take all of it.

"February. You got my word, brother," Mississippi said, his eyes searching the room for the high-yellow girls. "My word is bond."

"I can't stand tha' fraud-ass-motherfuckah," Ethan told Lester as they left the basement. "His word is bond, aw'ight. Them punks are always tryin' to copy som'um from the Muslims."

As they climbed into Lester's blue 66 Lincoln, they saw a brand new white Fleetwood pull up and stop. A tall slender man in a grey pin-stripe suit emerged from the driver's side. A slender white woman got out of the passenger's side, and they both went into Ms. Mamie's.

Ethan got out of the Lincoln and walked over to the white Fleetwood. He looked inside, then went to the back and wrote down the tag number. "Ben-E-67."

# CHAPTER XIII

Looking into her eyes, Wade whispered her name as if it were a prayer. For the fourth time since they'd arrived home, their naked bodies, covered in a blissful sweat, intertwined with one another's. She, now atop him, piercing herself, eased down upon his sore but still sturdy erection.

Frankie had been surprised at how well kept the apartment had been. "It looks great," she explained upon entering their three room abode. Immediately, her eyes had gone to the wall covered with her well dusted bookshelves. She looked around their little informal open kitchen, before settling on the couch and kicking off her shoes.

"Wanna shower?" Wade asked.

"Let's take one together," she replied, knowing they wouldn't make it that far. As soon as their clothes came off, Frankie took him by the hand into the bedroom. Pressing herself against his hard body, she felt him rising against her stomach. His body, slender but strong, pressed into the soft grooves of her's. Maybe it was the length of time since he'd last been with her, or just the love he'd always had for her, but the intensity was unlike anything he could've imagined.

"Damn, girl. I missed you so much."

"It shows," she replied, with a hint of a smile, slipping her hand between their bodies and rubbing up and down the length of him. "Don't talk, baby, it's been too long for words."

Wade sat on the bed and stood her between his knees. She gasped as he licked at her naked breasts, her nipples, sticking out like little chocolate kisses, one after the other, flattening under his tongue. She held his head and moved it to where she wanted his tongue to be. Roaming his hands over her wide hips and around the big soft cheeks of her ass, he inhaled her scent and tasted her inner flesh. She responded by pressing her lower stomach against his face, and moaning loudly as his tongue lanced out again.

For the next three hours, they made love that was beyond the senses. And though Wade knew he'd soon have to be at work for the Saturday crowd, he knew he would cling to her, until the last sweet moment. She was now in control, atop him, and he watched as she slowly rode, her eyes closed, her breath coming and going with each impelling movement. Three times already, during the night and in the early morning hours, they had exhausted themselves only to recover again. This was the final curtain call and he would not fail her now. Whispering his name over and over, as her body, like liquid warmth, spread and boiled atop him until neither could no longer hold back; again, they fell into the quiet moment of exhaustion.

Showered and dressed, Wade kissed a sleeping Frankie on the forehead and staggered out the door to work.

\*\*\*

A few hours earlier, just as the sun was rising over the city, Simon Hobbs walked slowly along an area north of Market Street, on 9th, called Skid Row. Laced with small discount stores, tailor shops and greasy-spoon restaurants, it was an area only a few blocks from, but in complete contrast to, Center City. There, the men little children often called bums and hobos could be found huddling around blazing trash cans, lying in doorways or walking up to cars stopped at the traffic light to beg for a cigarette or a dime for a cup of coffee.

Simon, an informant and agent provocateur for the FBI, was as cautious as ever. Paranoia having become second nature to him, he naturally showed up early to make sure no one other than Agent Alfred Doss would be there. It was supposed to be his last meeting with Doss, and he was anxious to get it over with.

Two times he walked around the block to let his nerves settle. In his pocket was the instruction sheet Doss had given him a few months ago. In part, it was a copy of a memo from J. Edgar Hoover, when this operation was first planned. Before leaving his hotel room that morning, Simon had read it again.

"The primary targets," the memorandum stated, "are leaders, member and followers of the Student Non-Violent Coordinating Committee (SNCC), Southern Christian Leadership Conference (SCLC), Revolutionary Action Movement (RAM), and the Nation of Islam (NOI)."

Of the four groups, it had been decided that RAM was the one Simon would first infiltrate because according to the agency, the members were espousing a bloody revolution. He had done his job and now wanted the rest of his money so that he could spend some time in Berkeley, getting high and fucking his girlfriend.

Mornings in Berkeley, California were so very different than any time spent in Philadelphia. In Berkeley, the mornings were fresh and cool with the scent of moistened grass in the air. Philly seemed hard and desolate, even for this supposed revolutionary who had told everyone that he used to be a Black Panther while in California. Actually, he was nothing but a fraud who used the money and information provided to him by the Feds to insinuate himself into the secret lives of those individuals dissatisfied with the disenfranchisement of Blacks in White America's social, political and economic system.

On his third trip around the block, he squinted his eyes and spotted Doss' pale blue Ford pulling into the deserted parking lot on the corner.

"Get in," Doss told him, when he reached the passenger's side of the Ford.

After bending down to peek in the backseat, Simon opened the door and slid in. His eyes again searched the windows of the surrounding buildings. "Are you gonna jus' sit 'ere, or wha'?" He asked. "This street will be crowded with people in a few minutes. I can't be seen sitting in the car with no white man."

"You'll be alright," Doss shrugged. "I have to drive over to Camden, anyway. I'll let you out before I cross the bridge." He didn't like snitches in general, and Simon Hobbs in particular. But both were necessary for him to do his job.

A pale-skinned, blond man, with a potbelly, Agent Doss had come to Philadelphia from the FBI's New York office. He hated all people of color, but especially blacks. And that made him the perfect agent to work closely with the Philadelphia Police Department. His assignment was laid out in the conclusion of an FBI memo, which ordered each field officer to assign agents to the new COINTEI.PRO. These agents were to submit an updated list of radical black organizations in its territory, and submit practical counterintelligence information suggestions to the FBI headquarters by April 4, 1968.

Pursuant to this new directive, Agent Doss and others were instructed to invent scenarios aimed at undermining these various black groups; specifically, the Black Panthers, Nation of Islam, and the Revolutionary Action Movement. Simon, who had met Doss while in New York hanging with a few members of the New Republic of Africa, or NRA, had started informing on NRA members, once he learned he could make a few dollars that way.

"Were you able to plant the stuff in Craig Sanderson's house," Doss asked, as he drove east on Arch, heading toward Front Street. As usual, he didn't make small-talk, he just wanted the details.

"Yeah, it's in his basement," Simon answered. "I didn't want his children to find it, so I placed it inside the box where he keeps all his revolutionary literature; you know, shit like Chairman Mao's Little Red Book and papers on Che Guevara and guerrilla warfare."

"How do you know that no one saw you down there? Were they home when you did it?"

"Craig let me stay with them for a couple of days," he said. "So when I got the chance, I just went down there and hid it in the corner of the box. For the few days I was in their home, no one went down there for anything. It's cool!"

"Is it still in the same bottle I gave you?" Doss asked, pulling over to the curb at Front and Arch Streets. He trained his cold blue eyes on Simon, staring as if trying to find some redeeming characteristics, only to be disappointed.

"Yeah. And the bottle is still wrapped in that cover, too. I guess that way no one will wonder why his prints ain't on it, huh?"

Craig Sanderson, along with his brother, Larry, were two of the leaders of the Philadelphia branch of RAM. Simon had been introduced to them by a low level member of the organization, who, by design of the FBI, happened to be arrested with Simon at a protest rally against police tactics, in South Philly, earlier that year. After being charged with inciting a riot and spending a week at the Detention Center, it was made to look as if Simon had arranged for both of them to be bailed out. The incident convinced the low level RAM member that Simon was cool, and soon afterward, Simon was introduced to the people the FBI were targeting.

Doss removed a wad of dollar bills from his pocket and counted off $500. "Of course, you know we're going to need your testimony at trial," Does said, while handing Simon the money. "And that will include you saying that you actually saw both brothers handling that bottle of poison while they plotted to kill police officers."

"I ain't got no problem with that," Simon replied, holding the money up in front of Doss' face. "I remember the whole scene about them putting the poison in the cop's food at the restaurant, and everything. But this 'ere's only five bills. I thought it was s'posed to be $1500?"

Doss hoisted his bulky frame. "You read what I gave you?"

"Yeah, I read it," Simon snapped. "You mean the memo, right? I kno' I'm s'posed to do the Black Muslim thing, too."

Doss raised an eyebrow. He didn't like Simon's tone, but again, he swallowed his hatred. "No, not the memo. The paper that was attached to it. Concerning this operation, four distinct demands were in place. Did you understand them?"

"I, uh. I thought, uh."

"Listen to me," Agent Doss interrupted. "You were to get close to the targets. Then allow us to position you in a safe place until the trial. After you've testified, you'll receive the remainder of the $1500. Then we deal with the Muslims."

"I just thought y'all would trust me, man. Like when I testified up in New York, y'all paid me ev'rything at once then."

"Though I met you then, you weren't assigned to me," Doss shrugged. "Plus, we can't allow you to go to Berkeley just yet."

"Wha'cha mean, man, my people's there. I need to see…"

"Listen carefully," Doss interrupted again. "You have to go to a safe house in Detroit. We will pay your expenses out of a separate fund, and you must stay in the area that we place you in. I can't tell you anymore than that. Just that we need to know where you are at all times."

Knowing that he didn't have much of a choice, Simon agreed to Doss' demands. But his mind was made up. They're not gonna control me, he thought, I'ma do wha' I wanna do, anyway.

Two weeks after Simon and Agent Doss had that conversation, the following article appeared in the September 27th edition of The Philadelphia Bulletin:

> *[Philadelphia Police disclosed an existence of a plot to poison "hundreds of policemen" during a planned racial riot last summer that never came off. The plot, told by an informer, was allegedly hatched by the Revolutionary Action Movement (RAM), a Negro extremist group. Four men have been arrested.]*

# CHAPTER XIV

The mirror reflecting America's barbaric treatment of her Negro was being held-up for the world community to see. The 1954 Supreme Court ruling banning racial segregation in the public schools, like the 1964 Civil Rights Act, prohibiting racial discrimination in hotels, motels, restaurants and gas stations, were laws not being enforced. By mid-March 1968, discontentment had become infectious. More and more people of color were realizing that power concedes nothing without demands on various levels.

From the hallways of the urban projects to the corridors of colleges and universities, cries of Black Power reverberated like shots being heard around the world. "I'm Black and I'm Proud " was being shouted out loud, even before James Brown made it famous in song later that same year. It was a renascent time in the ghettoes, where people were being revitalized by self-expression. Even in the middle class communities, where brotherly thoughts were often confined to one's immediate family, protest music and cultural awareness were in the air.

Bleaching cream companies now lost money because blacks now took pride in their skin color. Many black men stopped their Friday and Saturday visits to places like Don's Doo Shoppe to get their hair straightened. The fad of the processed, dyed, fried, parted to the side conked look was abandoned and replaced by the natural. And though their heads continued to turn when one of those fine wide hip sisters bounced by, brothers on the corners now showed respect for the women they saw in the street.

Martin Luther King, who normally conducted anti-segregation campaigns, was now speaking out against the war in Viet Nam and issues of poverty in the nation. Muhammad Ali was being honored by many as a hero for standing up and refusing to be inducted into the Army. Civil rights groups were staging mass demonstrations against civil rights violations. At the same time the Black Liberation Army, the New Republic of Africa, the Black Panthers, and Nation of Islam, groups the U.S. Government considered radical, were expanding their membership.

It was in this awakening period that Wade and Frankie planned to wed. He had proposed marriage months ago, right after receiving his "X." Now known as Wade 2X, in the mosque, he had tried to share his excitement with Frankie, but it was difficult. Though she accepted his marriage proposal, it was obvious to Wade that she remained apprehensive about becoming a Muslim.

"We can't continue to live together," he pleaded. "Islam forbids it. I love you and I want you to be happy. If you're not absolutely sure…"

"It's not just that," she answered, interrupting him with a look of sadness. "It's just that I've been a Christian all my life. My mother would have a heart attack. I know it!"

This conversation continued throughout January and part of February. Frankie had heard all his arguments but had he really heard and understood her reasons for being unsure of conversion? She understood the need for blacks to protest against racial discrimination in this country. While in high school, she had even marched against it herself, and they were all Christian. Her question now was why was it necessary to become a Muslim to advocate equal justice? She'd been tempted to ask the minister that question on one of the occasions she had gone to the mosque with Wade, but she didn't.

Wade knew that he'd never convince Frankie to forsake the teachings of her family and church. He believed that the most difficult part for her was in being asked to accept God as a being other than the image she had always seen nailed to the cross. That became obvious to him when he asked her to agree to a civil marriage ceremony, which excluded references of Jesus Christ, or the Holy Trinity.

Like so many of the men joining the Nation of Islam, Wade was attracted more by its Black Nationalist ideology than its spiritual teachings. He felt that in order to convert Frankie to the religion, he'd need the assistance of sincere Muslim women. Someone who could better express the spiritual side of the religion from a woman's point of view, and answer any questions Frankie may have.

"Why not talk to some of the Muslim sisters?" Wade cautiously suggested. "Sister Geraldine 3X has a bachelors degree in human services, and a couple of the other sisters are also college educated, and they had no…"

"What," Frankie interrupted, "You think just because I'm in college and they went to college, I'll be influenced by them?"

"Naw, Baby," he pleaded. "That's not what I meant. Just talk to them about women in Islam, please. I'm a man, and it's not easy for men to understand what women feel sometimes."

Though apprehensive, Frankie reluctantly agreed to go with Wade to Brother Ethan's home and meet Ethan's wife. What concerned her most was knowing she'd be alone with a bunch of Muslim women. Wade had told her that he and Brothers Ethan, Lucius and Josh had a planned meeting with the minister that afternoon. "But Josh's wife, Deborah, will be there, as well."

The swirling March wind lifted the bottom of her raincoat as she exited the car and followed Wade up the steps. He was right, she thought, this is a beautiful neighborhood. Trees lined both sides of the small street, and most of the homes were done in huge dark and light grey masonry stones. Ethan and his wife had the corner house, which usually meant it was more expensive because the outer side wall was covered with masonry stones, as well.

Frankie was even more impressed when she saw the house's interior. The furniture was modern, the walls were decorated in African art. Upon entering the foyer, a striking portrait of young Fulani girls carrying water jugs on their heads immediately greeted one's eye. And on the opposing wall was a beautiful portrait depicting a Hausa Village, done entirely in varying shades of green and orange. Under it stood a two-foot wood carving of a Ghana Sankofa Bird.

Wade introduced Frankie to the three men sitting in the living room. But she was so nervous that she barely heard their names. All she knew was they were dressed in suits, one was really tall, and they were now standing, smiling and giving her the greetings.

The greetings of "As-Salaam-Alaikum" used to seem foreign to her. But since she'd gone to the mosque a few times with Wade, she had become accustomed to it, although Wade rarely used it at home. He usually just greeted her with a hug, a kiss and a cheery, "Hey, Baby?"

"Wa-Alaikum-As-Salaam," she responded softly, glancing briefly into their faces.

Sister Geraldine entered the room and was introduced. She was a beautiful woman and seemed very polite. Smiling broadly, she greeted Frankie, gave her a warm hug, then immediately guided her out of the living room and into the dining room.

"Wanna get'cha away from all those men," she joked, trying to make Frankie feel a bit more at ease. Frankie could hear female voices coming from another room. The kitchen, she thought. She heard music, too.

Sister Geraldine pulled some folded cloth napkins from one of the drawers of a walnut china cabinet and motioned for Frankie to follow her into the kitchen. The scent of singed hair in a hot comb, mixed with the sweetness of Dixie Peach, reached her before she saw the other women.

"Welcome to Gerri's Beauty Salon," a light-skinned woman grinned, looking up from the kitchen chair as another woman slid the hot comb through her hair.

"That's fast mouth Fanny," Sister Geraldine laughed. "And this is Gussie, Deborah and Brenda."

Just as Frankie opened her mouth to speak, she heard a harmonious, "As-Salaam-Alaikum," come from all the different female voices in the room. They almost sounded like a singing group, she thought, as she retuned their greetings.

Sister Gussie, who was obviously the elder of the women, laid one of the cloth napkins on Fanny's shoulder. Deborah, her hair combed out, as if in waiting, sat in the corner, patting her foot and bouncing her head to James Brown's, "Outta Sight." And when Mr. Brown got to the part, "You gotta shapely figure momma," Deborah stood up, put her hands on her broad hips, and wiggled them as she grinned.

"You better stop that girl," Brenda joked. "You know Mr. Muhammad don't abide no loose women in the Nation."

"And Brother Josh ain't too keen on'em either." Fanny laughed.

Shrugging her shoulders and continuing to shake, "Shoot, Josh loves all my moves," Deborah grinned.

"You tha' sister who's getting' married to tha' fine new brother?" Gussie asked, glancing over at Frankie and pulling Fanny's hair along the back edge of the hot comb.

"What brother?" Fanny asked, bending her ear out of the way of the hot comb.

"Oh, you don't kno'im," Geraldine replied, as she began thoroughly greasing Brenda's scalp with Dixie Peach.

"Shit, I need to find me a good brother," Fanny said, looking up and grinning as she saw Wade entering the kitchen.

"As-Salaam-Alaikum, sisters," he said nervously. "I, uh, jus' gotta give Sister Francine the car keys. I'ma ride with Ethan, and I…"

Frankie blushed at seeing how nervous Wade was. She wasn't used to hearing him call her Francine. "Okay, I'll see you later," she said, being careful not to say at home. She knew Wade would've been embarrassed if these women knew they were living together. Somehow seeing him so nervous about their secret living arrangements empowered her. Shit, she thought, these women are no different than me. They straighten their hair, cuss, talk girl talk and wiggle their hips too.

# CHAPTER XV

During the next four hours, the records kept spinning on the turntable of the floor model Hi-Fi stereo. And, Frankie actually found herself enjoying her visit with these sisters. They did one another's hair, danced, laughed and talked about everything from the new Muslim school that was scheduled to open soon, to the work they would be doing to help pay for the camping trips the Muslim children would take that summer. Even the sex they shared with their husbands, enjoyable or not, was not off limits.

"Y'all need to hush," Sister Gussie would say every time the conversation got too graphic. Then she'd smile as if remembering some dark personal secret.

It was obvious to Frankie that all four women absolutely adored and respected Gussie. Even when she joked with them, the attention they gave each word was as if there might be some underlying meaning there. She was much more than their hairdresser, she was their teacher and counselor.

Between bites of fish fried rice, navy bean soup and sips of orange juice, Gussie relived the story of meeting the founders of the Nation of Islam when she was a child. Some of the sisters had heard this many times before, but always out of respect, they never interrupted her.

"When I was a child, Negroes were being lynched almost daily in this country. Not jus' in the South, either. My momma and daddy were first followers of Marcus Garvey. And the white man deported 'im 'cause he was trying to bring us black folks t'gether." Gussy told them that after her parents heard about Master Fard Muhammad and the Nation of Islam, they joined. She was just a little girl, she said, but remembered going to the meetings and admiring the strong black men who refused to call themselves Negroes and bow down to white folks. "They held their heads high and looked the white man in his eye when they talked to him. They weren't afraid, and we chill'un saw dat."

Frankie listened as the elderly woman spoke of how Fard had preached that Islam would supplant Christianity as the predominant faith of black people. "He called us the original people, and said that whites were devils for their treatment of our race. And those black folks that refuse to let go of the white man's ways, he called imps."

Frankie couldn't take her eyes off this woman. Her bushy white hair, thick around her dark face made her look almost angelic. As she spoke, her eyes darted from one sister to the other, always capturing and holding their eyes.

"And I remember when I first saw the Honorable Elijah Muhammad. He spoke on Sunday afternoons when Master Fard was out of town. He told us that the true religion of Allah and his prophets, Abraham, Noah, Moses and Jesus was Islam and that whites had used Christianity as a tool to enslave black people."

Gussie looked directly at Frankie when she spoke of how Christianity, and its belief in the Holy Trinity served to weaken the spirit of blacks instead of strengthening it. "We think of ourselves as inferior to all other peoples," she said. "We never think of God as lookin' like us. We think of him lookin' like the man who enslaved us. The Messenger says that, by Allah's will, Prophet Jesus performed many miracles and was obedient to Allah in every way. Jesus spoke only the truth and his followers were Muslims. Never did Jesus say he was Allah, the son of Allah, or that his followers should pray to him or to anyone other than Allah. Jesus was a man, and he had no father. Like Adam had no father and no mother."

As Marvin Gaye's "Pride and Joy" played in the background, Gussie began talking about her husband, and other husbands' work in the Nation of Islam. With tears in her eyes, she told them how dedicated her husband had been before he died from cancer, six years earlier.

"You know," she said, blinking her eyes, "Our men are true soldiers in the fight against dis 'ere white devil. Not unlike those pioneers or revolutionaries white folks always sayin' built dis 'ere country. Our brothers are soldiers in suits. To them, the Nation of Islam's security is a callin', not some profession. Most money they get goes to the cause of buildin' our nation. And though some might not like how they git tha' money, they git the job done tha' others are too scared to do."

"That's right, Gussie," Deborah chimed in. "Every army has an elite squad, and that's who our men are."

"Our brothers don't walk timidly," Fanny added. "They walk heavy. They lay their feet down and stand tall, strong and firm."

"And not only do they watch one another's back," Sister Brenda declared, "they'll pull a brother's coat, if he starts goin wrong."

Though confused about Gussie's statement concerning the money their men got, Frankie found these women's support for their husbands both refreshing and encouraging. She was also touched by how comfortable they all seemed in their own skin.

Though Sister Geraldine rarely spoke, when she did, her words were thought provoking. As the women were leaving, and Geraldine handed Frankie her coat, she whispered, "You know sister, before I was Muslim, I would notice that look men often gave me; and some women gave it, too. I admit, I felt flattered. But it wasn't until joining the Nation that for the first time in my life, I noticed others noticing me as a woman."

These are fascinating women, Frankie thought. Spiritual, yes, but not pious zealots. Instead of being submissive, they are more supportive of their men. Frankie compared Gussie to her mother. Both were about the same age and had come from the South. But her mother never spoke of events that affected black people's lives, like Gussie had today. She could remember one time when her father had mentioned that Negroes had to work in the cotton fields from can to can't, and her mother told him to shut up. "Don't tell the child that!" Later, when she was alone with her father, she asked him what he had meant, and he told her that can to can't meant from can see to can't see. "In other words, Negroes worked from can see the sun to can't see the sun." He had a real sad look in his eyes, he looked almost pitiful as he said, "The acts whites committed against Negroes were so barbaric that they brought national attention to themselves, but no shame to themselves." She hadn't thought about that conversation in years. Afterwards, when she'd try to get him to talk about those times, he would shy away.

As she drove home, Frankie recalled the look on Gussie's face when she said, "Evr'ybody else has had their time, now it's ours. The Hereafter is not som' place in time wit' a different meaning. It means right 'ere, after the destruction of the devilish power tha' has ruled over the righteous people of the earth."

Gussie's look had reminded her of the Sunday school teacher back in Virginia. The experience with the sisters was not unlike some of the bible study groups her mother would take her to when she was little. Only then, they were talking about and bowing down to Jesus. The strange thing was, it didn't seem strange then that so many black folks were bowing down to a white man on Sundays, and cussing white folks under their breath the rest of the week. She recalled the pictures she had seen of Africans bowing down to the Pope when he visited Africa. And how many times she'd heard Africans take pride in themselves for speaking what they called the Queen's language. Are we that messed up? She thought. Where is our dignity and identity? What happened to it? How did we lose it? Or should I be asking, who stole it?

# CHAPTER XVI

Wade and Ethan rode in the back seat of the black Riviera Lucius had accepted from Fat Hank. Josh sat in the front passenger's seat and joked with Lucius about letting him drive.

"You gotta be out'cha mind," Lucius grinned. "You put so many dents in that red Mustang som'body let you drive last week tha' dents were all over the roof."

"I was being chased by the cops," Josh laughed. "And the damn car kept flippin' over, anyway."

"Fuck that! You ain't gettin' behind this wheel."

Bits and pieces of a more serious conversation between Ethan, Josh and Lucius and the fact that they seemed headed in the direction of South Philly, confirmed Wade's belief that they weren't headed for a meeting with the minister. This came as no surprise to Wade. A few weeks earlier, while at the West Philly mosque with Ethan and Chris, Wade overheard Ethan mention something about a meeting with some brothers from downtown. Chris had said that he couldn't be there because Brother Minister Uriah wanted him to stay over in Chicago after the Savior's Day Convention. And now twice since they'd gotten in the car, supposedly headed to a meeting with Minister Milton, Lucius had mentioned the brothers from downtown.

During the months Wade had to wait to receive his "X" and Acceptance Letter from Chicago, he had spent quite a bit of time with the brothers. Ethan, who was still serving his six month suspension from the Temple for fighting, saw Wade more than the other brothers. Though it had been Lucius who first suggested to Ethan that he spend time teaching and quizzing Wade on his required Nation of Islam Lessons, it had been Ethan's decision to really befriend Wade and take him under his wing. He even paid for Wade's flight to Chicago for the February 26th Savior's Day Convention. Wade had never imagined anything so spectacular and so beautiful.

It was bitterly cold in the Windy-City. There were lines of people circling all the way around the block, waiting to get into Chicago's International Amphitheater. In one line, little children balled up their gloved hands and stuffed them in their pockets as they huddled around Muslim women dressed in long white dresses that hung beneath their overcoats. In another line, Muslim brothers, most of whom were dressed in suits, waited patiently, while Brother and Sister Lieutenants patrolled the sidewalks. Security was extremely tight. In the street, brothers dressed in F.O.I. uniforms directed traffic. Some cars were checked and even searched, if the brothers thought it necessary.

Upon entering and being searched, Wade saw brothers who had set up concession stands in order to sell books written by the Honorable Elijah Muhammad, books on the Savior, and the Muhammad Speaks newspapers. Uniformed Muslims guided people who were not in uniform, to seats behind an area reserved for Muslims who were in uniforms. Looking around, Wade saw huge pictures of Master Fard Muhammad and Elijah Muhammad hanging from the balcony and podium. Surrounding the stage, at the bottom, were seated brothers in F.O.I. uniforms staring into the audience.  On the stage, he saw rows of ministers and other dignitaries sitting around the chair he suspected was reserved for Messenger Muhammad.  Wade stared in awe when he recognized Muhammad Ali, who blacks still considered as the Heavyweight Boxing Champion of the world, regardless of what white folks said.

Attending Savior's Day had been an experience like none Wade could've imagined.  He loved watching the documentary they showed on the Nation of Islam's businesses.  The restaurants, bakeries, schools, temples and farms in the south.  And the speech given by The Honorable Elijah Muhammad captivated him.

"The Jews are not God's chosen people," he said to the audience.  "Nor the seed of Abraham because Jesus said the Jews did the work of the devil and not of Abraham."

Wade immediately thought of his Jewish co-workers at the clothing store.  They walk around as if they were the world's gift to humanity, he thought, but their hearts are filled with hate and arrogance.

"If you can accept Abraham, Moses and Jesus as prophets," Messenger Muhammad continued.  "Why can't you accept me?  I am here to do as Moses did, to tell Pharaoh to let my people go."

By giving him this trip, Ethan had bestowed upon Wade the gift of convergence.  After hearing the Messenger in person, he would forever feel indebted.

After returning to Philly, Ethan and Wade again began their sessions.  But they talked about much more than The Lost Found Fruit Lessons Number One and Two, and the Actual Facts, all converts to the Nation of Islam had to learn and commit to memory.  While talking to Wade, Ethan often quoted scriptures from the Bible in support of the Messenger's teachings.  He also spoke often about the history of Blacks in this country.

Once while defining what he believed Malcolm had meant when he said, "by any means necessary," Ethan made a compelling comparison to the pioneers in the Nation of Islam and those white pioneers who did whatever was necessary to steal America.

"Both purposes was and are to remove any obstacle blocking the path to nation building," he said.  "The only difference is the white man wrote the story that we've been trained to internalize.  For instance, if Nat Turner had been a white man fighting those who had enslaved white people, he'd be seen as a national hero.  However, black folks rarely mentioned his name.  The brothers you see today, those unafraid to stand up, speak up and act up in the cause of their people, are like those men, though forced into bondage, had the nerve to rebel against both the institution and the mentality of slavery."

Wade enjoyed hearing Ethan speak.  Sometimes they would go out in search of people to preach to.  They were like Jesus of the Bible fishing for men.  Only the waters they fished in were the places where black folks hung; on the rough street corners, in cut-throat bars, and greasy-spoon restaurants.  Of course, some brothers would go directly into the homes of the few middle class people they knew. But mostly, the heart and soul of the black community existed where most were afraid to journey and these brothers had come from there.

Wade admired the brothers he had come to know and respect as religious men, outspoken husbands, fathers and courageous Muslims. However, Wade found it difficult to reconcile some of the things he had come to suspect about them, with those tenets he thought he understood about the religion. He felt that they were serious about Islam, but he had also noticed another side to them. One that suggested a subtle, but genuine ruthlessness, that indicated they might go beyond what was necessary to advance what they believed in. And, though feeling honored that they had accepted him as one of their own, even offering him a manager's job in one of their North Philly store front businesses. Wade still doubted that he could measure up to their expectations. Especially if what he sensed was true, and they saw nothing as being off limits when it came to the advancement of the Messenger's teachings. Wade wasn't sure he could handle that.

Turning off 25th Street, on to Wharton, Lucius pulled in behind "Mo's" green 67 Fleetwood parked at the curb. As they exited the car, Josh extended the greetings to a tall slender woman in a pants suit, who was leaving the house they were about to enter.

"As-Salaam-Alaikum, Sister Jacie."

"Wa-Alaikum-As-Salaam, Brother Joshua," the sister responded. "Mo's in the living room. Go on in."

Increased membership at Temple 12, raising funds for the purchase of buildings, school buses, and the maintenance of equipment already purchased was what the meeting was all about. Since Wade was the only one there who didn't know the downtown brothers, introductions were brief.

Lucius, who had been instructed to conduct this meeting, introduced Wade to all the downtown brothers in the room. By doing so, he assured those who didn't know Wade, that he was trusted by those he was with. And though it was never a need to say or imply it, everyone there, with the exception of Wade, understood that this meeting had the blessing of certain brothers in Chicago, and Temple 12, in Philly.

Everyone took a seat, either on one of the couches or in one of the armchairs that were sporadically positioned around the large decorative living room. Two portrait hung on the wall; a small one of The Honorable Elijah Muhammad, and a larger one of the man Wade would come to know as Maurice "Mo" Barton.

Wade nodded and gave the greetings as he shook Mo's hand, then the hands of Cecil "Big Cil" Sampson, and Rushard "Rus" Braxton. It was his first-time seeing them, but he had heard their names mentioned many times on the street.

Mo walked over to the windows and pulled the cord on the Venetian blinds, then closed the curtains. "Harv will be late gettin, ere," he said. "He was in Detroit and jus' flew back in this mornin'. But he called and said he'll try to be 'ere befor' y'all leave."

Mo was wearing a blue and green Bill Blass, Scottish plaid sports jacket, a white shirt with no tie, and a pleated pair of green silk slacks. Having an appreciation for fashion, it was easy for Wade to recognize and appreciate the fashion sense all the downtown brothers seemed to have.

"No problem," Ethan shrugged. "This is important enough, we'll wait for 'im."

"In the meantime," Lucius began, "The Minister sends his greetings. And he asked me to tell y'all how good it was to hear that y'all was in Chicago for Savior's Day. He said that the Dear Holy Apostle was made aware of the $10,000 donated by y'all, but hope you'll understand that he can't personally thank you for it."

"Aw, we ain't expectin' no thanks, Lucius," Mo said, glancing around and stroking his walrus-like mustache. "It was done 'cause we believe in wha' the Messenger's doin' for our people."

Five minutes into the meeting, Wade heard someone coming down the steps from the second floor. It was Dalton Landers, a clean shaven, immaculate dresser, who Wade had met about six months earlier, at the mosque on South Street. As always, he was well dressed, wearing a French-blue dress shirt, with a white collar and cuffs, lavender suspenders and matching tie, and a grey shadow-striped silk suit. Crossing the room, Dalton greeted everyone and then quietly took a seat in the corner of the room.

Big Cil, always one to get straight to the point, leaned forward in his chair. "Okay, we're all 'ere now." He asked in his raspy voice, "Wha's the message you got for us, Lucius?"

"Simply put," Lucius said defiantly, "Y'all gotta come in outta the rain."

A muffled sound of a ringing of the phone interrupted the conversation. Big Cil, who was closest to it, picked up the receiver. "Yeah," he said, then frowned as he whispered to Mo. "It's yo'r weak-ass brother-in-law, again."

"Hang it up," Mo said, with a wave of his hand. "He's jus' beggin', like always."

"If it wasn't for Jacie," Cil grumbled, hanging up the phone. "I'd deal wit tha' maggot. I can't stand his punk-ass."

"That's my wife's brother," Mo sighed. "Som'times I gotta overlook shit."

"Even when it's stickin' to yo'r shoe?" Dalton snarled.

# CHAPTER XVII

"Wha' tha' mean?"      Russ asked. "Com' in outta the rain?"

"It means you brothers are appreciated for the support you give to the mosque." Ethan said, speaking softly. "But we don't need associates, wha's needed is yo'r participation."

"I don't like wha' I'm hearing," Rus spouted. "it's like som'body's tellin' us wha' we can do, and wha' we can't do."

"Rushard, we mean no disrespect," Lucius assured. "But som'body is tellin' us all wha' we can and cannot do. And how we should be doin' it!"

"Hold-up a minute," exclaimed Cil, turning toward Wade, and handing him a hundred dollar bill. "Wade, right? Brother Wade, do us a favor. "Round the corner, there's a deli. Could you go git som' tuna hoagies for ev'rybody? Dalton, show'im where it is."

It was obvious to everyone, including Wade, that BigCil wanted him out of the room. Cil knew Dalton would go along with whatever they decided, and wouldn't feel snubbed by being asked to leave the meeting. Right now, getting Wade out the room, was more important.

Wade watched as Dalton grab his suit coat and plum colored high crown fedora hat, with its lavender band, and motioned him toward the door.

"I like yo'r suit," Wade told'im, as they left.

"Thanks," Dalton replied, allowing Wade to walk out the door first.

"So wha' y'all is sayin'," Mo paused long enough to allow the door to close, then swallowed as if suppressing some hostile moment, before looking directly at Lucius. "is tha' to keep from getting' wet, we gotta git under the umbrella."

"Damn man, we're not enemies?" Josh interjected. "But as it stands right now, we're workin' against one another. We're aware of the problem y'all are havin' wit the Italians. First of all, they're over-chargin' y'all for the dope. And even though you're givin' them all yo'r business, they're using others to make it difficult for y'all to move the shit."

"So wha' is y'all sayin'? Russ asked. "How's going' into the mosque gonna help us deal wit' them white boys?"

Seeming to take exception to the way the conversation was going, Big Cil rose, holding his huge hands palm-up on both sides of his barreled shaped chest. He wasn't as tall as Lucius, but he was just as thick. And like Ethan, he had a cold penetrating stare that often instilled fear in many men.

"Whoa, whoa," he said, speaking directly to Josh. "Hold on a minute. "Did y'all forget tha' I'm also a Muslim? I was in the temple before sum' of y'all was. As a matter of fact, I went in at the same time you and Ethan did, Lucius!"

"We ain't forgot, Cil, you kno' tha'. Mo and Harv came in 'roun tha' time, too. But after Malcolm was killed, y'all left and never came back. Now, simply put, in order to keep wha' you got going' privately, y'all have to again follow Muhammad publicly."

Point gotten, Mo, Rus and Big Cil settled back for a less confrontational discussion. Lucius explained a plan they had come up with to eliminate the Italians from the equation and at the same time allow the downtown brothers direct access to Big Frank Matthews' people in New York.

"First and foremost," Lucius began, "Y'all know tha' the drug thing, ain't really our thing. Realistically speaking, we can't go to our people with Messenger Muhammad's life-givin' teachings in one hand and poison in the other. Actually, our thing is takin' money. But only illegal money from illegal people. But we've come' to the conclusion tha' we must combine our efforts to fight this devil. The Italians control all the drugs in our communities. The Jews control all businesses and cash flow and the Irish cops are their muscle. In order to take back our communities, and gain the respect of black people, we have to eliminate white folks control over us."

"You said y'all came to the conclusion tha' we must work together," Big Cil asked. "Was the decision really yo'rs or som'body else's?"

"We all work for the same people," Ethan said. "And you kno' as well as I do, tha' men protect the people they work for."

"I'll tell you this," Josh added. "By workin' wit us, not only would yo'r costs go down, the quality and quantity of yo'r package will go up."

"So wha' we gon' do?" asked Rus. "Replace the white boys influence in our neighborhoods?"

"If the dope and other shit gonna be there," Ethan responded. "We're gonna control it."

"We've dealt wit Frank before," Mo said. "What makes y'all think you can git a better deal than we got then?"

"It's not jus' about dollars and cents," Ethan said. "In other words, to put yo'r stuff out at a price tha' undercuts them white boys, you'll need cost-free muscle, right? If your opposition think tha' we are some' how involved wit y'all, you won't need tha' muscle. No one wants war wit the brothers, and that includes the Italians. Plus, our good brother Lucius 'ere, already got family dealin' wit Frank's people, and they like him enough to cut prices for'im."

"Who's tha'?" Mo asked Lucius.

Getting up and walking over to where Mo sat, Lucius leaned forward and smiled. "Fat Hank. He's like family. Plus, we'll persuade the Italians to put up the first $75,000 toward y'or first purchase. Of course, they won't know it."

"How the fuck you gon' do tha'?" Mo asked.

Lucius looked at Ethan and smiled. "Ethan opened the door, so I'll let 'im tell you."

Remaining seated, Ethan told them about Mississippi, the man who approached them for help with the Italians. He said that Mississippi not only ran their card games in the black neighborhoods, but also stored their number money for them.

"Because everyone at the shipyard knows tha' Mississippi works for them, he feels protected. Now he's storing their numbers money at his house, in Mt. Airy."

"How you kno' the money's there." Big Cil asked.

"Cause Mississippi likes women," Lucius added. "And he runs his mouth between their legs and their ears."

"Y'all want us to handle him?" Rus surmised.

"Yeah, 'cause if we do it, he'll have to go," Ethan said. "We'd rather keep him around for while, 'cause right now, he's like a cash-cow."

Rus and Cil looked over at Mo, who was rubbing his walrus mustache, and thinking. The room remained quiet as they all waited for his response.

"How do we kno' tha' this Mississippi niggah won't go runnin' to the Italians or the cops?" He finally asked. "If we don't slump this niggah, we might be settin' ourselves up for a bust. Especially if he's handlin' tha' kinda paper for them white boys. Shit, he'll be too scared not to tell'im."

"He's long strokin' one of them white boy's woman," Josh offered with a grin. "Dude name Vinnie Cato. Vinnie took tha' slick-ass Mississippi niggah to one of their picnics, and Mississippi pulled his wife. He's been fuckin' her for months now. We kno' wha' nights she goes to his spot. She usually stays for an hour, then leaves. They'll be naked, so jus' make'um get back in bed, and you take som' pictures. He won't tell tha'. He'll make up som' story 'bout how he got robbed 'cause he don't want Vinnie knowin' he been bangin' his wife."

"How y'all kno' all this shit?" Rus asked.

"Lester is bangin' one of them secretaries down at the shipyard. She sees a lot and tells him everything. When we started sittin' on Mississippi house, we got lucky. Vinnie's wife started showin' up three nights a week. At first we had no idea who she was. But the secretary knew that, too. But tha's also the reason tha' joker can't be slumped. If you hit him, you gotta do her, too. The secretary is down wit' the robbery. She'll get real nervous if people start dying."

The doorbell rang. Mo peaked out the window and saw Harv standing on the steps.

"Open the door," Harv yelled, seeing Mo at the window.

"Fuck you punk," Mo joked. "You shoulda been 'ere over an hour ago."

Standing just a little over six feet tall and wearing the wire-frame plum colored shades he' become known for, the neatly dressed Harvey Rollins surveyed the room, then flashed a big grin. "Aw'ight, ev'ry body empty yo'r pockets and git on the mothfuckin' floor." He shouted.

"Sit down, man and shut-up," Cil laughed. "Listen to this shit. They tell funnier stories than you."

After being brought up-to-date on the agreed merger, and the decision to cut off the Italian connection, and rob their front man of the number money, Harvey agreed to go back in the mosque, also. Like Mo and Cil, he'd been in before, and had left when Malcolm X was killed.

"I kno' Vinnie Cato," Harv offered. "He was in Lewisburg Federal Penitentiary when I was there. Maybe he's a killer out 'ere, but when he was in lockup, certain people called 'im Vinnie Vaselinie."

"Why is tha?"

"Cause, he's a joint!"

"You serious?" Mo laughed. "Tough-ass gangster, taking dick up the ass? You telling one of y'or stories, man?"

"He's a closet joint," Harv repeated. "I'm tellin' you."

Though relaxing by joking and laughing with one another in a respectful manner, these friends had taken this meeting seriously.

"If this is gonna work," Lucius told them, "We need to clear a way for Hank to approach Frank's people, again. Y'all kno' how close Hank is to me, but that has nothin' to do wit' this. If this is business, we have to protect him. There's a snitch workin' with the police so tha' he can keep pressurin' certain dealers and then resell their product as his own. Now he's pullin on Fat Hank's thing. He has to go befor' Hank can even think about approachin' Frank's people again."

"Wha's the maggot's name?"

"Dabney," Lucius said. "I don't remember his last n...."

"I know 'im," Russ interrupted. "I thought tha's who you were talkin' 'bout. The fat punk owns a little barbecue joint jus' offa Broad and South. I'll see'im for ya."

As if on cue, just as the serious discussion was winding down, in walked Dalton and Wade with tuna hoagies and sodas for everyone. The remainder of the meeting was to discuss what sisters they thought best to work with, and keep an eye on Stanley Coulter, executive director of the Community Activity Center. The center had been established to assist with the development of various community programs for inner-city children during the summer months and to aid low-income families with year round medical support and counseling.

"When tha' state and government fundin' starts com' in," Josh weighed in, "Tha' slick Negro, Stanley Coulter will try to grease his pockets. We gotta make sure tha' the sisters are involved so the money goes to the families in the neighborhoods, like it's s'pose to."

Now that he had everyone talking about Stanley Coulter, Josh leaned over and whispered in Rus' ear. "Oh yeah, keep this under yo'r fez. Lester's woman says Mississippi is a stuffah."

"He's a junky?" Russ asked.

"$100 a day habit. The white girl is probably one, too."

"Thanks," Russ nodded, getting the message. "Tha's jus' between you and me."

# CHAPTER XVIII

The apartment was dark and quiet. Wade walked to the couch and sat down. At first he thought Frankie hadn't gotten home yet. Then he heard the raspy sounds of Nina Simone's rendition of "I'll Put A Spell On You" coming from their bedroom, and noticed a slither of light beneath the bedroom door. Though anxious to hear about her day with the sisters, his thoughts were clouded with bits and pieces of the meeting at Mo's, and some things Ethan had said to him on the drive home.

After they'd left the meeting, Lucius drove everyone to Ethan's, so they could pick up their cars. Since Wade had given his car keys to Frankie, Ethan drove him home. It was the conversation during that ride that Wade was now remembering.

"How's everything at the store?" Ethan began. "I hope them Mighties are not givin' you no problem."

Wade knew Ethan was referring to the teenage boys around Warnock and Somerset who were part of the street gang called the Mighties Mothafucka's, one of the many gangs populating that particular North Philadelphia area.

"Naw, they cool," Wade answered. "Actually, they like comin' in to play the pin-ball machines and the jukebox. The only time there was any problem was when som' dudes from 8th and Norris came up to see som' girls. But it was cooled out."

"We picked up three more jukeboxes from them Italian boys yesterday," Ethan said. "They think we gonna place them in three mo'r stores, but actually, we already rented them to some speakeasies cross-town."

About five minutes of silence interrupted the conversation before Ethan spoke again. He was purposely waiting, trying to gauge Wade's reaction. Wade didn't ask a lot of questions, and that was one of the things Ethan liked about him.

"I like you," he said. "You're thorough, I can tell that by the way you handle yo'rself. And though you may not have come up like som' of us did, in gangs and juvie-hall and all, you don't scare easily. You look a man directly in his eyes when you talk to him. I like tha'."

"Thank you," Wade said, unsure of what else to say.

"Do you have a gun?" Ethan asked, surprisingly. "Have you ever fired one before?"

"Naw," Wade stammered. "I mean. Yeah, I've fired guns before. My uncle, he taught me ... But I don't own a gun."

Ethan then reached in the glove compartment and took out a blue steel .38 Smith and Wesson revolver, and handed it to Wade. "This is now yo'rs," he told Wade. "It's clean. Keep it down at the store. We got it registered for there."

As Wade sat on the couch staring down at the .38 he was now holding in his hands, he recalled what Ethan had said to him about the meeting.

"You won't be excluded from any future meetings," he said. "We'd like your input on some things. You got a good head on your shoulders, and you kno' a lot 'bout business."

"Yeah, if I can help," Wade managed to say, not knowing where the conversation was going. He flinched a bit as Ethan looked directly into his eyes, that penetrating transfixing stare.

"You ever able to get som' of them suits from off the rack," Ethan asked. "I mean without havin' to pay fo'em outta yo'r own pocket?"

"Sometimes I can," Wade answered. "All depends on who's there. Why?"

"Cause I may need you to help me wit som'um next week," Ethan continued. "I wanna introduce you to som' business people, and a couple of lawyers we deal wit' som'times. I may need to take them a few suits. Aw'ight?"

Hearing Frankie moving around in the bedroom, he took the gun to the living room closet and quickly stuffed it into one of the sweater boxes he kept stacked there. I'll put it in my briefcase later, he thought, turning just in time to see her coming through the door. Hands on her hips, she was dressed in a long white dress, with a matching head-scarf draped delicately over her head and around her smiling face.

Wade whispered her name softly. "Frankie." He couldn't believe how beautiful she looked. It was like seeing her for the first time, all over again. Though the dress covered her completely, her wide womanly hips pushed at the material in a caressing manner. Nina Simone was now singing about the "Forbidden Fruit", and Wade stood for the moment, completely hypnotized, then moved closer. Just as she had planned.

"You look absolutely beautiful," he whispered, leaning closer to her ear. "Beautiful. You're so … so beautiful." He pulled her closer to him, slipping his hands into the opening in the front of her dress. His fingers sliding around to her back, gently caressed her spine. She pressed against him, her skin soft, and her fragrance intoxicating. Their lips finally touched, and soon they were both naked.

"They made love, and talked, made love, and talked some more. She told him how much she'd enjoyed meeting the sisters and how she looked forward to seeing them again. "Especially Sister Gussie and Geraldine," she said. "They really made me feel like one of them. I had decided to join the Temple with you when you asked me, but it was Sister Gussie's talk that removed my fears and truly convinced me."

"Som'thing she said?" Wade asked, rubbing her hair, as her face laid upon his naked chest.

"More the way she was with us," she answered, lifting her face and looking up at him. "But, yeah, it was something she said. She asked me to look around at the world. To look at the oneness of the universe. Its unity in design. At first I didn't know what she meant. Then she said, the universe's existence proclaims the unity of its maker. The oneness of us, of life proclaims that God neither begets, nor is he begotten."

"What did that mean to you?" Wade asked, embarrassed that he had no idea what it meant, himself.

"She was saying that just as God didn't have a father, he also didn't have a son. That He would never require that our prayers go through an agent just to reach his ears. But what really got to me was that this was coming from Sister Gussie, an elderly woman doing hair. And everyone, all of the sisters there, looked up to her."

Wade kissed her face, from her forehead to her chin. He told her how good she looked when she stepped out that door in all white, the light behind her. "I actually felt som'what conflicted," he said. "You standing there in white Muslim garb, looking so sexy, enticing me, and making me rise."

"You know I'll have to go home and tell my parents what I'm about to do," she said, as she returned his kisses.

"Yeah, I hav'ta see my mom, too. I haven't told her yet." Frankie fell asleep listening to Nina Simone's, "I Love You, Porgy" and feeling Wade's fingers gently playing in her soft hair. He watched as her chest rose and fell. Her warm breath upon his chest was soothing and relaxing, like a sedative.

But the thoughts continued to rage. He was glad they both had decided to join the Nation of Islam. However, it wasn't the convergence that troubled him, it was his transformation as soldier. It seemed he would be called upon to do things he wasn't sure he was man enough to do, or stomach.

Gently twirling Frankie's hair around his fingers, again he recalled Ethan's penetrating stare and the words accompanying it. "We don't play games," Ethan had said, as he pulled up in front of Wade's apartment building. Switching off the engine, he turned and looked at Wade. His words came fast, and his stare was direct. "The brothers are for real, Wade. We don't play games. There's an inner-circle within the circle, and we take care of one another, and one another's family. If som'um happens to one of us, it happens to all of us. Remember this brother, no one will ever relinquish power freely. We have to take our fate in our own hands. I don't hesitate when I say that we'll die for one another. And more importantly we'll kill for one another."

"What's wrong, baby?" Wade heard Frankie say, rising from her sleep. "You look worried. You don't think we made a mistake do you?"

"Nothin's wrong, baby," he whispered. "No, I don't think we made a mistake by joining the Nation of Islam. I love the Messenger's teachings, and I trust the brothers and sisters in the Temple. At first, I admit I had some reservations, but after thinking about it, and looking at what has been going on in the world, I came to believe that it is the right thing for me. It's time for black folks to look at the world in a realistic light. We have to stop this singin', marchin', and beggin' white folks for our rights. We've been victims for too long, and its 'bout time we took our fate into our own hand."

Watching Wade's reaction, as he spoke, caused Frankie to feel a sense of pride in her man. "I love you, baby," she said, as she laid her head back down on his chest.

# CHAPTER XIX

Dressed in a green windbreaker and skull cap, Brother Kirk X Dickson pushed against Detroit, Michigan's late night wind, easing his way up Conner Street near East McNichols. He had flown in from Philly with Harvey Rollins over a week ago.

When Harvey left Philly for Detroit, he told no one except Mo where he was going, and why. "They busted my cousins in this thing 'bout poisonin' cops," he said. "The punk tha' set 'em up was spotted in Highland Park, Michigan. And I'ma deal wit 'im."

"Yo'r cousins? Who? Craig and Larry? Dey caught up in tha' revolutionary shit? Tha' RAM Organization?" Mo asked.

"Yeah," Harv answered, sticking a .357 in the waistband of his pants. "Silly as they are, I can't let 'em go down for som' shit like tha'."

"How long you gon' be there?" Mo asked. "You kno' we s'pose to meet wit' Lucius and the other brothers."

"Minister Uriah gave them the nod, huh?"

"Yeah. But you kno' he can't be there."

"I'ma try to do this as quick as possible, so I can git back. But jus' in case I hav'ta leave Detroit befor' seein' this snitch, I'ma take Kirk D. wit' me, he'll handle it."

"Tha' the young brother from up in Frankford?"

"Yeah."

"I guess you can depend on him," Mo laughed. "I heard 'bout tha' New Jersey shit."

"Yeah, but this has more to do with him havin' no connection to my cousins."

"No connections? Yeah, right."

Actually, Harv hadn't chosen Kirk just because he thought the cops wouldn't see a connection, and Mo knew it. He knew that Harv wanted someone with him that wouldn't hesitate in taking that snitch out, and Kirk D. was that person.

About a year earlier, while working with a drug dealer in New Jersey, Harv gave Kirk half a kilo of heroin to handle over there. Kirk proved to be a dependable worker, and soon was making quite a bit of money for Harvey. Then one day, a few so-called friends of Kirk's came up with a plot to steal a stash of uncut dope they'd heard Kirk was holding. They put a fine young red-bone on him, hoping she would discover where the dope was. After about a week of fucking Kirk, she had the information she needed. When she told his so-called friends where the stash was, they stole it. A few days later, one of the thieves came out of the back door of his house and found the red-bone draped across the hood of his car. She was naked, and her throat had been cut. That very same day, the package containing the stolen drugs was dropped off at Kirk's door, along with some money to compensate him for his trouble. The so-called friends relocated, and from that time on, Harvey viewed Kirk as an asset.

Kirk didn't like being in Detroit, at all. It was windy, and much cooler than Philly. Perhaps if he had been there on a regular visit; meeting some girls and partying a little. But as it was, he was there taking care of business, and had to lay low. Before leaving to go back to Philly, Harvey had given Kirk enough money to live on, but he chose to sleep in his rented car, see no one, and eat sandwiches from a Jewish delicatessen he found. Now that he had a visual on his target, he just wanted to handle this mess, and be on the first thing smoking back to Philly.

On the day Harv had to leave, they had spotted Simon Hobbs and trailed him from Highland Park to an apartment building in Detroit. Skyview, an apartment complex on the corner of Conner and McNichols was surrounded by low-cut hedges. It sat back off the street, just enough to create a shadow along the side wall. Kirk's eyes drifted across the street, toward the dilapidated shell of what looked like another residential hotel. Over the last couple of nights, while carefully stalking the area, the only people he'd seen hanging out around there were black and white prostitutes and their tricks.

Evidently, Simon liked hanging around the prostitutes in this town. Over the last two days, Kirk had watched him visit and get high with quite a few of them. But at night, Kirk noticed that Simon seemed to prefer the big butt dark skinned girl that hustled at the Skyview. He'd stay all night, then leave early the next morning. So on the third day, Kirk decided not to trail Simon, he would get himself some sleep, instead. He figured Simon would be at the Skyview Apartments later that night, and all he had to do was wait for him to show up.

Again, he glanced up and down the street before ducking along the shadowy wall behind the hedges. It was 2 a.m., and he saw no one, not the prostitutes or their tricks. Pulling the .357 Magnum from beneath his jacket, he squatted and waited.

Crouched along the wall behind the hedges, he didn't have to wait long before he saw a taxi pull up, and Simon Hobbs staggering out. Kirk could tell Simon was high. He swaggered from side to side as he followed the cement pathway between the rows of hedges. However, just before he reached the door, he heard a faint rustling noise coming from the hedges.

"Yo, Simon!" Kirk called out. "Hi ya doin', man?"

Simon stopped, his body weaving back and forth, his eyes trying to focus. "Who the fuck?" he murmured, his eyes finally adjusting to see a short slender man in a windbreaker and skullcap, standing before him. The man had a smirk on his face, as he gripped Simon's arm with his left hand.

"I don't kno' you," Simon slurred, trying to pull his arm free. "My name ain't Simon."

"Don't matter," Kirk frowned, extending the gun toward Simon's face. "The Sanderson brothers send their greetings."

Realizing what was about to happen, and why, Simon's eyes widened and filled with fear. "Don't do dis, man. The cops, the cops are watchin' me. I'm not gonna go to court."

"I kno'," were the last words Simon heard, as Kirk pulled the trigger and felt the magnum jerk in his hand. He quickly looked around before pulling Simon off the pathway and into the hedges. Putting the barrel of the gun in Simon's mouth, Kirk pulled the trigger again.

Moving swiftly and staying low, he removed his jacket, wiped off the gun, and dropped both into the sewer at the curb, before driving off in the rental car.

***

A week later, loud banging on the door startled Mississippi and Sharon. They had just finished screwing, and now sat naked on the side of the bed, preparing to speedball another mixture of heroin and crystal meth.

"Who the fuck?!" Mississippi grunted.

"Make sure you look out that window befor' opening that door," Sharon cautioned. "We don't need Vinnie finding me here. He'll kill us both."

"Fuck Vinnie," Mississippi mouthed to himself, as he put on his robe. "Som'body's fuckin' up my high."

Just the same, he pulled back the curtain on the window to make sure it wasn't Vinnie standing out there.

"Open the fuckin' door," he heard the man flashing the badge at him, say. "We're detectives from homicide. Don't make us kick this mothafuckah in."

Once Big Cil received the call from Dalton, telling him that Mississippi and the white girl were in play, Cil picked up Rus and headed for Mississippi's house, in Mount Airy. But first Rus needed to stop by his Cousin Nate's apartment, in the projects, to pick up some police badges he'd left there.

Nate and his woman lived in one of the two-story apartment buildings, at the Richard Allen Projects, in North Philly. He was a part-time dealer and full-time junkie, but Rus liked him and often used him to cut his heroin and deliver it to some of his workers in that area.

The living room was cluttered. It seemed everything Nate and his woman ever owned, bought, or stole, was right there. On the floor in the corner of the dining room, Rus saw two 16oz. yellowing bags of lactase, that were there the last time he visited.

"Wha' happened to the quinine I dropped off?" he asked Nate.

"We're usin' it!" Nate shrugged, scratching a much used needle track that was now a scabbed over scar. "Junior's usin' it now. It gives a much better rush, plus, dem jokers like to feel the itch."

Peeking into the kitchen, Rus saw Junior, a frail dusty dark dude with sunken eyes and dry lips, sitting over at the table. Spread out on top of the table were four large serving platters. On one of the platters sat four plastic spoons that someone had stolen from a McDonald's restaurant, and three sifters. One of the other platters held the raw heroin, and on the remaining two were quinine and bonita, used in cutting the heroin. Leaning over Junior and watching, was an equally frail, but kind of pretty, light-skinned girl, who looked as if she could be a teenager.

"Who the fuck is she?" Rus asked, noticing that the girl was holding a metal soda-bottle cap, with a knot of cotton in it. Rus knew it was their cooker. He watched as Junior put a lit match under the soda cap while she gently shook it until all the dope inside dissolved.

"Aw, she cool," Nate grunted. "Junior likes her to help him cut yo'r shit. She's testing, now. Young thing kno's how'ta polish the wood, too."

"I need those badges I asked you to hold for me."

"I got 'em right 'ere," Nate said, his eyes searching, as if trying to penetrate the cluster.

Rus glanced over at the girl, again. A cigarette hung from her lips, as she now used a hypodermic needle to draw up the dope from the cooker. Turning the needle upside down, she pushed the liquid up toward the needle until she was sure no bubbles remained in the syringe.

"How com' you let 'em take-off in 'ere?" Rus asked, as Nate brought him the police badges. He found himself feeling a twinge of conscience, but quickly shook it.

"'Cause it's better to have 'em already high while dey're cuttin' yo'r dope, then tryin' to steal most of it, 'cause dey noses be runnin'."

Standing motionless, they both watched as Junior tied a belt around her arm, then pierced the scabbed track with the needle. He poked around until he got a hit, her blood appeared, mixing with the contents inside the syringe. Slowly he applied pressure, pumping the syringe and pushing the dope inside her vein. Almost immediately, the young girl's eyes closed, her lower lip drooled, and the cigarette fell to the floor, as she went into a nod.

"Tha's som' boss shit," Junior growled, picking up her cigarette, then using the needle to draw up his shot. "I gave it a six, like you said, but dis 'ere shit can easily stand an eight."

"You still got som' raw left, right?" Russ asked Nate.

"Yeah. Why? We're puttin' a six on it, already."

"Bag me up a bundle wit'a two cut. I'ma take it wit' me."

# CHAPTER XX

As soon as he opened the door, Mississippi knew he was in trouble. Upon entering the foyer, Rus and Dalton immediately abandoned all pretense of being the police.

"Where's the bitch?" Dalton menaced, pushing Mississippi against the wall and sticking a blue steel snub-nose .38 in his face.

"She's upstairs," Mississippi managed. "In the bedroom."

"Is there a phone up there?" Rus asked, looking around until he spotted a phone on the table. He picked up the receiver and listened. Hearing nothing, he took the steps leading upstairs, two and three at a time. Sharon was starting to get dressed, and about to hide in the closet when the bedroom door flung open.

"Take dem clothes back off," Rus told her. "Vinnie said you'd be here naked. So get naked."

Keeping her eyes diverted, Sharon turned her back to him and started removing her clothes. She could feel his eyes on her body, and wondered if Vinnie had told him to rape her before killing her.

Rus picked up the bathrobe she'd obviously had on before, and tossed it to her. "Here, put this back on." Then he called downstairs. "Bring him up 'ere."

As soon as Dalton pushed him in the room, Mississippi began crying. "Hey, man, please, don't ya'll kill me. Tell Vinnie I wasn't..."

"Shut the fuck up," Dalton warned. "I told you before, don't say nut'in unless I ask you a question. And when I ask, you better answer right. Understand?"

"Yeah, yeah. I understand."

"Okay. Is the pussy good?" Dalton asked, grinning and looking over at a trembling Sharon.

"Yeah," Mississippi said, answering quickly.

"Good enough to lose yo'r life fo'?" Rus asked. "Vinnie want you dead, man. He said we could fuck her as long as we wanted, then kill her, too."

Dalton grabbed Mississippi and turned him around to face the mirror. Pulling open his robe, he whispered, "You kno' wha' dem white boys like as trophies from black men who fuck dey white women?"

"Yeah," Russ chimed in. "He said to cut off yours before killin' you. I asked him how he would kno', and he laughed and said, he could tell."

"We don't wanna kill ya'll," Dalton told them. "We jus' want the money Vinnie told us to find. He said you had it in this house, and we should bring it to him after we kill you."

Noticing the tray Mississippi had put the heroin, meth, and needles on, Rus moved it to the back of the room. He then pushed Sharon toward the bed, and told both of them to sit down and listen. Pulling out his gun and crossing his arms, he leaned his back against the dresser, and spoke quietly.

"We don't kill no brothers for fuckin' white women, and we don't rape no woman, no matter how good she looks. I'ma say this once. Give us the money, and we'll leave ya'll to do wha'ever you feel is right. Lie to us 'bout the money, and you both will die."

"How much you holdin' for tha' white boy?" Dalton asked.

"Eighty-five."

"Thousand?"

"Yeah."

"And how much you got?" Rus demanded.

"Twenty-five thousand."

"Show it."

Mississippi pulled back the curtains covering the window in his bedroom, and slid a wooden panel under the windowsill to the side. There, in a compartment, they saw two circular rolls, as large as car tires, containing bills that had been packed tightly together. Rus picked one up and saw that the bills had been wrapped around and around each other until all of them together formed a small wheel-like shape.

"Damn," he said, looking over at Dalton. "This mothafuckah must've had nut'in but time on his hands. Look at this shit."

As Dalton took Mississippi and Sharon into the other room to get the twenty-five grand, Rus put water in the two needles laying in the tray. He then replaced Mississippi's heroin with the dope he'd brought with him. When they came back with the other money, Rus was unwinding the wheel of money and packing it in bags. Before leaving, he suggested that they all take a hit.

"Before we leave, ya'll wanna share som' of yo'r dope wit'us?" Rus asked Mississippi.

"Yeah, tha's cool," Mississippi replied, glad that he hadn't been hurt. "Ya'll can take a hit."

"You wanna speed-ball this shit?" he asked Dalton.

"Yeah, wha' the fuck. But you gotta skin-pop me."

Rus skin-popped Dalton with the water he'd placed in the syringes, then himself. He then told Mississippi to prepare his own.

"You gotta fix yo'r own poison, my man," he said with a pretended slur. "Shit, this is aw'ight. Who you cop from?"

He and Dalton watched silently as Mississippi mainlined a hit of the meth mixed with the dope, then pinched the meaty part of Sharon's upper arm and skin-popped her.

Rus stayed in the room and watched as they nodded off, and Dalton took the money out to Big Cil, who was parked in the next block up, but close enough to watch the house. He then returned to help Rus search the house for more money. They found an additional fifteen grand, and some jewelry.

"Leave the entire bundle of raw," Dalton told Rus. "It'll look like dey got hold of som' bad shit and OD'd."

"Yeah. Tha' should satisfy the brothers, cause the girl who put them on to this thing in the first place, won't think she's responsible for somebody dyin'."

"Dey still ain't gon' like it."

"Fuck 'em. We got them the money, now we can deal wit Dabney, then git a real connect outta New York."

"Wha' about that Italian boy?"

"Vinnie will think cops got the money. Shit, they came in and found a naked black man on the bed wit' a naked white woman."

"Yeah," Rus laughed. "And the cops will think Vinnie did it, when they find out tha' the girl was his wife, sneakin' a ride on black dick."

After checking to make sure Sharon and Mississippi were dead, they placed their naked bodies in the bed, locked the doors from the inside, raised the window in the bathroom, and climbed out.

As planned, the Muslim Bazaar was held on March 30th, the last Saturday in the month. The Blue Horizon on North Broad Street was filled to capacity, with black folk and Puerto Ricans, Muslims and non-Muslims, all in a festive mood. Local talent donated their appearances. Each wall of the hall was lined with concessions stands and booths, where people could buy the Quran, Bible, Black History books, pictured t-shirts for the children, and prayer rugs. Women, holding babies in their arms, stopped to look at the jewelry, and to examine the various types of colorful material being offered for sale.

It was a jubilant atmosphere. Accompanied by Ethan and his wife Geraldine, Wade and Frankie walked hand in hand through the crowd. Halfway through the afternoon, they ran into Josh and his wife Deborah, who were headed for the area where Minister Sharrief was about to speak.

He spoke of the accomplishments of the Nation of Islam, and its intended direction. "The Messenger had inspired a nation within a nation that is now worth more than we could have ever imagined. With millions of dollars in businesses and assets, and ten times that in potential. We've purchased farm land, we're opening our own banks, purchasing our own Temples, our own schools, restaurants, bakeries, and supermarkets. In this city alone, we have bought school buses for our children to ride in, and by this time next year, will have opened three new Temples."

When the audience began to applaud, Minister Sharrief held up his hand, and said. "No. Don't applaud my words! Applaud the divinely guided actions of the Honorable Elijah Muhammad."

Everyone there was so moved. Some women, including Frankie and Geraldine, had tears in their eyes.

"C'mon, Wade," Josh said. "Let's go talk to the Minister." Wade was speechless. He had never actually spoken with the Minister before. Like most of the brothers in the Temple, he had greeted the Minister in passing and that was only when one of them happened to be on door post when the Minister arrived at the Temple. He was always surrounded by security and rarely stopped to talk.

But now he was standing there being introduced to Brother Minister Sharrief, and listening to Brother Josh laugh and joke with him. Before leaving, Josh told the Minister that he wanted to make Wade a squad leader so that he'd be in line to become a Lieutenant. "Brother Wade is a fast learner," he told the Minister. "And he's dedicated, Sir."

"Well, Brother Josh," Minister Sharrief said, "you're a lieutenant. Make him your squad leader. But run it by Brother Captain Philip first, just so he won't feel left out. He is the Captain."

"Thank you, Sir," Wade said, finally realizing that he'd been standing there almost too afraid to breathe. It was like standing in the presence of greatness.

Before leaving, some brother in a brightly colored dashiki and huge Afro, approached the minister with a question. He wanted to know why Muslims didn't seek funding from the State and Federal Government for their schools.

"We're not beggars," the Minister replied. "Beggars mounted run their horses to death."

Wade had never been as impressed with anyone, as he was with Minister Uriah Sharrief. He liked everything about this brother, even the way he dressed. Every suit he had ever seen the minister wearing, had been tailored, and the Windsor knot of his ties always fitted perfectly inside the spread of his shirt collar. But it was the dignified manner in which Uriah Sharrief spoke to people and delivered the message of his topics that really had gotten Wade's attention. Regardless of what I do in life, he thought to himself, as he watched the Minister leave, I'm gonna study to become a man who can speak as well as he does, and be as committed as he is.

Wade thanked Brother Lieutenant Josh for introducing him to the Minister, and for promoting him. But later, when he mentioned to Ethan what Josh had done, he thought he detected a bit of resentment in Ethan's tone.

"Yeah, for a man with a head as hard as a rock, he can have a soft heart at times."

# CHAPTER XXI

Date:         March 31, 1968
To:          All Special Agents in Charge
From:        FBI Director: Hoover, J. Edgar
Subject:  Black Nationalist Hate Groups

> [An earlier memo, dated July 26, 1967, to advise all field offices of the expansion of the Counterintelligence Program, (COINTELPRO), against militant Black Nationalist Hate Groups to profile the "Goals" of the program. Those Goals are to now include the prevention of the Coalition of Militant Black Nationalist Groups. Such a coalition might be the first step toward a real Mau Mau in America, and the beginning of a true black revolution. It is this agency's job to prevent the rise of a "Messiah" who could unify and electrify a Militant Black Nationalist Movement. Malcolm X, could have been seen as a Messiah, but is now only the martyr of the movement. Now Martin Luther King, Jr., Stokely Carmichael, or Elijah Muhammad might all aspire to the position.
>
> All field offices are ordered to assign new agents to the COINTELPRO, submit a list of radical black organizations in its territory and submit practical Counterintelligence suggestions to FBI headquarters by April 4, 1968.

On the morning of April 4th, two agents from the FBI met with two undercover officers from the Philadelphia Police Department's Task Force. The purpose of this meeting was to discuss the recent deaths of two of their informants: Simon Hobbs, and Steward "Mississippi" Franklin.

Pursuant to their new directive, the agents from the FBI had already formalized and submitted their scenarios aimed at undermining Martin Luther King, Jr. and Elijah Muhammad. However, due to a lack of trust, and agency policy, that topic was not subject to discussion with the Philadelphia police.

"We might have to shut down the R.A.M. case," Agent Doss said, his blue eyes glancing around at the other three men in the smoke-filled room. "Hobbs was the only person who could directly connect the Sanderson Brothers to that plot."

"Yeah, but I'm more concerned about this Franklin guy," the red-faced, pot-belly, Philadelphia detective, Joe Napoli, spouted. "Wasn't he on your payroll, too? Did he O.D., or did the mob find out he was screwing Vinnie Cato's wife?"

"We don't think that was a hit, Joe," Doss interrupted. "But we know that Hobbs was hit in Detroit. The question is, did it come from Philly?"

"I got a few informants up at the Detention Center that know the Sanderson brothers," Napoli said. "I'll see what I can find out from them. But in the meantime, we really should prioritize this Mississippi thing. I gotta feeling about it."

"What kinda feeling, Joe?" Napoli's partner, Detective Stacy O'Connor, asked.

"Remember that black guy, Dabney Richards? He feeds me information for protection of his little drug operation. He called me last night and said that he'd seen Mississippi with two Black Muslims a few weeks ago, and they were talkin' to him sorta secretively like. What makes this info important is, one of these Muslims was Lucius Please. He's that big son-of-a-bitch I told you about -- a real dangerous character."

"Can you share this Richards, guy?" Agent Smith, asked, his thick eyebrows rising as he peeked over his horn-rimmed glasses. "You may have people at the Detention Center, but we got people inside Temple 12. We're going to bring down the Sanderson brothers for that Hobbs hit, and we might be able to help get this Muslim guy, if we can put Richards to good use."

"As long as I don't lose 'im," Napoli said. "I need 'im to keep tabs on Lucius. I was using this girl, but she..."

"How you spell his name, L.u.c.i.u.s.?"

***

At 5pm, that same day, Wade and Frankie were joyfully frolicking in their huge bathtub. He, carefully running his fingers over the soft and firm parts of her warm wet body, and she, massaging the flat of his stomach and gently rubbing down between his muscular thighs. Their lips kissed away the beads of perspiration as quickly as it formed on their faces. Eyes closed, they used only their hands and mouths to stimulate each other's body in preparation of another sexual marathon.

They had gotten married earlier that morning, and since arriving home three hours ago, they'd done nothing but laugh, play, and make love all over the apartment. They were like two little kids, giggling, and playfully rediscovering one another's intimate secrets.

A few days prior to their wedding, Frankie had called her parents, and Wade his mother. Both explained the necessities of a quick civil ceremony. The fact that they were Muslims and could no longer live together as an unmarried couple was understood and accepted by their families. But only after a sincere apology and promises of a future family gathering.

Since no one in the Temple, but Lucius, Ethan, Chris and Josh knew that Wade and Frankie weren't already married, the brothers and their wives were the only ones to attend. Lucius, wasn't married, but he surprised everyone by bringing Babysis with him. After the ceremony, the normally tight-fisted Josh treated everyone to an expensive mid-day dinner at Rotunda's on City Line Avenue. Registering a look of surprise, when Josh picked up the check, Lucius mocked, "Damn man, break a brother off!"

"This is at the expense and compliments of Minister Uriah," Josh whispered.

"Did the minister get that package?" Ethan asked.

"Yeah, five grand," Josh grinned.

Whispering in Josh's ear, Ethan said, "We gotta talk 'bout tha' Mississippi thing. Tha' wasn't s'posed to go down like tha'. They had no..."

"Yeah, but we gotta do it later," Josh interrupted, not wanting to get into it with Ethan, and thinking it best to change the subject. "Sister Gloria seems to really like Big Lucius, huh?"

Glancing over at Babysis, Ethan didn't answer Josh. He was angry. Mississippi was dead, and he felt that those brothers wouldn't have acted on their own. Someone told them it would be aw'ight to take him out, he thought.

Babysis was enjoying herself. For a couple of weeks, she had been searching for Lucius. Then finally, the day before the wedding, she had tracked him down at his third floor, one room apartment, atop the South Philly Temple, on 15th and South Streets. He'd transferred there from the Temple in West Philly so he could help with the maintenance of the building.

The knock on his door sounded almost familiar. His breath caught as he saw her standing there in the khaki colored coat with a long blue skirt beneath it. Her hair was covered with a blue scarf, and her face shined like a brand new penny.

"Can I come in?" she asked, brushing by him, not waiting for a response.

As he closed the door behind her, she moved to the far wall and removed her coat and head scarf. She was wearing a white blouse that narrowed inside her skirt and hugged her breasts tightly. When she reached out her arms to hug him, he didn't know why, but he shivered and froze for a moment.

"You're surprised, huh?" she grinned. "Too surprised to give your little Babysis a hug?"

"What are you doing here?" he asked, walking away and leaving her arms waving in the air. "How did you kno' I was down 'ere?"

First she told him why she had come. She had wanted him to know that she had seriously considered converting to Islam and was no longer into the life.

"I would go to the Temple in North Philly lookin' for you. Hoping to see you there, but I didn't kno' you were in the South Philly Temple now. Anyway, I was there so much, tha' people thought I was a Muslim, and soon, I was dressin' and actin' like one."

"You look good," Lucius told her, feeling a bit confused. "I wanted to com' up and see you, but I was busy down 'ere."

"Napoli has been after me," she told him. "When he saw that I was no longer available, he blamed you. He said that no matter how long it takes, he was gonna put you in prison or kill you."

Lucius, avoiding the Napoli comment, focused on her. He was seeing her in a different light. He had always wanted her, but had always fought off the urge. Now seeing her standing there dressed in a long blue skirt that didn't even show off her voluptuous figure, as much, he found himself excited, and this confused him. And Babysis noticed his nervousness.

"Can I get my hug, now?" she said, moving to him, as he moved to her. He put his arms around her and held her tighter than he ever had before. She was on her toes and very much alive. Her heart pounding against his chest, her lower body involuntarily pressing up against his. She could feel his breathing, and then, the full erection she had caused him to have. Surprisingly though, this time, he didn't pull away from her. His strong arms lifted her body until she was pressed tightly against his bulge. Babysis put her arms up around his broad neck, stretching her body out against his tall frame. He wanted her, and for the first time, she felt that he would finally admit it to himself, and to her.

"Do it, baby," she whispered, her hot breath massaging his ear. "Take these clothes off me."

They made gentle love all through the night, and only left the bed for Wade and Frankie's wedding the next morning. Babysis had beamed with joy when Lucius introduced her to the Muslim sisters as, Sister Gloria. Now they were back in his bed, and he was fucking her with that vigor and energy she had prayed he'd bring to her bed the night he was released from prison. But none of that mattered, now. She had him deep inside her, and she would work as hard as she could to keep him satisfied there, forever.

His muscled back flexed as he pounded years of frustration into her soft body. Though the bed springs violently squealed and squeaked, only sweet moans and gloriously sobs escaped her lips. Her hands encouraging him on, her mouth giving a sultry sustenance as a reward, until finally, his muffled grunts turned vocal enough to bounce off the walls. Babysis' sweat-bathed body heaved and jerked beneath him. The blood rushing to his temples, the slapping sound of naked bodies ringing in his ears. Was it all coming from inside his room? Or was the eruption he heard coming from the quiet streets below? By the time their unrestrained gallop had drawn to a leisurely gait, they finally realized that the distressful cries their lustful utterances had evidently drowned out, were coming from outside on South Street.

Likewise, in Germantown, another part of the city, Wade and Frankie heard the ominous cries coming from outside their apartment building, as well.

"THEY DON' KILLED KING! THEM BASTARDS DON' KILLED MARTIN LUTHER KING!" Voices shouted from the streets below. More than one voice, yelling. There was a chorus of them. People were screaming, crying. People were in pain.

# CHAPTER XXII

Unlike the night before, the morning air was still, silent, and not a sound to be heard. The acrid stench of burnt wood ash, scorched bricks, and roof-tar greeted those who ventured out in the lonely streets to be surrounded by quietness. It was as if even the birds knew that black folks were in mourning, and that the slightest sound or movement might awaken their sensibilities and justifiable wrath.

From his third floor window, Wade could see that Stein's Hardware Store and Levin's Drug Store, directly across the street, had been torched and completely gutted. And he thought he caught a whiff of rotting flesh coming from the rubble of Masserman's Food Market. Masserman's two sons stood outside searching for the watch dog they kept in the building after they had closed the store.

Frankie had turned on KYW News Radio, and Wade could hear the disturbing accounts of yesterday's events.

> "Civil Rights Leader, Dr. Martin Luther King, Jr. was shot and killed last night at 6:01 pm. The official report coming in from KWY's affiliates states that the civil rights leader was in Memphis, Tennessee, and delivered a speech at the Mason Temple Church, on April 3. He was staying at the Lorraine Motel, when he was gunned down while standing on a balcony. Reports of rioting in..."

Wade turned the dial to WHAT Radio, one of the local black stations in Philly, where the DJs not only played the music, but announced the news and gave the weather report, as well.

> "Last night, our beloved civil rights leader, and dear brother, Dr. Martin Luther King, Jr., was shot and killed in Memphis, Tennessee. He leaves behind, a wife, Sister Coretta Scott King, and four loving children...."

Wade could hear the DJ's baritone voice breaking as he struggled to make this painful announcement to his audience.

"People, this morning before I
came to work, I asked the Lord
how long must we continue to
endure the killing of our black
leaders: Medgar Evers, Malcolm X,
and now our beloved Dr. King. He
was a giant, y'all. The Prince of
Peace. He was one of the symbols
of our hope, and the
exemplification of our patience...."

With the soft melodic words of Sam Cooke, "I was born by a river, in a
little tent, whoa, and just like the river, I've been running ever since", Wade
heard sobbing mixed with the DJ's words:\

"When Dr. King spoke to us, he
spoke from his heart, and we
listened. Well people, he's still
speaking to us now, and we must
continue to listen. We must not
self-destruct, we must build on his
legacy...."

Wade heard the phone ringing and suspected that it might be Ethan. He
was rights. "We got a meetin' at the West Philly Mosque," he said. "But first,
drive out to Minister Uriah's house and follow him in. You got his address,
right?"

"Yeah, it's in East Mount Airy, not too far from here."

"Okay, and be careful," Ethan cautioned. "The cops are on the prowl,
lookin' to bust all black men."

News reports of rioting in Newark, Detroit, and more than 75 other
cities, were already hitting the airways. Deaths had been reported in rebellions
in Washington, DC, Chicago, and Cleveland.

As he drove through the streets, Wade saw overturned cars, burned-out
buildings, and smoldering furniture littering the sidewalks. Broken glass from
store windows, torn awnings, and unclothed mannequins lined the intersection
of Germantown and Shelton. Off in the distance he heard sirens blaring and saw
people running. But it was not until he drove through North Philly that he saw
police cars parked on just about every other corner. And every cop he saw along
the way was white.

Words from Dr. King's April 3 speech being broadcasted from WHAT
on Wade's car radio, sounded almost prophetic.

"So I'm happy tonight. I'm not worried
about anything, I'm not fearing any man.
Mine eyes have seen the glory of the coming
of the Lord."

As Wade pulled into the minister's driveway, he wondered if Martin Luther King knew that white folks would assassinate him. He heard a car horn and looked over at the cocoa brown Cadillac pulling out of the garage. Brother Lt. Lynton was behind the wheel of the minister's car, and Minister Uriah was in the back seat of the passenger's side.

"We've been waitin' for you," Lynton yelled from the car window. "Follow behind us and keep your eyes open."

"Yes, sir."

As the Cadillac pulled out of the driveway, Wade noticed a pale blue '67 Oldsmobile parked in the wooded hilltop area on the other side of the minister's house. Though he could only see the silhouette of the person sitting in the car, it looked like Brother Chris' Olds. As Wade pulled out to follow the minister's car, he saw the silhouette wave to him, and he waved back. The Olds never moved, so Wade thought, Chris must be there to protect the minister's family.

The temple was already full of Muslim brothers, lined up and standing at-ease by the time Minister Uriah, Lynton, and Wade walked in the room. Just about every Muslim brother in Philly was there. To Wade, it looked almost like the Fruit of Islam classes on Saturday mornings. Ethan and Lucius were standing off to the side of the room, talking, while Josh approached Brother Lt. Lynton, who usually conducted the Fruit classes.

Standing in the middle of the floor was Brother Assistant Minister Milton issuing instructions. When he saw that Minister Uriah had entered the room, he yelled, "Attention!" And every brother there assumed the position of standing erect, arms to their sides, heels together, and eyes front.

Minister Uriah spoke briefly about what would be the Nation of Islam's position during this critical time.

"I spoke with our dear beloved leader and teacher this morning," Minister Uriah began. He told the brothers that the Messenger had insisted that we be aware of how much Martin Luther King was loved and admired within the black community. He said that black people all over America will be deeply disillusioned by this, and Muslims should be mindful of their feelings.

"Later today, Brother Milton and I will be flying out to Chicago, and while we're gone Brother Captain Phillip will be in charge here."

After both ministers left the room, Brother Lt. Lynton gave the order to stand at-ease, while issuing assignments to squad leaders. He then stood straight, head bowed, positioned his hands palms up out in front of him, and led the prayer. Afterwards, he took Wade over to the corner of the room.

"Brother, do you kno' yo'r general orders? He asked.

"Yes sir," Wade answered, a bit confused as to why he was being quizzed.

"Wha's yo'r first general order?"

"To take charge of this post and all temple property in view. Sir!"

"And wha's the first line of yo'r fruit lesson?"

"A fruit is obedient to the laws of Islam and those in authority. Sir!"

"So in order to walk yo'r post in the proper manner, keeping always on alert, you gotta be on time, right?"

"Yes, sir!"

"And wasn't it someone in authority who called you and told you to proceed to Minister Uriah's house, immediately?

"Yes sir, but..."

"Then why were you late this morning?" he snapped. "The minister had to sit there waitin' while you took yo'r own sweet time."

"Brother Lieutenant, I came as soon as I got the call."

"I understand that you've been made squad leader. And I want you to kno' tha' had it been up to me, you..."

"It wasn't up to you," Lieutenant Josh interrupted, as he walked over to where they were standing. "It was up to me."

"Oh, I see why this brother don't kno' the meaning of protocol. He's one of yo'r recruits."

"Back-up off this brother, Lynton. Minister Milton has instructed me to place him with Minister Uriah's security."

Lynton was shocked, but not as shocked and surprised as Wade was. One moment he was being called on the carpet by a lieutenant, and in the next, being placed on a special squad by a minister.

"I don't think he likes me," Wade told Josh, as Lynton hurried off in search of Minister Milton.

"Don't worry 'bout him," Josh said, with a wave of his hand. "He jus' wants recognition as an authority figure. We got you placed on security because you live closer to the minister's house than we do. And Ethan seems to think you're alert and dependable."

"Thank you. I'll try to be..."

"It ain't gon' be easy," Josh interrupted. "You'll be spendin' a lotta nights parked outside his house. Okay?"

# CHAPTER XXIII

Over the next few days, rioting continued in black areas in over 100 cities. However, in the city of Philadelphia, black community leaders like Cecil B. Moore, Reverend Leon Sullivan, and others were able to keep the violence to a minimum. But even before his funeral, some who had always disagreed with Dr. King's "passive resistance" philosophy had begun to criticize his methods.

Revolutionary-minded brothers and some Muslims -- though told they should learn from Malcolm X's mistake and not say anything that would be considered insensitive -- began deriding Dr. King for wanting to integrate into a racist society. The same society that killed him. Wade overheard some Muslims reciting from their English Lesson number C-1, in reference to King. The purpose of the lesson was to ask why the so-called American Negro likes the devil. The answer was, "He likes the devil because the devil gives him nothing."

However, their disillusionment over Dr. King's love for white folks was trumped by their anger over white society's murder of the man.

"Maybe I'll start collecting my four heads," one brother remarked, referring to Lost-Found Muslim Lesson number 2, about receiving a Star and Crescent lapel pin for delivering four devil's heads to the temple. Most brothers understood the lesson to mean killing the vices white society had imposed upon our society: activities like drinking, smoking, gambling, and committing fornication. But there were brothers who took this to mean actually killing white folks, and did so.

"I've already started," another brother replied. "Even befor' dem devils killed King, I was takin' their heads. I jus' got two more to go befor' I git my lapel pin."

Five days after the assassination, a horse-drawn carriage carried King's body from the Ebenezer Baptist Church to Southview Cemetery, opened by blacks for blacks because they were excluded from burial at other cemeteries. As the funeral cortege wound through the streets of his home city, thousands of blacks and whites joined together in honor of the man.

Wade watched the funeral on TV at his mother's house. She was devastated. Like so many black people, and especially those from his mother's generation, she had a special love for Martin Luther King. Not only was he a man of peace, for her, he was the one black civil rights leader who whites might have eventually listened to.

Though he personally disagreed with Dr. King's "turn the other cheek" philosophy, Wade still recognized him as a black man and his brother. His mother continued crying as he held her hand. Her sorrowful sobs, so powerful, that they tugged at him in such a way as to cause a trickle of water to flow from his eye as well.

Two months after King's death, escaped white convict James Earl Ray, the man believed to have fired the shot that killed Martin Luther King was captured at London's Heathrow Airport. And of course, black folks wondered how this poor-white-trash of a man had made it that far without help. Allegations of a conspiracy were plentiful.

The day after Ray's capture, Brother Chris and Wade were selling *Muhammad Speaks* newspapers on the corner of Broad and Erie Avenue, when an elderly woman approached to buy a paper. Looking up at the brothers with a sad expression on her face, she shook her gray head from side to side, and asked, "Why in the world would dat white man shoot 'em like tha'? Dr. King was a good man. He spoke fo' ev'rybody. He loved whites, blacks, ev'rybody."

Wade just looked at her with a sympathetic eye. He wanted to say to her that one man hadn't killed Dr. King. He wanted to say that it was an old fashioned lynching, pure and simple. That when the policies of an entire country are predicated, both covertly and overtly on a systematic destruction of a people by refusing to give them basic human rights, the racist acts of any of their citizens, in the furtherance of such policies, are the result and the responsibility of that country. But he didn't say it. She wouldn't have understood, and anyway, it wasn't the right time to say it.

Chris gave the elderly woman a big hug and a few extra *Muhammad Speaks* newspapers and asked that she give some to her friends.

\*\*\*

For many, Dr. King's demise brought about a significant change in direction. As tragic as his death was, it gave some the opportunity to further their own agenda. With Malcolm and King both gone, the FBI was able to turn its attention to its third major target.

One day after the assassination, FBI agents overseeing COINTELPRO's "hate group" agenda, launched a campaign of mass mailings to various Muhammad Temples around the country. Their plan was to disrupt the operation and growth of the Nation of Islam by anonymously mailing letters and booklets to create suspicion and distrust among N.O.I. members.

White segregationists, also seizing the opportunity to speak out, made it clear that they too had achieved victory with Dr. King's death. They felt it had shown integration-minded blacks, and their white supporters, that no one was safe while opposing their white supremacist values.

There were also segments in the black community who sought advantage in King's murder. Groups like the New Republic of Africa, the Black Panther Party, the Nation of Islam, and a few others also viewed this as a circumstance that, though tragic, was favorable for their purpose. These groups now experienced a rise in membership. Black people, who had previously embraced the Southern Christian Leadership Conference, under Dr. King, now questioned his nonviolent approach to the Negro problem in America. Many of them, mostly young black men, who brought with them their wives and girlfriends, joined either the Black Panthers or the Nation of Islam.

Throughout the hot and humid summer of 1968 the brothers launched their own recruiting plan. The timing was right for Brother Lucius to accomplish what Brother Captain Khalid had asked him to do. Since that meeting in Chicago, Lucius had only succeeded in bringing the downtown brothers back to the fold. But now it was time to produce some real numbers.

Quoting from something he'd read while in prison, Lucius told the brothers, "As fire is kindled by bellows, so is anger by words." And though they might not have understood exactly what he was saying, they knew he meant for them to teach the brothers and sisters on the street about the white man being the devil. And what better way to do that than to use the murder of Dr. King.

"Every day that the sun sets," Lucius said, "it sets on the white man's hatred of the black man. So blow on that flame."

Brothers Ethan, Josh, Chris, and Wade joined with Brothers Mo, Big Cil, Dalton, and Rus to design a way of getting every young brother who was affiliated with a street gang in Philadelphia to attend Muhammad's Temple.

Knowing all the gang areas, they focused on the roughest in the city. Camac & 8th and Diamond/Camac & 8th and Norris/21st & Norris/21st & Diamond/the Valley/the Village/the Avenue/the Hundreds/the Mighties/Warnock & Somerset/12th & Oxford/Master St./Marshall & York/the Morrocos/Tioga Ts/21st & Westmoreland/South Philly/15th & Clymer/Point Breeze/ 20th & Carpenter/Christian St./West Philly/the Top/the Bottom/Germantown/Summerville/the Brick Yard/and others.

They began pulling up to the young corner boys as they gathered on the corners. Be they singing, drinking, or just hanging out waiting for girls, the brothers would call them together and speak to them in ways that they knew would get their attention.

"Wha' cha' punks doin' standin' out 'ere?" Ethan asked.

"Who you callin' a punk?" would usually be the reply.

"You don't get mad when the white man call you a punk and ask you why you standin' on his corner," Wade told the youngster. "You give the man more respect than you give yo'r own mothers and sisters."

That challenging tone would usually set the stage for a dialogue with the young men. Sometimes, the brothers would drive up on the sidewalk real fast and jump out of the car like they were the police.

"Up against the fuckin' wall," Josh would yell. "Wha'cha got in yo'r pockets?"

Once the youngsters were up against the wall, Ethan and Wade would pat them down and tell them to get in the car. The young brothers would actually think they were being taken to the police station. But the car would pull up in front of a Muhammad's temple, and the brothers would be escorted inside. After the services were over, they would be driven back to their neighborhoods. The downtown brothers, Big Cil, Mo, and the rest, were doing the same thing in their areas. Soon the young brothers began looking forward to seeing the Muslims and having them come by just to talk to them and take them to the Temple. If some of the young men complained about not having the proper clothes to wear to the services, Wade would steal suits from the clothing store for them to wear and keep.

It worked. Young brothers from all over the city responded to Muslim brothers, not much older than themselves, because those brothers took the time to talk and walk with them. Many of these young gang members began to come to the Temple on their own. And soon their attitude about themselves and their communities began to change. The word niggah had almost disappeared from their vocabulary. And they began referring to black women as sisters and black men as brothers.

The benefit of having this many young men filter into the Temple was enormous. Not only had the Muslim brothers reached out to stop most of the gang wars in the city, but they filled the chairs of Muhammad's temple with young men and women, who in turn, would spread the teachings of Islam and brotherhood, as taught by the Messenger. They had also enlisted foot soldiers to their own cause, which was to take control of the black communities from the Jewish businessmen, the Italian gangsters, and the Irish cops.

\*\*\*

It was while taking some of the new brothers down to the South Street Temple for orientation that Lucius ran into Rus.

"I been waitin' fo' you," Rus said. "I'm registered down 'ere, now."

"Wha' about Mo and Big Cil?" Lucius asked. "Did they register down here, too?"

"Cil is," Rus replied. "Mo and Dalton are out West."

"Why you waitin' for me?" Lucius asked. "Som'um up?"

"Dabney, remember? I told you I'd help you wit' tha'."

"Yeah, I remember. But I didn't think you did."

"A Muslim's word is his bond, right?" Rus grinned.

"When we talkin' 'bout?"

"T'morra night," Rus said. "He wants me to get Monster Dave to sell 'im som' monster. I told 'im to meet me at 10:30 in the Hi-Line Club on Broad and Belfield."

"Then wha'?" Lucius questioned.

"We take 'im out to the park. I'll go in his car, while you follow in mine. He'll think we're gonna pick up the meth from Dave. He kno's Dave won't sell it to 'im without me."

"Tha' joka see me, he ain't gettin' in no car wit' you."

"Yeah, but he ain't gon' see you. He gon' see a couple of red-bones I'll bring wit' me. Don't worry! They won't kno' wha's goin' down. They'll get in my car like they gon' drive, but get out once we turn the corner. I done it befor'. Tha's how I give them their package so nobody'll see 'em git it."

# CHAPTER XXIV

The crowd inside Sid Booker's Hi-Line was thick. It wasn't just the usual Saturday night partiers. Tonight people had come to see The Intruders, an R&B singing group from North Philly that had made it big, and whose latest song, "Cowboys to Girls" was climbing the charts like a bullet.

Dabney had arrived around 10pm. Like a scavenger, he was already scoping out the scantily dressed ladies. Circling the bar and dance floor, he leisurely sauntered, as if stalking prey, while anticipating licking the bones of any woman his buzzard eyes found along that night.

When Rus picked Lucius up in a rented Bonneville, he wasn't surprised to see Josh there with him. Though he hadn't been told that Josh would be coming, he figured that it had been Lucius' intention all along. Rus suspected Lucius wanted Josh along in case things didn't go as planned, and they had to improvise. Rus also felt that because he'd killed Mississippi and that white woman, neither Lucius nor Ethan trusted his judgment anymore. However, what they didn't know was that it had been Josh who had secretly told him to handle it that way.

At 10:30 they met the girls outside of the club. Rus told them that upon leaving the club, they should head straight for his car, as they had done before, while picking up a package. But this time, they were to stay in the car.

Pointing toward the car, he said, "There are two brothers already in the car, crouched down in the back seat. Don't worry 'bout them. Jus' take the bundles of scag from under the seat and follow me. I'll be driving the other guy's car. When you see me make a turn at Broad and Hunting Park, you get out of the car. Don't make the turn! Jus' get out and split."

As Rus escorted the women into the club, he whispered, "You don't have to pay me for the dope. There's 12 bundles there. Y'all can keep the money to re-up, if you want."

The girls knew that each bundle contained 25 bags, and at $10 a bag, they would pocket the entire $3,000 to re-up with. They never asked any questions before and saw no reason to start now.

The club's circular-shaped bar was located in the center of the floor, and dancing was in the back part of the club. But as thick as the crowd was, no one was dancing. All eyes were focused on the stage to the right of the entranceway.

The place was jumping. Men were yelling and the women were screaming at Lil Sonny and the rest of the group. The rhythmic vibrations could actually be felt coming up from the floor.

"Hey, hey," Dabney called out from across the club upon seeing Rus enter with the two red-bones wiggling and snapping their fingers.

Usually cautious when dealing with the men most hustlers now referred to as "The Brothers", Dabney's suspicions of Rus were lowered as he admired the two fine red-bones, locked arm in arm with the stylishly dressed Rus.

Wearing a chocolate-colored silk suit and yellow crew-neck silk knit, that the club's lights embraced, Rus looked as if he'd come to party.

As The Intruders opened up with, "I remember! ...When I used to play shoot 'em up! ...Bang, bang, baby!" Dabney bounced his way through the crowd towards Rus and the girls. "I'm diggin' this 'ere shit, more and more!" he said. "Gotta pocket full of dollars, and you got the girls and the monster."

"Wha'sup?" Rus asked nonchalantly. "Look like you're already on."

"Things lookin' better," Dabney crooned, as he eyed the women and openly licked his lips. "Wha's yo'r name, sugah?"

"This 'ere is Yvonne, and this is Yvette," Rus pointed to one and then the other. "They both are ours for the night."

"Damn, kinda sound like twins," Dabney grinned.

"We often do things in tandem," the one called Yvette seductively teased. "Comes kinda natural like, you kno'."

She looked no older than 18 and enjoyed the dumbfounded, open-mouthed look she'd placed on Dabney's face.

"We gotta get out of 'ere," Rus said, "we have to catch Lil Sonny n'other time. I got shit in my car."

"How far we gotta go?" Dabney asked, barely tearing his eyes away from Yvette's fine body.

"Mr. Silks," Rus said, trying to hear himself over the noise of the crowd. "Monster Dave's been waitin' there for awhile, now. We'll go pick the shit up, then all of us will head for the motel out by the airport. How tha' sound?"

"Hey, tha' sounds good to me."

"Okay. We'll drive yo'r car," Rus told him. "The girls will follow in mine. Tha' way we can talk money."

"I'm good," Dabney responded, putting his arm around Yvette's small waist, and purposely brushing her wide ass in the process. "How tha' sound to you, sugah?"

Slowly looking him up and down, Yvette whispered, "Sounds like an all-night party to me, daddy."

As instructed, upon leaving the club, both girls walked to Rus' car and got in. As Rus got behind the wheel of Dabney's grey Continental, he reached in his pocket and pulled out a small packet wrapped in aluminum foil. Sliding it across the seat, he said, "Open tha'. It's a spoon of the monster you'll be gettin' from Dave. Crystal meth. So pure, it'll dissolve by the time it hits water."

Dabney retrieved a razor-blade from the glove compartment and dumped a bit of the meth out on a small mirror. "It's crystal," he mouthed, watching it fluff up as he chopped it with the edge of the blade. "Looks jus' like pure sugah."

Rolling up a dollar bill, he snorted a couple of tracks and winced from the burn. "Damn, that's som' good shit."

Rus, watching the oncoming cars, waited until Dabney had composed himself before pulling away from the curb. He drove south on Broad.

"You like tha', huh?" Rus said. "Well, the whole package is like tha'. They don't call 'im Monster Dave for nothin'."

Dabney pushed the button, turning on the radio, and the Four Tops' "Bernadette" flooded the interior. "Damn, I like listenin' to tha' piece when I'm high," he said. "Check out this high note when the background screams out her name, 'Bernadette!'"

Reaching the corner of Broad and Hunting Park Avenue, Rus turned left. A moment later he saw the Bonneville make the turn. He could tell that it was Lucius behind the wheel.

"Take another hit," he told Dabney.

"Shit, I'ma ride dem girls all fuckin' night wit' shit like this," Dabney mumbled, snorting four more tracks. "You think Monster Dave'll give me a good deal?"

"I don't see why not, you're coping weight."

"Last week, som' boys from Washington, DC came up 'ere wit' some shit they called Bam. Ever heard of it?" Dabney asked, rewrapping the package and placing it in his pocket.

"Yeah. The high is similar to monster, but you can sleep with it. Most people 'ere don't like it though, 'cause you can't snort it."

"Yeah," Dabney said, clearing his nose. "You gotta shoot it 'cause it comes inside tha' little pill."

Turning off of Hunting Park onto 33rd, it took less than ten minutes to get deep inside Fairmont Park. On a dirt path near where there's a spring water fountain, Rus stopped the car and looked out the back window.

"Som'um wrong," he said, turning to Dabney. "I'll be right back."

When Dabney looked back, he saw that the Bonneville had stopped and its headlights were blinking.

"Wha' goin' on?" he asked, as Rus exited the car and headed back toward the blinking headlights. "Are the girls aw'ight?"

Dabney hadn't seen Josh exit the Bonneville because Josh had did so right after Lucius stopped the car, but before he started blinking the headlights. In a crouched position, Josh rushed up along the passenger's side of the Lincoln, yanked the door open and gripped Dabney's coat collar.

"You're in the way fat boy," he growled, as he quickly pumped two shots, point blank, behind Dabney's right ear.

Dabney never had a chance to react. He died slumped over the front seat, with his right hand touching the floor.

Rus quickly wiped his prints from the Continental, removed the meth from Dabney's pocket, and dropped a pair of lady's panties on the floor of the car, right under Dabney's hand.

\*\*\*

Each of the new converts, or brothers and sisters on Forum who had yet to receive their "X", was assigned to brother and sister lieutenants and squad leaders. Visiting neighborhoods and homes to speak to and socialize with the new arrivals to Islam, was an assignment taken very seriously. Sisters spoke with new female converts about the Muslim Girl Training (MGT) lessons they'd have to learn: grooming, hygiene, nutrition, and child care. Brothers spoke to the men about maintaining employment, caring for, and protecting their loved ones. They also spoke on how black men should stop the white insurance men and salesmen from disrespecting their families, by just walking into their homes, unannounced, and calling their mothers, sisters, and wives by their first names. They said, "A black man can't go in the white man's neighborhood, walk in his house and call his woman by her first name. The white man won't allow it and we shouldn't either."

Some brothers often took a more aggressive approach while visiting the families of old friends or corner boys who had yet to convert. If a picture of Jesus hung on the wall, a brother might snatch it down and stand on it while talking about the blond-headed, blue-eyed devil who presented himself to the world as a look-a-like of Jesus Christ.

The brothers would say, "If Jesus was to walk in this room today, he would look nothing like this 'ere picture."

They told how blacks had been lied to about religion and divinity, and how the so-called American Negros were the only people on the planet to embrace a God that looks remarkably like the people who enslaved them.

The orientation was designed to teach the new converts how to respond to questions from their family and friends. They were told they were better than the white man and didn't need him in their affairs; that the five letters in the word "Islam" stood for "I Self Lord and Master"; and that they were the original people of the planet; capable of mastering their own destiny.

Brothers Lieutenants Josh and Lynton, also spoke with new converts. However, they were looking for brothers who would fit into their plan for raising funds for Muhammad: brothers who were already streetwise and street-tough, and they found such brothers in Brother Theron and Brother Anthony.

Lil Theron was a short light-skinned brother, about 5'5", with leadership ability resulting from being a former leader of a gang called Demarcos. And Anthony, who had been from the 24th & Thompson Street gang, was streetwise and also a leader among his peers.

Josh put together squads for both brothers. Theron's squad became known as the Four-Footers. It became an inside joke because all the brothers in this squad were short. Anthony's squad was a little older and a bit slicker than Theron's, but would receive their assignments from both Lynton and Josh.

## Chapter XXV

In the fall of 1968, the practices of the FBI's insidious COINTELPRO program were unknown to the brothers in the Nation of Islam, Black Panthers, and others. Still there were some inside those groups who suspected that something was going on. Brothers who had been involved in the struggle were being targeted. Some had been sent to prison, and others had been shot down in the street because of disputes between so-called conscious-minded organizations.

In October of that year, the Nation of Islam, the Black Panther Party, CORE, and SNCC joined with the Hopi Indians and Hispanic-American activists in Chicago to discuss how to prevent these disputes and government interference into their organizations.

Though Josh, Lucius, and Big Cil were among the brothers attending this meeting as security for some of the Assistant Ministers, it had been agreed that Wade, Ethan, and Chris would not attend. Instead, they would stay behind to oversee the brothers plan to convince local businessmen to form a Business-Black-Community Alliance. They would also inform the local hustlers and drug dealers that they would have to come over to their side or perish.

There was a three-part strategy to this plan. First, they knew that the owners of these grocery stores, dry cleaners, and neighborhood bars wouldn't meet with them. So the key was to convince the true power base within the black communities; the black women who had lived there the longest. These women would be asked to speak with the white owners about forming a community alliance. They would be asked to voice their legitimate concern for better services and for business contributions toward community centers for their children. Instead of playing in the middle of the street, the children would have recreation centers in which to play and learn.

The expectation was that the women would be ignored, and this would allow the brothers to get involved. They planned to convince these owners to either sell or rent their businesses to respectable black men and women willing to buy.

Persuading the owners to sell would involve creating a real psychological fear for their personal and business safety. First the owners would be visited by some big afro-wearing brothers, dressed as revolutionaries in camouflaged sweatshirts and dyed army fatigues. They would say nothing, just show up a few times, look around, and then leave. After the owners had time to absorb this, some well-dressed, well-mannered brothers would visit them with a message.

"We can't keep this area safe from violence any longer and suggest that you take precautions. There's a climate of racial strife and the word on the street is you're going to be hit hard. We asked that you at least consider selling to some respectable blacks or rent your business so that the neighborhood won't lose the benefit of your services."

To bring this point home, Wade and Ethan had paid some young gang members to break the windows and cause minimal fire damage to a few area cleaners and stores.

"Our next target will be easier to convince," Ethan told the brothers. "Them white boys are getting rich from all the drugs and alcohol they got in our neighborhoods. Well, we gonna flush 'em out. If we gotta take it over to do so, tha's wha' we'll do."

The brothers began forcing the hustlers working for the Italians to pay rent. But the money wouldn't go to them, it was used for loans to the neighborhood women with children and no husbands. The women were advised to use the money to give dinners and selling parties to raise rent money. The loaned funds were not to be repaid to the drug dealers or hustlers. If the women were able, they were to donate it to Muhammad's Temple. Local Jewish jewelers, who had been buying back the same stolen merchandise they had sold in the neighborhood, were told to stop. All boosters were told to bring all merchandise that was stolen only from downtown stores to the brothers. They would buy it, and if the boosters were arrested, the brothers had bondsmen who would get them out.

The last part of their plan was targeting the Italian gambling houses located in the black neighborhoods and run by front men or women. After learning from the women who worked the games which cards would be used, the brothers would buy that brand, already marked, from a dealer on Market Street. The girls working the games would replace all backup decks with the brothers marked ones. The brothers would then have their people come in to work the games. At least three were needed for each game. Though appearing not to know each other, two of them would sit at opposite ends of the table, so they could control the game. The third brother was there to watch their backs in case something went wrong. Soon after the game was underway, one would either spill a drink on the cards or fold an edge so that the deck would have to be removed. The decks coming in as replacements were always the brothers'.

The Jewish store owners and jewelers, as well as some of the bar owners, felt that it was better to compromise with the brothers than to lose everything. A few of them sold their stores and bars under a management-buyer's plan; most replaced old white managers with new black ones. And they all agreed to fund the recreational programs for the children and send them to day camp every summer.

The dope dealers and boosters presented no problem at all. The dealers complied by lending a portion of their money to the women with children, at no return rate. And boosters brought all their stolen goods to the brothers.

The gambling houses proved to be more profitable than the brothers could have imagined. Once the sisters working the games saw how much money they could make, they began telling the brothers about the safehouses the Italians used to store gambling money until it could be laundered.

The brothers didn't have to ask how the women knew about these houses. Experience had shown them that those white boys loved running their tongues over black women about what they had. It was their way of trying to impress upon a black woman how successful he was in comparison to the black man.

Still, after hitting one of the houses for fifty grand, the white boys changed locations. However, the brothers were satisfied with their accomplishment so far.

But, like the saying goes: "There is no gathering of the rose without being pricked by the thorns." The brother now had to deal with the police. Jewish store owners and even the Italian gamblers were complaining about them "nigger Muslims" who were cutting in on their action. The brothers found that some of the security at the safe houses were actually police officers working for the police commissioner. They learned this while disarming the security at the safe houses they took off, and came up with a few badges and guns.

It was around that time that the brothers' first heard someone refer to them as the Black Mafia. It had been at a meeting Minister Uriah had with some businessmen, community leaders, and the Philadelphia Police Commissioner, at the Philadelphia Savings Fund Society Building (PSFS) on Market Street. Evidently, the commissioner was upset about his men being relieved of their guns and badges, but dared not make it public because they weren't supposed to be there in the first place. Being an Italian himself, the mob had called on the commissioner to intervene with the Muslims.

Although the Italians had known for some time now who that black-hand robbing their pocket belonged to, they didn't want to confront the Muslims head on. All they knew was that these particular brothers called themselves "The Inner Circle". But the Italians didn't know exactly who they were or how strong they were in numbers.

According to one of the inside community leaders at that meeting, the police commissioner pulled Minister Uriah aside and spoke to him in a not-so-pleasant manner.

"What's going on?" he asked the minister. "Muslims trying to take over the city?"

When the minister replied that he didn't know anything about any of this, the commissioner reportedly yelled, "Well you damn well better find out. Them boys of yours are running around the city like they the Black Mafia or som' um!"

Soon the newspapers began labeling the brothers the Black Mafia, but the brothers only laughed at that. They were men; black men who hated the white influence over their people, and they would have never selected to call themselves by a name which conjured up images of some white organization.

"What," Chris once commented, "if we burned crosses on white folks' lawns? Would they call us the Black Klan?"

\*\*\*

While in Chicago attending the conference with the other organizations, Lucius also met with Brother Captain Khalid. He took that opportunity to tell the Brother Captain about their new recruitment program and how well it was working. After that meeting, and unbeknownst to Lucius, Khalid met with Brother Lieutenant Lynton, who had snuck into town to meet with him.

"How are things working out?" he asked Lynton.

"Jus' as we thought," came the reply. "No one knows who is calling the shots. As long as we keep Josh up front, we'll be able to control everybody, including Lucius."

"You know, its kinda funny how committed those brothers are. They're making a lot of money and giving most of it away."

"It's blind commitment," Lynton said. "All them brothers are so thorough to one another and their cause. They don't even think about trying to get rich. They got nice cars, wear nice clothes, and care for their women and children. But most of everything they can steal goes to the Temple."

"Yeah, and into Uriah's pockets and yours, too."

"Naw, mine comes from being left alone by the feds."

"Well, it's working to our advantage. Temple 12 is about to become the number one money earner in the country. And as long as we keep the feds happy, they'll leave us alone."

"You talked with Uriah, yet?" Lynton asked.

"Yeah. He told me about Phillip leaving for Boston. Do you know this new Captain y'all are getting?"

"Yeah. Brother Terence. He's smart, very smart. So watch yourself around him. He loves Lucius and Josh."

"Oh, yeah, Uriah said to remind you to work on keeping Josh and Ethan at odds. Ethan is as dangerous as Lucius."

"I know. And Brother Lucius is close to both of them."

"What about the brothers Lucius told me about? The ones who just came back in."

"They're from down my end of town. Good brothers who love making money as much as I do. But I have to keep them out my business, 'cause they're also close to Terence."

"Captain Terence, now."

"Yeah, Captain Terence."

"We'll just have to deal with those we think have some leadership ability," Khalid said, getting up from his chair and heading for the door. "If possible, get 'em outta the way. This thing is too sweet to let some zealous brothers fuck it up."

"We'll have to be careful," Lynton cautioned, "long as they think instructions are coming from the right people, they'll follow protocol. They're thorough. They been that way all their lives. They're not the kinda brothers who'll give you up or take you down with 'em if they get busted. But they will kill you without batting an eye if they think you went south on them or tryin' to set 'em up."

## CHAPTER XXVI

The last Monday in November was kind of breezy but not too cold. It was 1:45 am. Wade stuck his head out the door of the store he operated on Warnock and Somerset and called out to the teenager standing outside with a cute brown-eyed girl.

"Salaam-Alaikum, Bop," he yelled. "Excuse yo'rself for a minute. Need you to take this 'ere over to Artie for me."

"Aw'ight," Bop replied, adjusting his coat collar and smiling at the girl. "Catch 'chu later, Babe."

Bop knew Wade wanted him to carry money across the street to Artie, the bartender and new owner of Eddie's Bar. He was glad Babe had been standing there when Wade called him. Most everybody in the neighborhood knew Wade and the rest of the brothers who were usually at the store. They respected them. Especially the women, because the brothers were always telling the men around there to respect the black woman.

It made Bop feel important that the brothers trusted him enough to let him be around them. Ever since last summer, he had been doing little jobs for them. He had been the one Wade came to when he wanted the windows in Greenberg's cleaners broken out. Greenberg got the message and for the first time since he'd been operating his business there, began meeting with the committee of women in the neighborhood.

Eddie's Bar had been one of the businesses the brothers targeted under the management-buy plan. It was important to them because Artie, who'd been the night bartender there for years, was a good friend of Ethan's. During that time, he would allow the brothers to use the cellar to store money and guns. Some nights, after the bar had closed, they would meet there. It was also the perfect hideout, one the brothers often used when cops were driving the streets looking for them.

Now that Artie was the owner, they didn't have to worry that the white guy, Eddie, would discover what they had been storing there. Occasionally, Wade would send over money and other items he didn't want locked-up overnight in the store for Artie to lock in the safe. The money was usually from the sale of hot merchandise -- ladies' jewelry, dresses, coats, and children's clothing. The store was also used as a pawn shop, where people could bring their items, get money for them, and retrieve them later.

Bop like taking money over to the bar because at his age, that was the only way Artie would let him in there. But once he was in, he'd enjoy looking at the women with their dresses halfway up their thighs, wiggling their hips, and dancing in the middle of the floor. The men would usually be standing around trying to impress the women with a fist full of money.

As he strolled across the street with the bag of money and jewelry, Bop hoped Artie would be closing up the bar. If nobody's in 'dere, he thought, shit, I can get Artie to give me a taste of dat wine. He liked working with the brothers, but he still liked getting high, too.  Sometimes, when they caught him getting high, the brothers would put the boxing gloves on and beat him up.  But they never tried to hurt him.

Just before Wade locked up the store, Bop rushed back in, all excited and breathing hard.  "Puncho stabbed Artie!"  He yelled.  "He jus' stuck 'im in the chest."

"Wha' Puncho?  He did what?!"

"He walked in and started arguing at Artie 'bout his woman.  He said Artie's been bangin' his woman or som'um.  Then he jus' walked up and stuck 'im."

"Call Ethan," Wade said, getting his gun from under the counter.  "The number's on the wall.  And stay here!"

In a crouched position, Wade ran across the street, his gun in his right hand and pressed against his thigh.  Cracking open the door to the bar, he peeked inside.  In the middle of the bar, he saw Artie lying on the floor holding his chest, as Puncho, legs straddled, stood over him.

Wade looked but didn't see a knife.  Puncho was holding a silver-plated, pearl-handled gun that Wade recognized to be Artie's .32.20 revolver.  Wade had seen that gun many times and knew that it had a cylinder that rotated left instead of right.  Ethan had accidently fired that gun once because he thought the cylinder rotated to the right, like most guns.  When Ethan didn't see a bullet in the chamber to the left, he thought it safe to pull the trigger.  He was wrong and he almost shot Artie.

"Put the gun down Punch," Wade said, walking in with his gun still pressed tightly behind his thigh.  "Don't do this man.  You don't wanna do this."

"The hell I don't," Puncho yelled.  "I told this 'ere old muthafuckah to stay away from my woman or I'd kill 'im."

Wade watched the gun carefully.  As a result of almost being accidently shot, Artie began keeping only four bullets in that gun.  There were always two empty slots on the right side of the hammer, so when the cylinder turned to the left, the hammer would fall on an empty chamber both times.  Only on the third pull would the gun fire.

Looking past Puncho, Wade caught a glimpse of Bop peeking through the side door.  He had a stick in his hand and was trying to motion to Wade.

"C'mon Punch," Wade pleaded, "put it down."

"You don't kno' me niggah," Punch said, this time while pointing the gun at Artie's head.  "Get the fuck outta my damn business fo' I give you som' of wha' I'ma give this niggah."

Although he couldn't see the cylinder turn, Wade heard the first click, as Puncho pulled the trigger.  He saw Artie's body tense up.  His chest was heaving hard and blood was now squirting out of him.

"Don't!" Wade heard Artie yell, as Punch pulled the trigger a second time, then looked at the gun to see why it hadn't fired.  When he pointed it at Artie's head again, Wade fired twice.  He heard a loud explosion, his shots striking Puncho in his side and once in his chest.  The gun dropped from his hand and Puncho crumbled to the floor.  Then it was eerily quiet.  The silence, startling, echoed around the room.

Again realizing that the crimson color continued oozing out of Artie's chest, Wade called out to Bop, while rushing over to check on Artie.

"Dial the operator and get Temple Hospital!  Tell 'em to send an ambulance!"

Though Wade could tell that Puncho was dead, he kicked the gun away from him, as he bent to press above Artie's wound to try and slow the bleeding.

"Is he dead?" Artie asked in a hoarse whisper.

"Yeah, he's dead," Wade answered, realizing for the first time, he had actually shot and killed a man.

"Say I killed 'im," Artie whispered.  "You can't get mixed up in this.  Say I did it."

Ethan met Wade and Bop at Temple Hospital.  Artie had lost quite a bit of blood, but he would live.  The police believed the story told to them – that Artie had shot and killed Puncho with another gun he had in the bar.

Bop standing there wide-eyed and excited said nothing.  He had been ready to attack Puncho with the stick, but Wade – not wanting him in the line of fire – shook his head, no.

"Wha'cha gon' say 'bout all this?" Ethan asked Bop as they left the hospital.  "You kno' yo'r corner boys gon' be asking wha' went down."

"I'ma say wha' y'all told me to say when I busted out tha' white man's windows," he grinned, "nuttin' at all."

*** 

"How you doin'?" Ethan asked Wade, as he drove him home from the hospital.  "You aw'ight wit' this?"

"I'm cool," Wade mumbled.  Though he wasn't sure how he felt, he gave no outward appearance that he was troubled about what had happened.

"You kno' if you hadn't downed Puncho, Artie would be dead right now.  Tha' jokah would've killed him fo' sure.  And all over tha' yellow-ass woman."

"I know."

"Wade, wha' we do is for a cause, man.  Though Artie's a Negro minded dude, he's someone who we can depend on for wha' is necessary.  No more, no less.  If he'd been taken out, we would've lost a lot of money and contacts."

"I know," Wade said looking over at him.  "I'm fine…"

"I might've told you this before," Ethan continued, "but it's worth repeatin'.  We're not murderers, man.  We're killers when necessary.  We're committed to Muhammad.  And our business is nobody's business.  Our motto is, 'Those who kno', don't say.  And those who say, don't kno'."

Before Wade got out of the car, Ethan asked him to say the Morning Prayer with him.  They both positioned their hands, palms up, elbows pressed in their sides, and Ethan began: "In The Name of Allah, The Beneficent, The Merciful surely I have turned myself to thee, oh Allah…"

***

As soon as he reached the front door to their apartment, Wade thought about Frankie. "She must be worried to death," he mumbled, looking at his watch. "It's 5 am, I've never stayed out all night without calling her."

His thoughts were confirmed as soon as he opened the door and stepped inside. Frankie was in her favorite easy chair, the one she always sat in when studying. Her knees were tucked to her chest, a book in her hand, and her tortoise-shell glasses hung from the thin gold chain around her neck. Before he could say anything, Frankie leaped from her chair and hugged him tightly with a sigh of relief.

"I was so worried about you," she whispered. "All night I sat here. Are you alright? Is there som…"

"I'm fine baby," he lied. "I'm sorry I couldn't call, but the Minister had us busy all night. I promise I'll never worry you like that again."

"Wade, we're pregnant!" she proclaimed with glee, her arms still wrapped around his neck. "I stayed up so I could tell you and see your face. We're going to have a baby!" She sung the words to him. *We're going to have a baby!"*

His jaw dropped. His gaze went from her eyes down to her stomach and back again. "For real!" he stammered.

"No stupid, for play," she grinned. A huge grin that made him forget all about the events of last night. In just a twinkling of an eye, he had gone from the lowest point in his life to the highest he could have imagined.

He gathered her up in his arms and kissed her face all over. "Thank you," he said. "Thank you, thank you, thank you."

"My pleasure," she laughed, rubbing up against him. "I think we better take advantage of this time before I get too big, huh?"

## CHAPTER XXVII

By the summer of 1969, Messenger Muhammad's teachings had reached just about every black community in this country. His ministers, most of them powerful speakers, were broadcasting his message on radio in most urban cities. On street corners, brothers with Muhammad Speaks newspapers under their arms, stopped to give sermons to crowds of listeners. Some who had previously criticized the message and simply moved on, now stopped to listen and buy the paper. Nationally-known singers were now singing about the beauty and pride of black people and an ensemble of men calling themselves The Last Poets created a new form of black music. They began rapping about the black struggle against oppression in the land.

Despite surreptitious tentacles of the government's COINTELPRO operation, as well as those of the Philadelphia Police Department's Special Unit, the brothers – now known simply as "The Brothers" – were also progressing. Under the tutelage of Brother Lieutenant Josh, Theron and the Four-Footers were earning at a modest pace. Their job was to harass and rob certain drug dealers in parts of the city until they agreed to come in under the umbrella. Trying to remain independent would prove costly for the dealers. Brother Anthony had his crew operating in other parts of the city.

Some frustrated dealers tried to hire hit men to get these new brothers off their backs and out of their pockets. The hired hit men turned out to be Brother Harvey and Big Cil, who took the money and reported the contract to Josh. The dealers were then visited and told that under no circumstances were they ever to put out a hit on a Muslim again. This proved to be an effective strategy for getting dealers under control.

The brothers also had a crew of women, some white, to apply for jobs at factories and department stores. Because they were never suspected, they could go into an office and steal blank payroll checks from the back of the companies' checkbooks. Because the checks came from the back of the book, most companies wouldn't notice the theft until their monthly bank statement came. This allowed Brothers Lester, Ethan, and Wade to open bogus checking accounts at various banks in Philly and New Jersey. With false identities, they would cash the payroll checks, usually written for less than $2,000, by depositing half into the bogus checking accounts. Working each branch of a particular bank, in just one day, they would clear over $25,000. And on the weekends when department stores were usually busy, they would use the checks from the checkbooks to make expensive purchases from stores like Macy's and Bambergers in Jersey. Because these accounts could only be verified during banking hours, the store wouldn't realize the hit until around Tuesday morning.

The brothers' efforts were soon recognized by higher ups in the Nation of Islam. In Chicago and other cities, when there was a need for a certain type of security, the call went out to the brothers at the top of the clock, Temple Number 12, in Philly.

Though a great deal of the funds being used for the growth of the Philadelphia Muslim community came from the illegal activities of an inner circle of brothers, most of the financing came from hard working brothers and sisters who avoided crime. Brothers like Josh, Ethan, and Lucius had always tried to discourage their more spiritual brothers from illegal activities. Only those who were bold enough to be pioneers and were willing to be sacrificed for the greater cause were ever called upon.

***

With the elimination of Dabney Richardson, Fat Hank felt comfortable enough to introduce the Brothers to his New York connection Frank Matthews. With a nod from Brother Lucius, Mo, Big Cil, and Dalton accompanied Hank to the first meeting, which was held at Loretta's Hi-Hat, in Longside, New Jersey.

Evidently Loretta's had hosted these kinds of meetings before, and profited well from them. Seated around the huge table adorned with a variety of meats, cheeses, and fruits, served with champagne and gin, were men who had been in the drug trade for years. Horace Jones, from Washington, DC, Lil Walter from Baltimore, Maryland, the Aikens Brothers out of Charlotte, North Carolina and Chester Slim from Chester, Pennsylvania.

"The stuff will be comin' outta Turkey," Frank said. "So I'ma be puttin' up a lotta paper. I need to be sure y'all can handle the weight."

Big Cil didn't particularly like Frank Matthews. Though he had been in the life for years, and most people respected him for his business sense. Cil felt that Frank was only powerful because he had been lucky enough to be with the right people when certain connections were made. The Aikens Brothers had been Frank's greatest asset. Without them, Cil thought, Frank would be just another dope dealer.

"Can we control all the products?" Frank asked, still holding the floor. "That's the most important thing of all."

"In Philly," Mo began, "I kno' we got control. We..."

"Yeah, but I'm talkin' 'bout over everything," Frank interjected. "It's called vertical union. I got snow comin' in with the heroin. I got grass in the waitin'. The only thing I don't have control over is speed. Tha' crystal stuff y'all call monster in Philly."

"Let me say this," Mo began again. "Your concern is whether or not we can handle the weight. We can handle the weight. We're willin' to offer you options. In other words, we'll offer you a present price for your product, and even if things slack off a bit, we'll still pay that price, and take the loss out of our profit."

Obviously impressed with what he was hearing, Frank looked over at Fat Hank and smiled. Mo was endearing himself to him by appealing to his business acumen. Frank knew it, and he liked it. He liked Mo.

"Wha'cha mean, if things slack off?" Frank asked. The value on this level stays the same or rises. I control the price."

Mo leaned closer to Frank and nodded, as if agreeing with his point. "I understand where you're comin' from, but tha's only if there's no outside problems. Them white boys is gonna throw everything they got at us. You kno' tha'. On yo'r level you might not feel it at first, but we will, and that will determine how people feel 'bout paying yo'r price. There's always a star, a cash cow, and a problem child when dealing with this kinda product. All I'm sayin' in...."

"How long you been in this?" Frank laughed. "You sound like a businessman. How much money you made?"

"I earned my first few dollars cutting grass, shoveling snow, and selling papers," Mo said, winking at Frank. "Now I plan to sell grass and cut snow, so I can roll in paper, like you."

That statement sealed the deal. Prices were set, and an agreement for a series of meetings over the next few months was made. The meetings would be held at The Tippin' Inn in Jersey and Mr. Silks on the strip in West Philadelphia.

*** 

The last day of July, Frankie gave birth to a little girl. She and Wade named her Rasheedah. Things had changed a lot in Wade's life. He was now a father. He had quit his job in the clothing store, and with Ethan, had opened two small jewelry stores known as Asian Enterprises. The jewelry, made by Muslim sisters and purchased at a discount by brothers who sold earrings, necklaces and bracelets in local nightclubs and bars, was profitable.

Wade also met a guy called Mailman Charlie around that time. Charlie delivered mail for the U.S. Post Office, and he was a $100-a-day heroin addict. When Wade found out Charlie was stealing checks out of the mail to pay for his drugs, he pulled Charlie aside.

"Look, man," he said, "taking one or two checks everyday is like throwing bricks at the penitentiary. Soon you'll get busted. Tell you what. Bring me $1,500 worth of checks every weekday, and I'll promise you $350 at the end of each day."

"How you gon' do tha'?" Charlie asked.

"Don't worry 'bout that. You got my word I'll give you half of what I'll get for the $1,500."

The scheme worked smoothly. Wade began meeting Mailman Charlie every morning at a pre-planned location to pick up the checks. Once he had them, he took them to various store owners that he did business with. The checks were endorsed using the name which appeared on the front of the checks and the store owners gave Wade $750 and deposited the entire $1,500 into their stores' bank accounts.

When the people who were supposed to receive the checks reported them stolen, the federal and state agencies that had issued the checks would always replace them.

Wade knew he had to be careful. Mailman Charlie was a junkie, and he often dealt with other people who were also junkies. These men knew

Charlie was a punk and sometimes they would strong-arm him into giving them checks, even when he didn't have enough to give.

# Chapter XXVIII

There had been changes in the lives of some of the other brothers as well. Ethan's wife, Sister Geraldine, had recently given birth to twin boys, Hassan and Hussain. Josh and Deborah had a new son, Anwar, and Lucius was planning to wed Babysis in the summer.

Wade and Frankie were at Chris' house listening to tapes with Chris and his wife, Christine, when the call came. Chris and Wade were to report to Minister Uriah's office, at the masjid, in an hour.

"Can we listen to the last part before we leave?" Wade asked Chris. He really enjoyed listening to the Messenger's earlier speeches. This one in particular because it was about the coming of the Mothership. When he first heard this speech he found it hard to believe but came to accept it as part of having faith. As so many religions require, he thought, one must sometimes just have faith in what is being taught.

"Yeah, we got time," Chris answered. "The minister is at headquarters, it'll only take fifteen minutes to get there."

Wade and Frankie listened intently at the Messenger's graveled voice. Hanging on his every word, as he pointed out that the story in the Holy Bible about Ezekiel's wheel was a prophecy about blacks. "The Asiatic Nation," he said, "has the Ezekiel wheel ready to destroy this devil in six hours. A wheel-shaped plane known as the Mothership is one half mile by a half mile. It has 1,500 small saucer-like planes that will escort it to the point needed to drop its bombs. Only those believing in Allah will be safe from these explosions."

Although he had heard him before, Wade was always excited to hear the Messenger speak. This was a man he had come to love and would give his life for. A man he felt was giving his life for black people. Standing up before the world and calling the most dangerous people in the history of mankind, a race of devils. As far as Wade was concerned, that took real courage.

Headquarters was now in North Philly on Park Avenue and Susquehanna. They had opened this mosque just after New Year's 1970. Wade followed Chris up the steps to the minister's office on the second floor; both of them wondering why they were being called in.

Sitting in the room with Minister Uriah, were Brother Captain Terence, Brother Lieutenants Josh, Lynton, and now First Lieutenant Harvey. Wade had just heard of Harvey's promotion and nodded his congratulations upon entering the office.

"Brothers," the minister began. "I wanted you particular lieutenants here because we have some important engagements coming up, and security has to be perfect. But before we get to that, I need to handle another matter that just came up."

At that point, he nodded to Josh, and Josh opened the door to the outer office and asked Brother Larry to step in. Larry had been one of the brothers who had come over from the RAM organization and was Harvey's cousin. The minister reached in his desk drawer and pulled out a copy of *Nite-Scene*, one of those publications that printed articles and photos of the night-life in the bars and clubs around Philly and New Jersey.

"Brother, the investigator showed me this paper," the minister said, pointing at a picture of a brother standing with two women inside a bar and holding what appeared to be a glass of liquor up to his face. "Is this you in this photo?"

"Yes sir, Brother Minister, that... uh"

"Are you sure that's you?" Uriah repeated.

"Yes sir."

"Brother, are you telling me that the man in this photo, standing between these women, grinning and appearing to drink liquor from that glass, is you?"

"Yes, sir," Larry answered, his head bowed.

"Then I have no choice but to suspend you from the temple for 90 days, brother. Do you understand?"

"Yes sir."

Minister Uriah then leaned back in his leather chair and stared at Brother Larry for a moment. "Let me ask you a very important question, my brother. Would you inform on people you know if the police asked you to?"

"No sir!" Larry answered emphatically. "I wouldn't..."

"Yes you would brother. You just told on yourself. I had no way of knowing if that was you in this picture. The white man could have doctored this photo. The only way I know it's you, is because you told on yourself."

"I uh..."

"No, now, don't say anything else, brother. Listen, if you get caught with your hands in a cash register, you deny it was you. If the man who caught you cut off both your hands and they fall inside the cash register, you still deny it was you. And when they take you to court and present the hands to the judge, you tell that judge that you were born without hands, so those hands don't belong to you. Understand what I'm telling you brother?"

"Yes sir," Larry mumbled, "keep my mouth closed."

Every brother in the room liked Larry, but they were finding it extremely hard not to fall on the floor laughing.

Wade, feeling a bit more at ease now, was seeing another side of the minister. He seemed personable. People genuinely like him as much as they respected him for his position.

The meeting had been called to inform the lieutenants that Minister Uriah would be speaking at Temple University's Magonigle Hall that Saturday, and he only wanted certain brothers with him. "This event will be filmed," he said, "and since Brothers Chris and Wade were the only lieutenants here who don't have a police record, they should be the only ones on the stage with me."

Though no one mentioned it, they all knew why the extra security was now required. On December 4, 1969, the Chicago Police, using an informant and infiltrator, had assassinated two members of the Black Panther's Party. Two months later, in Chicago, three men had attacked Captain Shabazz, the chief of security for the Nation of Islam. It was widely believed that those men were sent by a group calling themselves the United Slaves or "US" and that they had actually meant to kill Captain Shabazz. However, when someone came to the house and interrupted them, the attack was turned into a robbery.

Although they had no real proof of just who those men were, they had the word of some former members of the group, "US", who stated that the FBI had once propositioned their leader to fight against the Nation and the Black Panthers. Still there had been too many recent incidents, and the Nation of Islam was taking no chances. Extra security was now required for all ministers.

On the first Saturday in May, Captain Terence took the podium at Temple University and opened up for Minister Uriah. He spoke to the racially mixed audience about Martin Luther King's dream, and how it dispels when one runs into the gate-keepers. He said that these gate-keepers acted as barriers, purposely positioned to deny access to a free market --- and that white society benefits from allowing their leaders to use classifications and generalizations to enable one group of people to constrain another.

After Captain Terence, Minister Uriah took the podium. Suave and polished, he spoke to the attentive students about the reasons one should follow Elijah Muhammad.

"The Honorable Elijah Muhammad is from the south," he said in his southern tone. "He saw black people in fear of those filled with segregationist zeal. He saw them walk the gauntlet of massive resistance toward integration. His black people were despondent and confused about the burdens they had to bear. Mothers, fathers, and children were enduring problems of poverty, despair, and powerlessness. He watched as their courage and racial pride met at the crossroads of degradation and self-pity and wondered if it was time for reconciliation or retaliation. So he offered us a solution that gives pride and dignity back to the black man. This is the reason we..."

During his speech, the brothers stood along the wall, and in every corner of the room, eyeing the crowd. Wade and Chris stood behind the minister and watched the expressions of those listening to him. While leaving the building a man, who obviously hadn't been in the auditorium, walked up and asked which person was Minister Uriah. He said that he just wanted to meet him. Wade pointed to an unknown person standing at the curb and the man went over to that person and shook his hand.

On the drive back to the mosque, Uriah whispered to Harvey, "I like Brother Wade. He's security-minded and seems to be trustworthy. Let him do the pickup from Chester Slim."

Wade noticed the interaction between the Minister and Harvey but hadn't heard the conversation.

Later that evening, First Lieutenant Harvey called Wade at home. "The minister wants you to ride with Chester Slim when he comes to Philly next month. It'll be your responsibility to make sure nothin' happens to him, so wear your shoes. Meet me one day next week at headquarters, we'll go over everything."

Wade felt a bit concerned. He knew that wearing his shoes meant to bring his gun. But why? Who is this Chester Slim, anyway? He wondered.

Chapter XXIX

In the early 1970s, the virus of violence now extended far beyond the alcoves of the ghetto. It was impossible to know how many brutal assaults and killings had occurred in black communities by unknown men in police uniforms. But once those numbers began rising in other places, people began noticing.

Anyone who considered the policies of the U.S. Government to be racist and imperialistic, and had the nerve to speak out against those policies, became targets. It didn't matter who they were, be they black or white, the U.S. Government, with impunity, often took drastic action against them.

On May 4th, two days after Minister Uriah's speech at Temple University, the Ohio National Guard Unit, ordered onto the campus of Kent State University, opened fire on students protesting the use of U.S. forces in Cambodia. The National Guard killed four and wounded eleven, all white. However, the National Guard and police were equal-opportunity terrorists.

It seemed a time of realization for the black renaissance. Instead of just advocates, more were becoming activists. This was something whites viewed as widespread arrogance, and their reaction to what they saw as black militancy was swift and vicious. Eight days after Kent State, police in Augusta, Georgia shot and killed six black protesters. And on May 15th, the police in Mississippi fired shots into a group of demonstrating black students on the campus of Jackson State University, killing two and wounding nine.

These occurrences did not escape the attention of the brothers and their revolutionary counterparts. In arranging a series of meetings with the Muslim brothers from Philly, the New York and New Jersey branches of the New Republic of Africa and the Black Liberation Army (BLA) were reaching out for support.

Ethan told Josh, Chris, Wade, and Lester that he had been contacted by Brother Sherman Bellamy, the defense minister of the BLA. "He needed to know if we could offer any safe houses here in Philly."

"Why here?" Josh asked, "and why us?"

"Cause they planned to retaliate against some cops in New York and would need to leave the city for a while. I told him we could provide a few spots."

"Wha'cha thinkin'?" Josh asked.

"I'm thinkin' we can ask Brother Arnold, he jus' got tha' spot down on Fawn Street. Nobody ever uses tha', and…"

"Naw, I mean why are they asking us and not the brothers in their own organization? Aren't they s'posed to be hooked up wit' the Panthers on Columbia Avenue?"

"They're having some problems. Some brothers are splittin' off from the Panthers. Sherman said they've been infiltrated."

"Ain't Arnold the shop steward on those renovating jobs 332 got the contracts for?" Lester asked.

"Yeah. In fact, he says he needs some brothers to come down." I told 'im 'bout Wade and Chris."

"Wha's this about the cops?" Josh asked.

"He said, be they cops or anybody else, if they're shootin' down defenseless blacks, they should be killed. He also said that we should be aware of the "incognegroes" the FBI is placing in certain organizations."

"Wha' the fuck is an "incognegro"?" Lester asked.

"A Negro infiltrator and informant. He said that the FBI set up som'um called a Counter Intelligence Program to infiltrate and bring down wha' they're calling black hate groups. In other words, brothers who love their own and wanna do fo' self are called hate groups."

"Well, that's cool. We hate white folks," Josh laughed.

"The FBI got these black so-called brothers and sisters goin' around joining the Panthers, SNCC, and any other group, so they can report back to the FBI."

Three weeks after this conversation, two cops were killed in Brooklyn, New York. A report came in that a female caller had stated to an operator that a woman, looking white or Hispanic, was being attacked by three black men in an alleyway in the 300 block of North Douglas Street. When the first police car arrived at that location, both cops were caught in a hell of gunfire and killed. The perpetrators took the cops' guns and were long gone by the time more police arrived.

***

On the same afternoon, in Philadelphia, FBI Special Agents Doss and Smith were meeting in a Holiday Inn motel room with Philadelphia Detectives Napoli and O'Connor. Although the U.S. Federal Building was just up the street, on 9th and Market, Doss and Smith had chosen to meet in the motel so they could speak openly about changes in their strategy.

"It's okay, Napoli," Doss said, while scribbling on a yellow legal pad, "We got time!"

"Yeah, but did you read the file I gave you on Lucius Please? I'm telling you, somehow, someway, that motherfuckah was involved in Dabney Richardson's murder. If we hesitate…"

"We already know what happened to this Richardson guy," Agent Smith cautioned. "If we become fixated on this Lucius Please, and move too soon, we'll blow the entire operation."

"Wha'cha mean, you already know?" Napoli snapped. "You said we would share information. How is it that you already know and we don't?"

The last place Joe Napoli wanted to be was cooped up in a meeting with these federal assholes. His stomach was hurting and his head was still spinning from the combination of liquor and coffee he'd been drinking for days. The coffee so he could sit up all night outside of Babysis' grandmother's house and the liquor in the mornings just so he could face the daylight.

For weeks now, he'd been trying to track down Babysis so he could get her in bed and also scare her into giving him information about Lucius Please. A snitch told him that Babysis sometimes visited her grandmother's house on 16th and Diamond. But he'd been sitting on that house off and on for seven days, and still no Babysis.

"Tell me this, Joe," Doss said sarcastically. "What if we had shared our information with you, how would it have made a difference in where we're at right now?"

Napoli shot him a frustrated look that said, I might have actually made some progress that would've kept me out of this damn meeting with you assholes. "That all depends on what you got," he said.

"Okay, listen," Doss offered. "I'm merely trying to determine how much of an effort we still have to coordinate. It's obvious that we have different sources and methods of dealing with what we get. But one thing is for sure, we want the same results."

"That still doesn't answer my question," Napoli frowned.

"You didn't read the memo I sent to your office?" Doss asked with a raised eyebrow. "I didn't name names, but tried to present you with an accurate picture of what was being done. We have people already in place. Now we must execute."

Trying to calm the tension in the room, O'Connor directed his rare question to Agent Smith. "These informants you speak of, how are they situated? Who are their targets?"

"They're more than informants," Smith assured. "They're paid provocateurs, so to speak. We've discovered that those men we thought were acting alone are already organized into a powerful group. We will first label them, so that people who might otherwise support them, will reject them. We don't want them being seen as Robin Hoods of the ghetto."

"These paid provocateurs, will they do what's necessary to place these men in our crosshairs?" Napoli asked.

"Dead center," Doss gloated. "This is the picture. The targets are already prone to crime and violence. Our people will be there to make sure that propensity continues. And by us orchestrating the activities from behind the scene, we'll be able to take some out, and put others away for good. We'll make sure they won't get away."

With a look of concern, O'Connor presented another one of his rare questions. "Are you sure your provocateurs will go through with this? And if they're caught, will our names come up? After all, they're informants, for Christ-sake."

"Yes, they will. They have already proven themselves in other situations. And no, our names will never come up."

"The good thing about this," Smith interjected, "is that the targets' own false sense of loyalty will aid us in their downfall."

"How's that?" Napoli asked.

"Our targets come from the streets and have a reputation for being thorough."

"But we knew that from the outset," Napoli said, "that's nothing new."

"Yeah, but once they embraced Islam they developed a new sense of brotherhood. One they're willing to die for, and with that death, take with them any and all secrets. They might discover that some of their own have set them up for us, but they'll never inform on them. They'll kill them, if given the opportunity, but they'll never sink to the level of the snitch. We're their enemy and they'll never give us that kind of satisfaction."

"So their thoroughness becomes a weakness for them and a strength for us?"

"Correct," Doss smiled. "Weakness is a strength contrary to itself. It's called the sequence of protocol and ties the hands of all true soldiers."

"By the way, Napoli," Smith offered as they were getting ready to leave the room.

"According to our people inside, it was this Lucius Please guy who gave the nod for the hit on Dabney Richardson."

"I'm gonna find Babysis if it kills me," Napoli mumbled to himself, as he left. "She's still in Philly. I know it!

# CHAPTER XXX

While waiting for Ethan and Wade to arrive, Brother Arnold 2X
Boyden playfully wrestled on his living room floor with his two sons, Ahmed
and Sabir. Ethan had called earlier and told Arnold that he and Wade would be
there in 15 minutes, but Brother Arnold figured it would probably take Ethan an
hour or so.

"He's never on time," he told his wife when she asked if he wanted her
to take the children upstairs when Ethan arrived. "When they do get here, we'll
go down in the cellar and talk." Then while pretending to struggle with his sons,
he added. "You kno' how Ethan is. He'll stop ten times befor' gettin' here."

Sister Anne did know how Ethan was. She'd grown up with both him
and her husband on 8th and Diamond Streets and had been the one to introduce
Ethan to his wife, Sister Geraldine when they were all teenagers.

Brother Arnold was one of the shop stewards for Union 332 and
figured Ethan was coming over to ask about getting Wade hired at the Center
City office building renovation site. He remembered Wade as being one of the
brothers with him when they were secret security on Cecil B. Moore, the head of
the local NAACP in Philadelphia. Moore had organized the march around
Girard College to protest its racist policies, and Minister Uriah had certain
brothers from the mosque act as security for Moore without him even knowing
it. Arnold also sat at the table with Wade at the F.O.I. celebration dinner last
year and had briefly talked about a job then.

As Ethan and Wade climbed the steps leading to the porch, they could
hear the laughter of the two little boys coming from inside the house. When
Arnold's wife opened the door, there was Arnold on the living room floor,
buried under both of his boys.

Seeing the short muscular brother clad in an undershirt and sweatpants,
tussling with his sons, reminded Wade of what Ethan had once told him about
Arnold.

"He's a fitness nut," Ethan said. "He kno's karate, and his basement
looks like a gym with all kinda apparatuses for strength training and muscle
development. He's serious 'bout that shit, too. He even stole som' of dem small
pickle barrels from a Jewish delicatessen and filled them wit' little rocks so he
could punch into 'em and toughen his knuckles."

"Salaam-Alaikum, Sister Anne," Ethan greeted, smiling at the boys still
trying to tussle with their father.

"Wa-Alaikum-Salaam, Brothers," the sister replied, as she picked her
sons up off their father and joked, "You can see what the brother does all day."

"Salaam-Alaikum," Arnold said, straightening his clothes and moving
toward the kitchen. "Let's go downstairs and outta this evil woman's way."

Following behind them, Wade could sense the closeness between the
two men. Both short and thick, with a stern but quiet ruggedness about them,
they were similar in many ways.

In the basement, Wade noticed the two 18-inch barrels filled with small fine stones. Glancing down at Arnold's hands, he was surprised that he hadn't noticed the hardened calluses on the brother's knuckles before. There were homemade weighted bars for weightlifting in one corner of the cellar. A heavy canvas bag with a full-length drawing of a cop pinned to it, hung from the ceiling. On the picture were kick marks from the midsection to the head.

Ethan walked across the room to where a floor model sound system stood. He pushed the button, and Cannonball Adderley's "Mercy, Mercy, Mercy" filled the room and became a delightful backdrop for their conversation.

"Did the brothers from New York arrive?" Ethan asked.

"Yeah," Arnold replied. "They came and went. I put them up in the spot over on Fawn Street. After a few days, they moved on. I didn't ask where to."

"I hear the man's turning over every rock in New York."

"Well, they're wasting their time," Arnold said. "Them brothers are long gon' from the city."

"Some people wants you to back up Wade when Slim comes in from Chester. Will you be available the first Saturday in June?"

"No doubt."

"He'll meet y'all at noon at the Brass Rail Restaurant."

"The one out by the airport?"

"Yeah. He should be in town for about two hours. After making his rounds he'll give Wade $14,000. Two apiece for y'all, one apiece for Lucius, Chris, Lester, and me."

Arnold didn't need to ask where the other six grand would go, he knew it was for the mosque.

"And from then on out," Ethan added, "we'll do the same thing every first Saturday of the month. Same players, only our roles will change so we'll all have a chance at equal pay."

"Does that go for the chief, too?" Arnold joked.

"Yeah, we wish," Ethan responded. "Wha'ever happened to tha' thing you were workin' on? Did you figure out what you would need?"

"Yep," Arnold said, moving over to the work bench in the back of the cellar. Lifting the tarp, he revealed a number of 1-inch steel washers, felt washers, and circled screens, all with a small hole drilled dead center. Locked into a vise attached to the table, was a 5-inch long copper pipe, with a 1-inch hole for the washers to fit into. Beneath the vise lay two end-caps, both with holes equal to those in the washers, and one with a 1-inch long treaded copper pipe attached to it.

"What the hell is all that?" Wade whispered to Ethan who was examining the end-cap with the attached copper pipe.

"It's the parts to a silencer," Ethan mumbled. "Damn, I thought you were jus' ... How many of these can you make? Will they work?"

"Already made four and tested one. They're fitted for an automatic. Not good for revolvers."

"Damn," Ethan mumbled again, picking up one of the felt washers. "Can you show me how to put these things together?"

"No problem. But let's do it later."

Sonny Rollins' album "Alfie" was now blowing through the sound system, and Sister Anne was coming down the steps with a tray of carrot cake and Shabazz juice.

"What about that job?" Arnold asked Wade. "Are you still interested?"

"Without a doubt."

"Well, give me a few days," Arnold said while stuffing his face with carrot cake, "and I'll get you on the detail with us."

"Dis som' good cake, Sister Anne," Ethan said. "I hear you and Gussie gon' host the Philly Muslim Sisters Annual Fashion Show and Luncheon this summer."

"Yeah, we asked Geraldine to help plan it, but she said she wanted to have some time with y'all's new twin babies."

"Who do y'all have appearing this year?" Wade asked.

"Uh, Dar-es-Salaam, The Delfonics. We wanted to get the Five Stair-Steps from Chicago, but Sister Supreme Captain won't let the sister in the group appear with her brothers."

"I thought that was jus' for stage shows. Since they're Muslims, seems she'd let her appear at a Muslim gala."

"You know how Sister Supreme Captain is. Plus, they are her family; her sister's children, I think."

***

"Are you listenin' to me, man?" Herc asked Lucius, as he turned his brand new mint-green Mark onto South Street from Broad. "We can't bang no cop!"

"Why not? He jus' a white devil with a badge who thinks he has the right to kill brothers and rape sisters. He's jus' a pale-faced white man, not a god."

"I'm talkin' 'bout how hot the city will get if we smoke this jokah, tha's all."

Motioning for Herc to pull over to the curb so he could get out, Lucius spoke to him in a quiet tone. "I'm about to get married man. I ain't gon' let this devil keep comin' 'round my wife 'cause of who she used to be. Tha' fat faggot's tryin' to use her to git to me."

Herc parked the car and turned to face Lucius. "I kno' all that, Lu," he said. "But he's not just'a cop, he's homicide."

"No, he's not a homicide yet, but he will be."

"He's a detective," Herc repeated. "If we fuck this up."

"So we don't fuck it up!" Lucius yelled. "You said you followed him a few times, right? Wha' does he do when he's not tryin' to scope my woman?"

"I been watchin' this cracker fo' two months, and the only time I ever seen him by his-self is when he was parked up the street from Sis' grandma's house. He'll sit there all night jus' drinkin' and watchin'."

"I can't him 'im there," Lucius mumbled.

"All dis cracker do is po-leece work. I think he's got a fat-ass wife, who he fucks around on, but only wit' black chicks. He goes to the Chesterfield Hotel som'times to meet wit' som' black trick. He checks in then waits for her. They stay for an hour or so, then leave separately. Other than that there's always som'body wit 'im. Either his partna, who he rides wit', his fat wife or the trick he's fuckin'."

"Tell you wha'," Lucius said. "Startin' today, we both gon' be watchin' this jokah. I kno' we can't be on him all the time, but we kno' at least twice a week he'll be parked outside Babysis' grandmom's house. So tha'll be our startin' point. Som' kinda way, we'll set 'im up."

"It would be helpful if we could git one of his tricks to help set 'im up," Herc said.

"The less people know 'bout dis, the better. Plus, no self-respecting black man should ever use a sister in som'um like dis."

"Yeah, 'cause if we did, we'd have to snuff her too."

# CHAPTER XXXI

As Lynton exited his Cadillac and crossed South Street, heading for Diamond's Men Store, he could see Mo and Big Cil through the display window. They were standing by one of the clothing racks looking at suits. Lynton readjusted his .32 revolver in the belt of his pants and zipped his waist-length blue gabardine jacket up. He had good reason to be paranoid.

When Mo had asked him to meet them at the clothing store to discuss Benny Pinter's upcoming party, Lynton had wondered why Cil would be there. He knew that Cil and Rus didn't like him and thought at first that they might have had some idea about his working with the Feds. However, he dismissed that thought because if they had, he'd be dead already. So, it has to be jealousy, he thought. I'm moving a lot of dope by using Benny to mix and match, and they have yet to figure out why the Minister protects me. They probably feel sum' kinda way 'bout tha'.

Still, the weight of the .32 on his side made him feel a bit secure as he entered the store with a faint, "As-Salaam Alaikum, my brothers!"

"Wa-Salaam-Salaam," Mo replied, while Cil, examining the silk suits, remained silent.

Taking Lynton by his arm and walking him around to the far end of the store, Mo whispered to him, "We heard 'bout dem white boys from upstate givin' Benny a party. Wha' dey trying to do increase distribution?"

"Yeah," Lynton answered, his eyes on Big Cil. "They got word out on the street tha' Benny's gon' be handlin' huge deposits from now on, and they want Goldfinger Brown, Big Melvin Taylor and Nard to funnel some of the stuff through Baltimore, New York and D.C."

"They all gon be there?" Cil asked without looking up from the suits.

"Su'posed to be."

"Can you git Josh and'nem in?"

"Yeah, I can get them in, but…"

"Nobody's getting' hurt," Cil assured, still fiddling with the suits. "We jus' wanna send a message."

"This time!" Mo added. "But if we don't git a cut, next time'll be different."

"I don't understand, man," Lynton finally asked. "Why y'all doing this? You jus' got the New York connect."

"You been playin' both ends against the middle too long now. This ain't how it was set-up. Remember? We don't tell the brothers that you're slingin' dope through Benny, and you make sure we benefit from any future connects. Well, when you hooked up with dem white boys on the sly, we jus' waited. Now they're trying to step on toes by spreadin' their shit to DC and Baltimore and hav' niggahs think it's all comin' from the New York connect. Well, it's time you bring us in."

"But why Josh and'nem? Can't I jus' handle it?"

"Nope. 'Cause you ain't got the heart. Ev'rybody kno's tha'. They'll jus' cheat you outta our piece. Josh and'nem don't have'ta kno' ev'rything. Just' tha' we're settin' Benny up for them to scare so that he'll contribute to the mosque."

Lynton figured that there was something Mo and Cil wasn't sayin, but he was in no position to resist. The brothers' policy was that no Muslim get directly involved with the drug trade. Though they protected some dealers for a fee and agreed to look the other way as long as the brothers from downtown came into the mosque. It was all done with the expectation of stopping the trade in the black community all together. But as for those Muslims who were already in the temple, dealing drugs was out. And being a lieutenant, Lynton knew better.

After leaving Mo and Cil, Lynton went directly to the bar on 15th and Venango. Butta's office was in the back of that barroom, and he was usually there around this time of day.

Leon "Butta" Johnson was one of the richest hustlers in Philly. Only in his midtwenties, he had been in the drug game since he was in high school. He was called Butta because he loved eating and his big belly attested to it. He had been just sixteen when he hooked up with some older dealers who turned him on to New York Frank. Because Frank liked him, and because he didn't have the kind of overhead and legal problems the older dealers had, he quickly outgrew them. Being able to buy in a much larger quantity was an advantage that allowed him to become a Philly supplier to some.

There were only a few male patrons in the bar when Lynton walked in. Dennis Jackson, Butta's top personal bodyguard, sat by the office door patting his foot to Junior Walker's, "Shotgun" and playing cards with two of Butta's other guards. Lynton had never seen Butta when these three men weren't with him. He'd often joked that they probably sat in his bedroom and watched his ass go up and down while he humped his woman.

"Wha's up Lynton?" Dennis asked as Lynton approached.

"Gotta see Butta," he said.

Dennis got up and entered the office. A moment later he opened the door and invited Lynton in. Dennis stayed in the room with Butta, while the others remained outside the door.

"Wha's happenin'?" Butta asked, looking up at Lynton and putting a fork-full of eggs and bacon in his mouth. He had no habits he would consider bad. Though he hated Muslims, he did like the way the true believers lived. So with the exception of eating port, he didn't drink, smoke or use drugs. He often patted his big belly while saying that women was his heroin.

"I need a favor," Lynton told him.

"Wha' kinda favor?"

"I need you to talk to Benny Pinter for me."

"About wha'?" Butta asked, chewing on another fork-full.

Lynton told Butta about his meeting with Mo and Big Cil, and how they wanted the brothers to make an example of Benny in front of the other dealers.

"Why should I get involved?" Butta asked. "Ain't nothing' in this for me. I don't need dem white boy's dope, and I don't fuck wit' dem outta-town niggahs. So why should I care if those South Philly niggahs take yo'r shit? You don't buy from me, you buy from dem Wilkes-Barre white boys."

"You kno' why I buy from them," Lynton said pulling one of the chairs over to the desk and sitting down. "Yo'r stuff is good, but the prices …"

"Yeah. My shit's best in dis town. You jus' wanna get tha' garbage from demI-talians at a low price. Then you give tha' weak shit to Benny 'cause he too scared and too stupid to go for self. You got him thinkin' that he got backup and he ain't got jac-shit."

"Yeah, you're right. I get it at a low price and sell it for the same thing you sell yo'rs for. But tha' ain't the main reason I stay wit dem. You won't let me push yo'r stuff through Benny."

"Tha's right, 'cause I don't wanna kil'im. His shit's garbage, and I ain't 'bout to let'im mix and match my shit."

"Do me the favor, Butta."

"Wha' is it you wanna say wit' my mouth?"

"Jus' let him know' wha' the brothers are gonna do, and tell him not to worry, they ain't gonna hurt him. As long as he kno's he ain't gon' be killed, he won't tell 'em nothing' tha' dey don't already kno'. But if he's scared tha' they gon' kill'im, he'll give ev'rything up."

"By ev'rything, you mean yo'r name and operation?"

"Right."

"Why can't you tell'im dat?"

"'Cause I've been told not to. They want him off-guard. They wanna make it seem real. But if you warn'im, well…"

Butta didn't particularly like Lynton, and it wasn't just because he was a Muslim. He didn't like him because he could not respect him. Butta felt that if he would cross his own Muslim brothers, he could cross him too.

"He can't say he got it from you?" Butta asked, wiping his lips. "What' do I git? You gon let me fuck yo'r sista?"

"I'll give you Monster Dave."

"Why would I wanna get involved wit' tha' speed shit. I make more wit' the heroin then I would wit' tha' powder."

"Monster Dave's a chemist, man. He's now making bathtub crank. Shit, it's jus' as potent as chrystal meth, and you can make three times the profit at less the cost."

"Who he getting' the chemicals from? … The I-talians?"

"Yep," Lynton grinned, "Tha's the reason I buy my dope from them. I can get the oil from them, too. Cheap."

Butta was no dummy. He knew that there was more to this plan than just the brothers trying to send a message to some weak drug dealers. The brothers hated him as much as he hated them and he figured this had more to do with them trying to move in on his operation. He made no contributions to the mosque when they asked him to, and they had taken that as an insult.

"Aw'ight, I'll talk to Benny for you. But you gotta do som'um for me, too."

"Wha's tha'?"

"One of yo'r brothers is workin' wit' the feds. I wanna kno' his name."

"How do you kno' …"

"I gotta girl workin' down at the Fed Building. She told me she overheard a conversation 'bout som' Muslim givin' up info on one of my houses. She thought she was warning me in advance, but wha' she didn't kno' was that dey had already raided it and took $75,000 and two keys. I'm sure dey didn't turn it in or she would've known they had already hit me."

"Aw'ight, I'll look into it," Lynton said, beginning to sweat, as he wondered if Butta really had someone working at the Federal Building. And if he had, Lynton knew he needed to find out, because he'd been the one who sent the Feds.

I gotta tell'em 'bout this woman, he thought, as he left the bar. Butta was right about one thing, they hadn't turned in the money or the dope. After giving Lynton $5,000, and a portion of the dope to put on the street, they had kept the rest for themselves.

The call he'd been waiting for came at 9:45 p.m.. It was from Pauline Sanders, the young barmaid who worked for Butta at the Venango Lounge. "He was here," she told Mo, "jus' like you said. He stayed 'bout an hour, then left."

"Was you in the bar when he got d'ere?" Mo asked.

"No, I was in the upstairs window. I saw' im from there."

Mo could hardly contain his excitement. He'd been right about Lynton running to Butta. Now, if things worked out like he had planned, Benny would believe Butta and think tha' the brothers were going to move on him and force him to give up his package. Knowing Benny, he'd be just scared enough to try and secure the dope he was holding by putting all the weight in one spot and have the Italians sit on it because he don't trust blacks.

Mo hung up the phone, clinched and pumped his fist in the air, and turned to Cil. "We got'im," he grinned. "Lynton went straight to tha' fat-ass mothafucka jus' like we thought he would. He don't want the brothers to kno' tha' he has any association with Benny, so he asked Butta to warn him."

"You kno' wha'?" Cil chimed in. I'd like to see the look on tha' punk mothafucka's face when he finds out tha' Butta's information is wrong and the brothers ain't even gon' show up d'ere."

"Yeah, but by then it'll be too late," Mo said. "'cause we gon' take it all. And Lynton better not say nothin' if he want us to giv'im his shit back."

"He can't say nothin' no way, 'cause he don't want Josh an'nem knowin' 'bout his connection with' Benny."

# CHAPTER XXXII

At 8:45 a.m., on the first Saturday in June, Arnold and Wade were on their way to the Brass Rail Restaurant, outside of Philadelphia International Airport. It was a rainy morning, and traffic was light on Island Road and they were making good time.

"He'll probably come in on the Industrial Highway," Wade told Arnold. "He told Ethan he'd be at the restaurant by nine."

"They said Chester Slim is known for being punctual."

"Did Ethan call you last night?" Wade asked.

"Yeah. He said tha' Minister Uriah and Brother Captain will be at the Society Hill Towers at four this afternoon. The Minister wants you, me, Josh, and Ethan to be there as well. I think he wants us to sit in on a meeting wit some of those civil leaders and business people."

"Which one? There's three of those buildings."

"Yeah, I kno'. I think it's the middle one. You ever been inside any of 'em?"

"Not inside. But one of the clothing sores I used to work at is right 'round the corner from 'em."

"I've been inside all of 'em." Arnold assured. "They're outta sight. Our union had the contract to remove the old heating system when they were converted to central air. The offices are plush: thick carpeting, long chestnut tables, high back cushioned chairs, that's high finance. The city's Chamber of Commerce has offices there, bankers, corporate lawyers and accountants."

"Why would the Minister want us there?" Wade asked.

"Because tha's his way of teaching us how to deal with people from all walks of life. He says if we're gonna be able to go for self, we must learn to speak for ourselves."

"Ethan also mentioned som'um 'bout Brother Mitchell and a dude named Fat Richard raping som' woman.

"Yeah, tha' was a couple of days ago." Arnold answered. "That idiot let Fat Richard talk'im and Brother Payton into helpin' im rob a speakeasy. There were women there pulling tricks. While Mitch and Fat Richard were robbing the place, they went upstairs and saw the women wit' their tricks. Both of'em forced one of the women to have sex with them, too."

"Did they get busted?"

"The very next day. But they weren't charged with rape 'cause the woman didn't want her people knowin' she was a trickster. The reason we know 'bout the rape is 'cause Payton was waitin' for'em in the car, and when they came out, the fools told'im wha' happened."

"Payton went straight to the Captain, huh?" Wade asked.

"Nope. He went to Brother First Lieutenant." Arnold said, as he looked out at what was now barely a drizzle. "He wasn't gonna take tha' shit to Terence. He would've gotten Mitchell kicked outta the temple."

"Yeah, I guess it was a better move goin' to Harvey. You think Mitch will be called on the carpet?"

"Damn right!" Arnold replied. "Both of 'em will. But not for the rape. Mitchell can thank Harvey for savin' his ass."

Chester Slim was standing under the awning outside the Brass Rail when Arnold's car pulled up. Wade couldn't help but notice how the man was dressed. Rumored to be rich, Slim stood there looking like an old-fashioned insurance man. He had on a faded blue suit that had been ironed so many times it looked iridescent. His tan penny loafers actually had pennies in them, and his black hat was a flat-top stingy-brim. "Damn," Wade mumbled, "he don't look like he's making millions."

"Tha's the point," Arnold said in response to Wade's comment. "If you don't look like you're doing wrong, you have a better chance of getting away wit' the wrong you do. He and his partna's been funneling drugs and laundering money for over 15 years, and they ain't never been busted. Only those jokahs who try livin' like millionaires on a few grand wind up in the joint, or dead."

After a brief mutual introduction, all three men decided to pass on breakfast and get started on their journey. Wade got in the front seat of Chester Slim's 63 Chevy Nova, and Arnold climbed back inside his 67 Buick Skylark.

"You been in the Nation of Islam for long?" Slim asked, as he made the turn back on Industrial Highway.

"About three years," Wade answered, wondering how much Chester Slim knew about the set up and what he thought of the Muslims. Did he think we'd hooked up with Frank Matthews in order to sell drugs? He wondered.

"Do you hate all white folk?" Slim asked. His eyes never left the road but seemed to Wade to be searching his face for effect.

"Can't say," Wade answered. "I've never met all white folks. But I feel tha' whites in this country has never meant black folks any good. That's why our Dear Holy Apostle says they're devils.

"You think he really believes that? Or is he jus' tryin' to change the way the white man thinks?"

"Minister Uriah once said that it was the Messenger's job to change blacks in America, not to try and change white folks. He said that the Honorable Elijah Muhammad teaches us that you cannot reform the white man. They are 100 percent disagreeable to live wit' in peace. They throw the stone then hide the hand. But if you look carefully around the world where conflict exists, you'll see that white hand stirring the pot of discontent."

"You kno', I make a lotta money workin' wit white folks in my business. Even got a Jew actin' as front man for one of my apartment buildings on City Line Avenue, here in Philly."

Wade smiled gingerly and replied, "You kno' if whites knew you owned that buildin' they'd burn it down. Let's jus' agree tha' making money wit white folks is one thing. But trying to make peace wit' them is a waste of time."

"I'll do this twice a month," Slim said, changing the subject and thinking that he liked this young man. "Each time I come I'm gonna ask for you. Is that aw'ight wit'cha?"

"Yeah," Wade answered, his thoughts again gong to what this man must think about Muslims. In a way we are involved in the drug trade, he thought.

"The reason I'ma ask for you is because I don't like too many people knowin' about me. If they send different people at different times, then soon ev'rybody will know."

"I can understand that," Wade replied. "But we don't …"

"Once in Delaware one of our houses was hit for $40,000 because too many people were involved. It's best to keep it real simple. I'll pick up money from six spots, pay you for your time, and be out of Philly in less than two hours."

"You ever find out who hit the spot in Delaware?"

"Yeah, but we didn't sweat it. Out of a sense of pride, a few people wanted to go kill'em. But I told them tha' you don't make millions by chasing pennies and chancing a murder rap over it. But still, som'body walked up on'em at a dice game and put two of'em in the ground, anyway."

The first of the six stops was at a small candy store in a quiet section of Southwest Philly. Slim was in and out in less than five minutes. The last of the stops was at the Venango Gardens in the Tioga section of the city. As he had done at all previous stops, Slim went into the building and exited without any trouble. In less than two hours, Chester Slim had deposited close to $350,000 into the trunk of his $2,000 car.

Back at the airport, they met up with Kirk D., Brother Lieutenant Harvey's cousin. He was not living in Chester and working as Slim's enforcer. Kirk removed the money from the trunk of the Nova and placed it in a Chester City taxi. Slim parked the Nova, then got into the back seat of the cab and Kirk drove the cab back to Chester. As Wade and Arnold pulled on to the highway, Wade recalled Slim's comment about, "som'body putting two of 'em in the ground." I bet that som'body was Kirk D., he thought.

Wade had the $14,000, plus an extra $5,000 he and Arnold decided to share between the other brothers involved.

*** 

When Josh and Ethan arrived at the Society Hill Towers with Minister Uriah and Captain Terence, Arnold and Wade were already there. As instructed by the captain, they had waited outside the building so that they all could enter together.

Waiting in the conference room on the 18th floor were two white men and one black. Al Hornstein, from Carlton Plastics, and J. Phillip Simon, from Rosenthal-Netter Ceramics, were there representing their companies. The lone black man at the table was Stacy Blankenship of the Urban Youth Development Program, recently established by him and Captain Terence.

Stacy Blankenship, known in Philly as an activist in the civil rights movement and sometimes city politician. He often acted as the go between for the mob and minority businessmen association. Two years earlier, it had been Blankenship who the mob had sent to Mo and Big Cil with an offer of a beer distributorship. The mob had heard that the brothers from downtown were about to join forces with the Muslim brothers from uptown and they wanted to thwart that move. What the mob didn't know was that the downtown brothers had an association with Muhammad's Temple all along. They turned down the offer of the distributorship because they would have never worked for the Italians, even had they not been Muslims.

With a friendly greeting, Minister Uriah and the captain joined those at the table. Chairs were provided for Wade, Arnold, Ethan and Josh along the far wall. They were there as non-participating observers.

It was obvious that the businessmen had already decided the agenda. Directing his comments to the Minister, Simon said that he, Hornstein, and Blackenship had met with the chairmen of John Wanamakers and The Philadelphia Saving Fund Society, the day before. "All are in agreement as long as you have people to effectively and efficiently operate the factories on the funds that are available."

The Minister assured them that the people he had in mind had both the credentials and experience. "To all prying eyes, their business plan will demonstrate the need for the funds and articulate the method and ability to repay all lenders."

Leaning back in his chair, Hornstein said almost in a whisper, "When Mr. Blackenship first came to us about the Government sponsored minority program, we agreed that any additional funds should come by way of contributions, thus requiring no repayment. However, if we are to accept government funding of this project, we have to first put up funds of our own. Funds that must be repaid."

"Excuse me, Mr. Hornstein," Blackenship said. "Are you friends of the Brotherhood?"

"I'm unsure of your meaning, Stacy." Hornstein replied.

Seizing the opportunity to speak, Blankenship smiled and spoke as if polishing each word. "We're at war on poverty in this city. And at this particular time, the U.S. Government has agreed to subsidize businesses that can prove they are owned and operated by competent minorities. We have presented to you a full list of businesses willing to place minorities in the position of ownership so that they may receive those subsidized funds. These people, some black, some white, mind you, who will be well rewarded for their contributions, are a part of the brotherhood fighting this war on poverty. We need part of the brotherhood fighting this war on poverty. We need friends, Mr. Hornstein. People in this city are hurting and we can provide them employment."

"And if you recall," Captain Terence reminded. "It was also agreed that it would be those minority structured companies that would be the contributing factor in urban community programs. That means that the government would be subsidizing them, as well."

The names of the financiers mentioned at the table were easily recognized by the brothers observing the meeting. They were the men who'd collaborated with NAACP leader Cecil B. Moore and Reverend Leon H. Sullivan, entrepreneur and founder of the Opportunities Industrial Centers and the Progress Plaza Shopping Mall, to raise well over $1 million dollars the day after Martin Luther King's assassination. It had been that money that established an agency which evolved into the Urban Coalition.

However, just as the meeting was ending, Mr. Hornstein, still not trusting of Stacy Blackenship, openly asked if Craig Newman, the lone black executive on his staff, could be substituted in Blankenship's position.

"It's nothing personal," he said. "Just that other backers might feel a bit more secure about our decisions. You know, running the process through an incubator system, and all."

"With all due respect," Minister Uriah replied, "Using Newman in that position would be like entering a mule in the Kentucky Derby and expecting him to win."

# CHAPTER XXXIII

Timing had been perfect for Minister Uriah's proposal to have minority businessmen represent themselves as the owners of white businesses. The backing he received proved to be an effective collaboration, which increased his bargaining power with other white companies seeking financial assistance from the government. Given the recent influx of college graduates now joining Muhammad's Mosque in Philly, the Minister had a wealth of intelligent business-minded brothers and sisters to assist in his negotiations.

Previously, Temple Number 12 had been referred to by other temples around the country as being at the top of the clock because of the large contributions coming from Philly. However, what most other temples didn't know was that some of those large contributions came from the illegal acts committed by certain Philly brothers. With the increase in membership of law-abiding, obedient-minded brothers and sisters, educated and working in various positions, Temple 12 now legitimately held that position.

On the streets of Philadelphia, people were noticing and becoming involved in the community development programs, safe street programs, and job training programs. Black folks were loving themselves and their identity and associating these changes, in part, with what they'd heard from the Muslims.

Brothers and sisters from the Nation of Islam were on the move in Philly. "Money for Muhammad" had become their slogan. 125,000 newspapers a week, a school, now called the University of Islam, eight Muhammad's Temples throughout the city to handle the growing influx of new members. And with it all came an increase in donations.

Community meetings were held at the temples to exchange ideas on how to get pledges from minority-organized businesses in support of the communities. School programs were working, gang membership was down, and Muslim membership was up. Even those who didn't particularly like the activities of some of the Muslim brothers noticed that the more negative things said about them, the larger their membership grew. And though some people considered them criminals, they had to admit that the brothers took care of the black communities. Many people admired them and would say things like, "As long as you don't mess wit them Moozlems, they'll respect you and protect you, too!"

The community recognized that those same brothers who used to terrorize the neighborhoods were now dressed in suits and going door to door selling fish and Muhammad Speaks. Brothers would go to the ice cream vendors and rent their trucks so they could keep the fish cold. They sold eggs that had come up from the Nation of Islam's farms in Georgia and Alabama. Kosher sausages from the Jewish meat distributors and their famous Shabazz juices from their own natural juice business.

The mosque brought a bakery on 60th Street. Sold dinners, first only at headquarters on Susquehanna Avenue, then at all the mosques which acquired kitchens. Sisters fed the brothers who came in late from selling Muhammad Speaks newspaper. Some enterprising brothers copying an idea from Muslim brothers in New York, even established a chain of restaurants in Philly called "Steak 'n' Takes." They also opened a furniture store and a few clothing stores.

Philadelphia had become a flourishing Muslim town and the spirit of black folks was in the air. People from different walks of life began participating in the Nation of Islam's school, programs, and businesses. Even children not born to Muslim parents were being given Muslim names.

***

It was 2 a.m., Friday morning. Wade was sitting outside Benny's Bar and Grill, on Seventh and Allegheny. Having been assigned to watch Benny's movements during the evening hours, he could barely keep his eyes open. Ethan would relieve him at 6 a.m. and he could hardly wait.

As he watched the patrons leaving the bar at closing time, Wade exhaled a sigh and yawned. His thoughts were elsewhere. How can I get everything done? he thought. We're scheduled to hit Benny's spot Saturday night. I haven't had any sleep and Frankie wants to go look at the floors in the new house after Fruit Class Saturday afternoon.

Not only did Wade have to be at Fruit Class because he was now a Lieutenant, he also had to go down to headquarters and wait for the Sister's MGT Class to end so he could sell them pastries and bread for the week.

A tired smile crossed his face as he thought of Frankie's initial response to seeing him waiting outside the sister's MGT Class with a table full of pastries. She didn't like it. A few of the more bolder sisters had made comments like, "Oh, sweets from the sweet." And, "Who tha' fine brotha?"

Though Frankie sometimes considered it a compliment, she also felt some of those sisters knew he was her husband and were just trying to make it known that they were interested.

Wade rubbed his eyes, stretched them opened, and yawned again. He saw the lights go out inside the bar. Only those in the windows remained on. The door opened and Benny and some female walked out. He watched as they both got into Benny's Cadillac and drove off. As he had done all week, he followed.

A half hour later, after dropping off the female, Benny pulled into a driveway behind a house right off 16$^{th}$ and Louden, in a quiet section of Logan. It was the first time Wade had trailed him to this house. The lights were already on inside and Wade wondered how Ethan would know to relieve him there.

He didn't have to wonder long. From behind him he saw car lights blinking. Suspecting it was the cops, he rehearsed his excuse for being parked there. "I got sleepy, officer, and just pulled over to keep from getting into an accident." But, it wasn't necessary. When he turned to look, he saw that it was Ethan.

"You knew 'bout this spot?" Wade asked, as Ethan pulled alongside him.

"Yeah," Ethan nodded, as he whispered. "You can roll, we got all spots covered. We think he's holding everythin' 'ere. If we don't meet tonight at the mosque, I'll see you Saturday morning at Fruit Class."

As he drove in the early morning hours, again Wade asked himself how he'd get everything done on time.

"Damn," he mumbled, remembering Mailman Charlie. "I'll hav'ta call the bail bondsman this morning. Charlie was now in jail. He'd gotten greedy and had started dealing with some local drug addicts from the neighborhood. One day three of them forcefully took some checks from Carlie and threw him and his mail bag out in the middle of 29th Street. People driving by saw this and thinking a mailman was being robbed, they reported it. When Charlie got back to the branch post office he was assigned to, and said nothing, his supervisor became suspicious and called in the FBI.

No sooner than he was arrested, Charlie gave up everybody he had ever given checks to. Everybody that is, but Wade. He didn't mention Wade's name, and Wade figured it was because he had been the only person who didn't take from him. He made sure that Charlie was paid, even when he couldn't get any checks. Charlie could come to him for money, when Charlie's girlfriend told Wade about the arrest, he promised her he'd bail Charlie out. In a way, Wade felt obligated. The checks he'd been getting from Charlie for well over a year now had enabled him to purchase the new house he and Frankie were about to move into.

# CHAPTER XXXIV

The call came fifteen minutes after Wade had gotten home. It was Ethan. "I need you to meet Josh at Artie's," he said. "I've already called Brother Mitchell. He'll pick you up."

"Wha', som'um happened?" Wade asked. He hadn't even gotten the chance to take off his clothes. "Mitchell's gonna drive me to Artie's Bar?"

"Yeah. Bring your shoes."

You still watching the house?" Wade asked, as he peaked into the bedroom. Frankie was still asleep and their daughter was circled up beside her.

"Yeah, I'm callin from a phone booth up the street from the house. I jus' realized how we can pull this thing off this mornin'."

This morning, he thought, as he tiptoed over to the closet and removed his briefcase. Mitchell? He just got suspended for 90 days 'bout the rape robbery thing. Instinctively, he bent down and gently kissed both his girls on their faces.

Seeing Mitchell from the window, he quickly descended the stairs and made his way outside. "As-Salaam-Alaikum," he said climbing into the 65 beige Electra 225. "Something happened?"

"Yeah, there's been a change in plans," Mitchell said, pulling away from the curb. "Ethan wants us to take that spot this mornin'."

Wade didn't say anything. He sat in silence and wondered how Mitchell even knew about this job. The last time he had seen this brother, he was being chopped up and chewed out by Brother First Lieutenant Harvey about that rape robber he'd gotten mixed up in.

Wade looked out at the lifting shadows of night with a smile as he recalled what Harvey had said to Mitchell before taking him up to see the Minister.

"You say wha?" Harv exclaimed. "Talk to the Minister fo' you! Shit, you gotta be crazy."

"But Brother Lieutenant, why y'all comin' down so hard on me? I've been in good standing for …"

"Hard on you?" Harvey snarled. "Actually, we're being soft on you. You lucky you ain't in the ground som'where. I can't stand brothers like you tha' take advantage of sisters 'cause dey ain't got no man to protect'em. When good-meaning brothers try to school yo'r ass, you don't wanna listen. The only time you half listen in when yo'r dumb ass is in trouble and you need help. Then you want people to go easy on 'ya."

"Nah, I jus' … It was tha' Fat …"

With a brutal stare, a menacing tone, and gravelled voice, Harvey cut him off again. "You kno', you remind me of when I was a little boy. My Momma, a good meaning woman tha' she was, always had som' medicine to give me and my brothers, whether we were sick or not. She always had som'um for us to take. It was always sum' bitter tasting, nasty castor oil lookin' crap tha' she'd use sweet words with, tryin to sugarcoat it and make it taste better. Make it easier for us to swallow, I guess. But, my Daddy, no nonsense, hard hittin' joka dat he was, would always yell, "Don't whisper no sweet shit to dem! Make'em drink it straight from the bottle, like men! Don't you make no sissies' outta my boys." And you kno' wha'? Every one of my brothers tha' continued to slurp from tha' spoon, sweet words and all, turned out to be punks, jus like you. So if you want this shit spoon-fed to ya, you gotta go find my Momma, 'cause I'm like my daddy. I don't play tha' shit."

No lights were on at Artie's. Sitting in one of the booths in semi-darkness were Josh, Chris, Rushard and Dalton. Artie was standing behind the bar. When Wade and Mitchell entered through the side door, he walked around and locked it behind them, then went down into the basement to get supplies.

Wade and Mitchell gave everyone the greetings. Rushard and Dalton stood and shook Wade's hand. "Haven't seen you in a while, brother." Dalton told him, while seeming to ignore Mitchell.

"It's been a while." Wade replied.

"Look like we finally gon' git to work together," Rus grinned.

Chris gave a warm hug and greeting to both Mitchell and Wade, while wondering like the others, why Josh had chosen to make Mitchell part of this operation. Though one of the Four-Footers, Mitchell had never really been tested. And the fact that he had let Fat Richard influence him said a lot about his character.

"We're on the clock" Josh reminded. "Ethan needs all of us in place in a half hour. He said Benny changed cars and left. He wants us to bring a big bag of trash wit' us."

"A bag of trash?" Dalton laughed. "How we gon' git dem to open the door wit' tha?"

"We ain't," Josh said, getting up and walking behind the bar. He pulled out two huge trash bags and filled them both.

"We gon' dump it on one of dem boys' car. Ethan says one of'em drives a red and black 69 Mustang Fastback, and he comes out ev'ry mornin' to wipe it off. Evidently Benny's Cadillac is in the garage, so the white boy's Mustang is parked right outside the garage door. And he always uses dat do'r when he comes out to check on his ride. When he sees the trash on his car, he'll think the trash man dumped it d'ere 'cause they come by at 5 a.m.."

"So when he opens the garage, we go in?" Rus asked.

"No. We go in when he starts cleaning his car. I'll walk by and speak to 'im. He'll follow me in, tryin' to stop me, and one of you will walk in behind 'im and jam'im. That way we don't have to wait until t'night, or pretend to crash Benny's party. We'll already have the stuff and gon'."

"How many of them white boys inside?" Chris asked.

"All week we've counted three." Josh answered. "Try not to git a body. If possible, we don't want no cops involved."

It was 6 a.m. when they executed their plan. When Josh walked past the tall dark-haired Italian kneeling to wipe trash from his Mustang, the man rose and followed him inside the garage in an attempt to stop him.

"Hey, Pal, where the fuck do you think you're going?"

- 136 -

Chris moved quickly. Coming from the opposite side of the driveway, he entered behind the man, closing the garage door behind him as he pulled his .45 automatic.

When the man felt Chris' gun pressed against the back of his head, he raised both his hands. Josh pulled a .32 from the man's waistband, then cuffed and gagged him. He then climbed the steps that led to the kitchen. Peaking around the kitchen door, he moved swiftly and quietly through the dining room. He saw no one but knew there were supposed to be at least two more men in the house. As he got to the living room door, he heard it. Snoring. Someone was sleeping on the living room couch. He circled around so he could take in the entire room. On the coffee table in front of the couch, Josh saw a spoon with cotton in it, a hypodermic needle laying beside it, and a half full quarter bag of what looked like heroin. He then looked for the man's gun and found it lying under the coffee table, on the floor.

With hands cuffed behind his back, and Chris pointing the gun at his head, the car cleaner followed instructions and entered the dining room. "Sit right there," Chris threatened. "You move and I'll put one in yo'r ear."

Chris watched the sleeping man on the couch and the one he had deposited in the dining room, as Josh moved to the front door and opened it. In came Ethan, Wade and Mitchell. Dalton and Rushard stayed outside in their car to make sure no one surprised the brothers inside.

Josh awoke the man sleeping on the couch, as Ethan, with his drawn .38 automatic, silencer attached, eased his way up stairs. He carefully looked in all the rooms, but there was no one up there. "I kno' I saw three different whit boys goin' in and outta this house yesterday," he mumbled, while scanning the rooms and closets again.

Running back downstairs, he immediately went over to where Josh was holding the man now seated on the couch, nodding from the dope. "Where's the third man?" Ethan asked.

"He left dis mornin'," the man slurred.

Ethan looked at Wade and motioned. Wade told Mitchell to take upstairs, while he searched the basement. "And take the phones off the hook," he whispered to Mitchell.

"Where's the stash?" Josh asked, leaning close to the man's ear. "You git one time to lie and then you die."

"It's not here." Answered the dope user. "They said …"

Josh punched the man in the face, knocking him off the couch. Before the man could gather himself, Josh hit him in the head again, this time with the gun and drawing blood. When he raised the gun for the second time, the man started crying. "I wasn't told where they put it 'cause they thought I might steal some of it." He whimpered.

Chris pushed the other man into the room and removed his gag. Seeing his partner on the floor bleeding, he immediately started talking.

"Both the money and dope is here." He said. "They didn't tell him 'cause he's a stuffer and might try to steal part of it."

"Git it," Josh told the man. He walked behind him as the man moved toward a wooden panel on the wall and nodded. From behind it they removed a tan suitcase. When Josh opened it, he saw stacked bills on the bottom and what looked to be three kilos of heroin in the top compartment. The suitcase had been labeled, "Goldfinger – NY."

"Where's the rest?" Josh asked.

"That's all of it," the man said.

Josh slapped the tall man in the face with his gun, then pulled a straight razor from his pants pocket. Ethan quickly moved over to the bleeding man and whispered in his ear. "If I was you, I'd cooperate. Tha' black man d'ere kno's how to use the razor, and he loves hurtin' white folks. All this' shit 'bout y'all cutting off moolies dicks ain't shit compared to what's 'bout to happen to y'all."

Mitchell had come back down stairs and reported that no one was up there. Wade had searched the garage and the basement and there seemed to be no others in the house. When he reached the living room, Ethan was pulling the man's head back so that his neck was stretched and his throat exposed to Josh's razor.

"Yo'r last chance," Ethan menaced. "Yo'r life or the rest of the stash."

"It's in the Cadillac in the garage," he moaned. "It's in the trunk."

As Josh got two suitcases from the car, Ethan and Wade took the two Italians upstairs. Ethan told Wade to put one of them in the other bedroom. "Gag 'im and cuff 'im to the bed in d'ere, so tha' they'll be apart."

Wade cuffed and gagged the man and just as he was about to leave, he thought he heard a noise. After looking around and seeing nothing, he figured it had been Ethan going back down stairs. But as he started down the steps, he heard the sound again. This time he couldn't dismiss it. He bent down trying to see someone downstairs to call out to but noticed that no one was down there, including Mitchell, who he was paired wit. "Damn," he mumbled. "Ethan, Chris and Josh had gone. "They probably think I'm with Mitchell." Inching his way back up the steps, he quietly listened until he heard the sound again. It was coming from the bedroom where Ethan had left the other man cuffed to the bed. When he peaked in, he saw that the cuffed man was watching the closet door, so he watched it too. A moment later the door opened and out walked a short husky Italian wearing a pair of pants with no shirt. Around his neck was a towel, which covered part of his bare chest.

Damn, Wade thought to himself, he don't even know what's going on. He watched as the man rubbed eyes, then widen them when he noticed his partner kneeling by the bed, handcuffed and gagged.

"Hold on," Wade whispered, jumping from behind the door with his gun leveled at the man. He was just as scared as the man facing him. He couldn't yell because he didn't know who else might be hiding someplace in the house. "Don't move a fuckin' muscle!"

The man's eyes registered hate as well as fear. Ignoring the warning, he reached under the towel into his waistband to where his gun was. Before the shock of the gun blast faded, Wade heard a car engine start up outside the house. Keeping his eyes on the falling Italian, he reached into the man's belt and removed his gun. Blood was streaming from the man's chest, and Wade kept hearing Josh's words. "Try not to get a body."

Gun in hand, Wade rushed to the closet and peaked in. He saw where the man had come from. There was an open access door in the ceiling of the closet, and hanging from it was a folding ladder. When Wade climbed up and peaked in he saw two more suitcases and two sawed-off shotguns lying in a small crawl space. He grabbed the suitcases, wrapped the two guns in coats from the closet, and got the hell out of there. He never looked back at the man he'd just shot.

Outside on the street, the early morning air hit him in the face as he ran up the driveway behind the houses. His eyes were wide as he searched every window, door and yard that he passed, expecting to see someone who'd heard the shot. The weight of the suitcases and shotguns seemed light compared to the burden he carried at that moment. He couldn't afford to get caught.

The driveway ended at 17th Street and was blocked on the other side by a taxi-barn. The Yellow Cab Company parked its off-duty cabs there for maintenance. Wade quickly ran inside the opened gate when he spotted a man parking his cab there.

"I need a cab," Wade said to the man, as he opened the front passenger's side door, opposite the driver.

"Sorry, my man, I'm off duty." The driver responded.

"I said I need a cab," Wade menaced, as he climbed into the front seat and pulled his gun. Aiming it at the man's mid-section, he added, "I'll pay you!"

After pulling out of the yard and turning onto 17th Street, high beams hit them. They were from a car following them down 17th Street. Wade looked back and saw what seemed like an unmarked police car, signaling them to pull over.

"Slow down, and then duck once that car pulls up alongside of you," Wade cautioned. "And don't try anything."

As the cab slowed and the car pulled alongside it, Wade realized that it was Chris's pale blue Toronado and breathed a sigh of relief. Chris had come back after realizing that Mitchell had driven off and left without Wade. When he drove back to the house and pulled up in the driveway, he spotted Wade crossing 17th Street and heading for the taxi barn.

As Wade exited the cab with the suitcases and guns, he gave the cab driver a $100 bill and the man smiled nervously and thanked him.

# CHAPTER XXXV

Temple services on Wednesday and Friday evenings were often conducted by one of the Assistant Ministers. The crowd was usually smaller, so on this particular Friday evening, the temple on Germantown and Butler Streets proved to be the ideal place for the brothers to meet and discuss the early morning events of that day.

Harvey had asked the sisters who were working the kitchen that night to prepare a dinner for the brothers. Pleased with the amount of money and dope gotten from the take, he wanted the brothers to celebrate with food. He also wanted to hear why Mitchell was even on this job.

After everyone had arrived and congratulations were said, especially to Wade, Harvey wasted no time in getting straight to the point. "Why was Mitchell involved in this?" He asked, addressing his question to Josh. "He could've gotten Wade killed, if the brother didn't know how to think on his feet."

"I thought he could handle it." Josh responded, shaking his head side to side. "He came to me talkin' 'bout he needed money. I felt sorry fo 'im 'cause he'd been suspended for 90 days, so I gav 'im som' money and asked if he wanted to earn a little more. I only thought of using him 'cause Lester was busted. He caught a paper case over in Jersey and they won't giv 'im bail 'cause he's from Philly."

Damn, Wade thought, I better go call Vernon White and tell him to go down and bail out Mailman Charlie.

"Well I talked to Mitchell earlier," Cil said, clearing his throat as he leaned forward to put more bean soup and rice on his plate. "I asked him 'bout wha' happened and he said tha' he thought Wade was in Ethan's car. He said when he heard the gun shot and looked around to see tha' all cars had left, he just assumed it was the Italians shooting at him and pulled off."

"Why ain't he here apologizing to Wade, now?" Rus asked.

"He can't com' to the mosque," Harv reminded. "He's on suspension. But he said tha' he apologized to Wade. Did he?"

"Yeah, he called this afternoon. He said he was sorry."

"Is Les out yet?" Chris asked.

"No, not yet." Josh answered. "We got tha' red-bone he's been bangin' to git him out by using her Aunt's address over in Camden. But she can't git 'im 'til t'morrow."

"Ain't tha' the girl, Pauline, who works for Butta?"

"Yeah, she helps manage a couple of his clubs."

"Wha's the breakdown?" Dalton asked, getting back to the reason they were all there. "I mean, we kno' wha' Muhammad gets, but wha' do we get outta this?"

"We split forty percent of the take," Harv said, not particularly liking Dalton's comment 'bout Muhammad. "We got 24 keys and $300,000 in cash. We can thank Wade for the extra 12 keys."

"And the two sawed-off shotguns," Dalton laughed.

"Ev'rything we do is for Muhammad," Cil said in a raspy voice, while looking directly at Dalton. "And, we kno' tha' the dope has to go wholesale. We can't go back into the retail business."

"We got som' white boys up in Allentown and Easton that will take a few keys." Mo said. "No need to worry, they won't kno' it's comin from us. We got som'body to handle it."

Getting up from the table to fill everyone's glasses with more Shabazz juice, Harvey told them that his cousin, Kirk D. could hand off 5 keys up in Norristown. He made no mention of Lynton's part in all of this, but knew he'd have to give him at least 2 kilos. Harv had a sneaky suspicion tha' Chris and Ethan suspected Lynton was involved through they had said nothing.

After eating their fill and handling the rest of their business, they all went upstairs to the main hall where one of the Assistant Ministers was already on the rostrum.

The tap on Wade's shoulder came just as he took a seat in the back row. Looking around, he saw Chris' broad toothy smile. "Minister Uriah wants us to stop by his house before goin' home," he said.

"Problem?" Wade asked, wishing there was more he could say. He'd already thanked Chris numerous times for coming back for him, but wished that there was more he could do to show his appreciation.

"Nah, I don't think so," Chris answered, sensing Wade's feelings. "I think he wants us to back up Brother Anthony at a meeting with Joe Larcardi. Som'um 'bout Lacardi's number writers being pressured."

It was near midnight when they arrived at the Minister's house. Brother Anthony, one of the younger brothers in Lieutenant Josh's squad, answered the door.

"Salaam-Alaikum," Anthony said, his grin as contagious as ever. Originally known as bow-legs from 24th and Thompson, Anthony had become a well-liked brother in the mosque. Polite and courteous, he was well spoken and well dressed.

It was because he was so well liked that Minister Uriah had chosen him to meet with Joe Larcardi. Licardi, who was the son of one of mob boss Angelo Bruno's chief associates, had met Anthony a year earlier, when he had sold him a truck load of wedding gowns. He liked the young black Muslim because he didn't seem at all threatening or arrogant like some of the other blacks he had dealt with. And unlike some of the other black, so-called hustlers he knew, Antony and the Muslims had refused to deal with his rivals from the Rufalino mob.

After talking with the Minister for an hour, the brothers knew what was expected of them. He told Wade and Chris that they were chosen for the same reason he had chosen Anthony.

"All you brothers, though serious, are disarming enough to calm troubled waters." The Minister never referred to his soldiers as dangerous. He always used words like serious and no-nonsense brothers.

He told Anthony to resolve the problem without disparaging our errant brothers. "We'll handle them," he said. "Although the Italians have no problem going to war with each other, Larcardi will respect you more if you don't speak ill of your own kind. Tell 'im he has my word, there will be no further Muslim interference with his number bankers."

***

It was early Saturday morning and Lynton sat silently on the side of his bed wondering how he could've been so easily fooled. They knew I'd get word to Benny and they counted on that punk moving his shit, and ev' ry body else's, to one spot.

Suddenly his thoughts were interrupted by the ring of his phone. "Yeah," he yawned.

"We got a problem here," Agent Doss told him. "The names of some of our informants have been compromised. So you won't be speaking with me any longer. From now on, you'll talk only to Khalid in Chicago."

Wiping the sleep from his eyes and pushing all previous thoughts from his mind, he replied. "Yeah, uh, I was recently approached by Butta about someone in your office giving up information about a servicer. He was told it was a Muslim, so of course, he came to me wanting to kno' who it might be."

"You know these guys, giv'em somebody." Doss said. "What's important now is that we get our elimination program working. The time has come to remove these players from the street, or put them under the ground. We got some people planted in the county prisons who'll start the ball rolling. They'll start by mentioning our first target's name as an informant. Then we'll start busting people around this target, but not the target himself. We'll get two or three birds with one stone."

"Who's the target?" Lynton asked.

"One of your brother lieutenants, Josh 8X Clarkson."

"Tha' won't work. Nobody will believe he's a snitch."

"It'll work if you do as we say. He'll listen to you, so you feed him jobs that will produce, and afterward we'll nab some of those involved by using only information that Josh would know. Soon someone will start looking at him. When they take him out, we'll get those who did the hit. Two or three birds with one stone."

"I'm tellin' you, man, tha' won't ..."

"No, I'm telling you! It's time to make things happen. You been making a lot of money because we've turned a blind eye to you and those you're using. Funding for our program will dry up if we don't start producing results. Understand?"

"Well, wha' bout Butta?"

"How important is he to our agenda?"

"Not only is he a millionaire who I can milk, but he's the one person who I can use to start a drug war. He hates the brothers and they hate him. I jus' gotta make sure tha' he'll survive the war or be able to pick up his gold if he don't."

"Then feed him somebody just to keep him dealing with you. Somebody who's available and you don't particular need or like. That way, it won't disturb your conscience, if you have one."

"Yeah, I kno' som'body," Lynton mumbled, while thinking of Lester. "Som'body who's been banging a red-bone tha' I want."

"Men who make decisions based on women have very clouded judgments," Doss warned, as he hung up the phone.

Immediately, Doss dialed homicide detective O'Connor's number. "How's Napoli?" he asked upon recognizing O'Connor's voice. "Is he still down in the dumps?"

"Yeah, som'um bothering him, but he's still on the job."

"I just talked with Lynton Thompson," Doss said. "He'll deliver Clarkson. Were y'all able to convince a judge to sign the probable cause warrant for Terence Folsom's arrest?

"Yeah, but he was reluctant because it's a five year-old homicide case. And all we have is a statement from a female junkie witness.

"Well, you just have to work on her some more. One thing for sure, she'll say anything for a fix. So offer her a heap of fixes. Bu don't give her any money or she'll disappear."

# CHAPTER XXXVI

After getting some much needed sleep, Wade and Chris met with Anthony to drive to Joe Lacardi's restaurant on 12th and Mifflin Streets in South Philly. The meeting they were now heading to was more of a formality than anything else. It was just to show respect and give assurances to Lacardi that his concerns had been heard and the problem solved.

When Minister Uriah was told that some brothers calling themselves Muslims had taken it upon themselves to pressure independent number writers into paying $1,000 per week for protection and assurance of more customers, he didn't pay too much attention to it. But after receiving a phone call from Joe Lacardi about those same brothers crossing the line over into his numbers operation, he had to put his foot down.

It had been Joe Larcardi's father who had arranged the meeting with the business people on the minority businessman deal. Stacy Blankenship would have never been accepted as a front man had not Larcardi' father intervened.

The Minister knew he couldn't personally speak to those brothers who were posing as connected Muslims and pressuring the number bankers. That would mean exposing himself to people who shouldn't know what he knew, so he called in Anthony.

Anthony went to the imposter's leader, Brother Gregory, and informed him of the problems their actions were causing. In no uncertain terms, he told Gregory that it would be in their best interests to stop what they had been doing. And that from then on, neither he nor his crew could accept money from any of the number bankers, not even the independents.

The smell of onions filled the air inside the small modest restaurant. There were a few fat men sitting at the counter eating Italian hoagies and watching the TV on the wall. Two younger Italians sat in a booth scarfing down cheese steaks and drinking orange sodas.

"Hey Anthony, my man," Larcardi said in a jovial tone, as he came from behind the counter. He was a short stocky man with a full head of hair, and he looked to be about 35. He wore a wide grin on his smooth face, as his eyes darted back and forth from Anthony to Wade, to Chris, before settling back on Anthony.

"It's good seeing you, Joe," Anthony said, reaching out his hand. But Joe brushed it aside and hugged Anthony around the shoulders.

"These are my brothers, Wade and Chris. This is Joe Lacardi," Anthony said as he stepped aside, allowing the men to greet one another with a nod and a handshake.

The silence was deafening, as Joe led the brothers through the restaurant, toward a closed door in the back. None of the men sitting and eating turned to look at the brothers, but they could feel their eyes. As Joe opened the door to the back room, he motioned to a buxom 40 year old looking blond woman in tight pants, and she immediately went out into the restaurant, closing the door behind her.

"I'm glad the Minister took my call," Joe said, pulling chairs up to a table for them to sit around. He joked, "You guys care for a beer?" Then he added, "Seriously, would y'all like som'um, sodas, pie?"

"Thanks Joe, but no," Anthony responded. "The Minister wants you to know he has a great deal of respect for you, Joe. That's why he acted immediately after receiving your call."

"I hated having to come to him," Lacardi said, leaning back in his chair, his hands clasped. "I detest emotional display. However, I thought it necessary for our friendship. In this business, we all need friends. And, I consider Minister Uriah as one of my much valued friends."

Relishing the fact that he knew Lacardi often treated his friends as if they might become enemies, Anthony hesitated, then countered. "Yeah, Joe, but som'times in yo'r business, there are no permanent friends, only permanent opponents."

After a moment of silence, Lacardi responded. "I think you will find tha' that condition exists within yo'r brotherhood, as well." His smile was broad and humorous, but his eyes were narrow and serious. "I've been told tha'one either takes a seat at Muhammad's table or becomes the menu."

"Hey Joe! The ponies are on the track," came a yell from the front of the restaurant.

Lacardi got up and turned on the TV in the room. Pausing briefly to glance at the beginning race, he then returned to his seat. "You fellows ever bet the ponies?" he asked.

"Nah, we don't have tha' luxury," Anthony joked.

"You know Anthony," Lacardi said, his blue eyes staring at the TV, as Wade and Chris stared at him. "Until now, we've had no territorial disputes 'cause you brothers don't deal in drugs. At least not retail. Oh, by the way, I've heard 'bout the Louden Street hit. But tha' don't concern us 'cause they were Rufalino's people. I can see that baldheaded prick now, runnin' around, looking like Quasimodo in a suit; cussin' and spittin'. ...Well, at least no one got killed."

"You lost me," Anthony said. "Louden Street?"

Chris and Wade remained as stoic as they'd been when first entering the room. Their facial expressions never changed and they never took their eyes off Joe Larcardi.

"Anyway, wha' I hope those brothers will understand is, I can't afford to have' em become an embarrassment to me."

Taking the opportunity to end the conversation, Anthony rose and shook Lacardi's hand. "Your people will have no more problems," he said with a reassuring smile. "And you and the Minister will hopefully break bread together, soon."

*** 

That evening Tony Rufalino called for a meeting at his cabin in the Poconos. Seated around the decorative living room on cushioned chairs were Otis "Goldfinger" Brown, out of New York City, Big Melvin Taylor, out of

Baltimore, and Benny Pinter, out of Philly. Two of Rufalino's bodyguards sat in chairs just outside the opened door.

The short, slightly humped-back Rufalino stood in the middle of the room surrounded by a circle of fear. While all three of the men meeting with him were terrified of him, only one of them felt that Rufalino might not allow him to leave that cabin alive. For over a year, Benny had been responsible for storing their product until they could convert it into cash. He was supposed to be a depository manager for Rufalino and those working for him.

It wasn't until Brother Lynton cut into Benny about moving heroin for him, that Benny started dealing it for himself. He wanted to be as big as Butta was in the game. And, in one year he had cleared over a quarter million dollars. He figured that Rufalino wouldn't mind as long as he didn't mix and match his stuff with theirs. But now he had lost his and theirs, and he was scared.

"Boy, I don't kno'," Rufalino said, as he paced back and forth across the room. "All I ever asked of you guys was to be straight wit' me. I treated each one of you good. Protected your asses from the cops and them punk-ass-niggers y'all scared shitless of. Now, why in the fuck did you let som' moolies take all my dope and money?"

"I, uh. Som'body told me tha' I was gonna get robbed, so I moved the stuff from the two spots I usually use. I thought nobody knew 'bout it. They must've been following me for weeks."

"How dumb can you be? Who told you, you were gonna be robbed? Was it one of them Moslems? He's probably the one who set you up!"

"Nah, it was a cop," Benny lied. He didn't dare mention Butta or Lynton as the ones who provided him with that information. To do so would mean certain death. "He's on the take. He always gives me good information."

"A cop? A black cop?" Rufalino asked.

"Yeah, he's black. He patrols the neighborhood where one of my bars is."

"Pour me a drink," he said, motioning to Goldfinger, a light-skinned black man originally from the Islands. Rufalino didn't know which island and he didn't care. Goldfinger was more of a pimp than a tough street hustler. His only value was that he could deal with the mob's prostitution ring in New York and Rufalino needed that connection.

Because it was consistent, prostitution had always been a cash-cow for the mob. However, drugs was now the rising star in a growth market and Rufalino wasn't about to accept this loss.

Unlike Goldfinger, Big Melvin was a tug that dealt only in the drug trade. He operated just below the Mason-Dixon line by handling the country boys who owned the little dance halls and night clubs. Benny knew that it would be Melvin who Rufalino would get to kill him, if he didn't give Rufalino the right answers. Six months earlier, he had been forced by Rufalino to watch as Melvin beat a man to death with an iron pipe, while Rufalino sat by eating ice cream.

"Now, I'm tellin you this!" Rufalino shouted, taking the drink from Goldfinger's hand, while staring directly at Benny. "You find these niggers who took my money. You got two fuckin' weeks to get me their names. In the meantime, 'till this shit is settled, I want fifty percent of the take from your three bars and cash payments of $50,000 to me, and $25,000 each for Big Melvin and Goldfinger."

"I don't kno' if I ... I think I can raise it."

"How?"

"I kno' someone who'll help me. I'll get it," he said.

"Up until now, I liked you, Benny," Rufalino said, as he reached behind one of the chairs and pulled out an iron pipe, which he handed to Melvin. "I thought you were a pretty smart guy. Please, don't make me hav'ta kill you. Understand?"

"Yes, sir."

"Two weeks for the names. One week to raise the money."

***

Dalton exited his car at 10<sup>th</sup> and Cumberland Streets and walked down Cumberland toward the Dew-Drop-Inn Bar. He felt the curious glare of a dozen pair of eyes. Something he was used to. On the corner across the street stood a gang of six black youths. He acknowledged them with a quick nod of his head. Believing that Dalton was there to see Rough-Ralph and collect for the mosque, they gave an admiring look and went back to their conversation.

Before entering the bar, he stopped to talk with an old man who was selling fruit and vegetables from the back of an old station wagon. Dalton picked out some strawberries and plums, handed the man a $5 bill, then turned and entered the bar. He was only in there for a moment. When he emerged, the eyes followed him and the neighborhood gangster, known as Rough-Ralph, across the street and into the Yorktown Housing Projects.

Rough-Ralph was one of Dalton's workers and had acted on his behalf to buy back some of the heroin that was taken from the hit on Benny's spot. Without letting the brothers know, Dalton, Mo, Rus and Big Cil had secretly made a deal with one of the buyers to buy back a couple kilos to put on the street. Because of First Lieutenant Harvey's position in the mosque, he refused the offer to get involved, but helped to keep their secret from the other brothers.

To avoid suspicion, they didn't set up in South Philly, instead they set up operations in two North Philly housing projects. If there were no problems, they planned to later expand their operations to South and West Philly.

Rough-Ralph lived at the Yorktown Homes and lent his name to the operation there, though he didn't run it. The dope was cut and packaged in an apartment on the top floor of one of the high-rise buildings and sold from an apartment on one of the middle floors. To guard against the police and stick-up men, a look-out team was stationed on the first floor and in the small park across the street from the buildings.

In the cutting and packaging apartment, they kept a bath tub filled with lye to dissolve the drugs in case the police happened to get by their spotters. Along with assurances of no shootings or fights, and special payments going to various tenants at different times, most of the people there kept their mouths closed.

Apartment 1801, on the top floor, belonged to Sylvia Syms who was in charge of the operation. Using only women for cutting and packaging, she also chose the men who were there as security.

"Wha' it is?" Ralph asked upon entering the apartment.

"You," Sylvia responded. She was a high-yellow slim girl with straight brown hair and stood out like prime rib at a hot dog stand.

"Ev'rythang on schedule?" Ralph asked. "Weather's hot, niggahs gon' be out lookin' to cop. We ready or wha?"

"Git the fuck outta 'ere," Sylvia frowned. "You always tryin' to impress Dalton, wit'cha raggedy-ass mouth. He kno' we got this 'ere thing right."

"Sylvia, I need to holla at'cha a minute," Dalton said, taking her aside.

"Wha 'sup," she asked.

"I'ma need you to train som' other people, 'cause in a few months, we gon' expand this thing to downtown."

"Tha' ain't no problem," she grinned. "Jus' tell me who and when. Sylvie already kno' how."

"But remember," Dalton cautioned. "No one can kno' who's frontin' this."

*** 

Under the pretense of feeling sorry about what had happened to Benny, Lynton invited him to his home to discuss a possible solution. Over dinner, he agreed to help Benny pay Rufalino the money Rufalino had demanded. However, Benny had to do something for Lynton. He wanted Benny to tell Rufalino that the man who had planned the robbery was an FBI informant named Lester Edwards.

"Is that true," Benny asked. "Is this guy a Muslim?"

"Yeah. But I want you to ask Rufalino to give you an extension of two weeks before you hav'ta pay him. That way you'll raise the money to pay for the hit yourself. Tell 'im not to worry, he'll hear about it when it happens. And he won't hav'ta worry 'bout no repercussions from the Muslims."

"Are you serious?" Benny asked, sounding concerned. "I can't pay for no ...plus Rufalino won't believe me."

Lynton paused before responding. He knew that no matter what the feds did, the brothers would never believe that Josh was an informant. Still, he had to do something to keep Agent Doss satisfied so that he could keep his drugs on the street. Sacrificing Benny was the key, he thought, to solving all his problems. He would kill Benny to keep his mouth closed, and Butta's people would kill Lester because they will think that Lester is the one who sent the feds to Butta's spot.

Ev'rything will be handled by other people," Lynton told Benny. "You don't hav'ta put up any money or have any involvement in the hit. Rufalino wants money. He'll go along wit' you and give you time 'cause he wants your bars."

After convincing Benny to go to Rufalino, Lynton called Captain Khalid in Chicago and asked that he speak with Agent Doss on his behalf.

"Ask Doss to find out the name of the woman who's been feeding information to Butta and plant Lester Edward's name in her mind."

When Khalid asked why he was doing this, Lynton told him about the conversation he'd had with Doss. "I have to make som'um happen," he said. "This is my way of satisfying Doss by starting a war between the brothers and Butta, and at the same time keeping his mind off tha' ridiculous plan to try and make Josh look like a snitch."

"You kno' that if the brothers find out you set this in motion, you're a dead man."

'Tha's why I need you to talk wit' Doss. Butta can't even say it came from me. The only other person who knows is Benny, and he won't be around to say anything."

"If this is about you keeping your shit on the street, won't you need Benny?"

"The end game for Benny don't mean that I gotta stop making money for myself." Lynton told him before hanging up the phone. "I got plans we both will benefit from."

# CHAPTER XXXVIII

Friday, August 28<sup>th</sup> at 10 p.m., Lucius arrived at the house he now shared with Babysis. He had just come from locking up the South Street Mosque for the last time. It had to be closed indefinitely so that money could be used to open a new mosque in another area of the city.

As he was about to climb the stairs to the bedroom, the phone rang. It was Hercules.

"Wha' sup, Herc?" Lucius asked.

"We got 'im!" Herc exclaimed. "The son-of-a-bitch is at the Chesterfield Hotel right now. I followed him to Locust Street where he met wit' the girl. It'll probably take 'bout 20 minutes befor' she gets 'ere."

"Can you intercept her?" Lucius asked, "And keep her from going inside?"

"Yeah, I can keep her from goin' inside. But how long will it take you to git 'ere?"

"Wha' about this other girl," He asked. "The one you say will keep the clerk from seeing me. Did you holla at her?"

"Yeah, I told you. I figured out ev'rything. Now how long will it take you to get 'ere?"

"Do I kno' this girl?" Lucius asked. "The one who'll be wit' the clerk? I can't take any chance of being recognized."

"Hey, Lucius, how long you been knowin' me?" Herc asked. "The girl knows nothin' 'bout nothin'. When we first decided to do this thing at the Chesterfield, I got close to the clerk. He's a snuffah who loves shootin' tha' boogie woogie. So I sent Linda at 'im. She's a freak. Every Friday and Saturday night, she goes by and shoots 'im up, gets him on, then gets him off."

"Linda who?" Lucius asked.

"Linda Johnson," Herc answered. "You kno' er. She used to be a spotter for the cops. That's why I chose her. They'll be more likely to believe her if they ask any questions."

"And she kno's nothin?"

"Nothin'. She thinks I sent her to him as payment for him letting me use one of the rooms to package my dope. And he thinks she comes around because he lets her do her tricks there sometimes."

"You're sure everything's fine?"

"Yeah, I'm sure," Herc said. "They kno' nothin'. Now how long will it take you to handle this? How long should I keep the girl outside?"

"Take your time wit' her. You kno' the deal, have som' fun until you see the window shade go up and down."

Fifteen minutes later, when the yellow cab with a pretty dark-skinned young woman stopped in front of the hotel, Herc rushed over and reached in to pay the bill.

"Keep the change," he told the driver, after handing him $20. Opening the door for the woman to step out, he held a $50 in his hand for her to see.

"Who are you?" she asked. "Are you the man or som 'um?"

"If I was a cop, would I pay for yo'r taxi," Herc grinned.

"Then why are you flashing the fifty, honey? If you want som 'um, I'm busy right now. I can meet you later."

"I don't do seconds baby," he said, pointing to his mint green Continental Mark III. "Lets me and you sit inside for a minute."

"A minute? Is that all it's gon' take?" she smiled while following him to the Mark. Looking up at this 6'5" man, whose suit was the same color as his ride, she was impressed with his car and his style.

Opening the passenger side door, Herc guided her inside and whispered, "You're probably goin' to meet som' old-ass man to give him pleasure while receiving none for yourself."

"Money, honey. That's pleasure," she said, pulling her skirt further up her thigh so he could see that she wore no panties. "You wanna do this here on your fine leather seats?"

"Don't worry." He whispered, laying the fifty across her thigh. I'm sure you'll take yo'r time and swallow ev'ry bit."

Parked in the shadows of the Progress Plaza Shopping Mall, across from the hotel, Herc watched Linda cross at the corner of Broad and Oxford Streets. She looked good. Her wide hips and sturdy bowlegs under the tight skirt. He watched as she sashayed up the steps and disappeared into the building.

Now, if only Lucius could get here on time, he thought. He had watched Linda work her magic on men before. He knew it wouldn't be long before she had that guy moaning in the back room.

Holding the prostitute's face in his lap and enjoying her manipulations, Herc saw Lucius pull up and entered the hotel ten minutes after Linda. Making sure no one was in the lobby, Lucius went up the stairs to the second floor and straight to the room Napoli always rented. He tapped lightly on the door then turned the knob when he heard Napoli say, "It's open."

Though it was dark in the room, Napoli, who was on the bed in his underwear could see the 6'5" outline of the person coming in from the lit hallway. He could tell it was no woman and immediately tried to reach for his .38 revolver which was on the night table. He was cut short by a blow to the head, which knocked him sideways off the bed.

"Get up," Lucius told him, as he grabbed Napoli's .38. I hear you been lookin for me."

Realizing who he was facing, Napoli didn't hesitate. He got to his feet as he'd been told. "I, uh, just wanted to, uh talk wit'cha, Lucius. You know …"

"'Bout wha'?"

"I wanted you to know that there was no hard feelings. I heard you were out and asked Babysis to tell you, that's all."

"She told me," Lucius said, motioning with his gun for Napoli to move over toward the bathroom. "I got 'cha message now I'ma give you one to take to O'Brien."

"What the hell are you doing, man? You know I'm a cop! You'll be caught!"

"Should tha' matter to me?" Lucius asked shifting his gun to his left hand and putting Napoli's in his right. "You done stepped over the line. You done touched Babysis for the last time."

"Look, Lucius. I understand. It won't happen again, you got my word on that."

"You sure?"

"Yeah, yeah, I'm sure."

"Good," Lucius said, ramming the .38 into Napoli's side and pushing him toward the bathroom. "Move."

"Sure, sure, Lucius," Napoli said, nodding his head. Lucius rammed the barrel of Napoli's .38 under Napoli's chin and stared in the man's eyes. "I came here to kill you white man."

"Please, Lucius, you can't do this." Napoli pleaded, while trying to grab hold of the gun. It was too late, Lucius pressed the gun against Napoli's flesh and pulled the trigger one time. The bullet tore into Napoli's chin, then traveled upward through the roof of his mouth and out the back of his head. Upon impact, Napoli's feet left the floor and he began sliding down the wall. Lucius immediately wrapped Napoli's right hand around the gun's handle. He then placed the gun on the floor to let Napoli's blood drip down on top of it.

Ten minutes after arriving at the hotel, Lucius signaled Herc with the window shade then casually walked out. Linda was still working her magic on the clerk in the back room.

***

The Last Saturday in August, Wade and Frankie's back yard was filled with fun, laughter and mouth-watering aromas. Sister Gussie hummed and swayed her body to Linda Jones' "Hypnotize," as she grilled chicken, steak and ribs. Sisters Brenda and Geraldine went about slicing the cakes and pies, while Sister Christine prepared her special potato salad.

It was a bright and sunny morning, not yet hot or humid. The sisters and their husbands had come to present Sister Frankie and Brother Wade with a housewarming party. The women refused to let Frankie do any of the work and the men, all but one, were busy doing nothing in the living room.

"You best git away from this 'ere grill," Sister Gussie told Brother Chris, as he tried stealing a chicken leg from the grill.

"I just' need som' nourishment so I can help wit' the work," Chris joked.

With one hand on her hip and a tong raised in her other hand, Gussie rolled her eyes and replied. "I'll give you som' nourishment up side yo'r head wit' this 'ere tong."

"I told you brothers to stay out this 'ere yard until we called y'all," Sister Brenda yelled. "Don't make me hav'ta tell y'all again."

"I never liked the woman," Sister Geraldine said, as she continued her conversation with Gussie. "The way she always stands with her hips jutted out to the side and her nose in the air like she Miss Five Hundred or som'um."

"Who you talkin' 'bout chile?" Christine asked, covering up a big bowl of potato salad.

"Miss Marion X," Geraldine said, pushing her long brown bangs away from her forehead.

"Do I know her?" asked Frankie. "Did she just join the mosque?"

"Sure you kno' her," Gussie replied. "She was the one who asked who yo'r husband was that day he was outside the MGT class tha' time."

"Yeah, when he was selling the pastries," Brenda added, raising her eyebrows. "Now she don' took off her holy clothes and ran off wit Sister Alberta's husband."

"Well," Gussie laughed, "at least 'till he come to his senses, again. You kno' he don' did this befor'."

As the women gossiped, the men sat in the living room and talked about Muhammad Ali's upcoming heavyweight bout against a known contender, Jerry Quarry.

"It's 'bout time they let the brother fight again," Ethan said. " He hasn't fought in three years. Dem devils stole his title, now he's gonna take it back."

"Can we get tickets?" Wade asked.

"Yeah," Josh said. "Minister Uriah will probably wanna go, too."

"I already got our tickets," Chris told them.

"You got tickets?" Josh asked. "You kno' the fight's in Atlanta, Georgia?"

"Wha' I say?" Chris asked. "I didn't stutter. I also got plane tickets. The fight's on October 26th. We can fly down a couple of days earlier. I already told the Minister."

"Who you git 'em from?" Josh asked.

"Stanley Coulter," Chris answered. "Because he's the executive director of the Community Activity Center, some people he's connected with threw 'bout ten tickets his way."

"Tha's what I like 'bout you brother." Ethan joked. "You stay on time."

"Well, old Stan the man is good for som'um," Chris said.

"You brothers ready to eat?" Brenda yelled. "Then c'mon out 'ere."

Later that evening while they were all sitting out in the backyard enjoying the cool air, and listening to Ray Charles' "The Night Time Is the Right Time," the phone rang. When Wade answered it he found it was Brother Lester on the other end.

"Did you hear what happened last night?" Lester asked.

"No. What happened?"

"Captain Terence was arrested for a body," Lester said. "It's a five-year old homicide. There's supposed to be some witness who picked out his picture. And, because it's a murder, they won't giv'im bail."

Wade immediately went to tell the others. Without any hesitation, the brothers decided to hire Milton Lerner, an old Jewish attorney with a reputation for winning. They also told their wives that as long as Captain Terence was in jail, they would regularly give them money to be delivered to Captain Terence's wife.

CHAPTER XXXIX

The police conducted an extensive investigation, trying to determine whether Napoli's death had been a murder or a suicide. Now, four months later, they were still no closer to making that determination. When the call had come into the Homicide Unit at the Police Administration Building, stating that a police officer had been found shot at the Chesterfield Hotel, police from just about every district in the city had responded. Police district vans, regular police cruisers and a battery of unmarked police cars were all over Broad Street and surrounding areas. However, investigators processing the scene and searching for witnesses had very little time before they were again overwhelmed. In less than 24 hours afterward, two more police shootings were reported. In two separate incidents, one cop had been killed and another seriously wounded.

The police were baffled. They didn't know if they were under attack by some radical group or what. A few days later, when three men, reported to be Black Panthers, were arrested for the later shootings, the Napoli investigation was somehow included. Lucius Please was never a suspect.

By mid-January, preliminary hearings were being held in Brother Captain Terence's case. The Minister instructed all brothers who had no criminal record to go to these hearings as a show of support. Each hearing room was filled with brothers and sisters. Though Brothers Ethan, Chris, Lester and Josh did not attend, Terence knew that it was their efforts that raised the money for his legal fees and family.

When the court set Terence's trial for late spring, the Minister appointed Brother Cecil, "Big Cil," as acting captain, until Terence's case was resolved. Most brothers were fine with the choice, but a few feared Big Cil would turn a blind eye to what Mo, Dalton and Rus were doing.

By now, it had become common knowledge that some brothers were involved in the drug trade. Ministers from Temple 12 and the surrounding areas had been ordered by Chicago officials to clear out those involved in drugs. As a result, Brothers Ethan and Chris were applying pressure to Mo, Rus and Dalton to clean up their act. Brother Lynton somehow remained under the radar.

Lucius had been Minister Uriah's first choice for captain, but Lucius had just married Sister Gloria and was now being considered as a personal bodyguard for the supreme captain in Chicago. Josh had desired the captain position, but knew that a couple of errors in judgment over the last few months had hurt his chances for a promotion.

One of those errors had come when Josh, wanting to raise extra money for Terence's family, decided to send Brother Antony and his crew to rob one of the Yellow Cab's branch offices in Center City. Brother Lynton had told Josh about the branch office, where money was brought in to be counted before being picked up by an armored car security company for bank deposit. Though the robbery went well, somehow a couple of the young brothers were later identified and arrested.

Ethan, Lester, Chris and Wade learned about the robbery only after Josh brought them their share of the take. Those brothers had no choice. They had to come down hard on Josh. He had gotten brothers involved in taking legal money and by doing so, he had created another financial burden on them. They let Josh know that because of his actions, they would now have to hire lawyers for the two young brothers, now in jail.

While submitting to their criticism, Josh secretly hoped that yet another decision he had made would not come back to haunt him. A day earlier, Josh had sent Brothers Mitchell and Theron to pressure a brother who had once been in the mosque. Brother Lamont was a man in his mid-thirties, not very tall, but about 225 pounds. While in the mosque, he had been a very popular lieutenant. After Malcolm X was killed, Lamont left the mosque, and since then he had made quite a bit of money as a numbers banker. Josh thought Lamont should be back inside the temple. It was for that reason Josh had sent Mitchell and Theron to talk with him.

However, what Josh didn't want to happen, did happen. Brother Lamont took exception to Mitchell's arrogant attitude and a struggle ensued. Mitchell, fearing he would be hurt and ignoring Theron's advice, pulled his gun and shot Lamont, seriously wounding him.

Two days after Josh had been criticized about the robbery, news of the shooting reached the brothers. This time, Brother Captain Cecil and Brother Lieutenant Harvey chose to speak privately with Josh. Though they out ranked him, and he had made a serious mistake, still Josh was a soldier and they had to show him the respect he deserved.

"You messed up, Josh," Cecil told him. "You should've never sent them brothers to talk wit' Lamont."

"Yeah, I kno'," Josh replied. "Lamont's no punk. He probably saw tha' as an insult."

"Probably?" Harv remarked. "Can a jackal offend a lion?"

"I really didn't mean it as an affront," Josh replied.

"Yeah, we kno' tha'," Cecil said. "It wasn't jus' tha' you thought he should come back in. It was the way you went about it. And by Mitchell shooting a tried and tested brother like Lamont, adds insult to injury."

"Some people don't kno' they've crossed the line until they've already gotten to the other side," Harv said.

"Wha 'cha want me to do?" Josh asked.

"He's gotta go," Harv said. "Actually, he should've left when he raped dat woman."

"Brother Theron tried to stop him," Josh assured. "He had nothin' to do wit' the shootin'."

"We kno' that," Cecil answered. "Theron's a good little brother and remains in fine standin'. The problem is Mitch. I understand he was one of yo'r fish, but sometimes you gotta throw som' fish back in the pond."

"I'll handle it," Josh assured him.

"No," Cecil shot back. "You both handle it. I want Harv d'ere when Mitchell leaves."

***

Lester drove slowly along East River Drive, listening to "Drums of Fury," by Michael "BaBa" Olatunji, on tape. He had just picked up a brand new $5,000 reddish fox fur from one of the female boosters, working for the brothers. She had sold it to him for just $1,800. Pauline's gonna love this, he thought, as he turned onto Lincoln Drive, it kinda matches the color of her hair.

He and Pauline were now secretly renting a duplex on the drive. Though they planned to get married next summer, they didn't want anyone knowing about the house until after their wedding. She respected his religion and he gave her space to pursue her studies to become a Licensed Practical Nurse.

Pauline, who now worked only on the weekends as a manager at Butta's club, attended nursing school during the day. With such a hectic schedule, Lester only went to the house on the nights she wouldn't be studying. Tonight was one of those he planned to stay until morning.

Lester turned left, steering his Cadillac Couple de Ville over to the snow-banked curb in front of the house. He shut off the engine, got out, and went to the trunk, removing the box containing the fur coat. The wind was lighter than it had been earlier that day, but still it blew his tweed Apple-Jack Jeff cap from his head. He picked it up off the snow-covered ground and stuffed it into the pocket of his tan London Fog raincoat. He turned the dark brown fur collar up around his neck and headed across the street toward the house. It was then he saw the dark colored Mercury Cougar slowly easing up the street. At first he thought the driver was just being cautious because of the ice, but when the car stopped, his instincts took over.

His gun was still in his car and he had to get back to it. As he turned two men jumped from the Cougar, leaving the driver, whom he now recognized as one of Butta's men, behind the wheel. Shots rung in his ear as he tried to make his legs move, but couldn't. He felt himself going down and turned over just in time to see one of the men aim and fire another shot, before darkness consumed him.

# CHAPTER XL

"We got two weeks to decide," Wade was saying, as the phone rang, interrupting his and Frankie's conversation about who would babysit their daughter while they attended Savior's Day in Chicago. "That's not a lot of time," Frankie said, as she handed him the pone. "It's Brother Christopher."

"As-Salaam-Alaikum, Wade said.

"Wa-Alaikum-Salaam, Chris replied.

"Wha 'sup?" Wade asked. "How's Lester? Did you go up with the Minister to see 'im?"

"The cops found Brother Mitchell's body in the Delaware River yesterday," Chris answered. "Said he'd been there 'bout a week or so. He had an icepick stuck through his neck."

"Wha 'cha think?" Wade asked. "You think it has anything to do with Benny? You kno' …"

"We don't hav 'ta think. We kno'," Chris replied. "Mitch fucked up when he shot Lamont. Tha' cost 'im. As for Benny, no one kno's who slumped him. The word is som'body was robbing his bar."

Wade thought about the time he'd followed Benny from that same 7$^{th}$ Street bar. And when the cops found him on the floor of that bar a month ago, Wade had wondered if he had been killed because of the money and drugs they had taken from his house.

"How is Lamont?" Wade asked, shaking the thought of Benny Pinter from his mind. "I heard he was released from the hospital a few days ago."

"His wife saw my wife at the mosque the other day. She said he was doing a lot better."

"Did you go to the hospital to see Lester?" Wade asked.

"Yeah, I went wit' the Minister," Chris said. "Lester is lucky to be alive. This 'ere shit's getting outta hand."

"Yeah, I kno'" Wade mumbled. "Jokah's shootin Muslims down in the streets."

"That'll be handled," Chris assured. "Lester kno's who the driver was, but he wants to talk to Ethan and Harv first."

"When can I go up to see 'im?" Wade asked.

"Minister Uriah said that any brothers going up there should be careful 'cause the police are hangin' 'round tryin' to git information."

"When are you goin' up again?" Wade asked.

"We can go up this evenin', if you like," Chris said.

While waiting for Chris to pick him up, Wade sat on his sofa staring at his wife combing and plating their daughter's hair. However, his thoughts were of a previous conversation he and Chris had with Brother Lester. It was on the night they flew back from Atlanta. Muhammad Ali had TKO'd Jerry Quarry in the 3$^{rd}$ round, and Wade, Chris and Lester were headed back to Philly. The other brothers who attended the match decided to stay over an extra day with Minister Uriah, who years earlier had been a Minister at the Atlanta, GA mosque.

"I think I'ma give it up." Lester had said. "I'm getting married soon and I believe it's best for me and Pauline."

"Wha' you sayin'?" Chris had asked him. "You thinkin' 'bout leavin' the mosque!?"

"Nah, I'm talking 'bout the hustle. Things are beginning to get crazy, man. The lines have become too blurred."

It soon became obvious to Chris and Wade that Lester was talking about the connection between the Muslim brothers and the drug world.

"I sometimes feel that we're causing more harm than good to our families and other people," Lester continued. "And if we're not careful, Allah will take us away from them."

"I agree wit 'cha," Chris responded. "Wha' I think is happening is we're allowing other brothers to define wha' we're supposed to be about. The teaching of our people into a knowledge of God is lost on us, if we fail to put the laws of Islam first."

As Wade and Chris took the elevator up to the floor where Lester's hospital room was, Wade recalled something else Les had said before they had separated that night. "We gotta talk to Ethan and Josh, man. We hav'ta git them to realize tha' we are now being pulled in the wrong direction. This ain't what we was supposed to be about."

Wade had said nothing that added to the conversation that night, but he knew that what Chris and Lester were saying was right. Actually, he was relieved to hear that he hadn't been alone in his thinking. Wade had often silently questioned certain things they'd done under the banner of Islam. However, he continued to go along because like others who might've had those same thought he had been taught to hear and obey. To openly question, he feared might be seen as being hypocritical about the religion. But he was beginning to realize that it was being hypocritical to ignore what he'd been taught about the laws of Islam. Mere belief, he thought, accounts for very little unless carried into practice.

Lester looked to be mending well. He had been shot in the chest and in both legs. Pauline had heard the gun fire and ran to the window just in time to see the men drive off in the Mercury Cougar. When she saw that it was Lester lying in the street, she grabbed her nurse's bag and ran to him. It had been her training in how to slow the bleeding that had probably saved his life.

\*\*\*

Saturday night, a week before Savior's Day, the Spinning Top nightclub on Germantown Avenue was filled with brothers and sisters from Temple 12. Redtop had contacted Ethan a week earlier, asking him to help her throw a combination wedding and going away party for Brother Lucius.

When Lucius decided to marry Babysis, Redtop had been the first person he told. Though Redtop loved him, she knew he and she would never marry. She understood that he was Muslim and his religion called for him to be married. She was glad he had chosen Babysis and not one of those uppity sisters from the temple. Babysis was from the street and would stand by him no matter what. And when she learned he had been asked to go to Chicago, she decided to honor him and his new wife with a celebration.

No alcoholic beverages were served, only juices of all flavors. A cornucopia of savory kosher meats and cheeses were available, along with fruit and vegetable salads. The entertainment was proved by local jazz musicians.

It didn't take long, setting back at the tables, for the guests to feel the magic in the air. The room was filled with much conversation and laughter. The festive event had some feeling as if they didn't have a care in the world. But a troublesome situation did linger and it needed to be handled.

"Wha 'cha think we should do?" Chris asked Ethan. "When I spoke with Josh 'bout this, he tried to pretend it wasn't a problem."

"Wha' did he say?" Ethan asked.

"You kno' how he is," Chris shrugged, a frown crossing his face. "He started philosophizing instead of responding to the question. He said that the only people complaining about what we do and how we do it were those who refused to accept the Messenger's teachings. He told me how we didn't come 'ere as barbarians or savages and that what we learned we learned at the feet of the slave masters." Pausing a moment, Chris then added, "But he never spoke to the question of how we've been moving in the wrong direction."

"I'll talk to 'im," Ethan said, pouring himself a pitcher full of Shabazz Juice and stuffing cheese and corned-beef into his mouth.

Across the room, Redtop was whispering to Babysis. "I'm glad he chose you," she said. "So am I," Sis replied. "I kno' that you and Lucius have feelings for each other. But I really love him. I've loved him since the first time I saw 'im."

"He's precious," Redtop said, as she handed a glass of juice to Babysis. "Take good care of 'im."

Wade sat with Lucius at Minister Uriah's table, listening to Billy Paul sing, "This is your Life, you're Living." Josh and Ethan joined them just as the Minister began explaining how important it was for the brothers to start making some adjustment in their lives.

"Take you brothers, for instance," he said, glancing over at their wives congregating at the salad bar. "You have good Muslim women and children depending on you. Your courage is commendable. One has to be courageous walking through the wilderness of North America. But one also has to be careful not to lose one's humanity."

Each brother knew that the Minister was about to impart some of his wisdom to them. Be it praise or chastisement, they knew it would be a learning experience. Leaning back in his seat, Minister Uriah took a sip of juice and savored it for a moment before continuing.

"The most insidious act the white race committed against our people was to rob us of our culture," he said. "Culture is what preserves humanity. The white man breached our culture by disrupting our birth and natural growth process. Also, committing such mutilations and assaults, so vicious, the mere brutality of it permeates our genetic makeup. It was such a complete distortion

- 160 -

that every black generation going forward was born with a defective gene in their minds. A gene that causes fear and distrust for one's own kin and kind. This defective gene causes us to create new ways of self-hate."

Again the Minister paused. He looked around the table at each brother sitting there. Then pointed as he spoke. "Like Marcus Garvey and the Honorable Elijah Muhammad, some of us were blessed to be born with a deficiency. A deficiency that caused us to miss having that defective gene which causes fear of the white man and distrust of our kind. But unlike Garvey and Muhammad, we can be self-destructive. Now knowing this, we must now allow our efforts to regain self-respect and dignity as black men cause us to mistreat and abuse our black people because they don't agree with us. We hav'ta to be a brother to our people and not become like the white race."

Josh knew immediately that his comment about learning at the feet of the slave master had been conveyed to Minister Uriah. He didn't mind the mild chastisement, though because as usual, the Minister hadn't made it personal. It came as a lesson to all of them.

As the last bit of the crowd was leaving, Fat Hank and Herc were just arriving. They had planned it that way so that they could have a little time alone with Lucius. Hank was also leaving Philly, but he was headed south. Herc was going to take over Hank's operation and pay him in increments for it.

"I wanna give you som'um." Hank said, passing Lucius an envelope. "I've been savin this for you since you went off to prison. I promised myself tha' when you were ready, I'd give it to you."

Lucius opened the envelope and saw a cashier's check for two hundred grand. "Hey, Hank, I can't take this." he said, trying to hand it back

"Shit, I'll take it," Herc grinned.

"No. This is Lucius' money. His mother had me put som' of her earnin's up for her befor' she passed. I invested it, and this is the result."

"I don't kno' wha' to say, Hank. You're a special kinda person, man. I love you like a father."

"Yo'r momma wanted you to have som'um from her, son. She was a good person. Just like you're a good person. Now you go on and make my little Babysis happy."

# CHAPTER XLI

A look of disappointment stretched across Brother First Lieutenant Harvey's face as he read the headline in the morning edition of the March 9, 1971, <u>Philadelphia Daily News</u>.

> " Fight of the Century: Joe Frazier wins a 15
> round unanimous decision over Muhammad
> Ali."

Harvey read the article out loud to Mo, Rus, Big Cil and Dalton who were all sitting in his modestly decorated living room, in his row-home on Opal Street in South Philly. They were waiting for Josh, Ethan, Chris and Wade to arrive so they could discuss the shooting of Brother Lester.

"For the first time ever," Harvey continued to read aloud from the article. "Two unbeaten heavyweight champions met for the crown. Ali clowned with Frazier during the bout but it hurt him in the scoring. His jabs puffed Frazier's face, but Frazier dropped him with a left hook in the 15$^{th}$ round."

"Damn Champ," Harvey said, as he flung the paper across the room. It landed on the floor at the feet of his wife Sister Monica who was serving the brothers coffee. Her glance was all it took for Harv to get up and pick the newspaper up and lay it on the huge marble-top coffee table in front of the sofa.

"Ali should've took tha' fight," Dalton said, getting up and taking the tray from Monica and placing it on the table.

"He'll beat Frazier in a rematch," Mo said, "wait and see."

"I should've went to tha' fight," Harvey said.

"Yeah, like that would've made a big difference," Monica laughed as she started out of the room.

Just then the doorbell rang. Sister Monica opened the door and in walked Ethan, Josh, Chris and Wade. They all gave a collective greeting of "Salaam-Alaikum."

"I see you read the news." Josh said. "The champ can beat that chump, man. He jus' gotta stay focused and stop tha' damn clownin'."

"Yeah," Ethan added. "Ali can't play wit' Frazier like he did wit' Jerry Quarry."

"I'm goin' to the rematch." Harv said. "As a matter of fact, let's all go."

"It's a date," Monica said before leaving the room and the men to their conversation.

While in the hospital, Lester had spoken with Harvey and Ethan about the shooting. He told them it had been Butta's lieutenant Dennis Jackson driving the car that night. He said he couldn't be sure who the dudes were who shot him, but he was sure about Dennis.

"I kno' tha' some of y'all will wanna retaliate," he'd said. "But before you do, kno' that I'm out the game. I was ready to quit even before I got shot. Now I know it's the right thing for me to do."

"Are you sure?" Ethan had asked him.

"Yeah, I'm sure," he answered. "And I don't want nobody feeling obligated to retaliate for me."

Of course those last words fell on deaf ears. However, sincere Lester might have been about quitting the life was one of no concern to Harvey. He and Butta had hated each other for years. Ethan and Lester were the best of friends even before they went into the mosque. There was no way Ethan was going to let this drop. If Dennis drove that car, he thought to himself, he did so with Butta's blessing.

"We hav'ta to be cautious about this," Chris said, after Sister Monica had left the room. "Somebody set Les up to be killed by Butta's crew and we need to kno' who and why."

"Sometimes caution borders on cowardliness," Rus said.

"Wha' the fuck you mean by tha'?!" Chris shouted.

"Whoa, I wasn't talkin' 'bout you." Rus explained. "All I meant is we hav'ta move on this quick or people will think we're scared."

"Nah, Chris is right," Mo said. "We have a lot to lose if we do this wrong and a lot to gain if we do it right."

"Dis ain't 'bout no advantage," Cil grumbled in his raspy tone. "I kno' som' of you are thinkin' dis will allow us to take over Butta's operation if he's gone, but dis ain't 'bout no money, dis 'ere is 'bout brotherhood. Dem maggots done shot down one of us."

Ethan, who had been sitting quietly and listening, finally spoke. "I'm probably closer to Les than any of you. Tha's not to say y'all don't lov'im like I do or tha' my word carries more weight than y'alls. But I think we should consider wha' Les is asking us. He kno's some'um going' down, but he probably wants to be in a much better position when it does."

"So wha 'cha sayin'?" Harv asked. "You sayin' we should wait? How long?"

"How about until after Frank Matthews gives his annual summer party," Mo suggested. "We're all invited. Butta and his crew will be there and we might get an idea who the shooters were jus' by watchin' them."

"Yeah," Rus added. "It'll show' on their punk-ass faces."

"Tha's cool wit' us," Josh said, motioning to Ethan, Wade, and Chris. "But we can't be seen at no player's ball. Y'all go and let us kno' who should be taken down wit' Butta."

***

On that same Tuesday afternoon, the one person not at the meeting was Brother Lieutenant Lynton. He was cruising by Camac and Diamond Streets, in his Cadillac looking for Monster Dave. Marvin Gaye's "Stubborn Kinda Fellow" could be heard coming from his car as he pulled over in front of the shoe repair shop on the corner. The little boy standing out front bouncing a ball was Dave's son.

"Where's yo'r pop?" Lynton asked.

"He down in the basement," the little boy answered.

"Go tell'im I'm up 'ere."

Monster Dave wasn't too keen on doing any work for Butta's crew. A few years back he had been kidnapped by Dennis Jackson and forced to make him a batch of speed. A week later, when they finally released him, they wouldn't even pay him.

"I don't like this," Dave said, as Lynton drove toward Broad Street. "You shouldn't have never mentioned my name to Butta.

"You do this for me, and I'll double wha' you would normally get," Lynton told him. "It's for a favor Butta did for me."

Lynton drove Dave up to the Poconos where Dennis Jackson and two other men were waiting. They had all the chemicals Monster Dave would need to make the crank. Lynton left him there promising to pick him up in three days. However, before leaving the Poconos, Lynton stopped at a phone booth to call Brother Captain Khalid in Chicago.

"How's things." He asked Khalid, knowing Khalid knew he meant Lucius.

"Fine," Khalid responded. "The brother and his wife jus' got an apartment on the south side and they're settling in."

Khalid went on to tell Lynton that the Supreme Captain and Lucius had become partners in one of the captain's clothing stores. "The Supreme Captain needed funds and Lucius had some to invest," Khalid said. "He has also been appointed to the Messenger's security squad."

"Damn, tha's good ain't it?" Lyndon asked. "Especially for you. Now you'll have eyes and ears close to the top."

"Yeah, but I still have to keep certain brothers from knowing where their instructions are really coming from. You got lucky, Minister Uriah's conscience is money. He'll look the other way."

"Well, I still hav'ta be careful. Uriah might look the other way on some things, but he's still about supporting the teachings."

"Greed overcomes a lot," Khalid said. "These people out here in Chicago are less corrupt. That makes my job harder."

"So what's our next move?" Lynton asked.

"Agent Doss asked me to send some people your way. When they contact you, they'll be presenting themselves as Ahmadiyya Muslims."

Lynton knew the name. And he knew that Doss wanted them to provoke a confrontation with the believers from the Philly mosque. The Ahmadiyya Movement started as a result of a book called Braheen Ahmadiyya written by the respected Muslim mystic and scholar, Hazrat Ahmed. After his death in 1908, his followers had spread out over the world and established communities, some in America. But in Philadelphia, members of any Muslim community, other than those of the Nation of Islam, were referred to as Orthodox Muslims. The difference in their religious philosophy often caused disputes that sometimes turned violent. The Orthodox or Sunni Muslims, as they called themselves, believed in and followed Prophet Muhammad of 1400 years ago. They spoke out against the teachings of Elijah Muhammad, saying that his were blasphemous and based on falsehood. That created a great deal of animosity between the different Muslim organizations. And, Lynton knew that any people calling themselves Orthodox or Sunni Muslims coming to speak with brothers from the Nation about Elijah Muhammad were in for trouble.

"Them the people you used to rob and scare the Supreme Captain?" Lynton asked.

"No, they were from the United Slaves," Khalid said. "I will be contacting them later. They will be sent to provoke a confrontation with certain brothers. The Ahmadiyyas are just to stir the pot."

***

However, what Brother Khalid didn't know was that the now highly paranoid Supreme Captain had become suspicious since the robbery at his house and what he felt was attempted murder. He had taken Brother Lucius into his confidence and asked that Lucius pay close attention to certain brothers, including Khalid. When Lucius asked why, he told Lucius about conversations he'd had with people that Khalid shouldn't know about, but somehow did. And that he found out from a sister who worked in one of his stores that Khalid was having secret meetings and talks with certain brothers, including Brother Lieutenant Lynton X. Thompson from Temple Number 12.

"I trust you," the Supreme Captain told Lucius. "You are not a part of this thing out here and you have no allegiance to anyone but the Honorable Elijah Muhammad."

Brother Lucius didn't know whether this was some kind of test or what. The Supreme Captain obviously didn't know that it had been Captain Khalid who had sent for him when he first got out of prison and had been giving him instructions since then. Still, if the Supreme Captain's suspicions were true, Lucius thought he should know what was going on. His loyalty did lie with the Messenger and the Nation of Islam.

# CHAPTER XLII

The last week of March, 1971, Brother Captain Terence went on trial in City Hall for first degree murder. Brothers Theron and Anthony had been instructed to accompany Terence's wife to the trial each day. The jury was picked and seated on Monday morning, the 29th. By the afternoon of the next day, the trial was over. It ended in a mistrial when the key witness for the prosecution failed to return from lunch and be cross-examined by Terence's attorney.

A motion to dismiss the case was filed by the defense and denied by the judge. Bail was also denied and Terence was to remain in custody while the judge entertained a defense motion to block a retrial based on something called double jeopardy. The defense argued that since it had been the state's witness who had caused the mistrial, the defendant should not be held accountable and the defendant should not be placed in jeopardy a second time.

***

That same afternoon, just four blocks away from City Hall, at the U.S. Federal Building, Agent Smith, with the latest FBI memorandum dangling from his hand, walked across the room and stuck his head in the open door of Agent Doss' office.

"Did you see this damn thing?" He asked Doss. "They just keep adding on and on."

"Yeah, I saw it," Doss replied, pointing to a copy of the same memo captioned COUNTERINTELLIGENCE PROGRAMS (COINTELPROS) INTERNAL SECURITY-RACIAL MATTERS lying on his desk. "It's no big deal, we just focus on the part entitled Black Extremists and let others concern themselves about White Hate Groups and that espionage shit."

"You think the revision came as a result of the Citizen's Commission to investigate the FBI breaking into the Media office to steal those documents?" Smith asked.

"What you think? The break-in was on the 9th, now three weeks later we get this crap."

"Well, I might have some good news for a change," Smith said. "I got a call this morning from Detective O'Conner, the one who worked with Napoli. Well, a plainclothes narc by the name of Kelly busted some guy two days ago for trying to sell 'im an ounce of heroin last night."

"So what's the good news? Doss asked impatiently.

"This guy is Maurice "Mo" Barton's brother-in-law. He also knows Rushard "Rus" Braxton and Dalton Landers."

"I know of 'em, so what the fuck?" Doss said, getting up and walking over to the filing cabinet to retrieve a folder.

"The point is this guy, Carl Hunter, is a drug addict and snitch. He's scared shitless of going to jail and will help us get around the wiretap issue with Judge Fogel."

"That old fart still ain't gon let us tap their phones without some substantial evidence on these guys"

"We don't need the old fart," Smith grinned. "O'Connor told me that because Hunter has federal and state priors, he would have his case transferred to us and we'll have a chance at this guy. We get Hunter to set up Maurice and the rest of his dope dealing brothers from this office phone. All calls going in and out of a federal building are taped. So we just get this Hunter guy to ask the right questions then we wait until the tapes are transcribed."

Grinning from ear to ear, Doss stood up and shook Agent Smith's hand. "You son-of-a bitch, we got 'em," he said.

"Yeah, and this Hunter guy probably knows how Maurice has been using his money. We know that Maurice's wife, who's the snitch's sister by the way, owns and operates a beauty salon. Maurice buys a new Cadillac damn near every year and owns, at least two restaurants and a small supermarket. How the fuck can he explain where he gets all that money."

Over the next three weeks, Carl Hunter was brought from the county jail five times to meet with Agents Doss and Smith at the Federal Building. Each of those times the agents discussed with Hunter the best way for him to get Mo to make a drug deal with him over the phone. But Hunter kept trying to tell the agents that their plan to get Mo talking wouldn't work.

"Y'all don't kno' 'im like I do," Hunter said. "Mo is very suspicious and he ain't no dummy."

"Alright, you know this guy, so you tell us, how can you get him to negotiate a drug buy over the phone?"

"While I've been up there at the Detention Center, I been thinking," Hunter told them. "Mo ain't gon' talk to me 'bout no drugs 'cause he don't trust me and he thinks I ain't gon' pay 'im back 'cause he married to my sister."

"So what have you come up with?" Doss asked.

"Y'all give me som' quinine. Tha's the shit ev'ry drug dealer needs to cut his heroin wit'. Put the word out on the street tha' I been sellin' it. When I call to speak wit' my sister, Rus or Dalton will ask me 'bout it. Tha's how I get dem to deal. And Mo won't say nuffin. He'll jus' let dem do the deal."

"Yeah, but our target is also your brother-in-law. We need him there and his voice on that phone." Smith said.

"I'll pull 'im in, you jus' get me out of jail and put the word out tha' I got som' good quinine for cutting dope."

"You listen up, black boy," Doss said, putting his face up close to Hunter's. If we put this stuff in your hands and you try to screw us, we'll kill you. No jail, no telling Mo on you. We'll just put a bullet in your fucking head."

Hunter just smiled. He had been threatened by much tougher men than Doss. But he had no intentions of crossing the Feds. He told them that they would have to arrange the call when they knew that Rushard and Dalton would be at Mo's house.

Carl Hunter's plan worked. Two weeks later, after keeping Rushard and Dalton under surveillance, getting Hunter out of jail, putting the word on the street that Hunter had been selling quinine at the right price, and having him report to their office every day to make the call, the call was made.

Rushard, Dalton and Harvey had come to Mo's house to talk about the planned hit on Butta. Harvey was at odds with Josh's suggestion about waiting to take Butta and Dennis out; but Mo kept trying to impress upon him the wisdom of waiting.

"Man, we stand to make millions if we do this right," Mo told Harv. "If we move too soon, we stand to alienate Frank, and no one's making money without New York Frank these days."

"Every time I think about wha' tha' punk did, I …"

"Are you sure it's 'bout Lester?" Mo asked, interrupting Harv, "Or is this jus' 'bout hatin' Butta?"

When the phone ran, Mo answered it. He immediately frowned upon hearing Hunter's voice. "Jackee ain't 'ere, man. You kno' she don't get in until late." Mo yelled into the phone.

"Who dat?" Russ asked. "Is tha' Jackee's brother?"

"Yeah," Mo said, about to hang up the phone.

"Wait, let me talk to 'im," Rus said.

"Wha 'sup," Hunter asked Rus.

"You got dat thing?" Rus asked, knowing Hunter knew what he was talking 'bout.

"Yeah, I'm still holdin'," Hunter said, winking at Doss.

"Wanna make a trade," Rus asked. "You still like tha' boogie woogie, right?"

"Damn' straight," Hunter said. "But only if Mo signs off on it. I mean, he's my brother-in-law, and I kno' he'll treat me right."

"He cool wit' it," Rus said.

"Nah, let me hear 'im, man. Y'all brothers don't play fair all the time."

Just to get the matter over with and at the urging of Rus and Dalton, Mo picked up the phone, approved the deal, then handed the phone back to Rus.

***

The trial judge hearing Brother Captain Terence's double jeopardy motion took two months to rule. He denied the motion and ordered Terence to be re-tried. The trial date was set for September 1, of that year. The brothers immediately paid the attorney an additional $5,000 to appeal the trial judge's double jeopardy ruling to the State Appellate Court.

# CHAPTER LXIII

Before joining the Nation of Islam, Brother Captain Khalid had been one of the leaders of the revolutionary organization known as the United Slaves (US). In 1968, while still using the name, Jonny Jamison, he became a paid informant for the FBI and was asked by them to join the Nation of Islam. He was to work undercover as an agent provocateur, provoking violent disagreements between the Black Muslims and other black groups.

The advent of organized crime into the Nation of Islam's affairs in Philly, made Khalid's job a whole lot easier. It was mid-June when the six men, all wearing Arabic garb and portraying themselves as Ahmadiyya Muslims arrived in Philadelphia to meet with Brother Lieutenant Lynton. They were told which temple meetings they should attend and disrupt.

"Only the meetings on Wednesday or Friday evenings," Lynton told them. "You'll meet less resistance on those nights because not a lotta brothers are there then."

When one of the men asked Lynton if they should expect any violence, Lynton told him no. "I don't expect any of tha'" he lied. "But jus' in case, don't take your real identification and use a rented car."

The men posing as Almadiyya Muslims were also told that they should distribute the fliers challenging the teachings of Elijah Muhammad and describing him as a false prophet. The filers had been printed by the FBI but made to look as if the Almadiyya sect had printed them.

The Assistant Minister at the mosque on Germantown Avenue and Butler Street was already on the rostrum when four of the men, dressed in Arabic garb, were escorted in the large room, on the evening of June 23, 1971. They had entered the mosque in pairs and were seated in the back row. At first they sat and listened quietly. But as the audience began responding to the Minister's comments, by shouting, "That's right Brother Minister, make it plain!" The men sitting in the back row in Arab clothing started to yell out, "That's wrong! He's wrong! That's a lie! You're lying! You're teaching falsehood! Elijah Muhammad is a false prophet!"

Once the brothers on post determined who were making these comments, they immediately confronted the men and asked them to leave the mosque. When the men refused to leave, the brothers on post sent for the two brother officers on duty that evening. Brother Lieutenants Arnold and Ethan, who had been upstairs in the office came down. After speaking with these men, Arnold, Ethan and another young brother escorted the men outside.

However, once outside, one of the men began shouting to the people who were standing around out there. "I challenge these false Muslims from the Nation of Islam to explain Islam as taught by the scholars of this religion," he said, turning to the brothers who had escorted him outside. "Elijah Muhammad ain't no prophet. Y'all running around talkin' 'bout Elijah being a messenger of God. He ain't none of those things. He's a damn fraud and ..."

"I don't think you understand what the Honorable Elijah Muhammad is teaching us brother, but this is not the time or place to discuss it," Arnold said in a whisper, while trying to move the men along. "Please, sir, would you leave from in front of the mosque."

"The time is never right for y'all because y'all don't kno' true Islam as taught by the scholars."

"And who determined the scholars?" Ethan asked, becoming agitated at these men's presence. "The Arabs? The Arabs who have always ignored the plight of black people, even those blacks who proclaim themselves Muslim. The Arabs come to this country and befriend the same people who are oppressing black people. The Arabs invest their money with our enemies. They sell pork and liquor in our neighborhoods and use the profits to party with Europeans."

"The Arabs represent the Sunna of the prophet," said one of the men passing out fliers. "It's you Black Muslims who cast a dark shadow over the religion.

Stepping up on the steps to address the crowd that had gathered, Arnold spoke clearly. "There are those who call themselves Muslims while trying to look like Arabs. Some of our people don't realize that Islam is practiced in every country just a little differently to comply with the various customs of the various countries. In Indonesia, China, and other places, Muslims don't lose their culture and adapt that of the Arabs. Only black s in America do that. We had been socialized to emulating the white man and now that Islam has come to us, our social training tells us to emulate the Arab in every way. We wanna dress in Arabic clothing, stop shaving, and even have our wives covering their faces with veils. It's the Nation of Islam, not the Arabs that are raising up the deprived ex-slave to a level of dignity and grace."

Watching the crowd cheering on Brother Arnold as he spoke, caused the man who'd been speaking for the Almadiyyas to drop the flyers on the ground and motioned to the two men who were still sitting in the car.

"Now, please, my brothers," Ethan was saying to the men, "everyone has had their say. Please pick up yo'r fliers and leave this property."

Ethan hadn't seen the other two men get out of the car and approach them. One of these men carried a baseball bat. When Arnold saw the man with the bat, he immediately stepped down to the sidewalk and touched Ethan on his arm, moving him away.

The man with the bat said nothing. He just swung it with all his mite. He missed both Ethan and Arnold with his first swing. But his second swing caught a teenage Muslim brother, who had just come outside, squarely on the side of his head. The teenager went down as the man raised the bat again. This time Arnold was able to catch it on his right forearm. He then pivoted on the ball of his right foot, turning his back completely to the man with the bat and side kicked him under his chin with his left foot. The blow caused the man to fall backward against the wall. Arnold continued delivering kicks and karate blows to the now defenseless man.

At the same time, Ethan caught the other man who'd gotten out of the car with a left jab to the forehead, followed by a left hook to the man's jaw. As the man went down like a ton of bricks, the other four men ran off, leaving the car and their two buddies who were now on the ground being beaten and stomped.

The police arrived just as the Muslim sisters attended to the unconscious teenage Muslim brother. Both men posing as Almadiyyas were arrested for trespassing, assault and battery with a weapon, and attempted murder.

Later that evening, the other four men met up with Lynton at a Holiday Inn to explain how things had gotten out of control. They told him that in light of what occurred at the mosque, they would advise Khalid not to send the other men to Philadelphia. Lynton was disappointed and though he tried, there was nothing he could say to change their minds.

The teenage Muslim brother hit with the bat, was named Derrick, and he remained unconscious for two days. The two men charged with assaulting him were first held without bail because it was determined that they were actually from Chicago and had no residence in Philly. Once the young Muslim brother regained consciousness, the men were given high bails and told that they could not leave the city if released.

*** 

Since the summer of 1967, when Lucius first walked into Wade's life, until the summer of 1971, the brothers had not faced one serious casualty within their inner circle. Though Brother Captain Terence's arrest was cause for concern, he was not a part of their inner circle. And neither was Brother Mitchell, who'd made the mistake of shooting a well-respected Muslim and wound up paying for it with his own life. But their luck was about to change and the brothers of the inner circle were now about to experience some devastating losses.

After the arrest of the men who had come to the mosque and seriously injured the teenage brother, Minister Uriah told Brother Lieutenants Ethan, Arnold and Josh to find out who had sent them. Using one of the bail bondsman he knew, Ethan paid the bail of the man who had swung the bat. While he and Arnold waited in a parked car along State Road, Josh went to the county jail and waited outside for him to be released. It was 8 p.m. when the jail got the call to release him.

When the man came out of the prison, the only person he saw standing under the light was Brother Josh waiting by a dark colored car.

"Are you Paul Weems?" Josh asked the man, knowing that was the name the man had given to the police.

"Yes, sir," the man replied. "Are you here to pick me up?"

"Yeah," Josh said, opening the door to the rented car. "I have to take you to the office so the boss can determine where you'll be staying while in Philly."

"Any place is better than jail," Weems said, climbing into the passenger's side of the car.

As he drove Josh asked Weems if he wanted the name of a good attorney. "You kno' Philadelphia courts are notoriously famous for convicting black men."

"Yeah, but first I hav'ta see some people," Weems said.

Josh turned off State Road onto a small cul-de-sac and pulled over. "We hav'ta talk," he said, turning to face Weems. "I need to kno' who you're working for."

"Wha 'cha mean," Weems said, not noticing the two men who had just exited a car and was now approaching from behind.

"I mean you hav'ta try and save your life," Josh said, as the back doors of the rented car opened and Ethan and Arnold climbed in.

"Remember us?" Ethan said. "I'ma ask you one time and if you don't answer me, you die right here. Understand?"

"Yeah," the man said. He was so scared he was shaking.

"Who sent you to the mosque?"

"A brother named Khalid. Khalid Jamison." Weems said. "I met him when we were in US."

"By US, you mean the United Slaves?" Josh asked. "Aren't they in California?"

"Yeah, but we have people in Chicago and Jersey now."

"Who is this Khalid Jokah?" Ethan asked. "He head of y'all Chicago crew or som'um?"

"Yeah, but he's also in the Nation."

"The Nation of Islam" Arnold asked. "He's a Muslim!?"

"Yep," Weems said, sounding a bit arrogant.

"You been to Philly befor'?" Josh asked.

"Nah."

"Then how did you come to pick tha' particular mosque?"

"We were sent to meet this brother at a Holiday Inn off of Fifth and Market Streets. He didn't tell us his name, just told us to follow him to that mosque. I think he's also a Muslim.

"Where's this jokah at now," Lucius asked, shifting the phone from one ear to the other as if trying to hear better.

It was midnight and Josh had called him from a pay phone so they could talk about wha Paul Weems told them about a Muslim in Chicago named Khalid.

"Oh, he's lying by the side of the road wit' three in his head," Josh said nonchalantly. "I kno' you don't think we let tha' maggot walk."

"Well you could have first tried to verify if wha' he was sayin' was true," Lucius said, "I think I kno' who tha' person might be. I've been hearin' stuff."

"Wha' kinda stuff?" Josh asked.

"I'll get back to you on tha'," Lucius said. "Right now y'all should be tryin to find out who their connect was. I have an idea 'bout him, too, but I'll let y'all give me the name first."

# CHAPTER XLIV

"Well, I see that the Feds are already here, mauling over my evidence," Detective O'Connor yelled to Agent Doss, as he and his new partner climbed out of their unmarked police cruiser.

"We've been here since dawn," Agent Doss said. "What took y'all so long?"

"This is Agent Doss of the FBI," O'Connor said, as he introduced Doss and his new partner. "This is Detective Al Jones, my new partner."

Detective Albert Jones, a tall muscular black man, nodded as he presented his right hand to Agent Doss.

"How's the Joe Napoli investigation going?" Doss asked O'Connor, while shaking Detective Jones' hand. "Did y'all find anything that changes the medical examiner's findings from suicide?"

"No, not yet," O'Connor said. "But I still believe he was murdered, and one day I'll prove it."

"Why is the FBI interested in this murder?" asked Jones, looking around at how many forensic people were working over the crime scene. "Was this guy someone y'all knew?"

Doss looked at O'Conner before answering detective Jones' question. "He was associated with someone we communicate with, yes."

"Was he on your payroll?" O'Connor asked, stepping away from the body to allow pictures to be taken.

"Nah. His real name was Wesley Gibson, a former member of a revolutionary organization known as United Slaves. We know he was sent to Philly to cause problems for the Black Moslems, but obviously he messed with the wrong people."

"Yeah, somebody paid $20,000 to bail him out of jail a couple of days ago," O'Connor said. "It looks like they paid the bail just to kill 'im."

"What else you know?" Doss asked.

"He was arrested 8 days ago for an assault and battery at that mosque on Germantown and Butler. We think the two men he fought with might be involved in this."

"We know they were involved" Doss said, as he squatted by the body long enough to examine the entrance wounds in the back of the man's head. "We have already spoken to a witness who thinks that the two men he saw get out of a dark-colored car with this man the night of the 29th, were the Black Moslems, Ethan Siswell and Arnold Boyden."

"How long you said you've been here?" Detective Jones asked curiously.

While examining the dead man's hands, Doss glanced up and said, "We canvassed the area when we first got here this morning. You see, your commanders had called us before you got the call."

"That's how you came upon the witness?" O'Connor asked.

"Yeah, he's an old man who lives just about a mile from here. He was driving home that night and just happened to pass by here when he saw the three men get out the car."

"How did he identify them?" Jones asked. "From photos or what?"

"Yeah, we have photos of every Moslem in Philly," Doss said, holding up two pictures for Detective Jones to see. "I laid an array of them out on this man's table and he picked out these two."

The pictures were mug shots of Brother Arnold and Brother Ethan from previous arrests. Detective Jones thought it strange that the FBI already had so much information about a body that was just found earlier that same morning and the men suspected in the murder.

"How long have you known about the fight at the mosque on June 23?" Jones asked Doss. "I'm not trying to get …"

"No, I understand," Doss replied. "You're just curious as to how we got the upper hand on this. Well, as your new partner knows, we have been on these guys for a while now. We were informed about the fight at the mosque on the same night it occurred. We've been watching this incident, but we didn't expect it to end like this. At least not this quickly."

Detective Al Jones asked no more questions. He wondered why Detective O'Connor hadn't asked more. For instance, he noticed the drag marks in the grass and that there was only a small amount of blood around the dead man's head. To him that indicated that the man was killed someplace else and the body then brought there. If he saw it, O'Connor saw it. And that meant that the witness' account, if there was a witness, was wrong. "I have no more questions now," Jones said to himself, "but I'll have some later on."

*** 

By the time Lucius called Chris that Saturday morning, he was convinced that Khalid had been working for the FBI and against the interest of the Nation of Islam. Once Khalid had been identified to him as the person who had sent those men to the mosque in Philly, Lucius began going over everything he had previously heard about Khalid. Whenever Khalid would leave the store, Lucius would search his office looking for anything that might indicate who his contact person was in Philly. Three days after Josh told him about Khalid, Lucius found a little phone book taped to the back of an old wooden desk inside Khalid's office. Inside the book was a list of names and phone numbers. The word "contact" was written under some of the names along with another list of phone numbers. Each of the second set of phone numbers had a different area code. When Lucius called the second set of numbers, he wasn't surprised to learn that in each city, the number being called was in the office of the Federal Bureau of Investigation.

Brother Lieutenant Lynton's X Thompson's name was on the last page of the book, along with his contact person's number. When Lucius called the number within the 215 area code, the call was answered by a man calling himself Agent Doss.

"The reason I'm calling," Lucius told Chris. "I've been tryin' to reach Josh all mornin'. He didn't go to FOI Class at the mosque on Susquehanna Avenue. Have you seen him?"

"Yeah, but I don't wanna mention where he is," Chris said. "I guess you haven't heard 'bout Ethan and Arnold being arrested, huh?"

"When?" Lucius asked.

"Last night after temple service." Chris said. "When leaving the mosque, four homicide detectives surrounded them. They had other cops hiding over by Elverson School in case the brothers tried to resist or som 'um."

Lucius had no need to ask why they had been arrested. He knew that might happen once Josh told him how they had left the man on the side of the road with three in the head.

"Did Josh give you a name?" Lucius asked.

"Yeah, he gave me two names," Chris said. "But he said you weren't sure about them."

"Well, I'm sure now," Lucius answered. "At least 'bout one of 'em. We gotta talk. I want you to come here. Try to fly out tonight and bring, uh, bring Brother Wade wit 'cha. He's trustworthy."

"You kno' tomorrow is the 4th, right?" Chris asked, referring to the Fourth of July.

"Yeah, tha's why I want y'all to get here tonight."

# CHAPTER XLV

During the late evening of July 4th, the sound of gunfire was clearly audible to the guests inside New York Frank's Oak Beach estate on Long Island. To the people enjoying the festivities in the huge yard of the walled estate and down on the beach, the gunfire was mistaken for the sporadic sounds of fireworks they had been hearing throughout the day and night.

A few days earlier, in Philly, Brother Kirk D. was at a meeting with his cousin Brother First Lieutenant Harvey, and the other downtown brothers Mo, Rus, Dalton and Brother Captain Cecil. Kirk D. was told to transport their guns up to New York on July 2nd by bus. He was to meet them at the hotel just outside La Guardia Airport on Long Island the night of July 3rd.

"It's just a precaution," Harv told Mo. "I kno' we agreed with Josh and Ethan tha' we wouldn't do anything until after Frank's party. But we don't have any control over wha' Butta and his punk-ass crew might try to do."

"I kno' all tha'," Mo said, slumping back in the chair and rubbing his walrus-shaped mustache. "But we did more than jus' agree with the brothers, we gave them our word. Plus we have to consider Frank. If we wanna continue doing business wit' him, we can't embarrass him. If we wait and do it right, we'll git rid of Butta and have his drug operation too."

"I'm jus' sayin' that I'd rather be caught wit' my shoes than without 'em," Harv said, turning again to his cousin. "So you make sure you're at tha' hotel on the 3rd."

Frank Mathews had flown some of his guests, including the downtown brothers, in on the morning of the 3rd. Every hustler on the East Coast knew that Harvey and Butta didn't get along, so Frank flew Butta and his crew in on the 2nd. He wanted to talk with Butta and get his assurance that he would control his men. When Frank spoke with Big Cil and Harvey the next day, he asked for the same assurance from them. "I kno' y'all feel tha' Butta might have been behind tha' Lester thing, but this is a celebration of our success." Frank told them. "So please, for all our sakes, let's jus' have a good time for a day or two."

One to pay close attention to details, Frank had spent a lot of money on this party. Every Fourth of July, he would have guests come out to the estate he had purchased from one of his Italian backers. He knew that he had paid a ridiculous price for the place, but it was his way of showing off. And every year it was something new. This year he challenged the interior design by converting the first floor into a night club, complete with intimate mood lighting, crystal wall art, and two connecting heart-shaped bars. Instead of booths, there were high-back plum-colored lounge chairs with long lavender curtains draped behind them. The second and third floors had private party rooms where caged female dancers, all of whom were of different nationalities, danced topless.

It was 10 pm when Harvey, Cil and Mo walked into the club-like atmosphere on the entrance floor. Like most of the other guests, they ignored Frank's security request that all guns were to be checked at the door. Rushard, Dalton and Kirk D. remained outside for a few minutes to mingle with the guests partying just inside the wall.

Sly and the Family Stone were performing on the first floor stage. The sound system pumped their "It's A Family Affair" throughout the three-story building. The crowd was thick. Young fashionable women in short glittering dresses sashayed back and forth across the floor. Men in open-collared silk shirts with gold chains around their necks danced right behind them. A tall, shapely white woman in a tight red dress and matching high heels slid over to where Mo stood with his light and dark grey glen plaid sport coat draped over his shoulder.

"C'mon honey, let's me and you show'em how it's done." She whispered.

He grinned and pulled the woman closer to 'im. As he moved her to a spot on the dance floor where he could better survey the area, he heard Frank's voice calling to him. He looked up to see Frank leaning over the upstairs banister. "Up here," he yelled. "You and the brothers c'mon up."

Frank's private room was huge. Across from the large bed where he sat with two other couples was a gold-colored cage with two topless female dancers in it. A long but low table was adorned with liquor, food, fruit and wine. He and his guests were dressed in silk pajamas and everyone but Frank had a drink in their hands.

I'm glad y'all made it," Frank said. "After I heard the news 'bout Brother Ethan and tha' other brother, I wasn't too sure you'd git here."

"Yeah, we heard about it right befor' we left Philly." Harv said, not really wanting to talk about it because it reminded him that he and Cecil shouldn't even be in New York at this time. He was a first lieutenant in the Nation of Islam and Cecil was a captain. And though he'd gotten Uriah's permission to meet with New York Frank, the Minister thought it was strictly a business meeting. He didn't know about the annual party.

"I got som' pretty good attorneys in Philly," Frank said. "I mean if y'all lookin."

"No, we got it covered," Mo said. "Some brothers will be meetin' wit' the lawyers first thing Monday morning."

"I arranged for your group to have the private room next to this one, if you like," Frank said getting up from the bed. "I have som' females who'll join y'all. The music is boss, the ladies are fine, and we got all night. In the morning we can sit down and discuss our plans for future business, but tonight we jus' party, party, party!"

Frank never mentioned Butta, but they knew he was there. As they had come up the steps, Cil noticed one of Butta's men going into a private room down the hall. So he figured it was Frank's intention to keep them apart from one another but close enough so he could watch both groups. And it worked for about an hour until one of Butta's men accidentally chased a half-naked woman into the private room where the brothers were enjoying the company of some women from Jersey.

"Whoa, wha'cha doin'? Rus asked, when the man ran into their room.

Butta's man looked around the room and recognized Big Cil and Harv immediately. He dashed back out of the room and Rus and Kirk D. followed him, bringing the woman with them.

"Yo, man," Rus yelled. "You got a half-naked woman out 'ere in the hallway."

"You ain't gotta worry 'bout tha', even if it was yo'r business," one of the men in Butta's room said as he stood up.

"Sit yo'r punk-ass down, you coat carryin' mothafuckah," Kirk D. told the man.

As Rus and Kirk turned to walk back toward their room, Mo and Cil, knowing how quickly the two younger brothers could become agitated and get into something, stepped out of their room to bring them back. But as they did, they heard someone in Butta's room yelling at Rus and Kirk. "You better get y'or phony Muslim asses' outta 'ere."

Frank also heard the insult and stepped out of his room to intercept Cil and Mo from proceeding into Butta's room, but it was too late. Stepping around Frank and into the room where Butta sat surrounded by six women and five of his crew, the brothers, Harvey now with them, surrounded the table.

"We're trying to enjoy Frank's hospitality, "Harv said to Butta, as he approached his table. "You're a man tha' can understand tha', right?"

"Yeah, I can understand that." Butta replied. He watched as Big Cil walked around the table and stood directly in front of Dennis and stared. With his arms folded in front of him, Cil said nothing, just gave an icy cold stare that caused Dennis to sweat and squirm nervously in his chair.

"We don't want no trouble," Butta continued. "Life's good and we're here to enjoy ourselves."

"Then enjoy it." Harv said, turning to walk away.

"Wha 'cha say," Dennis yelled, still nervous almost to the point of panic. His shirt now soaking wet with sweat.

"Best check yo'r boy," Cil told Butta, while pointing at Dennis. "He's 'bout to self-destruct."

"He's cool, Cecil," Butta said, waving his hand at Dennis in a gesture for him to calm down. But it was too late. The fuse had been lit.

"Who y'all talkin to. Don't nobody need to check me," Dennis yelled, now completely out of control. "I, I check my mothafuckin' self. We kno' wha' dis is about. Y'all think we don't kno'. We kno' y'all want our dope."

"You the only one runnin' his gibs," Rus said menacingly. "You ackin like you tryin' to put som' work in, or som'um."

"Don't say anything," Harv whispered to Rus.

As the brothers stood and stared in silence, Frank's men, seeing that the situation was beyond Frank's control, got him out of the room and down the stairs toward the back door.

None of the brothers said anything for a full minute or so and to Dennis it seemed like an eternity.

"Hey, look, Harvey," Butta said, finally breaking the silence. "Back up off my man. He ain't no punk. We ain't no punks, and y'all ain't no punks. Ain't gon' be nothin' done to us or by us. So let's jus' forget this shit."

"Fuckin' right" Dennis shouted, as he sprang to his feet while lifting up the bottom of his shirt and revealing the handle of the .45 automatic stuck in his waistband. "I ain't no punk and y'all don't scare me, man. Y'all don't scare me!"

It proved to be the wrong move. Both Rus and Cil pulled their guns and cut loose wit an onslaught of bullets hitting Dennis squarely in the chest. He never got his gun out of his pants. As he went down, two of the other men sitting at the table fired back but hit no one. They too went down in a hell of bullets, mostly coming from Kirk D.'s .357 magnum.

Before the shock of the first shots faded, all six women and one of the other men took off running. They brushed past Mo, who had taken up a position at the door. Butta was left at the table as an open target. Too large to move swiftly, he tried pulling his weapon from the back of his pants. He never got it out. Brother Harvey who'd been waiting years for this opportunity, stepped up, his adrenaline pumping, and fired two shots into Butta's chest. As he heaved as if trying to catch his breath, Harvey coolly fired another round into the wounded man's head. "Die mothafuckah," he said, as he stood watching Butta take his last breath.

Cil had caught the last of Butta's men trying to crawl out the room. Grabbing him by his shirt collar and standing him up against the wall, Cil said, menacingly, "I been lookin' fo' you maggot. You was in on tha' hit wit' Dennis."

"I wasn't in on no hit," the man said with a whimper, breaking away from Cil and running toward the door. He ran straight into Mo, who hit him with the gun barrel, knocking him down. Cil placed the man up again and asked him where his gun was. Shaking as he tried wrenching his arm out of Cil's powerful grip, he said. "I ain't got no gun."

"Well, you should've had one." Cil growled, as he shot the man point blank in the head.

Guns drawn, Mo and Kirk D. led the way down the stairs and out the front door. Those people who were still inside the house were cowering in the corners of the room. Some had scrambled beneath tables and others hid behind the two heart-shaped bars. Fear and panic was written on their faces as they silently watched the brothers leave.

Just outside the door, Kirk D. and Mo came face to face with a man in a crouched position, aiming his gun at Kirk and claiming to be a police officer. The man who had been one of Frank Matthew's guests was indeed a New York Police Officer.

"Drop your weapons," he yelled. "I'm a police officer, and ..."

The cop never finished his statement. Brother Dalton, who had already gone outside to pull both cars around to the gate, saw what was happening and fired twice, hitting the cop in his chest. But as the cop went down, he got off a single shot which struck Kirk in the heart. Kirk was dead before he hit the

- 180 -

ground. Cil ran over to where the cop lay and took the gun from his hand. He then pointed it at the cop's head, but didn't pull the trigger since he seemed to be already dead. So Cil tossed the gun and ran over to where the brothers were lifting Kirk's body up off the ground.

"We can't leave 'im here." Harvey yelled. "Get 'im to the car."

"He's dead, man," Rus said.

"Put him in the fuckin' car," Harv yelled again, as he opened the back door to one of the rented sedans.

# CHAPTER XLVI

It was a spectacular display of fireworks high in the night's sky. People watched the bright and brilliant colors cascading downward over Lake Michigan. Brothers Lucius, Chris, and Wade sat among them at the Naval Pier, on the north side of Chicago, watching the Fourth of July celebration and talking murder.

Chris was still having trouble believing all that he was hearing. He had met and talked with Brother Captain Khalid at the annual Nation of Islam Officers' meetings. To him, the man seemed genuinely devoted to the Messenger. After hearing the teachings of the Honorable Elijah Muhammad, Chris wondered, how could anyone turn around and try to dismantle his work.

Wade was also shocked but more so about the possibility of Brother Lieutenant Lynton being an informant. He never really liked Lynton, but that was personal. He didn't know Brother Captain Khalid well enough to form an opinion, but still it was disturbing to think that a black man could work wit white folks against the interest of black folks.

"If he's working for the Feds," Chris said, "then we have no choice. He's gotta go."

"Yeah, but that's the problem," Lucius said. "I only have information connecting Khalid to the Feds. Lynton might not be an informant. He might be someone being set up by Khalid."

Another explosion of colors caught their attention for a moment. They sat silently and watched. All somehow feeling a bit indifferent about the patriotism that so reminded them of the contemptible manner in which their ancestors had been treated by those being honored on that day.

A black woman and her little girl walked by with sparklers in their hands. Tough it was past midnight, little children were running around in their bright colored clothes, stopping only when there was another colorful blast of brilliant lights high in the sky.

Lucius was angry. Despite his instincts, and regardless of what he had found behind the desk in Khalid's office, he still couldn't be absolutely sure. He wanted to do something. He wanted to hurt the man, but if he was wrong he'd be damned for harming a Muslim.

"Can you be certain?" Wade asked, speaking more about Lynton than Khalid. "We see him almost every day at the mosque and nothing ever seems ..."

"Nothing 's carved in stone," Lucius said, knowing that if he didn't handle this correctly, he would become a maximum target for either having the truth and not acting on it, or mistaking what he had found and acting in error.

There was no question in his mind that someone had infiltrated the Nation of Islam and was causing a cancer to spread throughout. Not only were those soldiers who because of their love for Messenger Muhammad would sacrifice and even kill, being put at risk; at risk also were those who because of their love and belief in his teachings would not kill or even break the law.

"You kno'," Lucius said, looking at Chris and Wade again, "we usually try to give a brother the benefit of any doubt. We try to do that kinda' thing if we're in a position to. Usually on the assumption tha' the favor might somehow be returned someday."

"Yeah, tha's called a blessing," Chris replied. "But are we in a position to giv 'im that benefit of the doubt? Brothers' lives are at stake here. If we don't act … well, tha' could easily be Ethan and Arnold lying in the morgue."

"We watch both of 'em," Lucius said. "Y'all are in Philly with Lynton and I'm out here with Khalid. We make sure that no brothers are influenced by them, but we can't reveal this to anyone. When the time's right, y'all com' back 'ere and take care of Khalid. He has to go first because he seems to be at the top."

"How can we make sure they don't influence anyone if we can't reveal what we know?" Wade asked.

Well, right now, we only hav'ta worry 'bout Josh." Chris said. "Ethan, Arnold and Captain Terrence are busted. Mo and the brothers from downtown don't mess wit Lynton anyway. So we'll jus hav'ta keep Josh away from Lynton."

"You can tell Josh." Lucius said. "He's impulsive, but he's thorough. He'll keep our secret."

"Why do you want us to handle Khalid? Wouldn't it be easier for us to handle Lynton, if need be?" Chris asked.

"I can't get involved in tha' way. I'm too close to the Messenger now. I don't wanna bring nothing like tha' in his presence. It'll be bad enough tha' once it's done, I might have to lie to him if he asks me if I kno' anything 'bout Khalid or wha' happened to 'im."

"So, it's a go, right?" Wade asked.

"It's a go," Lucius replied to the man he had brought into the Nation of Islam. "We jus' hav'ta bide our time."

As the images of the American Flag and Statue of Liberty were flashed into the sky in the center of another thunderous explosion, people began to stand and applaud.

"Man, do you know tha' the Statue of Liberty first had a black face." Wade said absent mindedly, speaking to no one in particular. "It was designed as a black symbol of our freedom from slavery. But white folks wouldn't have it. They sent it back to France and told 'em to whiten her face."

"Who gon' see the lawyers for Ethan and Arnold?" Lucius asked.

"Me and Wade," Chris answered. "Josh can't show his face 'til we know wha' the cops know."

***

Harvey looked around the room they were in. Though he was disoriented, it was slowly coming back to him. The building they were in was a small abandoned church about ten miles off the beach. After forcing open the wooden back door, they had hid down in the church's basement. The night had passed slowly. Despite trying to stay awake, the stifling air had made Harvey groggy. He blinked at the darkness through heavy eyelids, woke with a jerk, and fought not to drowse again.

The next time he woke, he remembered hearing the groans, seeing blood splatter, and women fleeing in panic. The scene from Frank's house played over and over again in his head. He blinked at a movement on the floor and reached for his .357 magnum. It was a mouse watching him watch it. It twitched its whiskers and then ran off under a table in the corner.

Fully awake, Harvey looked around the room at the others sitting on the dust-covered floor. Everyone was there except Kirk D. and Dalton. He recalled that all of them had blood splattered on their clothes. They had decided that since Dalton had the least, he should be the one to go find a car so that they could try and escape the Island.

They had caught the local news on an old radio in the church. It was reported that three Philadelphia men had been shot dead at Frank Matthew's house party on Oak Beach. "Shot and seriously wounded," the report said "was an off-duty New York City police officer, 3 other Philadelphia men were also shot, but their injuries were not life threatening." The reporter gave the names of the dead and wounded and the only name the brothers weren't familiar with was the cop's.

"He's still alive, huh?" Cil said. "He might be able to identify us."

"We'll worry 'bout tha' if it happens." Harv said.

They still had Kirk D's body with them and had decided they would bury him in the woods before leaving.

"Where the fuck is Dalton," Cil asked, pacing back and forth across the squeaky floor.

"He'll be back soon," Mo yelled. "Stop tha' damn pacin', man, I can't stand tha' noise."

"Ten-to-nine," Rus answered. "I'm hungry as a mother jumper."

"Wha' the fuck is a mother jumper?" Mo said, sharing a temperate laugh with everyone.

Hearing a noise, Cil pulled his gun just as he turned to see Dalton coming in through the back door with an arm full of bags.

"Wha', you gon' shoot a brother?" Dalton joked. "After I don' found a way to save yo'r asses?"

"You gotta car?" Mo asked. "And wha's all tha'?"

"I got a car, plus got som' clothes so we can get out of 'ere. Shit, we can drive to the airport now. I got all you no dressin' jokahs som' pants and shirts. Jus' get the blood off yo'r shoes and we're in business."

"Wha 'cha mean, airport?" Rus asked. "The place probably crawlin' wit' the man."

Dalton gave Rus the dumb look, then said. "Yeah, looking for five or six men in bloody suits. We can't drive back to New York on the Long Island expressway 'cause the cops will be cruisin' all up and down there. I stole a car and drove to som' local stores to get this food and these clothes. No one even looked at me twice. I seen two cops in a Suffolk County police car, and they were sittin' there eatin' donuts."

"Wha 'cha say, Mo?" Cil smiled. "He's probably right. We can fly out like we flew in. The cops don't kno' we're from out of town."

"They will if Frank's people talk," Mo answered.

"Or if Butta's crew starts squawking," Rus added.

"I say we try LaGuardia," Cil said.

"I hav'ta bury my cousin first," Harv said, sadly.

"I bought a shovel," Dalton said.

***

Flight delays at O'Hara's Airport in Chicago, caused Wade and Chris to miss their Monday morning appointment with the lawyer. Arriving back in Philly at 3:30 that afternoon, it was 5 pm when they walked into the law offices of Roundtree, Banks and Clark.

Ruth Banks leaned back in her leather chair, her long tan legs crossed, wearing sheer stockings, a pale blue business suit over a pink blouse, and listened to Wade and Chris apologize for being late. The tall light-skinned woman looked more like she should be in movies than a court room. Her dark hair pulled back into a bun made her look even sexier.

They had chosen her because the law firm in which she was a partner had a good reputation and wasn't afraid to represent the Brothers in court. Most of the Italian and Jewish lawyers now shied away from the Brothers since the police and newspapers had stared referring to them as the Black Mafia. One Jewish attorney had told them, "You Brothers can't get a Judge to take any money from y'all. No politicians, not even the few black ones will work wit 'cha like they do with the Italians."

"Why did you choose me, Mr. Coleman?" Ms. Banks asked.

"We need a fighter, Ms. Banks," Wade answered. "You have a reputation for being just that. Plus, we hear that you have connections. Our Brothers will need all the help they can get."

We don't come cheap," she said. "And I won't be able to represent both men. Ms. Veda Clark will handle Mr. Boyden and I'll handle Mr. Siswell's case. That is if you want us and have the aforementioned $5,000 retainer for each man."

"We want you." Chris said. "The $10,000 will be in your office by noon tomorrow."

Ruth Banks smiled a smile that had both men shaking their heads as they left her office. "Damn, I could never go home to a woman who looked like that." Chris grinned. "I'd never wanna leave again."

# CHAPTER XLVII

Having gone straight from the airport to the law offices, Wade and Chris hadn't heard the news. It wasn't until they went to see Josh at the safe house that they learned what had happened at Frank's holiday party in New York.

"Shit, it's all over the news" Josh told them. "They keep sayin' it was som' men tryin' to crash Frank's party, but I kno' it was Harvey and Big Cil. They lied to us, man. Harvey gave us his word tha' they wouldn't move on Butta yet."

"Nobody's heard from them?" Wade asked. "Not even the minister?"

"He would be the last one they would contact," Chris said. "Jus' in case someone was listening. They wouldn't wanna involve him in som'um like tha'…"

Well at least they got tha' much sense," Josh said.

After they had calmed Josh down, and Chris had told him about the conversation he and Wade had with Lucius, all three men sat silent for a long time. It was as if they all had come to the conclusion that their world was falling apart. Then as suddenly as the dread had come upon them, it was gone.

"We gotta do som 'um 'bout the Negro in Chicago frontin' as a Muslim," Josh said.

"Yeah, but tha's a delicate matter," Wade told him. "We can't move on the little information we got. Khalid is a captain in the Nation of Islam. You can't even imagine wha' would happen if we're wrong about him."

"And Lucius wants us to wait," Chris added. "He's tryin' to find out if Lynton is involved."

"I'll never believe tha' 'bout Lynton," Josh said. "He may be an idiot sometimes, but he's no agent for the man."

"Wha' about you?" Chris asked. "You hear anything about who the cop's witness is on Ethan and Arnold?"

"Nothin'," Josh said. "But som 'um is strange 'bout all this. My name ain't com' up, and I'm the one who got outta the car and banged the dude. If a witness would've seen anybody, he would've seen me."

"Well, you jus' lay low," Chris told him. "At least 'til we can find out wha' all they got. The preliminary hearing should be in a few weeks, well kno' by then."

As Josh was trying to avoid the Philadelphia police, the New York City police were trying to learn the identity of the men who had shot up Frank Matthew's party, killing three and wounding four, including an off-duty New York City police officer.

After a few days of interviewing Frank Matthews and his crew, as well as Butta's remaining crew, the police learned absolutely nothing. It wasn't in Frank's interest to talk and Butta's men knew that they wouldn't be able to live in Philly if they talked. It was only after someone had mentioned that some of the men at the party could have been from New Jersey or Pennsylvania that the police got a break. A month later, after reviewing previous arrest photos of black men from both states and New York, the wounded New York City officer who'd been shot by Dalton, identified Cecil Sampson, known as "Big Cil" from Philadelphia, as one of the men he'd seen with a gun that day. It was September when the arrest warrant was issued, and Cil, learning of it from a Philly lawyer, went on the run.

***

"The punk probably saw my face when I went over to make sure he was dead," Cil said, as he packed his bags to leave town.

"Where you gon' be?" Harvey asked. "Jus' so we can get money to you."

"I'll be in Detroit," Cil said. "Tell Minister Uriah tha' I'm sorry I let 'im down."

"We both did," Harvey said. "I can't keep this position if I got the police looking over my shoulder."

"Yeah, but you should think about it first," Cil said. "The Minister needs strong men around him."

"He still has Josh and Chris," Harvey said. "And Lucius jus' might decide to come back to Philly to help out."

***

After hearing about what had happened in New York on July 4th, Lucius stayed away from Philly. He only communicated with Wade, Chris, and Minister Uriah who had tried to get him to come back to Philly as acting captain because Cil was on the run. He told Lucius that Brother First Lieutenant Harvey had also given up his position because he too might be subject to arrest. But Lucius had declined the offer – not only because he was needed on the Messenger's security staff, but also because he didn't want to deal with what was now going on between the brothers in Philadelphia. "They're at odds with one another," he told Minister Uriah, "I don't wanna be there when they self-destruct."

It was late winter when Lucius finally got the chance to speak with the Supreme Captain about Brother Khalid. What he learned surprised him. It had been the national secretary who had actually vouched for Khalid, through a thorough check of his background and revealed some questionable connections to the United Slaves Organization and their surreptitious activities within the California branch of the Black Panthers.

Lucius also learned that Khalid's name had come up when the two brothers from the Black Panthers were gunned down in Los Angeles. It was believed he had something to do with them being set up. However, soon afterward, Khalil was vouched for by the National Secretary of the Nation of Islam as someone who could help with the recruitment of professionals into the Nation.

"I had opposed it," the Supreme Captain said. "But the secretary carried more weight at the time than I did."

"Was it just the rumors about the Panther's death that made you oppose his coming into the Nation?" Lucius asked.

"No, it was the fact that he also had been rumored to have been an inside man of the Black United Front when they were raided in Cleveland. Two women and one man were killed by the police in that raid."

"Were there's smoke, there's fire, huh?" Lucius asked.

The Supreme Captain looked Lucius straight in his eyes and said, "Confront him and see what you get. The only reason I never have is because I wasn't prepared to eliminate him if I had gotten the wrong answers."

"I hear he's supposed to help with operations at Temple 66 in Jacksonville, Florida, next summer." Lucius said. "You heard anything about that?" he asked.

"Yeah. He's going down to assist the new ministers and the captain. They're opening a Steak 'n' Take restaurant down there as well."

"Could you keep me updated, sir?"

"You have my word on it." The captain said. "But be very careful. Remember, you're a part of the Messenger's security."

\*\*\*

During the next six months, Brother Terence's Motion for Release under the Double Jeopardy Clause was heard and taken under advisement by the State Supreme Court. He would have to wait another six months to find out whether he was going to trial or would be released.

Ethan and Arnold were being held for trial. The witness in their case had turned out to be a near-sighted old man, so now the prosecutor's office was now saying they had new evidence from a jail-house informant. According to Ethan and Arnold's attorneys, the state was now claiming that an informant had overhead a jailhouse conversation between Etna and Arnold admitting to the murder.

However personally disheartening these legal setbacks were to these brothers, they didn't allow it to extinguish their fire. In fact, the more pressure placed upon them, the more determined they became. As a result of the racial policies, past and present, the Philadelphia County Prisons were filled with black men. Brothers like Captain Terence and Lieutenants Ethan and Arnold became outstanding teachers of the religion while in prison. Out of 1200 plus black men in Holmesburg Prison, over 800 of them became followers of the Honorable Elijah Muhammad. The same thing happened in the other two county prisons and eventually inside the state penitentiaries, as well.

Black men who had gone to prison with no political thought whatsoever on their minds now returned to their communities to teach and preach Islam and Black Nationalism. They found that they were embraced by Philadelphia's black communities.

Over that same six-month period, Dalton and Rushard had spent their time muscling in on Butta's prior territories and recruiting some of his old workers. Under the direction and leadership of Mo, they were able to convince New York Frank that things would run smoothly and that there would be no retaliations over Butta's death. Being a business man and knowing that nothing would stop because Butta was dead, Frank had no objections to Mo running the operation in Philly.

To avoid any problems with the mosque, Dalton and Rus decided that a front man would be needed for the operation. Monster Dave was chosen as he was street-wise and already had plenty of his own customers buying his speed. But the main reason they wanted him was because he was easily controlled and too scared to cross them. It was during one of their negotiations with Monster Dave that they learned something about Brother Lieutenant Lynton.

"Yeah, he took me up the Pocono Mountains to cook som' speed for Dennis Jackson," Dave told them. "I was a little scared cause Dennis had kidnapped me about a year ago and made me cook for'im. He didn't pay me a dime. I even had to pay for the P2P myself."

"The P2P?" Dalton asked. "Wha' the fuck is tha'?"

"The oil. Phenol 2 Propynol," Dave replied. "It's …"

"I was jus' jokin', fool. I kno' wha' it is."

"Why did Lynton want you to do this?" Rus asked. "They ain't never been tight like tha', have they?"

"No, not tha' I kno' of," Dave said. "But Lynton said it was because Butta had did him this big favor."

"Wha' kinda favor?" Dalton asked.

"I don't kno'," Dave said. "But it was right after tha' brother, um, um, Brother Lester got shot. I didn't think no mor' 'bout it 'till I heard 'bout Butta and Dennis getting' blown up by dem dudes in New York." On their drive back to Mo's house, Rus asked Dalton, "You thinkin' wha' I'm thinkin'?"

"Yep." Dalton smiled. "This might be a way of smoothin' things over wit' the brothers. They got an attitude 'bout this thing in New York. But wait till they hear 'bout Lynton and Butta."

# CHAPTER XLVIII

Wade sat silently watching the shadows projected by his thoughts of the upcoming events play out on his living room wall. Though darkness had crept upon him, his thoughts were clear and unclouded. He could hear Frankie upstairs talking with their daughter, Rasheedah, as she put her to bed. Their voices distinct but distant. The words most audible in his mind came not from his wife and daughter, but from Brother Lucius.

"I did the follow up as protocol required," Lucius had said over the phone. "It's a go. You and Chris will fly out to Jacksonville in the morning. Chris has the instructions."

Even after speaking with Chris a few minutes ago, Wade's misgivings continued. And though Chris seemed as determined as Lucius, Wade thought he had heard those same misgivings in Chris' voice as well.

Controlling the pressure swelling in him, Wade got up and went to the hall closet. He removed the locked briefcase he kept there and then headed upstairs to his bedroom. Pushing the briefcase under the bed, he sat down and began staring at the nap of the carpet on the floor. The troubling thoughts continued, until suddenly the room was filled with music. He looked up to see Frankie standing in front of him, wearing a sheer white nightgown. She had a hair brush in her hand and was mouthing the words to a Linda Jones' song, "Hypnotized."

"There's a spell that you cast," she mumbled. "Please, please make it last ..."

A wide grin crossed Wade's face. He opened up his arms and she fell into them. The faint fragrance of her perfume filled his nostrils and voided his thoughts. His night was spent in her delight, not in his doubt.

While joining her husband for the Morning Prayer, Frankie asked him why he seemed so troubled. "If something's worrying you about this trip, then don't go," she whispered to him.

"I'm not troubled," he assured her. "Jus' hate leaving you alone for an entire week."

"We'll be fine," she smiled. "You just be careful.

Their guns wrapped in a box and shipped to Jacksonville, by Trail Way, Chris and Wade took an early flight that would stop over in Atlanta, Georgia. From there, they flew on to Florida and were walking in Hemming Park, a 1 and 1/2 acre plaza in downtown Jacksonville by that afternoon.

Lucius had told them that he would call when Khalid left Chicago for Jacksonville. That would give them time to look around after picking up their guns. Chris figured that they had at least a couple of days to work with. They rented two rooms at the Ambassador Hotel on West Church Street and then checked out the area around Muhammad's Temple 66, on Kings Road.

"When we get the call," Chris said, "We'll jus' watch the Temple. Khalid will hav'ta come here, then we can follow him all over Jacksonville and pick the best location to slump im."

"How's Christine," Wade asked.

"Upset," Chris answered. "She seems to sense tha' som'um is wrong."

"Tha's why I asked," Wade replied. "Our wives are a lot closer to us than we think."

"I'm leaving Philly," Chris said. "After this, I'm out of here. I'm putting too much pressure on my family and we're not doing the things we su'pose to be doing anymore."

"I get the same feelings." Wade said. "But I just can't pick up and leave. I jus' bought a house."

"So did I," Chris said. "But Sister Brenda is a realtor and she'll take over the mortgages and give us a lump sum payment."

"You fo' real?" Wade asked. "Sister Brenda 5X?"

"Yep."

The call from Lucius came on Monday. By Tuesday night they had sighted Brother Khalid when he came out of Temple 66 and followed him back to the same hotel they were staying at. The next morning, Wade followed Khalid to breakfast and stayed with him until Chris picked up the surveillance in the park that afternoon. They figured Khalid would go to the Temple for Wednesday night services, and they were right.

Sitting outside the Temple that evening, they went over the places Khalid had been during that day. They discovered that both of them had followed him to the post office and to Hemming Park, which was only a couple of blocks away from the post office.

The next day they followed him together. He didn't go to the Temple, but he did meet with an old white man in a dark blue suit and yellowing white shirt for over an hour in the middle of Hemming Park. Chris followed the white man when he left the park, and Wade stayed with Khalid. Again, that night, they went over the day's details.

"You ain't gon' believe this," Chris grinned. "The man in the park is an FBI agent."

"How you kno' tha?"

"I followed him to the post office and guess wha'? The FBI has an office on the top floor. The man walked right inside like he belonged there. I waited outside until he came out again, and he was with two other white men I had watched go in and out of there. They all went in that little restaurant on Julia Street. He's an agent alright."

"We'll call Lucius in the morning." Wade said.

They both knew where this would lead. There was no doubt in their minds now. Their next move would be to kill Khalid and make it look like a robbery. All day Friday, Khalid had spent with the brothers from Temple 66. They drove over to where the Steak 'n' Take Restaurant would be opening and then back to the Temple. Later that night, after Temple services, Khalid drove back downtown in his rented car. He stopped by a topless bar and emerged about an hour and a half later with a tall, shapely, black woman in a bright orange dress. After stopping at a few bars, they drove out to the suburbs near

Edgewood and parked in a wooded area behind the Edgewood Apartment complex.

It was just after 2 am, the air was cool and clean from the early morning smells wafting down from the trees. The overhead lights from the apartment complex cast broken shadows across Khalid's car and patches of grass, which revealed many tire tracks. At first Wade and Chris thought Khalid had driven the woman home, but they could see from the amount of tire tracks in the grassy area that the place was probably a make-out spot.

They looked around and saw no other cars parked in the area. After about twenty minutes, they saw the door on the passenger's side open and the woman got out and headed for the bushes.

"She's goin' in those bushes to pee," Chris said, as he eased his car door open. "Grab her and make sure she thinks we're trying to rob and rape her. But don't let her see yo'r face and don't let her get back to tha' car."

Watching as Chris ran up to Khalid's rental and swung open the door on the driver's side, Wade then snuck up behind the woman and caught her just as she was about to stand up.

"Don't move," he said in a menacing tone. "Lay y'or ass down on y'or stomach, and git naked."

When the woman tried to protest, Wade put his foot in her back and pressed her down into the ground. He rubbed the gun barrel alongside her cheek and told her if she tried to get up or look around she would die. The woman was scared out of her wits. She was a prostitute and had experienced a lot, but never anything like this. She began whimpering as she slowly started removing her clothes.

The fear in Khalid's eyes was real and palpable as he saw Chris' dark face staring at him from behind the .45 automatic with a silencer attached to it. He knew that he must have been followed from Chicago and that meant they had come to kill him. I have to keep talking, he thought. I have to try and control this situation until I can get my gun from under the seat.

"What's going on?" Khalid asked Chris. "Why are you ...?"

"Just tell me who yo'r contact person is at Temple 12 and save yo'r miserable ass life, Chris said through gritted teeth. "I don't have time to ask again. If you wanna live, give me his name."

"Contact person? Please. I don't know wha' you're talking about," Khalid said, trying to inch his way toward his .38.

"You kno' exactly wha' I'm talkin' about," Chris said.

"Are you saying that I'm a snitch?" Khalid asked, trying to keep the conversation going. He knew Chris wanted a name and that he might not shoot until he got one.

"No, you're no snitch," Chris said, gritting his teeth. "You're worse than a snitch. There's a big difference between wha' you do and wha' a snitch does. You're a Judas. Now tell me the fuckin' name!"

Both Khalid and Chris could hear the woman's pleas coming from the wood area.

"Please don't hurt me," she was crying. "I'll do what you say, jus' don't hurt me." She was now completely naked with her face pressed down in the dirt. But Wade was trying to see what was going on at the car. He could see Chris' back silhouetted against the light coming from the inside of the car, but couldn't see Khalid at all.

"Spread yo'r legs and don't move, bitch," he said. "I'ma take off my pants so I don't git no dirt on 'em."

But instead, Wade backed away from her. Moving closer to where Chris and Khalid were, he could hear Chris' yelling to Khalid not to move. Wade ran up to the car just as Khalid was trying to reach under the seat for his gun.

"He's got a gun!" Wade yelled. Chris was already firing. Without hesitating, Wade reached around Chris and pumped two from his .38 automatic with its attached silencer.

Khalid's eyes registered shock, then pain, as his body did a brief dance across the front seat of the car before slumping over dead in a pool of his own blood. Neither man said a word. As Chris reached into the car and took Khalid's gun, watch and money, Wade ran back to where the woman lay trembling and crying on the ground. He looked down at her and spoke, as if speaking to his accomplice. "Dam! Too late to fuck her now. That punk should've gave up the cash. Well, jus' grab her money and jewelry and let's git the fuck outta 'ere."

Later that morning, they threw the guns and the clothes they had worn into different sewers and flew out of Jacksonville to New York. They went to Penn Station and took a train back into Philadelphia.

# CHAPTER XLIX

Two days later, when Lynton got a call from Agent Doss, he knew that it must be important because Doss had previously told him his contact would only be with Khalid.

"Khalid is dead." Does said, without hesitating. "So we must assume you may be compromised. Have you heard anything?"

"Nah, I, uh, I haven't seen or heard anything out of the ordinary." Lynton said, trying to wrap his mind around what Doss was saying. "Look, uh, wha' happened? Where was he at? I had heard he was supposed to be in Florida helping with ..."

"He was in Florida," Doss said. "I don't know, it might have been a robbery and an attempted rape on some woman he was with, but regardless, we can't take any chances."

"Look, get back to me on this," Lynton said. "Nobody up here did it. I'm pretty sure of that. Unless, well, ... unless Lucius left Chicago and ..."

"He didn't leave." Doss said. "As a matter of fact, we have him on tape at two of the supreme captain's appearances at two different universities on Friday and Saturday."

"I'll see wha' I can find out," Lynton said. "Call me tomorrow."

"Yeah, and when I call you, I'll have some information on something I'll need you to handle for me, Doss said. "We got to rid ourselves of someone who is no longer useful. Since I don't have Khalid anymore, I'll need you to arrange it."

"Who you talkin' 'bout?" Lynton asked. "Wha' city?"

"You know him," Doss said. "His name is Jacob Lawrence."

"You serious?" Lynton asked. "Isn't he the witness used in tha' recent federal drug case here in Philly?"

"Yeah," Doss said. "This has to happen now. He's been talking to the wrong people about how that was arranged."

"Yeah, but, I've used him to sell som' stuff ... and ..."

"No buts." Doss ordered. "Use some of your people and make it happen. Use Josh, the brothers will follow him into hell and back. Tell him that Lawrence is the jailhouse snitch the D.A. is planning to use against Siswell and Boyden in that murder case."

"Perhaps I can get Jacob to meet me on the roof of that old hotel we use to exchange packages in," he suggested to Doss. "I'll tell 'im I got som' dope I want 'im to sell."

"I don't care how you do it," Doss said, pausing for a moment before hanging up, and adding, "I shouldn't have to call you tomorrow. Just get it done. Think of it as a way of showing me that you're still useful."

As soon as his talk with Doss was over, Lynton called Josh to set up the hit. "As-Salaam-Alaikum, he said. "I need to see you right away. Som' body's been spreadin' som' vicious rumors 'bout me, man. And I..."

"Yeah, I heard them," Josh interrupted, still believing Lynton was thorough. "But don't worry, we gon' speak to the Minister and get this stuff straightened out."

"Cool," Lynton said. "But I'm also callin' 'bout that jailhouse snitch in Ethan's and Arnold's case. Som'body said you was trying to find out where he's at."

"Yeah, you kno 'im?" Josh asked.

"Yeah, he's a junky from down 13th and Dauphin Street," Lynton said. "He used to sling for me. If I put the word out tha' I got som' bundles for 'im to sell, he'll meet me."

"When?" Josh asked, excitedly.

"Will you be at the meeting the Minister called?" Lynton asked. "It's tonight at Brother Lamont's house."

"Yeah, I'll be there." Josh replied.

"Okay, we'll talk then."

***

They sat crowded around the dining room table in Brother Lamont's house, a three-story row house just off of 13th and Olney Avenue. Summoned to the meeting by Minister Uriah were the South and West Philly brothers: Mo, Rus, Dalton, Harvey, and Lynton. The brothers from North Philly were Josh, Anthony, Chris, Wade, and Theron. Brother Lamont sat beside Minister Uriah, who was at the head of the table, drinking from a tall glass filled to the brim with Shabazz juice and ice cubes.

There was little in the way of small talk. Everyone waited for Minister Uriah to open the conversation. But the Minister took his time. He called Harvey into the other room and asked him about Brother Cecil.

"Is our brother alright," he asked, with a solemn look on his face. "If there's anything he needs, tell'im to get word to me. You kno we got a pretty good Muslim lawyer out of Ohio that we can send for."

Not waiting for Harvey's reply, the Minister led the way back into the dining room, took his seat, and immediately began speaking to the brothers.

"It has come to my attention that some of you brothers may be having problems with one another," he said. "Let's all be perfectly clear about one thing. We're all Muslims and we don't get caught up in no territorial conflicts and we don't deal drugs. We're followers of the Honorable Elijah Muhammad and that's all. Our focus should always be on the growth of our religion under the leadership of our dear Holy Apostle. Now, regardless of what might've gone on in the past, for the purpose of that growth and regardless of who may have looked the other way and allowed it to go on, it all stops now."

Wade watched and listened as the Minister spoke to some of the most dangerous men in Philadelphia in a tone that most people wouldn't dare use with them. The brothers looked the Minister directly into his eyes, as he spoke and nodded their heads in agreement. They considered themselves soldiers and they loved and respected this man, who, though in his fifties, still exemplified the strength and courage of a defiant black man.  And more importantly, they loved and respected who he represented.  He was not only the man who had allowed them the freedom to act as they had, but also he was the man Elijah Muhammad had placed in authority over them.

Minister Uriah went on to say that he had been appalled to hear what had happened to Brother Lamont.  "A Muslim being shot down and almost killed by another Muslim.  Well, now our Brother Lamont has rejoined us in the temple and will be the Assistant Minister at the Susquehanna Avenue mosque."

The meeting had started at 7 pm and didn't end until around 10 pm.  The Minister's words were meant to step on the toes of each man in the room, and they had.  Theron, who had been with Brother Mitchell when he shot Brother Lamont, felt a twinge of guilt for not being able to stop the shooting.  And it was no surprise to anyone that Brother Mitchell's death was never mentioned.

Despite the Minister's appeal, his words about the Muslims and the drug trade had little effect on Dalton, Rus, and Mo.  On their way to the meeting, Dalton and Rus had dropped off a cellophane-sealed two-kilo bag of heroin with Monster Dave.  There was another cellophane-sealed kilo bag in Mo's Cadillac that he intended to drop off when the meeting was over.

Brother Lynton never really heard what the Minister was saying.  His mind was preoccupied with thoughts of the Jacob Lawrence hit he'd just got Josh to agree on.  While pretending there was something he needed to write down, Lynton borrowed Josh's ink-pen but never used it.  He took hold of the pen by its top and held it for a moment before slipping it into his coat pocket.  Josh, who was listening intensely to what the Minister was saying, never even noticed.

When the meeting ended, Harvey again spoke with Minister Uriah in the other room.  And though he mentioned no names, he promised Minister Uriah that he would do all that he could to get the brothers out of the drug game.  The Minister thanked him then left in his car with Brother Anthony driving.  Theron followed them in Anthony's car.

"After making sure the Minister is home safely," Josh told them, "I want y'all to meet me and Lynton at my house."

Outside of Brother Lamont's house, Wade caught Rus, Mo and Dalton just as they were about to get into their cars to leave.  "I got something in my car you need to see," he said, pulling Mo aside.  Reaching inside his car, he pulled out a copy of a Today Magazine, which was scheduled to appear as an insert in the upcoming Sunday edition of the Philadelphia Inquirer newspaper.

"I think you should see this," he told Mo.  "I got hold of it last night."

Mo's eyes widened when he saw what was on the cover of the magazine.  It was an array of photos, his picture dead in the center, surrounded by shots of other brothers, including Big Cil, Rus, Dalton and Harvey.  The caption on the magazine read: "Philadelphia Black Mafia."

"Where the fuck did you get this?" Mo asked, passing the copy on to Harvey.  "The date says it's for Sunday.  That means it ain't been printed yet."

"Oh, it's been printed." Wade told him. "I got a man who works at the Inquirer. He called me last night and told me about this magazine. They printed it Wednesday to appear as an insert in Sunday's edition of the Inquirer."

"Did you show this to the Minister?" Harvey asked.

"I haven't shown it to anyone but Chris," Wade told him. "The article is a bunch of crap about Muslims who they refer to as the Muslim mob, but our pictures aren't in there, only y'alls."

"Them devils never quit, do they?" Dalton smirked.

"Yeah, but it's best to take this seriously," Chris said.

"Well we got some news for y'all, too." Rus said, as he walked between Chris and Wade and grabbed both of their arms, pulling them closer to him. "According to Monster Dave, Lynton set Lester up for tha' hit. Dave said Lynton did som'um for Butta and Butta okayed the hit. I didn't wanna say anything at the meeting, but since he's already gon', and the Minister is gon' … well, y'all can do with it wha'cha like."

Brother Chris nor Wade responded to this revelation. They had already suspected that a Muslim was somehow involved. And in light of the information Lucius had come up with, hearing that Lynton might be that Muslim was no surprise to them.

"Wanna call Lucius now?" Wade asked. "It's only 9 o'clock in Chicago."

"Yeah, I'll call 'im." Chris said. "This 'ere shit is disgustin'. I wish Rus would've said som'um before Josh left with the sukkah."

"Yeah, I kno," Wade responded as they walked to their cars. "Josh still thinks Lynton's legit."

# CHAPTER L

On the southeast and northeast corners of Broad and Dauphin Streets stood apartment buildings directly across from one another. The building on the southeast corner was where white people lived. The other housed blacks. Both buildings were five stories high, and though both were owned by the same people, there were noticeable differences. The one where whites lived was always clean and well kept. The outer door stayed locked and to gain entry one had to be buzzed in. However, it was easy to get in the building where blacks lived. Buzzers didn't work, and most of the locks were broken. This was the apartment building Lynton had told Jacob Lawrence to meet him at around 1 am to pick up the drugs.

"I'll advance you 50 bundles at $75 a piece," Lynton told Lawrence. "That means you'll make $50 on each bundle. If the money comes back right, I'll advance a 100 bundle the next time at $65."

"Com' by yourself," Lynton told him. "I don't trust too many people these days."

"Solid," Lawrence said. "Jus' me, myself and I."

Once Anthony and Theron were told that Jacob Lawrence was the jailhouse informant scheduled to testify against Brothers Ethan and Arnold, they wanted to go with Josh and Lynton. It was decided that they would take two separate cars and Anthony and Theron would remain inside the cars so they could watch both sides of the apartment building.

As Lynton and Theron pulled up on the Broad Street side of the building on the northeast corner, Anthony and Josh parked on a narrow driveway behind the building called Watts Street.

Lynton had told Josh that he could enter the building by taking the back steps that led into a fire escape.

"The fire escape steps are inside the building," Lynton said. "And the door to the fire escape is never locked. Go up to the fourth floor and wait inside there. I'll jam'im and bring 'im to you. If he sees me comin' I'll chase 'im to you and you hold 'im 'til I get there."

Josh, leaving Anthony in the car to watch the rear of the building, followed those instructions. He slipped into the fire escape door and into darkness. Passing several lidless trash cans and a few rats that didn't bother to scurry out his way, he took the steps two by two, until he'd made his way to the fourth floor. He briefly stepped out the door and onto the ledge to survey the area. Other than seeing the car, Anthony was in, he saw no other cars parked on watts Street.

Theron watched from the car, parked out front, while Lynton entered the building through the unlocked front door. As he crept past an open door of a first floor apartment, he saw two middle-aged women in housecoats and slippers, popping their fingers and dancing to Sam and Dave's "Soul Man." There was an aroma of fried chicken and alcohol in the air, and he could hear females laughing and men arguing as he continued up the shadowy staircase.

Lynton headed straight to the roof where he and Lawrence had agreed to meet. Jacob Lawrence, his coat pulled tightly around him to block out the cold morning air, was already up there. He heard the sound of little stones crackling under Lynton's feet as he stepped out of the door and onto the roof.

"Right on time, man," he said, turning to greet Lynton. "I hear tha' shit you got is outta sight, brother man."

"You're right 'bout tha'," Lynton replied, "My shit's off the hook."

"I'ma test it myself," Lawrence said.

"You remember the terms, right?" Lynton asked, glancing around the roof as he approached Lawrence.

"Yeah. 50 bundles for $75, then 100 for $65," Lawrence grinned. "The money gon' be right, brother. You ain't gotta worry 'bout no shorts 'cause I ain't takin' none."

Pulling a brown paper bag from inside his overcoat, Lynton moved over closer to the edge of the roof. He sat the bag on the ledge and motioned for Lawrence to move closer. When he did, Lynton pulled a .45 automatic from the bag and fired point blank into Lawrence's face. As his blood splattered, Lawrence's scream was cut short when Lynton fire another shot into his forehead. Lawrence stumbled backward and over the edge of the roof on the rear side of the building. Lynton dropped the ink-pen he had borrowed from Josh on the little blood stained stones and then headed for the fire escape.

Josh heard the scream and looked out the fire escape door just as Lawrence's body fell past the ledge. He watched the dead man's body splatter on Watts Street in front of his car. Then he turned, gun in hand, as he heard footsteps approaching from the other direction. It was Lynton, all out of breath and yelling to him. "He came at me. I had to shoot, man. Let's get the fuck out of 'ere." Both cars pulled alongside the fire escape exit and then sped away as soon as the car doors closed.

*** 

It was a little past 5 am. A uniformed officer waved FBI Agents Doss and Smith into a parking spot at the curb. Turning off the light on the roof of their car, they got out and walked over to where Homicide Detectives O'Connor and Jones were sitting in their unmarked Plymouth parked partially on the sidewalk on Dauphin Street, facing toward Broad.

I somehow expected we'd see you here," Detective Jones said to Doss.

"Better be careful you don't get a ticket for parking the wrong way on a one-way street," Doss said with a smirk.

Though Jacob Lawrence's body had been removed around 3 am, the crime unit was still there going over the scene. Yellow crime-scene tape had been stretched across Watts Street to block any traffic, and there was a wooden barrier in front of a chalked outline where the body had landed. Blood and other human matter could be seen inside the outline.

Two cops stood on each corner in front of the taped-off barrier to hold back onlookers who were trying to edge their way closer to the street.

"It's a mess," O'Connor remarked as he got out of the car and walked over to the barrier. "We have to wait for the sun to come up so we can make sure we got everything."

Stepping around three women with rollers in their hair, and clad in housecoats, Doss whispered to O'Connor. "You know we got two witnesses to this murder."

"O'Connor reached in his pocket and pulled out a pack of Pall Mall cigarettes. Shaking one from the pack, he curled his lips around it and held it there. He glanced back at his partner who was standing outside the Plymouth talking with Agent Smith.

"How is that?" he asked, almost afraid of hearing the answer. "You know the victim?"

"He's one of ours," Doss answered. "He was due to go in front of a judge next month to answer questions about some possible illegal activities of a few agents."

"Inside the bureau?" O'Connor asked. "Had he mentioned any names?"

"Sadly, no." Doss said. "For his own protection, we had been ordered to keep a tail on him. But every once and awhile, he would slip it to go buy drugs. Our people had just caught up to his car, when this went down."

"What, someone saw this happen?" Jones asked, having walked up behind Doss and O'Connor, hearing part of their conversation.

"No, they didn't see it happen." Doss smirked. "But they saw three men drive off in two separate cars."

"Any idea who they are?" O'Connor asked.

"We got a tentative I.D. on one," Doss said. "His name is Joshua Clarkson. Just so happens we been investigating him for some other crimes. We don't know how he's connected to the victim, but suspect it's drug related."

"But no identifications on the other two?" Jones asked, looking at Agent Smith and wondering why he had nothing to say.

"Not yet," Doss answered. "Joshua is a Moslem, so they're probably Moslems too. As soon as we can identify them, we'll give you their names. After all, this is still your case."

"Don't want the embarrassment, huh?" Jones remarked, as he strolled over to speak to a crime-lab technician who was gathering human matter off the ground, now that the sun was up.

"I don't like him," Doss said to O'Connor and Smith.

"I believe it's mutual," Smith laughed.

"Are these witnesses reliable?" O'Connor asked. "I mean, I remember the old man you spoke with in that other case. He turned out to be damn near blind. If we hadn't got a break with those jailhouse witnesses, we'd be up shit's creek."

"Look, O'Connor," Doss said, pulling O'Connor by his arm and away from the other detectives. "You've been aware of our investigations and what we've been trying to do for as far back as when Napoli was alive. We're not the bad guys here."

"Yeah, I know," O'Connor said. "But I just don't wanna wind up the subject of any investigations myself. I got a pension I'm depending on. We understand each other?"

"You're safe," Doss said. "Just pick up Joshua Clarkson and hold him for first degree murder. We'll pull the photos of every Moslem in Philadelphia and before the day is over, you'll have those other names."

"And this is our case?" O'Connor asked.

"I want no credit," Doss smiled, while looking in Jones' direction. "It's your case to share or not to share, makes me no never mind."

# CHAPTER LI

Special Agent Alfred Doss had been right. Before the day was over, Stacy O'Connor had the names of both lookout men in Jacob Lawrence's homicide. Doss had sent two young FBI Agents to O'Connor's office with pictures of Anthony Black and Theron Moore.

Based on the previous conversation with Agent Doss, about Joshua Clarkson, Detective Al Jones had already assembled a team of detectives and uniform police and was meeting at that very moment about how to arrest Joshua Clarkson. A detective had found an ink-pen with blood on it, lying on the roof at the exact spot where it appeared Lawrence went over. The pen was now being dusted and the blood analyzed.

The agents now sitting in O'Connor's office were telling him that they had been on assignment when they saw these two men, Anthony Black and Theron Moore, sitting in separate cars, parked outside the apartment building on Dauphin Street about 1:30 a.m.. While observing them, they said they heard gun shots and then saw Joshua Clarkson exit the building from the fire escape steps.

"He ran to the last car first," said one of the agents. "He threw what looked like a gun into it and then ran to the first car and got in the front seat passenger's side."

The other agent told O'Connor that both cars pulled off and headed east on Dauphin. "However the lead car, the one Joshua Clarkson was in, turned south on Park Avenue. It was too dark to get the license plate numbers, but the lead car was a dark Lincoln Continental, and the second looked like a Mercury Cougar, black. "… But as you know, sir, we can't testify to this because we're still undercover and were not supposed to be there."

Both young FBI Agents were only following the orders they had received from Doss. They had been told that an informant had been on the scene and that his name could not be revealed.

"In order to make sure this murder is solved," Doss told the two agents, "we have to provide the names of the suspects to the homicide detectives."

O'Connor had no reason to doubt what he was hearing from the agents, but still he was skeptical. Detective Al Jones had earlier interviewed the two women who lived on the first floor of the apartment building, and they placed another man inside the building at about 1 am. According to these women, they saw a chubby dark-skinned man walking by their apartment door and heading up the steps. Neither of the pictures that the agents had shown to O'Connor fit his description. One of the women said she got a pretty good look at the man when he turned to look at her. She told Detective Jones that she believed she would recognize him if she saw him again.

Both agents, feeling satisfied O'Connor had bought their story, were surprised when O'Connor asked them if they were sure they hadn't seen a fourth man at the scene. Startled, they hesitated for a moment before shaking their heads and answering, "Yeah, we're sure."

"If there were two cars," O'Connor mumbled to himself, after the agents left his office, "there could've been a fourth man."

Studying the two pictures in his hand, O'Connor yelled for an officer. "Pull the files on both these men," he said. "I need to see any photos we have of them, and any addresses and names of people they may be associated with."

***

When the two agents reported back to Agent Doss and told him what O'Connor had asked them, he became concerned. Doss wondered why O'Connor would have asked about a fourth man. Had he found an actual witness to this murder?

Without hesitating, Doss dialed Lynton's number. He got no answer and tried again. "I need to know everything that happened at that building," he mumbled, as he hung up the phone.

"What was that?" Agent Smith joked, as he walked into the office with some papers in his hand. "You talking to yourself again, huh? I thought we had gotten you help with that."

"I got a problem," Doss said. "I may need you to cover for me for a couple of days."

"Anything serious?" Smith asked. "The family alright?"

"No, I mean, yeah, the family is fine. I just may need to handle a former subject."

"What do you mean by handle?" Smith asked, his bushy eyebrows rising up over his horn-rimmed glasses, as they did when his suspicions were raised. He knew that Doss often used the word "subject" when referring to federal infiltrators and informants who worked for them. A former subject meant that someone had become a matter in dispute.

"You know I'll cover for you," Smith said. "And if you need my help, I'm here. Just let me know."

Doss knew that Agent Marvin Smith wouldn't push him for answers. They had been friends for over twenty years and had kept each other's secrets without questioning what they meant.

"I'll let you know," Doss said. "I may have to leave the city for a few days. When I get back, I'll call you."

"Well, at least let me give you a bit of good news first," Smith grinned. "That's why I came in this den of iniquity in the first place."

"What, you finally found a woman that'll give you sex?"

"Nope, still looking," Smith shot back. "But we've gotten an indictment against Maurice Barton, Rushard Braxton and Dalton Landers."

"When? This morning?" Doss asked, leaping to his feet and grabbing the indictments out of Smith's hand. "I checked with the Assistant U.S. Attorney yesterday, he said nothing had come down from the grand jury yet."

"It came down late yesterday afternoon," Smith said. "We got 'em on conspiracy to possess heroin with intent to distribute."

- 203 -

"Yeah, it also says we got 'em on substantive counts of using a telephone to facilitate the unlawful distribution of heroin," Doss said, reading aloud. "Based on Agent Marvin Smith's application that there was probable cause for an electronic wire intercept, subjects Maurice Barton, Rushard Braxton, Dalton Landers and other unknown individuals who were involved in trafficking heroin in the City of ... How about Cecil Sampson and Harvey Rollins? Are they the other unknown individuals?"

"We don't have them on electronic intercept," Smith said. "Cecil Sampson is now being sought in New York State for possible involvement in that police shooting and multiple homicide on Long Island. Right now, we've nothing on Rollins."

"If Sampson was involved, they all were."

"I know."

"I see you back dated the Affidavit." Doss said.

"Yeah, I had to," Smith answered. "That's the only way the federal judge would have allowed us to present this to the Assistant U.S. Attorney's office."

"Well, I won't tell if you don't." Doss laughed. It was the first good feeling he'd had in a week. Now to handle that damn Lynton, he thought as he handed the papers back to Smith.

Before leaving his office, Doss tried Lynton's number again. This time he got an answer.

"Yeah," he heard Lynton say.

"We need to talk." Doss said. "Meet me at the cabin."

Lynton knew that the cabin meant the Pocono Mountains. He wondered what could be so important that they had to leave town, especially just after he'd gotten rid of Jacob Lawrence for Doss.

"Can it wait a day or two?" Lynton asked. "I've got an abscess on a tooth I need pulled. I really would like to take care of it before I travel anywhere."

"Handle it today," Doss said. "I'll call you again this evening."

\*\*\*

Police cars blocked the 4500 block of North Bouvier Street at both corners. Three homicide detectives, wearing vests and carrying shotguns stood in the alley behind the house where Joshua and his wife and children lived. Detectives O'Connor and Jones were paused at the front door, guns drawn, wearing vests and breathing heavily. O'Connor nodded to Jones who hit the door with the butt of his gun.

"Police officers" they yelled, then kicked the door open. Jones went low, rolling on the floor, while O'Connor, gun raised out in front of him, stayed high. Four cops, their guns also drawn, ran by the detectives into the dining room, knocking over furniture, looking in closets and then going throughout the entire first floor and basement. O'Connor and Jones, taking the steps two by two, went to the second floor and found no one there. The house was completely empty.

Josh's neighbors gathered out in front of his house and began asking questions about what was going on. Another neighbor was on the phone calling over to where she knew Josh's wife, Sister Deborah, was. Since Brother Ethan's arrest, Sister Deborah and her children had been staying with Ethan's wife at her house.

Sister Geraldine answered the phone and gave it to Deborah who was told what was going on at her house. Deborah then placed a call to Josh who was at one of the safe houses.

"What's going on, Josh," she asked, her voice revealing her panic. "They say the whole block is filled with police, looking for you."

"I'll explain when I see you." Josh said, not knowing what he was going to tell her but just trying to calm her down. "I hav'ta see the Minister, then I'll call and tell you where to meet me."

Embarrassed that his open display of police power had failed, Detective O'Connor told his men to squeeze the street informants they knew. He told them to sit outside of every mosque in the city to see if those brothers showed up. And to go around to the black bars and speakeasies and show the photos of all three men to every hustler, prostitute and drug addict they knew.

"Talk to anybody who needs a favor from the police," he told them. "I want these killers off the street."

# CHAPTER LII

Lucius didn't particularly like the position he found himself in but he was determined to see it through. It was Saturday afternoon and he had met with Minister Uriah earlier that morning at the Brass Rail Restaurant, just outside of the Philadelphia International Airport.

Over breakfast they talked about Brother Lieutenant Lynton and former Captain Khalid. The conversation wasn't one Lucius thought he should be having with a minister as well respected in the Nation of Islam as Minister Uriah was. But, he knew it was necessary if a war between the brothers was to be diverted.

"There's been a protective shield around Brother Lynton for a long time," Lucius told the Minister. "And you hav'ta be the one who removes that shield, sir. He and Khalid have divided the brotherhood here in Philly, and you have to speak out before more good brothers are busted or killed."

"But if he and Khalid were together in this, and Khalid is no longer a treat, why is it necessary for me to say anything?" Uriah asked. "What's going to happen to him will happen regardless, won't it.?"

"Appearances, Brother Minister." Lucius said. "With all due respect, your hands haven't been exactly clean in all this. For the longest time now, Lynton has been able to use your name for protection. Without you in his corner, he would have never survived to rise through the ranks. He would have had no influence. If he leaves this planet, and he will leave very soon, your image will be muddled if it seems like you were completely fooled by him and still supported him."

"I'll take the podium tomorrow." Minister Uriah said.

That conversation had taken place over an hour ago. Lucius had since left the Minister and drove to North Philly to meet with Josh at the safe-house Chris and Wade had hid him in.

Sitting in the living room of a row house on Park Avenue and Lehigh, Lucius could see that Josh hadn't slept. He looked as if he hadn't shaved in a week and he had only been one day in hiding. Still, as Lucius handed Josh a hot meal in a box, he pulled no punches.

"You should've seen this, Josh," he said. "As a matter of fact, both of us should have. But of all the senior lieutenants and knowledgeable brothers, you've always been the one with his ear to the ground, and for that you were the most liked and respected. When a brother would join the Nation and have trouble relating to everyone else, we could always depend on you to bring him around."

"I know I let brothers down." Josh said. "I wish I could make it right, but I don't know how. It's embarrassing that it took the cops raiding my house to see that it must've been Lynton setting this whole thing up. There's jus' no way they could've had a make on me that soon, unless he …"

"Unless wha'?" Lucius asked, displaying his displeasure at Josh, someone he had known and loved all his life. "A man can be forgiven for being fooled in the dark, Josh, but not for being fooled in the light. You were repeatedly warned about Lynton."

Hesitating for a moment and staring at the wall, Lucius calmed himself, then continued. "Lynton was a cancer inserted by the Feds to spread inside Muhammad's Temples. He and Khalid helped the Feds target certain members to send false letters and drawings to. They created jealousy among the sisters and instigated a war from within. We can't ..."

"How can I make it right?" Josh interrupted. "Tha's wha' I wanna kno'."

"I'ma tell you how'ta make it right." Lucius said. "We can't let them young brothers go down because of Lynton. They busted Anthony and Theron this morning. And it was because of Khalid and Lynton that Ethan and Arnold are down. Like I told the Minister, first of all, Lynton has to go."

"Yeah, but he's gotta be hidin' by now," Josh said. "He has to kno' that I kno'."

"He ain't hiding." Lucius answered. "He kno's you can't do too much on the run. He's greedy, so he'll be back on the street. Tha's his nature. But I got Wade and Chris on 'im."

"They gon' bang him?" Josh asked.

"No. They gon' follow him for a few days first. Oh, he's gon' get slumped but first we wanna find out who he's been meeting wit."

"Then wha'?" Josh asked.

"Then we deal wit Mo, Rus and Dalton." Lucius said with a groan. "I love 'em, but they lied to us. They still slinging tha' powder, and their greed has caused problems for us in Chicago. People there have taken notice."

"I ain't gon' say I told you so," Josh grinned with a fork full of food going in his mouth. "But I did. When you first came home, I told you to leave dem dudes alone or we may find ourselves goin' to war wit 'em."

"Yeah, I remember." Lucius said, reaching over and taking a bit of Josh's food for himself. "You, Chris and especially Ethan, told me this might happen."

"I gotta talk to Deborah," Josh said. "She's worried to death."

"A word to the wise," Lucius responded, while getting up to leave. "Let Sister Gussie speak wit her first. After we've handled our business, then you'll be in a better position to convince her tha' things will be alright."

"Are you goin' back to Chicago?" Josh asked.

"Nah, I'ma stay here until this thing wit Lynton is settled. But I'm goin' to leave you my car outside so when its time for you to move, you can."

"I appreciate it Lu," Josh said, with a serious look in his eyes. "I kno' I really fucked up this time. I'm glad it's you pullin' my coat."

Lucius pulled Josh to his feet and gave him a big hug. As he walked toward the door, he turned quickly and said, "Oh yeah, we got news from Terence's attorneys Friday tha' the Supreme Court seems to be leaning Terence's way. He might be coming home soon, In-sha-Allah."

"In-sha-Allah," Josh repeated.

***

As the Philadelphia Sunday Inquirer was being delivered to newsstands throughout the city, a Federal Task Force was meeting on the third floor of the Federal Building a 9th and Market Streets. An hour or so later, heavy rain pounded the four beige sedans and four white federal vans that pulled out of the lot behind the building. Their headlights were on and their windshield wipers repeatedly slapped aside thick steams of rain water.

Heading the task force operation to arrest Maurice "Mo" Barton, Rushard "Rus" Braxton, and Dalton Landers were Agents Marvin Smith and Alfred Doss. A team of six men and two backups were assigned for each suspect. The fourth team of six men and two backups was to proceed to the home of Cecil "Big Cil" Sampson to apprehend him on a fugitive warrant issued by New York.

At Maurice's home on Walton Street, agents, with their backs against the wall, guns drawn and flak vests under their jackets, inched their way toward the front door. They knocked once and was surprised when Mo opened the door and invited them in. It was the same at each of the suspects' homes. The agents found absolutely no resistance. And because the brothers had been warned by Wade giving them that "Black Mafia" article three days earlier, they had removed everything the Feds might consider illegal from their homes. The Feds found no guns, no drugs and no money.

***

When Lynton finally called Agent Doss' office, it was 9 am Monday. Lynton, and every street hustler in Philly, had heard about the Sunday morning raids on the brothers' homes. He knew that Doss would be tied up for a few days, and he would use that to his advantage.

"I've been trying to reach you," Lynton told Doss once he had him on the phone. "I took care of that abscessed tooth. I can meet you at the cabin anytime you say. This evening if you like."

"Don't fuck with me, Lynton," Doss whispered into the phone. "You're becoming a disappointment. You were supposed to call me back Saturday night. We have to talk about what went down at that apartment building and we have to talk as soon as possible. However, I have to stay in the city until Wednesday morning, so I'll meet you there Wednesday evening."

"Wednesday evening," Lynton repeated. "Okay, I'll leave around four o'clock Wednesday afternoon. Hey, just in case I beat you there, is that key still in place?"

"Yeah it's still there." Doss said, glancing up to see a couple of agents signaling to him through the office window to join them in the outer office. "Please don't make this thing a problem, Lynton."

"Don't make it a problem, huh?" Lynton mumbled after hanging up the phone and reaching under the bed for the briefcase with his guns in it. "I kno' exactly wha' you wanna do to me you white motherfuckah, but I'ma do it to you. If I'm right, you probably gon' leave tomorrow so that you can be waiting for me when I git there. But I'ma leave now and be waitin' for yo' ass. I'ma blow yo'r head off."

Lynton pulled his Cadillac out of the garage in the back of his house and turned left at the corner. Wade didn't move. He waited until he saw the Cadillac reappear around the block and continue down toward the Expressway. Wade had learned by following Lynton before, when they worked on Minister Uriah's security squad, that Lynton always made a left turn at the first four corners he reached. That would bring him back to his starting point and he could see if anyone was following him.

Wade and Chris were following him, but he never saw them trailing four to five car lengths behind him on Ridge. They followed as he turned onto the Schuylkill Expressway, heading west on the Northeast Extension. By the time they passed through Allentown, PA, heading toward Hazelton, a slight drizzle had started.

Lynton's eyes scanned the campgrounds, but his thoughts were on Doss. He knew he would have to kill Doss because he knew too much about the agent's corrupt dealings. I can't hide from 'im, he thought, as he pulled in behind Doss' cabin, he's the fuckin' FBI. How in the hell am I gon' hide from them? Plus, he'll probably make sure the brothers know about me, so they'll be tryin' to kill me too. No, I gotta kill'im and bury his ass up here in these mountains. Just like he had me snuff Jacob Lawrence for him, he might be sendin' som'body here to kill me. But I'll already be here checkin' out whoever comes near this cabin.

As he raised the top from the porch lamp and removed the door key, he thought about what Doss had said while telling him to get rid of Jacob Lawrence. "Show me that you're still useful." He said.

Lynton opened the door and instinctively put the key back under the lid of the lamp.

"I'll be cool for tonight," he mumbled, feeling his eyes getting heavy. "I'll get me som'um to eat and som' sleep, then be ready for his ass when he shows up t'morrow, or maybe Wednesday. After tonight, I won't sleep again 'til this shit's over. I'll show the motherfuckah how useful I am."

## CHAPTER LIII

The call from Mount Pocono to Lucius came late Monday afternoon. Wade stood inside the phone booth down the street from the restaurant Lynton had just entered.

"How long did it take y'all to get there?" Lucius asked.

"'Bout two and half hours," Wade answered. "We can tell that he's nervous. He keeps looking around every few minutes or so, but he ain't seeing nothing."

"Good. Y'all stay on him until we get there," Lucius said. "I'ma have Josh meet me outside the city. If he makes it that far, then we'll kno' he's not being followed. The cops would pick him up before they would let'im get outside the city limits."

"Okay, the cabin he's in is off to the side of a lake called Lake Wamopompack, 'bout two hundred yards beyond the campgrounds. But just before you get to the campgrounds, off to the right, you'll see a lumberyard. There's a sign on the fence saying they sell logs, so I guess these people go there to buy logs for their campfires."

"So his cabin's 'bout two hundred yards from the lake or the campgrounds?"

"The campgrounds." Wade answered.

"Don't worry, we'll find you," Lucius said. "We're goin' to leave 'round eight, so we should get up there 'bout ten or eleven. Anyway, I kno' we'll be there befor' midnight."

"As-Salaam-Alaikum." Wade said into the phone.

"Wa-Laikum-As-Salaam." Lucius responded, then added. "Listen, if anything happens, or if the cops pick us up or som'um and we don't get there, Lynton's not to leave there alive. I want yo'r word on tha'."

"You got it." Wade said.

"But most of all," Lucius said. "Make sure y'all stay safe."

"We'll be cool."

*** 

Agents Smith and Doss stood to the right of the Assistant U.S. Attorney who read from the indictment and complaint filed by the government. The name of the informant was never mentioned, though every defendant and their family members knew who he was.

At another table on the left side of the room, stood three attorneys hired by the defendants. Attorney Joseph Santori spoke first. "Your Honor, I'm here to enter the plea of not guilty to all charges for defendant, Maurice Barton. Attorney Lee Simone, for Rushard Braxton, entered the same plea for his client, as did Attorney Nino Tragotti, for Dalton Landers.

When the attorneys asked about a bail hearing for their clients, the Assistant U.S. Attorney told the Judge that his office would oppose any request for bail. "This case is based on information about a continual criminal enterprise," he said and we have to consider the safety of our confidential informant." The judge denied bail and said that the defense could renew its request for bail at a later date.

***

Lucius and Josh had no problem finding the area Wade had describe. Even though that slight drizzle was now a biting rainfall coming down really hard, they spotted Chris' Toronado parked just near the far end of the campground. Lucius pulled alongside the car and rolled down the window.

"Any problems?" Josh asked, looking around to see if he saw anyone. "Police or anybody?"

"No. No police," Chris answered. "Not even a suspicious look from anybody. Probably 'cause it's dark. Wouldn't wanna be out here in the daytime, someone would be calling the cops yellin', 'Niggahs in the campground'."

"How the cabin look? Lucius asked. "Which one is it?"

"It's the one on the end." Wade said, pointing to the row of cabins situated at the level top of a gentle slope and bordered by shrubs. "There's a brick wall in the back like a fence around a yard or som'um. I went back there and looked around for a minute, but didn't stay because I didn't wanna take a chance that he'd see me."

"Good," Lucius said. "If he had seen you, he would've broke camp and we wouldn't be able to find out who he came up here to see."

"Is anyone else in there?" Josh asked. "Who let'im in?"

"I don't think anybody else is in there." Wade said. "He took a key from out tha' porch lamp and opened the door."

"Where's the key?" Lucius asked. "Did he put it back?"

"Yeah. He put it back under the lid, I think."

"Wha 'cha wanna do?" Chris asked. "We can go in there or we can wait to see who he's meeting."

"S'pose it's a woman?" Wade asked. "Wha' then?"

"He ain't com' all the way up here for no woman," Josh said. "He got a spot over in Jersey where he takes all his women."

"Nah, this ain't no female thing," Lucius agreed. "This is 'bout money or life. Me and Josh will go in first. Y'all wait 'til I com' back to get you."

Through the darkness, in the rain, crouching behind the bushes, Lucius made his way up the slope to the cabins. The shrubs and the night made it very difficult to see some of the cabins, and no lights were on in any of them. Josh waited in the shadows until he was sure Lucius was in place before he inched alongside the cinderblock wall behind the cabins and made his way into the backyard. The cold wind and rain had his face stinging as he peeked in the window. He saw a kitchen table and chairs in the middle of the floor. There was a small refrigerator and stove by the far door leading into another room, but no movement inside. Staying low, Josh crept along the cement wall of the cabin until he reached the side window. Lucius was already there.

"He's in there on the bed," Lucius whispered. "Must've fallin' asleep."

"How we gon' do this?" Josh asked. "Want me to guard him from here while you go in the front?"

"Yeah, I'ma get the key outta tha' lamp and go in the front door," Lucius whispered. "You watch 'im from the window to see if he pulls a gun. If he turns toward the back door, you go around there and make sure he don't break."

"We can't take any chances wit'im." Josh cautioned, as he accepted a pair of rubber gloves from Lucius and put them on. "If he sees you comin' in tha' door he'll kno' he's 'bout to die. He'll shoot, shout, scream or shit tryin' anythin' he can to get away or make a whole lotta noise jus' to bring attention to us."

"He won't get a chance," Lucius said, putting on a pair of gloves as well. "Like I said, you watch'im, through tha' window. But just' in case he tries to make som'noise, I'll put one in his brain. He won't make any sounds after that."

Lynton had no idea that Lucius had entered the cabin. He never heard the squeaking floor boards, nor did he awake when Lucius removed the gun he had placed under the pillow and the one lying atop the night stand by the bed.

When Josh saw that Lynton hadn't moved, he walked around to the open front door and went inside. He searched the cabin for other guns and anything that would tell them who owned the cabin. He found nothing and joined Lucius in the bedroom.

"Should I wake 'im?" he asked Lucius, who was standing in the corner of the room holding Lynton's two .38 revolvers in his hand. Lucius nodded and they both moved closer to the bed.

"Wake up, you fuckin punk," Josh yelled, standing over Lynton. "You try anything and I'll blow yo'r fuckin' brains out."

The shock alone almost killed Lynton when he was shaken from his slumber to see Lucius and Josh standing over him with guns pointed at his head. Breathing heavily and rubbing sleep from his eyes, he tried to think. Damn, two of the most feared men in Philly got their guns trained on me. How the fuck am I gon' get out of this shit?

"As-Salaam-Alaikum, brothers," he managed. "Wha's ..."

"Whose cabin is this?" Lucius asked, cutting off Lynton's faint attempt at normalcy. "Who you meetin' here, the Feds?"

"Why the fuck you do this?" Josh screamed, the emotion in his voice obvious. "We loved you like a brother and you been sellin' us out, selling out all the brothers and sisters in the Nation tha' trusted you."

"I love the Nation, man," Lynton protested. "I'm still a Muslim. I jus' got caught up in som'um wit this federal agent name Doss, man. He had som'um on me and I ..."

"Is tha' who you're waitin' for?" Lucius asked, his eyes revealing nothing but a stone cold stare.

"Yeah, he wants me dead 'cause I wouldn't kill Josh. He said tha' uh, I ..."

"You're a fuckin' liar," Josh said, slapping Lynton across his face with the barrel of his gun and drawing blood. "You took me there to set me up wit a body. You gave dem our names and because of you Anthony and Theron are busted."

"Don't hit 'im," Lucius said, grabbing Josh's arm. "He has to look presentable when tha' agent walks in the door."

"What, we gon' wait here for the Feds?" Josh asked. "We should jus' slump this maggot and get the fuck outta Dodge."

"Not yet," Lucius said. "Doss, tha's the name I saw in Khalid's book. Because of tha' devil, we don' lost som' good brothers. I'ma kill tha' son-of-a-bitch."

Josh tied Lynton to the bed and gagged him. "If you lyin', yo'r punk-ass gon' die a miserable death. I'ma take a piece of you every day for a week. But if you wanna live, you better act normal when tha' Fed gets here. Understand?"

Lynton nodded his head and swallowed hard. His fear was palpable. Sweat poured from him like water and he couldn't keep his legs from shaking, as he watched Josh looking at him with disgust.

Going back to where Wade and Chris sat waiting in the car, Lucius told them to park both cars on the other side of the campground so that the Fed wouldn't see them when he arrived. They parked Lynton's Cadillac there, as well, then they all returned to the cabin to wait. Lucius told them to make sure they kept their gloves on at all times.

"Touch nothin' wit yo'r hands," he said. "And if you've already touched som'um, go back and wipe it down good."

***

Lynton had been right, Doss had planned a sneak attack on him. Like Lynton, Doss thought of arriving early so that he could surprise Lynton when he walked in the door. Around 9 pm, right after finishing up his paperwork on the hearing for Mo, Rus and Dalton, Doss left his office and drove straight to Mount Poconos, nonstop. But as he pulled up in front of the cabin, the headlights of his car gave him away.

Lucius had been sitting by the front windows and Josh by the window in the back of the cabin. Wade and Chris kept watch on Lynton. When Lucius saw a car pass by the front of the cabin and pulled alongside the wall, he suspected that it might be who they were waiting for. A moment later, a shadow came around the opposite end of the wall. Lucius held his breath. The figure stopped, then moved closer to the front door of the cabin. Lucius signaled everyone to be still. He knew this was the man they were waiting for and had already made his mind up to kill him. There would be no threats, no time for last thoughts or conversations about why this was happening. As far as Lucius was concerned, both Lynton and the agent knew why they would have to die.

When he heard the key turn the lock and saw the door come open, Lucius stepped out of the shadows and grabbed Doss by his collar, taking note that the agent wore no protective vest.  Before Doss could do anything, Lucius kicked the door closed and then asked, "Do you know me?"

Doss knew immediately who this big man was.  He looked up at Lucius with an attempt to say something, but it never came out.  Lucius pressed one of Lynton's .38's against Doss' chest and pulled the trigger twice.  Blood splattered the door behind Doss as Lucius held him up and looked into his closing eyes until there was no more life in them. Turning to Wade and Chris, he told them to bring Lynton there so he could ID the man on the floor.  A frightened Lynton, still with his mouth gagged and hands tied, looked down at Agent Doss' body and nodded his head, confirming who the man was.

Without saying a word, Lucius then searched Doss, removed a .32 colt snub nose from the dead man's waist and handed it to Josh who was kneeling beside the body.  Josh wrapped the fingers of the dead man around the gun's handle, then looked up at Lynton, whose eyes were wide with fear.  Josh then stood up and placed the gun's barrel against Lynton's forehead and fired one shot. Chris and Wade released Lynton's body and let him fall to the floor, dead. In a matter of seconds, they were out the door and heading for their cars.

# CHAPTER LIV

It had been a week since Agent Doss and Lynton had been found dead in Mount Pocono. The Pennsylvania State Police had yet to confirm it, but their thinking was that the FBI Agent had walked in on Lynton burglarizing his cabin, and a shoot-out between them had resulted in both their deaths.

However, FBI Agent Marvin Smith, who had been Agent Doss' partner for 15 years, felt differently. He knew that Lynton Thompson had been Doss' informant and had been inside that cabin before. But since he couldn't place anyone else at the cabin when they were killed, he couldn't rule out the State Police's theory that they may have killed one another. He also felt that he should keep quiet or Alfred Doss' reputation as a respectable and honest FBI agent would be tarnished.

Homicide Detectives O'Connor and Jones had a different take altogether on the death of Doss and Lynton. Doss had fed them erroneous information about a murder and now evidence had surfaced that was pointing them in a different direction. Detective Jones had mixed Lynton's picture in with pictures of other men and taken them to the woman who had said she saw another man at that building the night of the murder. She was sure Lynton had been the man she'd seen going up the stairs toward the roof. It appeared to both homicide detectives that Doss had arranged the hit on Lawrence with Lynton Thompson and tried to incriminate Joshua Clarkson, Anthony Black and Theron Moore. But they couldn't act on their suspicions yet, not until they could speak with Joshua Clarkson face to face.

"We got a problem, though," Jones said, speaking to his partner about their suspicions. "Those brothers are notorious for keeping their mouths shut."

"Yeah, I know," O'Connor responded. "They would rather go to hell wearing gasoline drawers than to cooperate with the police."

"What about that lawyer?" Jones asked. "The one who said he was representing Joshua Clarkson? When did he say he was coming in to talk?"

"He said he would be in town tomorrow," O'Connor said. "But I don't put much faith in that. He's a Moslem, too. Calls himself Abdullah Pasha. I checked him out, he's from Ohio."

"Well, it might be a start," Jones said. "At least, we'll be a little closer to finding this Joshua Clarkson guy."

***

Minister Uriah sat at the head of the table giving thanks to Allah for the dinner his wife had prepared for the brothers and their wives. It was a special evening because Josh was due to surrender himself to the authorities the next day. The Muslim attorney, Abdullah Pasha, from Ohio, had been hired to negotiate the surrender and represent all three brothers.

Over plates of brown rice and lamb stew, with macaroni and cheese, and bowls of navy bean soup, the brothers and their wives laughed and joked for what seemed like the first time in a long while. After dinner they sat, ate ice cream and carrot cake, and drinking Shabazz Juice.

As the sisters helped the Minister's wife in the kitchen, Minister Uriah, Wade, and Chris sat at the dining room table watching a chess match between Josh and Lucius. The Minister looked worn out, but not from an evening of dining and joyful conversation. He felt exhausted just thinking about all that had occurred in the last year. However drained, he was also thankful to have had brothers like Lucius, Josh and Harvey in his corner. Without the loyalty of all the brothers inside his inner circle, he too could be facing prison or even death.

Indirectly, he'd sanctioned all that the brothers had been doing to raise money. Though he didn't tell them to do these things, he never seriously used his authority to discourage them. In fact, he had benefited greatly from their actions, and the Feds would have loved to hear his name mentioned by any one of the brothers so he and other ministers could be arrested and discredited.

If the brothers hadn't been loyal to the Nation of Islam and each other, the Feds would've tried locking up Muslims from Chicago as well. But instead of trying to make deals for themselves with the police, brothers like Terence, Ethan and Arnold concentrated on spreading the teachings of Elijah Muhammad to those brothers who were in prison. And Uriah counted his blessings and thanked Allah daily for the thoroughness of these men.

"You gon' move, or wha'?" Lucius asked Josh "You been staring at the board for five minutes already."

"Don't rush me, chump," Josh said, moving his white pawn from king's 2 to king's 4. "You kno'," I'ma win this one so yo'r tryin' to distract me."

"Yeah, right," Lucius said, moving his pawn from King 7 to King 5, facing Josh's pawn.

Wade and Chris, who had played chess often, watched as Josh moved his King side Bishop to his Queen side Bishop 4, and Lucius countered by moving his King side Bishop to his Queen side Bishop 5.

"You heard from Harvey," Josh asked, moving his Queen from Queen 1 to King side Rook 5. "He went up to New York to talk with New York Frank, didn't he?"

"Yeah, he called me last night," Lucius said, while moving his King side Knight to King side Bishop 6. "Frank wants him to help put together a group to take over his operation when he leaves."

"Tha's checkmate," Josh said, making his final move with his Queen capturing Lucius' King side pawn on Bishop 7. I told you I was gon' win this one."

"I hope you kno' I let you win," Lucius laughed. "It's been so long since you had a victory, I felt sorry fo' ya."

"Well, if Pasha can deliver like he say he can, I'll have a much needed victory."

"Frank's leavin' New York?" Chris asked Lucius.

"Yeah, he has no choice," Lucius shrugged. "Tha' July 4th thing brought a lot of attention to him. I mean they already knew he was one of the biggest drug dealers in New York, but until then, his name had never been mentioned in no police shootin'. I guess they don't care 'bout those who was killed. But when a cop gets shot all hell breaks loose."

"Well, doesn't it seem kinda funny tha' Frank would ask Brother Harvey to help him find some people?" Minister Uriah asked. "Given what happened involved Harvey."

"At first I thought so too," Lucius said. "But Harv told me tha' Frank understood tha' it wasn't jus' Harv's fault. If Butta's people hadn't panicked and pulled their guns, they might all still be alive. Anyway, Frank likes strength. He sees our brother as an honorable man and he'd rather deal with him than someone he feels is untried and untested."

Josh gave himself up to police the next morning. He was accompanied by his attorney Abdullah Pasha, and chose not to make any statements. Having investigated the case, the attorney discovered that Lynton Thompson had been positively identified as the man seen going up to the roof of the apartment building where Jacob Lawrence was killed.

Meanwhile, Brother Harvey was meeting with Frank Matthews on the top floor of a large brownstone in Harlem. The inside of the heavily guarded house was decorated with expensive furnishings. The rooms were large and spread out with a center hall, living room, and dining room dominating the wood-paneled first floor. A mahogany staircase led to the bedrooms on the second and third floors.

It was in the middle bedroom of the third floor that Harv and Frank sat alone in discussion.

"I appreciate you coming here," Frank said. "I know you might've felt tha' I was angry about that thing on the beach, but I kno' it wouldn't have happened if Butta's people hadn't panicked."

Harv, who at first, felt apprehensive about this meeting, said nothing. He just shook his head in agreement and continued to let Frank talk. He was a firm believer that the less a man said, the less others knew what he really thought.

"This is business for me," Frank continued. "I don't have the luxury of being emotional about the loss of a Butta or anyone else, for that matter. I have already recouped my losses from that and moved on. However, I was hurt by it in another way. My name has been placed on the endangered list by the federal government. I will be arrested soon, make bail, and disappear. This is why I need your help."

"How do you know all this?" Harvey asked. "It sounds as if you've planned it."

"I have," Frank grinned. "My life wouldn't be worth a nickel if I didn't know what was going on around me. I have to leave the game and I chose to do so on my own terms."

"Since you have things so well planned out why do you need my help?" Harvey asked.

"Because my one mistake was putting so much of my money in the hands of an associate from your neck of the woods."

"Philly?" Harvey asked. "Who?"

"Cadillac Sonny," Frank sighed. "He has always been a good friend and partner as long as I was available, but now that he knows I'ma be leaving soon, he's been showing me his ass."

"Wha 'cha mean?" Harvey asked. "If he's your friend ..."

"Money and women," Frank said, interrupting Harvey. "A man can always judge his true friends by how one acts around his money and his women, especially if he thinks he's alone."

Frank rose from the couch and walked over to a door that led to another room. He opened it and waved to someone he called, "Badia."

Harvey stood up when he saw her. She stared and smiled as she entered the room and stood facing Harvey. Her complexion was dark, like soft rich chocolate surrounding her large brown eyes. Her black hair was combed straight back, hanging down over her shoulders. She wore a tight white knit dress that showed off every curve of her tall fine body, and her high heels made her almost equal Harvey's 6' 1" frame.

"Badia, this is Harvey," Frank gestured. "He's the one I told you about."

"Hello Harvey." She said, in a husky voice, extending her hand. "I've been hearing a lot about you."

"Don't believe the bad," Harvey said, smelling the faint scent of her sinful fragrance as his large hand enclosed her soft small fingers.

After they were seated again, Frank told Harvey how he had sent Badia to see Cadillac Sonny about the money, and Sonny had propositioned her.

"I don't know if he was trying to create a diversion by trying to make me think he was after my woman or not," Frank said. "But I don't have the time to play games with him."

"Wha' is it you want from me," Harvey asked.

"When the time comes, I'll send Badia to Sonny again, but this time I want you to go with her to make sure he gives her my money."

"How much are we talkin' 'bout?" Harvey asked.

"$1.5 million," Frank answered with no hesitation. "I got enough to pay the cash bail they'll set, but I'll need that $1.5 million to disappear with."

Harvey didn't ask if Badia was gon' disappear with him, but he could see why Sonny would try her. She was fine.

"What's in it for me?" Harvey asked. "I might have to slump Sonny, and for what?"

Badia got up from her chair and went to the closet. She pulled out a briefcase and opened it. "There's $100,000 in here," she said. "It's yours. All you have to do is give us your word that you'll be there for me when Frank calls."

"You mean I can take that now?" Harvey asked, surprised.

"Your word has always been good." Frank said. "I know that I'm asking a lot, so I'm willing to take the chance that you'll continue to keep your word. I know that you need money for Cecil and the others who are facing federal charges. So, I'll give you this money in advance. All you have to do is accompany Badia when the time comes."

As Harvey headed to Detroit to give Big Cil part of the money he'd gotten from Frank, he thought the situation through. He had known Cadillac Sonny since he was a little boy. Sonny had been one of the first hustlers in South Philly to start making real money slinging powder. Ordinarily Sonny wouldn't go up against me, he thought, as he turned off the turnpike into Detroit, but since so many brothers are now busted and others are on the run, some suckahs might try to get bold.

"Damn, I can still smell her perfume," He mumbled.

# CHAPTER LV

It had taken three months, but the Federal cover up of Agent Alfred Doss' involvement with Lynton Thompson, coupled with the investigations conducted by the Pennsylvania State Police and the Philadelphia Homicide Division, finally led to the release of Brothers Joshua, Anthony and Theron. There had not been enough evidence to hold them for murder. Detectives O'Connor and Jones believed Lynton had killed Jacob Lawrence and that Agent Doss had covered it up to protect his informant. They weren't sure that Joshua Clarkson and the others had not somehow been involved in the murder. But for now they had to accept that the evidence showed they had been setup by Lynton Thompson and Agent Doss.

Though disappointed by the outcome of that murder case, Detectives O'Connor and Jones were able to get some measure of satisfaction from another murder case. The trial of Ethan Siswell and Arnold Boyden had proceeded as scheduled and both had been convicted of the murder of Wesley Gibson, the man who had come to Muhammad's mosque, swinging a baseball bat.

Because Lynton Thompson, at the urging of Agent Doss, had identified the wrong man as being the jailhouse informant, the real informant had lived to testify against the brothers. His name was Sean Yates, and he had been placed under protective custody while the trial was going on. However, two weeks after the jury convicted the brothers, based on Yates' testimony, that he'd overheard them talking about how they did it, Sean Yates was found shot to death in North Philadelphia. Someone had fired two bullets into his mouth and left him lying in the middle of a rat-infected alley.

The word on the street was that the brothers had dumped Yates' body there. But when the police tried to get someone to talk to them about the murder, the conversation suddenly dried up. No one was about to snitch on the brothers about possibly snuffing a man who had snitched on the brothers.

***

In January, 1973, just as New York Frank had predicted, he was arrested for conspiracy to possess and distribute cocaine and heroin. And like Maurice "Mo" Barton, in Philadelphia, the Internal Revenue Service also charged Frank with income tax invasion.

New York Frank's bail was originally set at $5 million, but on the day it was cut to $400,000 cash, Brother Harvey got a call from Badia later that evening.

"Where do you want me to pick you up," she asked. "I'm in Philly and can drive to your house, if you like."

After thinking for a moment, Harvey asked her if she knew where City Hall was. When she said she did, he told her to pick him up there. He would be standing on the Southeast corner of Broad and Market Streets. He wasn't sure why, but thought it best that she didn't come to his house. "Maybe I don't wanna have to introduce her to my wife," he mumbled, as he unlocked the closet door to remove the briefcase containing his guns. He hesitate, then put the briefcase back in the closet. I don't need my gun for this, he thought, this is Cadillac Sonny, I'm meetin wit, he's no threat to me.

The weather was cold, but he didn't mind waiting. He had parked his car in the garage on 16th Street and walked down to Broad. As the wind swirled around the buildings on the corner, he broke the brim of his gray felt fedora all the way around, turned up the collar of his black maxi-overcoat, and pulled his gray suede gloves from his coat pocket. He felt content knowing he'd already divided the $100,000 he had gotten from Frank. Mo, Rus and Dalton had received $10,000 each. And if he was able to, Harvey planned to get more money from Frank. After all, he thought, without me, Cadillac Sonny might try to keep all Frank's money.

As he stood on the corner, he wondered had Badia already spoken to Sonny? Is he waiting for us at his house or someplace else?

He saw the car coming toward him and somehow knew it was her before she even got to the corner. She drove a red, 1972, Cadillac Eldorado with beige interior. Very befitting, he thought, as she leaned across the seat and opened the door on the passenger's side, inviting him in. Her smile was broad, her blue skirt short, and her silver-fox fur was flung over the back of his seat.

"You look good, Harvey," she smiled, as she removed her coat. "Just as good as you looked when I saw you at Frank's that day."

"Hi, you look good, too," he said, feeling embarrassed and really not knowing what else to say. His eyes nervously glanced up and down her body before settling on her healthy brown thighs protruding from her short blue skirt. She wore a blue cardigan sweater that showed off the fullness of her breasts.

Harvey didn't like what he was thinking. This is supposed to be a business meeting, he thought, with someone else's woman picking up someone else's money. I'll just keep my word to Frank and that will be that.

"How's Frank?" He asked, watching as she turned on to the Expressway. "Why are you turning here? Sonny's spot is on Washington Avenue."

"Frank's fine." She answered. "And we're not meeting with Cadillac Sonny until tomorrow morning. Right now I'm taking you to where we can sit down and talk. You and I have to have a meeting of the minds before seeing Sonny."

"Where are you going?" Harvey asked.

"To the Embassy," she said, turning to look at him.

"The hotel?"

"Yes, I needed a place to sleep. Tomorrow I have to pick up a lot of money from various places around the Philly area, then go to get my man outta jail so we can disappear."

"Wha', he's still in jail?" Harvey asked, a bit confused as to why she hadn't waited until morning to call him. "When you called, I thought he was already out."

"Uh, uh," she said. "You don't mind spending a little time with me, do you? I mean we can talk, get a bite to eat, then I'll drive you back. I'm a lonely girl from outta town, Harvey, humor me."

The drive out by the airport wasn't long at all, but to Harvey it seemed like an eternity. He sat quietly, almost as if he was afraid to speak. She talked nonstop, however, about how she had met Frank and how she enjoyed the Ali-Quarry bout in Las Vegas last June. "That was just before you came to Frank's party on the beach, wasn't it?"

Harvey didn't answer her question because she already knew the answer. "I didn't see tha' fight." He said. "I saw Ali in his comeback, when he stopped Quarry in Atlanta in 1970."

When she stepped out the car, Harvey could see her full body again. The skirt was tighter than he had imagined, her thighs, pushing against the material, seemed to be stretching it. As they walked across the lobby toward the elevator, Badia nonchalantly took his hand and pressed it against her ass and held it there. Then as casual as speaking about the weather, she whispered, "I'm a nontraditional woman, Harvey. I like things a bit differently, if you know what I mean. I do what I like, when I like, and most importantly, for as long as I like." With her other hand, she placed her fur on his shoulder then let that hand gently slide down the front of his pants as she watched his reaction. "Is that alright with you, Brother Harvey?" She asked. "Can you handle it?"

The morning came much too quickly for Harvey. He had never been with a woman like her. No shame, no blame. She was true to her word. The only thing he didn't learn from her that night was her complete name. Each time he asked her, she'd whispered, while tonguing him someplace on his body. "Just call me Baby and I'll come."

On the way to Sonny's Harvey asked Badia if she had told Sonny that he would be coming there with her. She told him no because that would spoil all the fun. Harvey wasn't sure what she meant, but left it alone. He had made up his mind about this woman, she was definitely unpredictable and he found himself liking that about her. She amazed him and in a way, he'd hoped to have more time to spend with her.

Cadillac Sonny was a big man and much older than Harvey but not as serious. He liked partying and spending money just to impress those around him. However, he wasn't impressed when he saw Harvey get out the car with Badia, who was carrying a small suitcase with a flowery pattern on it. Sonny had hoped to have one last chance at convincing her to leave Frank and be with him. He had been so desperate to have her, his last attempt had almost resulted in him raping her.

He was alone in the house now because she'd told him she would be alone when she came to pick up the money. He'd taken that as a sign that she might stay awhile and talk. But now that he had seen Harvey get out the car, Sonny wasn't sure if he'd have a chance to really talk to her the way he wanted to.

As soon as they walked in the door, Harvey could tell that Sonny wasn't glad to see him. Their greeting, while normally cordial, was polite, but obviously strained. And, Badia seemed to rub in the fact that she was with Harvey by flaunting her sexuality and repeatedly touching Harvey's arm as she spoke.

"We're here to pick that up for Frank," she said in her huskiest tone. "I've been here since yesterday but had other business to attend to, and now I must rush back to New York."

"I got yo'r money," Sonny snapped. "I told you on the phone that there would be no problems, you didn't have to bring nobody wit'cha."

Harvey knew from Sonny's reactions that something else was going on between these two, but he said nothing. He would do what he came to do, make sure all the money was accounted for and leave.

"Just give me the money," Badia said. "I don't wanna go over anything else, okay."

Cadillac Sonny handed a shopping bag to Badia, and she gave it to Harvey. "Count it for me shugar," she said, her eyes never leaving Sonny's face. The money was in big bills, and once Harvey had verified that it was $1.5 million, she told him to put it into the suitcase she'd brought with her. But as Harvey transferred the money, he was startled by the loud sound of a gunshot. He looked up and saw Badia holding a .32 silver plated automatic in her hand, and Sonny sliding down the wall with blood flowing from his neck. Before Harvey could react, Badia nonchalantly leaned over Sonny and fired another shot into the side of his head. She then turned and looked at Harvey sort of casual like, as if she had done nothing out of the ordinary, and wiped her prints from the gun and dropped it on the floor.

"What the fuck!?" Harvey yelled, as he stood frozen in place. "Are you outta yo'r mind, girl?"

"He tried to rape me that time when Frank sent me to see him" she said, looking at Harvey with an utter indifference that shocked him more than some things he'd seen in the eyes of ruthless men.

"He started off by saying that he admired my sense of style and the way I didn't seem to have too many airs about myself. Then the next thing I know he's trying to force me to suck his dick." As Badia turned and looked down at Sonny's body, she paused for a moment, then said. "Don't make a big deal of it, Harvey. He won't be trying to rape no other woman, that's for damn sure."

As if in a daze, Harvey stood staring at this beautiful sexy woman who had just the night before given him the best fucking he's ever had in his life, and couldn't believe what he was seeing. He wasn't sure if he believed what she was saying about the attempted rape, but it made no difference because Sonny was just as dead. However, he was sure that he was in awe of her, it was almost erotic. He wondered if he'd brought his gun would he have killed her out of fear that she might've tried to kill him. I guess not, he thought, after all, she picked up the casings, wiped off the gun and dropped it.

"What are you waiting around for, the cops?" she asked, standing bow-legged and putting her hand on her hip. "Grab the damn suitcase and let's get the fuck outta here. I gotta go get my man, honey."

Badia convinced Harvey to ride with her to Norristown to pick up additional money. She didn't talk about Cadillac Sonny, instead she talked about what she and Frank would do once they were out of the country. After picking up two more shopping bags of money, Badia packed it all into two suitcases and drove to the Greyhound Bus Station. She asked Harvey to drive her red Eldorado back to Philly and park it at the 30th and Market Street Train Station.

"Someone will pick it up," she said, as she handed him an envelope with $50,000 in it. "Thanks for spending time with me, shugar. I really enjoyed it."

Harvey could only smile as he watched her board the bus for New York and wave goodbye.

# CHAPTER LVI

*A Night Out With The Fruits of Islam* had become an annual celebrated event. A notable occasion of observance of those men who had assisted in establishing the teachings of the Honorable Elijah Muhammad in Philadelphia.

As Wade and Chris arrived at Muhammad's mosque on Park Avenue and Susquehanna, they could hear the applause coming from the building. The celebration had already begun and most of the brothers had already arrived.

It was early March and the night spent out with the FOI had actually begun earlier that afternoon. Brothers had begun arriving at the mosque that morning to set up for the day and evening celebration. It would be special this year because the State Supreme Court had recently ruled in Brother Captain Terence's favor and he had finally been released from prison and was scheduled to speak. And there would be group pictures taken of all brothers who in the previous year and the first quarter of 1973 had sold a weekly average of 500 copies of <u>Muhammad Speaks</u> newspaper. Their pictures would appear in the next edition of <u>Muhammad Speaks</u>.

It was a relaxed atmosphere, more than 100 young Muslim brothers, all casually dressed. The tables were crammed with pitchers of various juices, bowls of bean soups, platters of fried chicken and beef ribs soaked in hot sauce. The sisters had even prepared salads and there were kosher hotdogs and hamburgers for those who didn't want chicken or ribs.

Captain Terence was a solemn and commanding presence in front of a room full of FOI brothers gathered in the assembly hall of the mosque. He spoke to them in a strong confident voice, articulating his frustration and regret about what he referred to as the loss of the Muslim focus. "We've lost it," he said. "We have allowed the devil to remove our focus from our people and place it selfishly on ourselves. Except for the teachings we have received from our leader and teacher, the Honorable Elijah Muhammad, we're unimportant. It is our lost found brothers and sisters who should be important to us because it's our responsibility to deliver the Messengers teachings to them."

The room was silent as the FOI sat listening attentively to this brother. He was a Muslim very much admired by other Muslims and non-Muslims for his straightforwardness. A gifted speaker who had stood up in prison against the brutal tactics of the beast and returned undaunted and unscathed. Instead of bowing to the white jailers while in prison, he, along with Ethan, Arnold and other brothers, had spent time teaching and organizing so that they could send out many new converts to the religion.

"We have to teach and teach, like the Honorable Elijah Muhammad has taught us to do," he continued. He spoke for an hour from the rostrum. But before joining the celebration, he spoke privately with the brothers for which his message had really been intended.

Crowded around a table in a rear upstairs' office were Minister Uriah, Captain Terence, Brothers Harvey, Josh, Wade, and Chris. Because it was a conversation not meant for the ears of others, they had Billy Holiday's "Strange Fruit" playing loudly, over and over again in the room.

Speaking from a position of authority that now unofficially exceeded his position as captain, Brother Terence knew he had to be firm, but flexible. Informed earlier that he was being considered for the position of minister over Temple 12 once Minister Uriah left, he knew he'd need the support of the men sitting in this office. They might have a reputation for being ruthless, but they were also courageous, thorough, and able to demand the respect of others. Terence was wise enough to know he'd soon have to rely on those qualities.

Still he began by telling everyone in the office that he understood why they had positioned themselves in the way they had. "I commend you because your intentions were honorable. However, you have created a separate living and breathing entity that differs from what the Nation of Islam stands for, and there's no honor or dignity in that."

Terence told them that he and others appreciated their willingness to sacrifice themselves for the cause of building the Nation, but that the Nation would survive regardless.

"I'm not saying we no longer need the money," Terence said, speaking softly and inserting flexibility. "Since we've lost certain brothers to the prison system, we've seen a huge drop in donations to the temple and also to local community programs. And I realize that the loss of these brothers has placed an added burden on you, but we have to be mindful of how we are perceived by those we're trying to reach."

"We're aware of the problem," Harvey responded. "Those we once counted on to fund the mosque's neighborhood programs now see us as being weakened by certain events and claim they have other priorities."

By certain events, everyone in the room, including Terence, understood that to mean the last year convictions of Brothers Ethan and Arnold in state court, and the drug convictions of Mo, Rus, and Dalton just three days ago in federal court. The fact that New York Frank was now on the run and South Philly Vinnie Cato was muscling in, trying to fill the void left by Frank, hadn't helped matters any.

"Priorities my ass?" Josh shouted. "I mean no disrespect Brother Captain, but by other priorities they mean they gotta pay dem white boys who took over New York Frank's thing, so they can work, and ain't nu'ffin left for nobody else, not even for the black neighborhoods, like they agreed to."

Minister Uriah said nothing. This was Terence's meeting and he needed to handle it. Terence had never dealt with the brothers under these circumstances, so this would be his test.

Taking a page from Minister Uriah's playbook, Terence allowed the brothers to state their frustrations and choose a course of action. He knew that their pride wouldn't allow them to bow to the white boys. To allow white guys to take over New York Frank's Philadelphia territories would take money out of the brothers' pockets and from the pockets of the families of the brothers now in prison. Terence also knew that he had to be discrete in his manner of being the first to suggest new methods to brothers who had their own way of solving old problems.

Speaking barely over a whisper, Brother Terence told the brothers that the method they had been using was flawed. He briefly paused, then continued. "There's no economic value in it; no long-term value that is. The economic concept is based on giving up something of lesser value to gain something of a greater value. However, we've been giving up something of a much greater value to gain something of a lesser value. We've been giving up dignity and respect in the eyes of the black community to gain money. That's unacceptable economics."

The brothers agreed that they had demonstrated very poor judgment in allowing the reputation of the Muslims in Philly to become tarnished. But they also knew that they couldn't allow Vinnie Cato to regain control over the areas they had taken and distributed to people like New York Frank and his workers at a price.

"What is it you want us to do, Brother Captain?" Josh asked. "We're opened to suggestions."

"The same things you did when we first decided to take over our communities," Terence replied. "Don't put the image of Muslims at risk. Y'all are all officers in the Nation. If you feel there's a job that you must do that deals with the activity of them white boys, or anybody else, then try to do it outside of the temple."

"Wha 'cha mean?" Harvey asked. "You're asking that we separate ourselves from the temple until the job's done?"

"As I understand it," Terence answered, "We still have Brother Lieutenants Chris and Wade who have agreed to handle what needs to be done inside. They have given me and Minister Uriah their word that they have stepped back from certain activities. I believe we can rely on that."

"Give us a month to put everything in order," Josh said. "Harvey and I will handle what needs to be handled."

"We still have a source of funds," Chris assured. "The money we have coming in from Asian Enterprises, and of course, the checks that we're working with Brother Lester will be made available to the temple as donations."

\*\*\*

Downstairs in the assembly hall, Brothers Anthony and Theron waited to talk with Josh. They had already agreed to help him train another group of brothers so they could raise the necessary money for Ethan and Arnold's continuing defense of the murder convictions. They were facing life sentences.

Harvey still had his connections with people who would be helpful in handling the appeals for Mo, Rus, and Dalton. But first he planned to speak with Big Cil about Carl Hunter, the informant who had set them up for the Feds.

"I hear that Captain Terence is in line to get the minister's post," Theron told Anthony, as they sat in the assembly room enjoying the rest of the celebration and eating fried chicken and potato salad.

"Yeah, I heard that, too." Anthony replied. "He could always out teach most of the Assistant Ministers anyway."

"Tha'll be good," Wade said, taking a seat next to them. "I've always loved hearing him teach."

"Me too," Theron said.

"Y'all sure you wanna roll wit' Josh on this job?" Wade asked. "I kno' it's about getting' things done for Ethan and Arnold, but you gotta be careful. Them white boys ain't scared of Muslims, they just been trying to avoid a war wit' us."

"It's on Vinnie Cato," Anthony said. "He ain't respecting any previous agreements. Even his own people don't think he should have those territories."

"People like who?" Wade asked.

"Joe Lacardi," Anthony answered.

"Mifflin Street Joe Lacardi?" Wade asked. "The guy we met with for Minister Uriah?"

"Yeah, he's setting it up." Anthony said. "Well, he gave us information about where we might find Vinnie on some Saturday nights."

"Be careful," Wade said, wanting to say more about Josh and his need to be controlled. But he said nothing because he didn't want them to tell Josh and possibly give him the wrong impression. It wasn't that he thought Josh untrustworthy, he just thought him hardheaded and reckless at times.

However, Chris and Wade couldn't leave that evening before warning both Josh and Anthony about possible problems they might encounter by accepting help from Joe Lacardi. "He's an Italian." Chris said. "They don't care anything about us."

"Lacardi's a businessman first," Anthony responded. "All he sees is the benefit he'll get from this. Plus, he don't have any respect for Vinnie Cato. Once he commented about the stories concerning Vinnie when he was doing that bit up in Lewisburg."

"You mean the Vinnie Vaseline jokes?" Josh smiled. "I think everybody's heard them."

"Well, where there's smoke," Chris laughed.

"How we gon' handle this thing? Theron asked. "Go after them jokas workin for 'im?"

"To kill a snake you don't cut off its tail," Josh said. "You cut off its head."

# CHAPTER LVII

Working within the window of opportunity given to him by Brother Captain Terence, Josh formed a new inner circle of brothers. But unlike the previous team, these brothers had not been tried and tested on the street and didn't have the infamous reputations of the original crew. Some of the new brothers had come from county jails where they'd been taught and trained by Ethan, Arnold, and others. For many of them, it had been their first time hearing the actual teachings of the Honorable Elijah Muhammad. However, from word on the street, most had heard of the original inner circle of brothers and hoped to be like them. But Josh, trying to be cautious, first limited their fund-raising activities to collecting from drug dealers and distributing Muhammad Speaks newspapers to local stores so the money could later be collected from the owners.

When it came to Vinnie Cato, Josh thought it best that he, Anthony, and Theron should do the hit. After all, both Theron and Anthony had kept their mouths closed when the rollers had them locked down about that Jacob Lawrence thing.

Joe Lacardi had given Anthony information about Vinnie's black girlfriend. Anthony told Josh that Joe Lacardi must've been having Vinnie followed on his own, because he knew where the girlfriend lived, when Vinnie saw her, and that Vinnie always used some old black dude to drive him to her house and park outside. "Sometimes, the black guy would leave and come back later," Lacardi told Anthony.

Over the next five weeks, Vinnie's girlfriend was followed every Saturday night. Her name was Linda Mae Johnson, a young attractive light brown-skinned woman who managed a few of the Italian pizza parlors in Center City. Vinnie wasn't the only man she was seeing. There were at least three other men visiting her on different Saturdays.

"Linda's a busy girl," Anthony said, sipping on a Coke and eating a donut. He and Theron were parked up the street from her house. It was late and one of her other boyfriends was inside with her. He was a black dude and he drove a blue Lincoln Continental.

"Tha' must be how she pays for her duplex," Theron said.

"Tha's a boss ride tha' dude got," Anthony said. "I might get me one like tha' when I make som' real paper."

Linda's duplex was on the corner of Wayne Avenue and Coulter Street. She lived on the first floor and the entrance to her apartment was at the side of the building. The pathway leading to the side door was lined on both sides with planted shrubs. Just outside her green leafy lawn, which was surrounded by a wrought iron fence, was a huge oak tree with low hanging branches that partly hid the house's front and side windows. It seemed Linda Johnson had picked the perfect spot for her many secret rendezvous.

The spot was also perfect for what Josh had in mind. The tree and shrubbery made it difficult for anyone to see who might be entering or leaving the side door. Josh told Anthony to pay special attention to the black driver. "How often does he leave Vinnie there? And how long is he gone?"

It was 9:30, the night of June 9, their sixth Saturday of sitting on Linda's house. Vinnie Cato had just arrived back in Philadelphia from Jamaica, New York, where he had watched Secretariat complete the Triple Crown at the Belmont Stakes. His spirits were high and all he could think of now was seeing his fine black girl, as he called her. He called Pops, the old black dude that always drove him through Linda's neighborhood.

When Josh got the call from Anthony saying that Vinnie Cato was inside Linda's house, it was a little after 11 pm.

"The old black dude pulled off," Anthony said. "Usually he's gone for about two hours."

"Wha' kinda car the black dude's driving?" Josh asked.

"A dark brown Ford Fairlane," Anthony replied. "It's got a leopard skin design on the roof. Foxtails hanging from the back fender. Real country lookin', you can't miss it."

"Okay, jam Vinnie," Josh yelled into the phone. "I'll be there in fifteen minutes. Don't let him or the girl get outta tha' house, and if the black dude shows up, let 'im in and jam 'im too."

"You want 'em tied up?" Anthony asked.

"You still got dem cuffs and badges, right!?"

"Yeah, in the trunk."

"Use 'em and take in those big plastic trash bags."

When Josh turned onto Wayne Avenue from Schoolhouse Lane, he stopped about fifty yards up from the house. Surveying the area, he didn't see the Ford Anthony had described. Josh parked his car in front of Linda's duplex, checked the street again, then walked the pathway to the side door. Inside the apartment, he found Linda and Theron in the living room. Her hands were cuffed behind her back and she had a frightened look on her face. From the conversation between Linda and Theron, Josh could tell that she still believed that the two men she'd let in were detectives from the Philadelphia Police Department.

Vinnie Cato was cuffed to the table leg in the dining room and he had no such assumption. "Who the fuck sent y'all? He asked, when he saw Josh. "Tha' fat hunchback motherfucker, Rufalino?"

Josh looked at Anthony who shrugged and said, "Yeah, he keeps asking me the same thing. I told im I don't kno' no Rufalino."

"You don't respect agreements," Josh said, taking a seat beside Vinnie. "Even yo'r own people don' loss respect for you, man."

"Wha 'cha want, a couple of keys?" Vinnie grinned. "No problem, you want it, I got it. But I want the fat hunchback motherfucker dead."

Josh stood up and pulled a silencer fitted .22 automatic from his waistband. "Joe Lacardi says you see too much," he said, as he fired one shot directly into Vinnie Cato's right eye. As Vinnie's head jerked backward, Josh caught it with his left hand and fired another bullet into Vinnie's temple.

"Bring the girl in here," Josh said to Theron who stood in the dining room doorway staring as if in shock.

Anthony hustled Linda into the room, and she immediately fainted when she saw Vinnie's body, still handcuffed to the table leg, laying twisted on the floor. Josh lifted her from the floor and shook her until she opened her eyes. Terrified, and thinking she was about to die, she attempted to scream, but Josh quickly placed his hand over her mouth.

"You wanna go where yo'r white boy is at?" Josh asked. "I ain't got time for this shit. You scream, you die."

"Wha' we gon' do wit' her?" Theron asked Anthony.

"Wha' the fuck can we do?" Anthony answered. "If she says the wrong thing, she's slumped."

Josh seated Linda in the chair closest to Vinnie's body and turned her back to it. "You gon' say the right thing if someone asks you 'bout Vinnie, right baby? You gon' say tha' Vinnie left yo'r house wit two white men, right?"

Linda tried to answer but no words came. Josh asked her again and finally she answered, "Yes ... two ...two white men."

"You sure 'bout tha?" Josh asked, putting his gun to her head. "You're too fine a woman to be dead. I don't kno' what a fine sister like you would want wit' a faggot like Vinnie anyway."

Fearing that Josh was about to pull the trigger, Theron stepped in and grabbed the woman's arm. "Do you understand tha' yo'r life depends on wha' you saw?" he yelled. "White guys, two of 'em took Vinnie outta yo'r house and tha's the last time you saw 'im, right?"

"Yes, I understand," she said, seeming to come out of her trance. "I was in the kitchen when Vinnie let them in, but I saw them when they left. Two tall white men in suits. They made Vinnie leave with them."

Josh picked up her purse and pulled out her ID and looked at her Social Security card. "We kno' how to find you if we need to, Linda. Please sister, forget you ever saw us."

"Go get the car and pull it around to the side of the house," Anthony told Theron. "We gotta bag this punk before puttin' him in my trunk."

# CHAPTER LVIII

Vinnie Cato's body was delivered to Joe Lacardi's people and never found. With Vinnie gone, Joe Lacardi teamed up with Hercules "Herc" Williams who would handle Lacardi's heroin coming from the Gambino crime family in New York. He would pass part of all proceeds to Brother Anthony for laundering. The money was to be used by legitimate Muslim businesses to make wholesale purchase of merchandise like clothing, jewelry, and furniture for resale. A percentage of the profits would then be distributed to the mosque to rent school buses and provide aid to needy Muslim families.

Things went well with that part of the operation. Anthony was dependable and only used brothers he thought trustworthy. But some of the brothers assigned to Brother Theron to collect from other dealers and number bankers were not as trustworthy. A few of them felt as if they could go off on their own and target dealers who had previously been given a pass by the brothers because of the favors they did for the brotherhood.

Many of the older drug dealers didn't have the same kind of respect for these new brothers that they had had for the original brothers, and didn't consider them a real challenge to their operations. Feeling disrespected by the older drug dealers who refused to pay, one of the new brothers, Brother Norman 3X, came up with an idea to start a drug war between dealers from West Philly and South Philly. Norman, who was a conventional coward, who drew his courage from the strength of others, believed he would gain favor if he was able to intervene and stop a war he had secretly started. His plan to arrange a robbery of low-level drug dealers from West Philly and have it blamed on rivals from South Philly, backfired when the dealer was shot and killed during the robbery. When the killing sparked incidents that threatened to explode into a war that would involve Muslims, Brother Josh was forced to step in and call a meeting between the warring parties.

The Sunday morning meeting, supposedly on neutral turf, was held in the back room of the "Dirty Old Man" bar at 10th and Old York Road in North Philly. Since Brother Theron's crew was involved in this mess, Josh told Theron to handle the meeting. "Don't let things get out of hand," he said. "Me and Anthony will be parked outside if you need us."

Try as he might, Theron couldn't keep things from getting out of hand. Too many enemies in one room yelling at each other about everything from a year-old drug hijacking to the recent killing and constant disrespect, was like being in a room holding a lit fuse while standing on a powder keg.

"I know you brothers realize that we can't afford to be at one another's throats," Theron offered. "Our purpose is to do what we can to settle these petty disputes, not …"

"With all due respect to you Brother Theron," a man from West Philly interrupted. "We don't owe dem motherfucahs who hang wit' you, nuffin'. Jus 'cause they now calls themselves Muslims 'cause they don' bought a new suit, dey think we don't kno' dat dey the same punks dey used to be. We kno' tha' it was punk-ass Norman who started dis shit."

"I ain't no punk," Norman shouted across the room.

"I can't tell, motherfuckah," the man shouted back. "You gotta prove dat shit to me."

It was then Theron realized he had made the mistake of not having someone take these men's guns. That had been the first thing Josh had told him. "Make sure you take their guns time they come in the door."

"You don't know me," Norman yelled at the man. "Ain't no punk in me. And I didn't start this shit."

"You ain't no motherfuckin' gangsta, tha's for sure."

As Theron rose again in an attempt to calm everyone down, from behind him he heard footsteps. Norman had gotten up and was now approaching the table. Realizing that was precisely the wrong thing to do, Theron turned to motion for Norman to sit back down, but it was too late. Another sound was heard, a click from a pistol being readied. A tall wiry man, his glance set, stepped from behind the man who had been yelling at Norman and fired two shots at Norman. One of the bullets struck Norman in the head, but the other hit Theron in his chest. As both men fell to the floor, others pulled out guns and bullets began flying. It was a melee, as the tall wiry man, cold eyes in a broad face, stepped closer, glancing down at Norman and then Theron.

When someone yelled, "C'mon, man, let's git the fuck outta 'ere," the men who were previously ducking under tables began running for the doors. Josh and Anthony, now outside of their car and aware of what was going on, fired on a few of those who were not Muslims spilling out onto Old York Road with guns firing and coattails flying in the wind.

It was broad daylight on a wide street. People were out walking with children and pets. There was no way there would be no witnesses to this shooting. Cars sped away as sirens were heard off in a distance. Guns drawn, Josh and Anthony entered the building to get their brothers out. While Anthony checked Norman, Josh gathered Theron up in his arms and took him out to the car.

Norman was dead, but Theron was still alive and conscious as Anthony drove him to Temple University Hospital, about six blocks away. The police had already been alerted about the shooting and were at the hospital waiting, just in case someone was brought there. Theron was admitted for surgery and all three were arrested. Other than Norman, the only other man to die in the shootout was the tall wiry man who had fired the first shot. The police determined that as he tried to flee out the door, he had been shot and killed by someone waiting outside.

\*\*\*

During the first week of January, 1974, Carl Hunter, having heard through the grapevine that the Brothers organization had been disbanded, returned to Philadelphia to see his family. It was his first time back since he had testified in federal court against Mo, Rus, and Dalton. Not trusting those in South Philly who knew him, he hung out mostly in North Philly.

It was a cold and windy night and wanting some companionship, Carl again decided to go to one of the local bars on Broad Street. But what he didn't know was that his visit to Philly hadn't gone unnoticed. From the first day he had come back to town, calls went out and his location was known.

The Twist bar was a nice clean little spot on Broad Street, right off Susquehanna Avenue. Carl had been there the night before and the Friday night crowd had been fun to be around. He had even met a girl who told him her name was Sandy and that she might be coming back Saturday night. Carl surely hoped that she would.

Like the night before, the fun crowd was out. Drinks were flowing, music playing, and people were dancing in the middle of the floor. The booths for couples were in the back of the bar on the top level, situated behind a 500 gallon aquarium at the top of the steps. As he waited for Sandy, Carl spent his time drinking and staring into the fish tank at the many different colored fish swimming under, around and through all the plastic apparatuses that had been place inside. So many different colors, he thought, so many different kinds of fish.

Carl liked being back around the familiar surroundings of Philadelphia. To him, it had a special feel to it. He briefly glanced back at the two men sitting behind him when he heard them laughing and joking about some woman they both wanted or had supposedly had.

"She said all you wanted to do was lick on her," joked the man wearing a tweed applejack Jeff cap, pulled down on his head and thick wool overcoat with its collar turned up. "So I told her she needs me to lay the pipe."

"Why you keep touchin' me when you talk 'bout her, man, I ain't strapped?" the other man, with his back to Carl, said. "Wha' you scared I'ma pop a cap in yo'r ass or som'um?"

"I'm jus' tryin to see if you still soft as you used to be, motherfuckah," the other replied in a raspy voice that sounded to Carl like an alcohol-induced slur.

"Hey, motherfuckah, the last time a jokah said som'um like tha' to me, I got fingerprinted," the man laughed. Then they both broke out in loud laughter.

Carl watched a big butt woman in a red wig stroll to the jukebox in the corner and heard someone yell, "Mamie, play 'I Need Your Lovin' Everyday'." And as the soulful lyrical incantation, "Whoa-whoa-whoa-whoa, whoa-whoa" that was Don Gardner and Dee Dee Ford's signature opening, loudly blasted throughout the bar, people began snapping their fingers and tapping their feet. A few gathered in the middle of the dance floor to show off their moves.

Wearing a bright red dress that fit her like a glove, Carl saw Sandy when she entered the bar. "Damn, she looks good," he mumbled, as she sashayed through the crowd. What Carl didn't see was the man wearing the applejack Jeff get up and walk down the steps toward the front of the bar.

When he reached the front door, he swirled around, placing his back against it, and pulled a sawed-off shotgun from beneath his overcoat, firing one round into the ceiling. As the patrons scattered in panic, the man yelled in a loud voice, "Aw'ight, ev'rybody on the mothafuckin' flo'!" To let them know he was serious, he fired off another round. "This 'ere gun fires indiscriminately," he yelled. "If you don't wanna get sprayed you best do what I say. Stay on the flo', empty yo'r pockets and keep yo'r eyes closed."

His attention diverted from the lady in red to the man with the shotgun, Carl's eyes widened with fear when, like an image slowly raising from the murky deep, recognition surfaced in his mind. The shotgun-wielding man was Big Cil.

Uncertain who the man still behind him might be, Carl rose in an attempt to flee, but it was too late. "Sit down, punk," the man wearing a pair of wire-frame plum-colored glasses said, as he grabbed Carl's coat collar, pulling him backward. "You got a debt to pay, maggot,"

Without hesitating, Harvey produced a long ice pick and plunged it through Carl Hunter's neck. Holding onto Carl, he plunged it again and again into his neck and upper chest, before finally allowing him to drop head first into the aquarium, turning the water blood red. They then left without taking anyone's money.

\*\*\*

Two weeks later, on January 28, 1974, Lucius, Chris, Wade, and Harvey, accompanied by their wives, met in New York City at Madison Square Garden to see the Muhammad Ali, Joe Frazier rematch. Ali was in top shape for this fight and won a 12 round unanimous decision.

"Well, I kept my promise," Harvey grinned, looking at his wife. "I told you I would bring you, and that Ali would win this time."

"Now all he has to do is re-capture his title," Wade said, huddling up with Frankie.

That night out was for their wives. The brothers wanted to spend time with them and make sure they had a good time. So after the fight, they enjoyed a late dinner and show. The next morning they all had breakfast together before sending the sisters out to do some shopping.

Once the brothers were alone, they discussed what had been happening within the brotherhood, and what would be expected of them. Acknowledging that they needed to help Josh and Anthony, who had been charged with murder. They also agreed to make sure that Big Cil, who was now back in Detroit, would have enough funding to keep him out of harm's way.

"We hav'ta disband those brothers running around using our names while doing nothin' for the temple," Lucius said.

"We'll be in Chicago on Savior's Day," Harvey said. "We can discuss how to handle it then."

"See you on Savior's Day," they said to each other upon leaving to pick up their wives and head home.  But little did they know that the upcoming 1974 Savior's Day celebration would be the last one they would ever attend.

# EPILOGUE

During the latter months of 1974 and first month of 1975, the Honorable Elijah Muhammad's health deteriorated rapidly. A diabetic for years and continuously on oxygen, on February 8, 1975, he suffered congestive heart failure and had to have emergency surgery. Though his Muslim followers in the Nation of Islam were made aware of his health problems, they were in denial concerning anything short of his recovery. After all, he was the Messenger of God and his prophecy had yet to be fulfilled.

On February 24th, Wade received a call from Brother Lucius telling him that the Honorable Elijah Muhammad had died at 8 o'clock that evening. And like so many of the Messenger's followers, Wade couldn't believe it. Two days before Savior's Day, he thought, almost ten years to the day Malcolm X had died. Wade remembered last year's Savior's Day address by Messenger Muhammad. Though he seemed ill, he spoke just the same, saying that "Our Savior, Master Fard Muhammad, was born on this day, February 26, 1877. So we are here to celebrate his glorious birth."

On February 28, more than 7,000 people gathered inside and outside of Chicago's Mosque No. 2 for the funeral service. A procession of more than 50 cars escorted the body to Mount Glenwood cemetery, in Glenwood, Illinois. Eulogies poured in from people like Jessie Jackson, Vernon Jordan, Roy Wilkins and other black civil rights leaders. Mayor of Chicago, Richard Daley, declared February 25, "Nation of Islam Day."

Like so many others, the Brothers Lucius, Chris, Harvey, and Wade watched with tearful eyes as Ministers could barely deliver their eulogies. And on the mind of just about every follower was the question, what's going to happen to us now.

In the weeks after the funeral, followers in the Nation of Islam began to hear that certain ministers were dissatisfied with the choice of Wallace D. Muhammad, one of the Honorable Elijah Muhammad's sons, as his successor. Everything seemed to be changing so fast. Followers were being told that the teachings they had studied and learned over the years had been false. They were purposely taught these lessons so that they would stop believing God was in the image of a white man and believe in their own black selves as being as worthy as anyone else.

The Nation of Islam, built by Elijah Muhammad and Malcom X's ministry, had constantly progressed financially and philosophically over the years. It evolved because of its dedicated and selfless ministers and followers. But it was now being dismantled both financially and philosophically under a wave of confusion, paranoia, and greed. Some members of the Messenger's own family were filing lawsuits in white courts in an attempt to gain access to the Nation of Islam property.

When the Messenger's son, Wallace D. Muhammad converted tens of thousands of black Muslims from what he said was the false teachings of his father to orthodoxy, some ministers and some followers remained mired in the teachings that demonized one race of people over another. When the former leadership departed, the sole victor was J. Edgar Hoover. The greed and selfishness that threatened the organization emerged at the top and quickly found its way down to the grass root followers.

Many understood why Messenger Muhammad had used reverse psychology on the Negro to make him believe in his own black self-worth. Still it was hard for them to face a world that now saw them as being duped by a lie. The realization that their dreams and aspirations of a world void of white folks' rule would not come to pass was even harder for them to take.

The brothers who dedicated themselves to the point of forming an unholy alliance under the guise of religion for the support of the Nation of Islam, now had to face this cold reality as well. The Muslim brothers now in prison and those still free had to watch as younger brothers misrepresented themselves by trying to live off a reputation they hadn't earned. Unlike the original inner circle of brothers, these newer brothers called themselves gangsters and dealt openly in drugs. Using the reputation of those who went before them to get their illegal gains, they contributed very little of their money to the mosque. Geographical boundaries that had been blurred by the original brothers now became defined and fought over.

Muslims were warring with each other over drug territories and insincere women who played one group of brothers against the other. Instead of being embraced by the community, these newer brothers soon became an embarrassment.

Wade, Chris, and Lucius retired from that life. And though all of the original inner circle of brothers remained loyal to one another, they all soon converted to orthodoxy and became Sunni Muslims, following Imam Wallace D. Muhammad, who had been chosen by his father to succeed him.

Harvey, who had heart problems all his life, died at an early age. And Big Cil, who would often come back to Philly to visit his family, was finally arrested and extradited to New York, where he was convicted and sentenced to 15 years.

Brother Terence replaced Minister Uriah as the Imam over the Philadelphia mosque, and the change was complete. The Nation of Islam was fragmented and most members now followed the son in "The World Community of Islam in the West."

Sadly, there were no more black leaders like Marcus Garvey and the Honorable Elijah Muhammad who were courageous enough to stand and advocate black self-interest for all people of African descent in America.

As for the brothers on which this novel is based, though they did form an unholy alliance and committed many crimes, they were not guilty of some notorious crimes that would later be attributed to them. But, in the minds of those who believed the FBI and police versions of events, they became the stuff of infamous legends. The Federal Bureau of Investigation's Counter Intelligence Program, with the help of some misguided and overzealous Muslim brothers, had done its job and was soon disbanded.